LIKE CHALK AND CHEESE

COLIN COLLIER

FERSEN
BOOKS

First published in the United Kingdom in 2025
by Fersen Books

Print ISBN   9798 3056 3515 7

Cover design by Danny Cazzato

www.colincollierauthor.com

This book is dedicated to anyone who has ever dreamt of being a pop star. Or of being an author, come to that.

It's also dedicated to the real Michael. You know who you are.

Chapter 1
Michael

Michael Hambelton sat in front of his dressing room mirror, wondering what was so special about his face that it should grace millions of teenagers' bedroom walls the world over. Although there were probably no official images of him that hadn't been enhanced, he realised that there was only so much that an editor could do to make someone look beautiful. He smiled as he remembered one of his grandmother's favourite sayings, 'You can't make a silk purse out of a sow's ear,' and was sure that she would have wasted no time in bringing him back down to earth with a jolt if she had been here right now. But she would also have been the first to admit that he was in great shape for his age. Especially since he hadn't yet succumbed to the plastic surgeon's knife, despite the fact that, heaven forbid, he was fast approaching his twenty-ninth birthday. The temptation grew stronger day by day though, and as he gazed at his reflection, he was sure that yet another very faint pair of crow's feet had developed overnight on either side of his face. He pulled a distorted expression at himself in the mirror; he couldn't believe some of the absurd things that ran through his head just before a show.

His dressing room was right at the back of the arena, behind the stage, and he could already hear the thunderous sound of his expectant audience. He shivered as a sudden rush of adrenaline ran through him. This was one of the smaller venues on his current tour. Someone had told him that the Stockholm Globe was a mere

16,000-seater, although audience numbers had stopped worrying him years ago. He could only ever see the faces of the people in the front few rows anyway. He had learnt early on in his career that making eye contact with them would often lead to disaster, since you could become so engrossed in the person you were looking at that you'd risk forgetting your lyrics. He remembered all too well the first time it had actually happened to him, shortly after he'd had his first global hit album. Panic stricken, he'd quickly pointed the microphone towards the audience and thankfully, on cue, they had responded by singing the forgotten words. Nowadays, he used the tried and tested technique of gazing at his audience's foreheads rather than into their eyes, to avoid any distraction.

So far, Michael was very impressed with this venue. He'd been told that it had opened eight years ago, in 1989, and it still had a very new feel to it. His dressing room was extremely plush and most unlike some of the dives he'd had the misfortune to occupy over the years. This was the first of two consecutive nights in Stockholm and he was pleased to have such a comfortable room to spend time in both before and after the shows. The city of Stockholm always made him feel at ease too: the people, the environment and the general feel of the place. It was much less stressful than the majority of other cities he'd visited. A sudden knock on the door brought him back to his senses.

'Who is it?' he shouted, as pangs of fear thunder-bolted through his body. What if another fan had managed to get past security? Just two nights ago in Berlin, his self-proclaimed 'number one fan' had been hiding in his dressing room when he'd arrived and had held him hostage for a good ten minutes before someone had rescued him. During that time, Michael had been forced to entertain her whilst she had showered him with small bottles of cheap German beer and bargain basement chocolates. God only knows how many things she had produced from her rucksack for him to sign. What on earth would she do with all those autographs anyway? He must have signed over a hundred photographs and CD covers for her, during what felt like an eternity.

There was another more impatient sounding knock on the door, this time accompanied by a man's voice announcing that it was just twenty minutes until curtain up. Michael's heart sank as he realised that he had absolutely nothing left to do to fill that time apart from sit and worry. He'd been dressed and ready for his opening number for over half an hour now and was sure he'd go mad if he ran through that damned setlist in his head once more.

Until a few weeks ago, somebody had been employed as his make-up artist, hair stylist and dresser. Her name was Misty and, although she had been rather outlandish with his make-up at times, Michael had got on really well with her and had enjoyed her company. She was very down to earth and he would have described her as the girl next door type, rather than a media luvvie, which was quite refreshing in Michael's world. His manager, Ricky, had fired her without even consulting him, saying that she didn't really fit the bill. Michael found it all very odd and had his suspicions that his manager had perhaps made a pass at Misty, who would have been understandably outraged and had probably resigned on the spot. Since Michael didn't have any contact details for Misty, he had no way of getting in touch with her to get her side of the story. A replacement had appeared the following night, a French guy called Fred, who Michael had promptly sacked when he had caught him sneakily taking photos of him with a cheap instamatic camera. Michael had only been in Fred's company for a couple of hours, but in that short time the guy had bored him rigid with stories of how his girlfriend's family didn't approve of him, which Michael actually felt was quite understandable. Ricky had thrown a hissy fit when he had found out, and unsurprisingly, nobody had been employed to fill the position since. Michael was absolutely certain that his manager was punishing him for firing Fred. Fortunately, there were only a few nights left of the current tour by that point and he was more than capable of taking care of his own make-up, hair and clothes.

Michael's attention returned to his reflection in the mirror and it suddenly dawned on him just how absurd this situation was. How many other international performers of his calibre would be waiting in their dressing room completely alone before a show? None probably, or at least very few. He knew he only had himself to blame though, since he'd given up asking people to come along to his gigs long ago. In the early days, when everything was still very new and exciting, he had invited the world and his wife to come backstage, both before and after each show. But he had very soon come to the conclusion that people basically fell into two camps: his true friends, who would decline any request because they were afraid that he would think they were only interested in him now because of his fame and fortune, and the hangers-on, who really were only with him because of it. As he'd become increasingly famous, the situation had just got worse.

He'd lost touch with all but one of his original friends, and even the meetings with him were now virtually non-existent, so much so that Michael felt far too guilty to even pick up the phone and try to contact

—

4

his best mate, Bowie, after all this time. He wasn't even sure if his friend still went by that name - the name given to him by his school friends because of his striking likeness to the iconic star. His parents called him Lee, but Michael couldn't remember ever hearing anyone else call him that. He'd never heard his friend complaining about the moniker either, but that was hardly surprising, since he was obsessed with the performer and even had a Ziggy Stardust poster framed on his bedroom wall. It was quite obvious that Bowie adored the nickname that had been bestowed upon him and Michael couldn't help but smile as he remembered some of the bizarre situations he'd found himself in with his friend. The funniest one had to be when Michael's father had assumed that Bowie was Michael's girlfriend, much to Bowie's delight. He absolutely adored ambiguity. Just the thought of it now made Michael laugh out loud. It hadn't helped matters that his friend sometimes daringly wore a touch of mascara and lipstick outside school. He was also quite keen on wearing a brightly-coloured Alice band in his long, blond hair. Once Michael's dad had realised his mistake, he'd made it very obvious that he wasn't impressed at all with his son's choice of a friend, and had advised Michael that a fella who wore make-up and hair ornaments was undoubtably very dodgy. Michael made a mental note to ensure that he touched base with Bowie as soon as he got back to the UK, deciding that with good friendships, it really didn't matter if there were long gaps between contacts.

If Michael was truly honest with himself, there were actually times when he quite enjoyed being on his own before a show, although most nights would end up like this one, with him feeling nothing but depression and solitude. It was definitely better than being joined by his manager and his cronies though and at least tonight he

—

had been left alone so far. He was sure his luck wouldn't last though; he was certain that he'd have the displeasure of Ricky's company after at least one of the two Stockholm shows. It was quite possible that the guy was out front of house right now, crowing about how important he was in the Michael Hambelton empire. In reality, he was so unreliable these days and did virtually nothing to support his client's global success.

He wondered if perhaps the cold, dark weather was adding to his melancholy. It did seem exceptionally bitter for March, even for Sweden. Whether it was because of the gloom and freezing temperatures or not, he couldn't remember when he had last felt so subdued. How ironic that just a few metres away there was a capacity crowd, about to profess its undying love for him. If only they knew how he really felt and could witness the empty nights when he would cry himself to sleep, or the hurried room service meals he would eat all alone in his luxury hotel suites. It felt good to have so much money yet, in a way, it seemed that as his bank balance grew, so did the wall between him and the real world. He wasn't even sure that he would ever be able to identify with someone from that other world now; in particular, enough to build a relationship.

As if to amplify his crippling loneliness even further, Michael could hear the raucous sound of his musicians and backing singers in the room next door. He guessed that his bodyguard was in there with them too, as usual, and it sounded like they were having a whale of a time. There were loud violins playing and lots of cheering. He sometimes wondered if the members of his band found him aloof, since he never joined in with their pre-show antics. But after some awkward encounters with them at the start of the tour, he now preferred to keep things on a professional level. They'd all been at the set up and sound check earlier though, and everything had been very jovial. He liked to think there were no hard feelings between them, but there was now definitely a dividing line drawn.

As for Clint, the latest in a long line of body-guards, he was about as much use as a chocolate teapot. A muscle-bound budding actor, he seemed to spend as much time admiring himself in the mirror as he did looking out for Michael. He was a very moody character too and could be quite unpredictable. There was no way of knowing if he would be in a chatty mood or not and, truth be told, Michael tended to prefer it if he wasn't. Rather than keeping an eye on Michael, he much preferred spending his time partying with the other band members.

Michael had come to the conclusion that the worst thing about his current situation was that he couldn't even go out now without being mobbed by adoring fans. He'd tried to disguise himself in the past by wearing hats and sunglasses but he never seemed to carry it off with any success. It just made him feel even more isolated and trapped in his allegedly charmed life. Sometimes the loneliness would become so unbearable that he would even contemplate suicide. Wouldn't the press have a field day with that one though? They'd probably accuse him of being a spoilt brat again and would create some fabricated story of how his death had been the result of a lethal cocktail of drink and drugs, despite the fact that in reality he never consumed either substance. The only thing that stopped him acting out his morbid fantasy was that he couldn't bear the thought of the Michael Hambelton name being tarnished for all eternity. At least whilst he was still in this world, he was able to fight his corner whenever the press printed their scandalous lies, albeit via his legal team. After all, there was no-one else to fight his battles for him now, especially since both his parents had died and he no longer had any contact with his brother and sister.

It really troubled Michael that both his siblings had turned their backs on him soon after he'd had his first few global hits and he'd therefore been unable to share his incredible success with them. If only they had stuck around, he would have given them anything they'd ever wanted and would have loved them to have been part of his new jet-set lifestyle.

His sister had managed to turn both their parents against him prior to their deaths too. He had spent so much time questioning her motives but had never resolved the issue in his head. Michael was sure that her hostility towards him was about much more than just money. She had ultimately been the sole beneficiary of their parents' estate, as conveniently for her, their brother Jake had also been written out of the will.

Michael had often considered trying to get back in touch with both his siblings, especially now that he had so much money that he didn't know what to do with it. But it was a matter of principle; if they didn't want to know him when he was a poor, struggling musician, then just how genuine was their love anyway? His brother Jake hadn't actually been that bad, but he knew now that his sister Alice was a really nasty piece of work.

Bringing himself back to his senses, he stood up, stepped back, and admired himself in the dressing room mirror again. He was already wearing tonight's first costume: a peacock blue two-piece suit embellished with rhinestones of the same colour, which he wore with a very tight-fitting cerise T-shirt underneath. He had polished his ultra-shiny black cowboy boots so well earlier, using some paper towels from the dispenser in his room, that when he looked down he could see his reflection in them.

Michael walked across to where the other three costumes for tonight's show were hanging and ran his hand across them. Truth be told, he was coping quite well without an assistant. Just how difficult was it to change from one suit into another, after all? One of these days he'd throw his crew into turmoil by deliberately putting the outfits on in the wrong order. But not tonight, since he didn't feel strong enough to face the consequences.

All Michael really wanted to do right now was to run away from all of this and hide. Rather than being proud of the expensive outfits hanging on the rail, Michael just felt guilty at the obscene amount of money these costumes had cost to make: one of the jackets alone was worth more than four thousand pounds. He would never understand why he couldn't just wear off the peg designer suits instead, and was sure that any top fashion house would happily donate their creations for free, just to be able to say that he wore their brand. Of course, he understood the amazing power of stagecraft and, as his manager often reminded him, albeit in a sarcastic tone, it was the theatricality of Michael's shows that made them legendary. But why on earth had he agreed to sing two numbers on the current tour dressed as Napoleon? Admittedly, both songs shared the same theme of him wanting to rule the world but he was still unconvinced that this was a smart move, especially since the only photo that had made it onto the front pages of the world's newspapers the day after opening night was of him in his imperial garb. It was very unfortunate that details of his current wealth had been leaked to the press on the very same day too. It had felt as if he'd played right into their hands by dressing as the French emperor, since it was that image which had appeared alongside such outrageous headlines as 'Britain's Top Earner Wants to Rule the World'. But then didn't someone once say that all publicity was good publicity?

He suddenly sensed that his mouth had gone very dry and that his chest was tightening. Why did the panic always start at this exact point before a show? He'd had some counselling for it in the past but it had got worse rather than better, although he hadn't shared this with anyone, especially not with the latest in a long line of therapists. As far as his management team was concerned, the shrinks had sorted him out good and proper and his panic attacks had gone. Yet in reality, that couldn't be further from the truth.

On cue, all his usual pre-show fears started to surface and he began to run through the things that he always scared himself with before a show … What if he fell down that precarious staircase at the centre of the stage tonight? Had the crew checked that all the heavy lighting was securely fixed above the stage? Were the electrics all safe? What if he did forget his lyrics again? That last question made him smile - he was pretty sure that nobody would even notice if he sang the wrong words, since the noise of the crowd usually drowned out his vocals completely. At least when he'd had Misty to assist him backstage, their light-hearted banter had kept his focus off his nerves.

He hated touring so much these days that, whenever there was bad weather, he would secretly hope that the gig would be cancelled. There was thick snow outside the arena tonight, but Michael was sure that there would be no chance of the show being axed. The Swedes were always well prepared for these conditions and he was sure that not a single person would have failed to make it here tonight.

Michael knew that, despite his fears, there was no going back now and before long he would have to be out on stage, giving it his all. He'd better pull himself together. He fumbled in his rucksack for his Sony Discman, headphones and portable CD wallet. He always travelled with his twenty favourite CDs and one of them was ABBA's *Super Trouper* album. The title track always managed to calm him down and he was certain that tonight would be no exception. He plugged in the headphones and selected the CD from the wallet, clicking it into place in the Discman. He tried to get comfortable in front of the dressing room mirror. The seat was remarkably cosy. *Typical Swedish design and comfort*, he thought. Taking a deep breath in through his nose and slowly blowing the air back out through his pursed lips, he put the headphones over his ears and pushed the play button on the device. Leaning back, he closed his eyes and tried his hardest to focus on slowing down his racing heart, as the title track from the album began to play. The beautiful acapella intro and jubilant opening music was like honey to his ears. Michael sensed that he was already beginning to relax.

Having been a big ABBA fan for many years, he had a real soft spot for both Agnetha and Frida. He'd met many other performers during his time in the public eye and always regretted that he hadn't yet had the chance to meet any members of the Swedish group.

Frida sang lead on this song and whenever he listened to it, he felt a real affinity with the character she was portraying. The lyrics really struck a chord with his own feelings of isolation in front of a capacity crowd and it always grounded him and made him feel more normal, just knowing that someone else may have suffered the same solitude that he had. Michael often experienced crippling loneliness when he was on tour. How he wished there was someone he truly cared for in the audience tonight. ABBA's music was truly magical and

Björn was so insightful with his lyrics, especially when set to Benny's amazing music. Michael was certain that nobody else matched their skill at song-writing, himself included. This track was no exception.

He was suddenly struck by how ironic it was that he should be listening to this song right now, just moments before he was about to step out on stage in ABBA's hometown. As the music faded, he found himself daydreaming that one of the members of the group could perhaps be in tonight's audience.

He pushed the stop button before the next song began and removed his headphones, taking the CD out of the device and carefully putting it back with the other discs in the wallet. He neatly packed everything into his rucksack, having wound the headphone wire into a neat loop so that it didn't get tangled up in transit. That was one of his pet hates - the number of times he'd had to untangle that cable in the past was nobody's business.

Michael stood up and carefully ran his hands over his black short-cropped hair. He then carefully opened his jacket with one hand and brushed his T-shirt with the fingers of the other hand in an attempt to remove any stray fluff. He checked himself out in the full-length mirror on the other side of the room and gave himself a sideways glance. He blew himself a kiss and stood back to get the full effect of his hair, make-up and clothes. He'd become quite a pro at getting himself ready now. He did look amazing. Even he could fancy himself tonight. He'd often been told that he had a real presence, both on and off stage, and he guessed this was helped by the fact that he was six feet two inches tall. He towered above the majority of other people he knew. He had never been one to exercise but kept himself in trim by trying to eat healthily, even when he was on tour. Seeing himself in the mirror tonight made him glad that he had looked after himself.

There was yet another loud knock and Michael looked up at the clock on the wall, realising that the time had come for the arena manager to lead him to the stage. He slowly walked towards the dressing room door. There really was no way of avoiding this any longer - it was time yet again for him to meet his public.

He unlocked the door and took his first few nervous steps outside. Clint was standing a couple of metres away and as Michael appeared, the bodyguard stepped a fraction closer. Michael gave him a half smile. Rather than creating a feeling of protection, security personnel always intimidated him and made him feel that he wasn't man enough to look after himself. The arena manager, whom Michael had met very briefly earlier when he'd arrived at the venue, but whose name he had now forgotten, nodded at Michael and did an exaggerated 'follow me' gesture as he led Michael away from the safety of his dressing room. Slowly but surely, they walked along the bustling corridor towards the stage, with Michael trying his hardest not to look at anyone on the way. He was grateful that nobody backstage stopped him to ask for an autograph.

Ever since the start of his music career, Michael had suffered from imposter syndrome. On a daily basis, he expected someone to randomly tap him on the shoulder and ask him what on earth he thought he was doing, playing the part of a global pop star. In the beginning, he had put it down to lack of experience, and had hoped that over time it would just fade away. If anything, it had got worse. There were moments when he really doubted that he had the talent to justify his incredible success the world over. The numerous therapists he'd seen over the years had put it down to low self-esteem, but this didn't stop his stomach doing somersaults every time he made his way towards another eager audience. He focused on his breathing once again and thought of how relieved he would be once the show was over.

They finally arrived at the edge of the massive darkened stage and the arena manager stepped aside to allow Michael to pass. A member of the crew handed him a wireless microphone, and in the semi darkness, Michael made his way towards the towering staircase that formed the centrepiece of the specially constructed set. Luckily, there was enough dim light for him to be able to find his way. He knew that his band would be in place by now behind a second black curtain at the back of the stage. That curtain would be pulled back and the band revealed after the first two numbers, once the staircase had magically disappeared.

He briefly stopped at the foot of the stairs and then carefully began to make his ascent, stopping about seven steps from the very top. He sat down, making sure that his suit was hanging right, and lengthened his back to make himself look more aloof. He took another deep breath and gazed ahead at the immense curtaining. Behind that black façade he could hear the sound of 16,000 people shouting their petty conversations over the pre-show music. They were all totally unaware of the fact that Michael was now on stage. He imagined them shuffling in their seats and packing their coats and bags out of the way, in preparation for the show.

He was always intrigued by the music that each venue chose to pipe through its sound system before his show. He listened to the song that was currently playing and was initially disappointed that it wasn't a track from his latest album. He had suggested to his manager on numerous occasions that this might be a good strategy to boost sales, but as usual, the suggestion seemed to have fallen on deaf ears. His mood suddenly brightened though, as he recognised the song. Michael prided himself in his knowledge of what the four members of ABBA had been doing since they had stopped recording together in the early 80s, and realised that the track that was playing was 'Även En Blomma', the lead single from Frida's most recent Swedish solo album. This had to be a good sign for tonight's show. Michael's record and CD collection was legendary amongst his peers and incorporated music by many other European artists, including solo work by Frida and her fellow band members.

The music abruptly stopped mid-song, waking Michael from his daydream and causing the audience to give a brief cheer. He noticed the manic beating of his heart again and just hoped that the microphone wouldn't pick up on the sound. He glanced towards the stage below and felt a huge wave of vertigo as he tried to focus in the semi-darkness on a hat stand which stood in the far-right hand corner. A bowler hat and a cane hung from it: his props for the third song.

He knew that the arena lights would now be dimming and seconds later, the thunderous opening section of his first number began. The curtains began to part and the blinding lights suddenly illuminated the stage. Michael carefully stood up, trying to ignore his dizziness and the thought of how high that bloody staircase was. A Swedish accented voice boomed out from the arena's sound system, as if to inform anyone who had managed to get in without knowing who they were about to see …

'Ladies and gentlemen … please put your hands together for … Mr Michael Hambelton!'

Chapter 2
Alice

The early morning sun was already streaming in through the bedroom window by the time Alice woke from her alcohol-induced sleep. Her eyes flinched at the brightness of the room, even though the thickly lined, heavy velvet curtains were tightly pulled shut. The room was very warm, mainly because she'd left the central heating on overnight as usual. Her head was spinning. Maybe going out with her gay friends the previous evening hadn't been such a good idea after all, even if she had managed not to buy a single drink all night. She loved the strength of the pink pound and the fact that her posse was always naïve enough to fall for her stories about forgetting her wallet or being too weak to put her hand into her money-packed pocket to buy a round of drinks.

If she had any sensitivity at all, she would have thought it sad that she only had this very small group of people left in her life. She'd created a void between herself and the rest of her former friends over the years with her vicious tongue and meanness. Even her mother had considered disowning her shortly before she'd died, after discovering that Alice had placed a personal ad in a local newspaper for her, hoping to attract a new man to replace her husband. It was the last straw for Alice's mother, who was still grieving the recent loss of her spouse. Her daughter had tried to explain that she was sure that it was just what her mother needed, which had only made matters worse. She really couldn't understand why the notion was so shocking.

Alice had had hangovers before, but today's seemed to be particularly bad. Trying to make sense of her thoughts, she suddenly remembered the drinking competition she'd had with her friend Nigel, one of the guys she'd been out with the night before, the memory of which made her head spin even more. She'd won the £20 at stake but that seemed insignificant now. Somehow, it seemed wrong that Nigel had even participated in the dare, considering he had a full-time job as a chauffeur. Despite this, he never seemed to refuse any of Alice's drinking challenges. She'd only recently allowed him back into her friendship circle after they'd had a massive fall-out a few months previously. He hadn't learnt his lesson though and had yet again unabashedly accused her of being a benefit cheat the previous evening. Outraged, she had screamed at him, saying that she never wanted to see him ever again, and he had stormed off. No doubt, he would come crawling back again in the very near future.

Alice couldn't remember when she had last felt this awful. There was nothing else for it - she would have to call a doctor out. Staggering from her bed, she tugged her food-stained, white towelling dressing gown down from the hook behind the bedroom door, pulled it over her chocolate-stained nightshirt, and made her way out onto the landing. Her head spun even more as she tried to focus on the telephone at the bottom of the staircase. Gripping the banisters tightly, she lurched her way down each step and eventually made it to the bottom. It really was too much effort sometimes to climb up and down those stairs. She'd have to make it a priority to research having a stair lift installed.

Reaching the phone, she seized it with her right hand and steadied herself against the wall with the other.

—

She hit 3 on the keypad with her thumb and the phone called the local surgery, whose number was safely stored in its speed dial system. Surprisingly, it only rang twice before a friendly, willing voice answered the phone, although Alice didn't quite catch what was said.

'I NEED A DOCTOR!' she yelled into the mouthpiece.

'Who's calling?' came the startled reply.

'It's Alice Hambelton and I need a doctor RIGHT NOW! I've been sick all night and I keep fainting.'

'Have you taken anything?'

'I've taken all my usual medication but I think I'm dying. You'd best send an ambulance!' She smiled to herself. She couldn't actually remember when she had last taken medication of any kind. All the drugs she was regularly given on repeat prescription always went straight down the toilet when she got home from the chemist. They all added to the legitimacy of her benefit claims though, and her bursting medical records certainly helped whenever she needed to apply for any extra support.

'Now calm down! How long have you been feeling like this?' asked the receptionist.

Alice was already tiring of this game. She wasn't just any old patient with a stomach upset. She might not be on speaking terms with her celebrity brother but hadn't the stupid woman heard her surname? Surely Alice had sold enough kiss and tell stories about her famous sibling by now to be instantly recognisable to the cow on the other end of the phone. And didn't she realise that this was an emergency?

'Listen - I just told you. YOU NEED TO SEND ME A DOCTOR.' Alice blinked as she spat each word out loudly. 'I feel far too ill to make small talk with you over the phone. I need to go back to bed.'

The woman was having none of it. 'I'm afraid I can't send a doctor out until I've checked your symptoms and have verified what you may or may not have …'

Alice cut her off mid-sentence. She recognised the woman's voice now; it was that awful Sheila, the worst of all the surgery's receptionists and someone whom Alice hated with a vengeance. Sheila had slurred her words during a previous conversation they'd had and Alice was certain that the woman had a drink problem.

'You'll send me a doctor right now or I want it on record that you refused to help me as I was dying!' Alice tried to say the words as threateningly as possible. 'May I remind you, Sheila,' she continued, saying the woman's name with as much venom as she could muster in her current state, 'that my brother is a celebrity!'

The receptionist sighed. She had lost count of the number of times that Alice had called out an emergency doctor over the years and, although the surgery was well aware of the fact that she was a time waster, they had no choice but to send someone out, just in case it was genuine this time.

'Alice, someone will be with you sometime today. I've got your contact details here.'

'SOMETIME TODAY ISN'T GOOD ENOUGH!' Alice falsely coughed for effect. She knew exactly how the surgery was run. She'd been employed there very briefly after leaving school after all, although hadn't had the displeasure to work alongside any of the current staff. She was sure that things couldn't have changed there much though and was well aware of which buttons to push to get priority treatment.

She smiled to herself as she remembered the short time she'd spent working at the clinic. Unfortunately, she'd been caught photocopying the confidential medical records of her friends and

19

neighbours to take home to show her parents. As a result, the manager of the practise had ultimately shown her the door. But Alice had been there long enough by then to learn everything she needed from some of the genuinely incapacitated patients to never have to work again. She'd made a good living since then from her fraudulent benefit claims, many of which were based on legitimate cases that Alice had witnessed during her time at the surgery.

'I'll try to get someone out to you as soon as I can, Alice,' sighed Sheila. Despite her anger and frustration, she was trying her best to keep her cool. The last thing she needed was for this deranged woman to report her for being rude. They'd had innumerable complaints come in from Alice over the years, pointing the finger at the majority of Sheila's colleagues. Fortunately, none of them had ever come to anything, although just hearing Alice's name was enough to strike fear in most of the medical centre's staff. Sheila's own mental health had suffered as a result of Alice's behaviour in the past too. Despite the fact that the powers that be knew what a fraud she was, it was very difficult to prove it. So, for now, they just had to put up with her.

Alice began to scream down the phone again. 'YOU NEED TO GET SOMEONE OUT HERE RIGHT NOW!' She coughed again, due to all the shouting, and then cleared her throat before menacingly continuing. 'You'd better make sure that they are here within the hour!' Laughing loudly, she slammed down the receiver, causing Sheila to jump at the sudden bang at the other end of the phone.

Alice staggered along the hallway into the kitchen. Picking up a pair of Emporio Armani sunglasses from the kitchen table, she put them on in an attempt to block out the dazzling brightness of the room. Shuffling over to the fridge, she opened the door and flinched at the white light which shone out from inside. She grabbed a can of diet cola from the top shelf and clumsily pushed the fridge door shut. Squeezing her index finger through the ring pull, she opened the can and downed the drink in one, gasping as she caught her breath afterwards. She belched loudly and pulled a face, totally bemused at where the burp had come from.

Those medical receptionists really made her blood boil; who did they think they were? At least she could console herself with the fact that she always had the upper hand. Without fail, an emergency doctor would be calling within the next couple of hours. She really hoped it would be that Swedish medic they'd sent the last time. With his rugged good looks and his very easy bedside manner, he had obligingly checked everything Alice had asked him to, including a few personal areas that hadn't been viewed by a medical professional, or anyone else for that matter, for a very long time. Maybe Alice should have asked Sheila if he was on duty today. But there was no way she was going to phone that useless good for nothing receptionist back now. She felt far too rough and there was no guarantee that they would send the Swedish hunk out anyway, even if he was available. Plus, she didn't actually know his name. He had been very bashful when she had asked for it on his previous visit. He'd eventually realised that Alice wouldn't be allowing him to leave if he didn't respond to her question and had coyly told her that his name was Dr Freud. She'd laughingly asked if that meant that the local surgery had now also employed Dr Jekyll and Mr Hyde too, which had made him guffaw loudly. At least he'd had a good sense of humour. She liked that in a man.

Alice unlocked the back door and wandered out into the conservatory, still squinting at the bright sunshine in spite of her sunglasses. She slumped down onto one of the padded chairs which overlooked the garden. Her parents had had the garden re-landscaped a few years previously and Alice kept it maintained with the help of a local gardening firm. She sometimes had to pinch herself whenever she realised that this house now belonged entirely to her. It felt so empty here now though. It was a real shame that she was completely alienated from both her brothers, but so much water had gone under the bridge since she had last had contact with them. She had been so disappointed with Michael when he had hit the big time with his singing career and had refused to share any of his massive fortune with his family. Her relationship with her other brother, Jake, had always been quite fragile anyway, but had worsened when their parents had become ill and Alice had refused to let either of her brothers see them. She knew that Jake had subsequently married a very wealthy woman called Sue, whom Alice loathed, despite the fact that she had never actually met the woman. According to what Alice had heard, the dreadful girl was a workaholic and had her husband waiting on her hand and foot. How could he be such a wimp?

When they were younger, Alice's brothers had gone to the local boys' school on the other side of town, and their father used to drop them off on his way to work. Alice's school was much closer, just a three-minute walk from home, which meant that she could spend a few more cherished moments with her mum each morning before setting out. She still remembered the permanent, downcast look on her mother's face. She was an amazing parent but always doubted herself, thinking she was making a terrible job of raising her children. Remembering those days now made Alice feel quite melancholy.

They had been such a tight family unit back then and Alice had been absolutely furious with her brothers when they had selfishly headed off into the sunset to their new charmed lives. Jake had gone to university to study law and Michael had moved in with a couple of friends not long after his eighteenth birthday. She felt such resentment towards both of them now. Deep down, she knew that she had also been partly to blame, but she had no intention of admitting that to anyone. She was the one who had been left stranded at home after all, whilst her brothers lived the high life. Michael and Jake had been far from innocent in all of this.

Alice remembered how exhausting it had been to convince both parents that her brothers were unworthy of their love. It had taken a lot of energy and inventive-ness, and she'd had to concoct umpteen lies about her siblings, the stories increasing in ferocity until their mum and dad had finally taken the bait and cut off both sons. When Alice's father had had a final fatal heart attack, Alice had successfully shielded their mother from Michael and Jake's attempts to make contact again and had even managed to keep details of the funeral service secret from both her brothers. This strategy had worked perfectly and their unintentional absence had played right into Alice's hands, as she was then able to tell their mother that her sons had cared so little about their father that they hadn't even bothered to turn up at his funeral. As a result, their mother had changed her will and left everything to Alice. When their mum had also died, not even a year after the death of their father, both brothers had tried their best to challenge the will, but had failed miserably. Alice had had very little pity for them, what with Michael already being rich from his singing career and Jake having a high powered job with a law firm at the time. Neither brother wanted for anything. In comparison, Alice lived on her own without a partner and considered herself genuinely in need.

It had been a total shock to Alice when she'd learnt exactly how much she was going to inherit. Both parents had been extremely hardworking and had allocated their money wisely over the years, both in property and well-chosen investments. Alice remembered her father poring over the Financial Times each morning during breakfast, choosing the right moment to buy and sell shares. Alice did occasionally wonder what he would have made of her idle lifestyle.

Following her parents' deaths, Alice had appointed a wealth management company to look after her fortune. More recently though, she had put a large sum of money into a secret venture that she hoped would ultimately boost her finances even further. The future was certainly looking very bright indeed. Her main bank account and investments were in her real name, Alicia, which was also her maternal grandmother's name. Since she was a child, she'd always been called Alice, and as an adult, she had cleverly managed to open a separate bank account using that name too. Her friend Nigel had been working at the Midland Bank at the time and had quite happily signed off her identification, without even noticing the discrepancy with her first name. That account had proved to be very useful indeed when she'd started to claim benefits, since she had been able to keep all her other money safely hidden.

Her parents had named the family home Malibu, following a wonderful holiday they had had in the city of the same name in California. Alice had been born about nine months after her parents had returned from the trip, just after they'd moved into the new house, and she'd liked to tease them by asking what had happened in Malibu and if it was where she had been conceived. She never had found out if that was the case. The property was in Rottingdean, an area which was very unlike California but still quite a desirable place to live. Located near Brighton, it had the advantage of being close to the hustle and bustle of town life, whilst still being a convenient distance away from it.

As children, Alice and her siblings would often be taken to visit nearby Drusillas Zoo by their parents. Their favourite attraction at the zoo was always the penguins, and their father had bought them a sculpture of the flightless birds which still sat to one side of the garden pond. It was looking worse for wear now, with bits chipped off and its once bright monochrome colours now completely faded. Alice sat there dreamily looking out of the conservatory window at it, remembering those happy family days out.

Alice absolutely loved living here - it was the only place she had ever lived, after all. She knew every nook and cranny of this house and sometimes got quite tearful, remembering the fun she used to have, playing hide and seek with her siblings when they had all lived here together as children. They'd had a sister back then too, Eva, who Alice tried not to think of too often, as it was just too upsetting. The four children often used to climb a big oak tree in the garden, where their father had built them a tree house. They would stay up there for hours, until the fateful day when Eva, who was two years younger than Alice, had fallen out of the tree and tragically hit her head upon landing, dying instantly, they'd been told. Alice could still picture her father running up and down the garden with Eva in his arms, desperately trying to revive his youngest daughter, as if running away from the tragic event would erase it completely. Needless to say, their father had destroyed the tree house and the old oak had been cut down soon afterwards. There was hardly anything left of the tree now, apart from a wizened, scaly stump.

Although Alice had only been a child herself when her sister had died, the event had forged a deep scar on her psyche. Before Eva's accident, the four children loved nothing more than pretending to be ABBA, which had worked out perfectly with them being two boys and two girls. When they had learnt that the band's name was an acronym of the group members' first names, they had decided to do the same themselves, and would sometimes refer to themselves as JAME - standing for Jake, Alice, Michael and Eva. She remembered how Michael, the eldest of the four siblings, had created a JAME emblem for the four of them, flipping the J to imitate the Swedish group's iconic logo with a reversed B. All four of them had absolutely adored ABBA, so much so that 'I Have A Dream' had been played at Eva's funeral. Alice hadn't been able to listen to the song since then.

It was actually during one of JAME's performances in front of their family that they had noticed just how well Michael could sing. Alice wondered if Michael still remembered that moment of discovery? He had always had such natural charisma and she could see why he had legions of fans all around the world. Even as a child, he had been well aware of his charms, and would use it to his advantage. During their youth, the rest of the family had fallen for this time and time again.

In recent years, Alice had made a vast sum of money from selling untrue stories about Michael to the world's press, but she now had plans to turn things up a notch. Recently, she had been working very hard at putting together a dossier about Michael. She had only shared details of the project with two other people so far, but she knew for sure that it was guaranteed to get a reaction from her brother. It included extracts allegedly taken from their father's diary, all of which she had completely falsified. In one of the excerpts, she had even gone as far as saying that Michael had been responsible for their sister Eva's death, and that he had encouraged her to climb out onto a decaying branch, even though he'd known that it was dangerous. With Michael being such a global superstar now, Alice was certain that her exposé would be quickly snapped up by a hungry publisher, keen to make an easy buck. It was going to be truly amazing when it all came to fruition. She felt no guilt whatsoever about the fallout her plan would ultimately cause - Michael had brought it all on himself.

Waking from her daydream, Alice noticed that she was feeling chilly. She made her way back into the warmth of the main house and stumbled from the kitchen towards the front door. She unlocked it, leaving it slightly ajar. It was her usual trick - leaving the door open so she could focus on perfecting her best dying pose upstairs for when the doctor arrived. With the porch door left shut but unlocked, the doctor would easily be able to let themselves in. In the meantime, Alice needed to get herself ready for the visit. Her head was still spinning from all the alcohol she'd consumed the night before but she needed to forget that now and put all her energy into giving an Oscar winning performance for when the physician arrived.

She returned to the kitchen and began rummaging in a drawer. She eventually found what she was looking for - a wheat-filled heat pack - and placed it in the microwave for a couple of minutes. It would be ideal for putting under her arm to bring her temperature up. When the doctor arrived, she would have to insist that they take her temperature there rather than by putting the thermometer in her mouth. It had worked the last time, when she had lied about a glass allergy which weirdly only affected her tongue.

Alice waited for the microwave to ping and then put the burning heat pack onto a tray, ready to take upstairs. She then took a couple of chillies out of a jar she found in one of the kitchen cupboards and popped them into her mouth, immediately sliding her fingers back into the jar for more as the burning sensation filled her mouth. She decided to bring the jar with her so added it to the tray. She was quite certain that the chillies would make her throat look inflamed. To be on the safe side she'd consume a few more whilst waiting for the doctor to arrive. She carefully lifted the tray and headed back upstairs, precariously climbing the stairs towards her bedroom.

She put the tray onto a chest of drawers on the landing. Now all she needed was something to redden her face. Fortunately, she remembered that she had just the thing in the bathroom cabinet. She'd been prescribed some cream a while back, although she'd long forgotten what it was for. Probably a flare up of eczema that she'd somehow managed to concoct. She vividly recalled that she had had a severe allergic reaction to the product on the one occasion that she had used it and it had made her face come up like a balloon. She was chuffed with herself now for keeping it - it would be perfect for creating a convincing rash on her face and chest. It was such a shame that she'd have to spend the rest of the day suffering as a result of using the cream, but she had no choice. She retrieved the tube from the bathroom cabinet and smeared some of its contents onto her face, décolletage and under her chin before scurrying into the bedroom, grabbing the items from the tray on her way.

She lay on the bed, practising a few positions

before choosing the one she would assume when she heard the doctor climbing the stairs. She writhed around uncomfortably and then finally propped herself up in a sitting position with the aid of two plump pillows. Putting the heat pad under her left arm, she dipped the fingers of her right hand into the jar of chillies once more, popping yet another couple into her mouth and letting the juice run down her chin. She never understood why people made such a fuss about chillies being so hot - she'd been known to consume a whole jar full before now and yet hardly break out in a sweat. Talking of heat, she could already feel that awful cream starting to do its work.

She carefully leant over to open the drawer of the bedside cabinet, reached in and removed a paperback copy of *The Stud* by Jackie Collins, which she chucked onto the floor. She needed to make room in the drawer for hiding the heat pack and jar of chillies when the doctor arrived. She chuckled to herself at the foolishness of the local medical team and hoped that they would never realise what she was up to. After all, she had paid her taxes for a few weeks before giving up work completely, so she felt she had at least made some kind of contribution to the system before starting to take anything out.

Alice was acutely aware that she needed to keep her medical records fully up to date in case the authorities ever decided to question whether she was truly unfit for work. In her mind she was absolutely certain that her GP would always verify any disability claim, especially since he knew she had the power to get him struck off. There was absolutely no way that he would ever refuse to sign any form that Alice presented before him. He had faltered once but had suddenly realised the error he had been about to make when Alice had threatened to sue him on the grounds of molestation. Alice would never forget the look on her doctor's face when she'd made those threats, despite the fact that it was all a pack of lies. She'd lost count of the number of forms the doctor must have signed for her since then and dreaded the day when he might announce his retirement. He'd done her proud - Alice couldn't believe all the benefits she now received. She found it hard to understand why people bothered to go to work - didn't they realise how simple their lives could be, just by telling a few white lies on a couple of meaningless forms?

It was hilarious really, since she had already been obscenely wealthy from inheriting her parents' estate when she'd started to make these claims. Yet it was so exciting playing this game of cat and mouse with the authorities, and then watching the extra money coming into her account, month after month. She had never revealed her enormous wealth to anyone of course, especially not to the benefits office or to her very few remaining friends. What did it have to do with them anyway?

Within a matter of minutes, she heard the chime of the doorbell. The doctor had made it in record speed this time. At least she wouldn't need to waste too much more of her day on this, especially since she was now beginning to feel so much better, apart from the awful burning caused by the cream.

Alice hastily removed the heat pack from under her arm and threw it into the drawer, carefully putting the lid back onto the jar of chillies and placing that in there too. She slammed the drawer shut and lay down, assuming her best dying pose. Over the years, she'd learnt that the best effect was achieved by feigning unconsciousness, so she turned her head to one side on the pillow and opened her mouth slightly. Those acting classes her parents had paid for in her youth had been worth their weight in gold. She could feel some of the chilli juice trickling out of her mouth and she tried her hardest to lick it back up without moving. Inevitably, some of it made its way onto her pillow.

As she heard the front door close, she wondered if she would recognise today's doctor from a previous visit. She really hoped so, since at least they would then have the foresight to come straight upstairs. Otherwise, it was anyone's guess how long it would take them if they searched for her in every room of the house. Alice heard the doctor call her name and she had to stifle a laugh. She couldn't quite make out whether it was a male or female voice but either way, she hoped they wouldn't be too long, as the effects of the heat pad and chillies wouldn't last forever. Luck was on her side though, and within seconds she heard someone climbing the stairs. She decided that the footsteps were too heavy to be those of a woman and allowed herself the briefest of fantasies that the hot Swedish doctor was making a return. As the visitor made their way across the landing, Alice smiled to herself and slammed her eyes tightly shut, preparing herself for the performance of a lifetime. She had no doubt whatsoever that this doctor's visit would be adding yet another impressive entry to her already overflowing medical record.

Chapter 3
Jake

The newspaper headline was screaming out at him from the newsstand and no matter how hard he tried to ignore it, it wouldn't let him go. 'Pop Star's Sordid Nights of Passion', it read. He had recognised his brother's photo on the front page of the daily as soon as he had walked into the supermarket. Thank God no one in the neighbourhood knew that Michael was his brother. He only hoped that his wife, Sue, wouldn't see the headline and that it wouldn't make it onto the television news, otherwise she would definitely want to make a big deal out of it. Sue had never met Jake's brother and that was how he wanted it to stay. Jake had fallen out with his sibling just before meeting Sue, after Michael had refused to lend Jake ten thousand pounds as a deposit for a house. It had seemed obvious to Jake at the time that the amount of money he'd asked to borrow was just small change to Michael. His brother had said that he didn't have much hard cash to lend and that the earnings from his chart successes hadn't started to come through yet. Jake hadn't believed that at all; it was clear that Michael just didn't want to help him. His brother was already a big star by then, and had had a number one single on both sides of the Atlantic, as well as a string of other top ten hits. The brothers hadn't spoken since then, yet despite this, Jake couldn't help but feel secretly proud of Michael. They were family after all. Michael was already to the 1990s what the Beatles were to the 1960s, ABBA were to the 1970s and Madonna was to the 1980s.

Jake's attention was brought back to the present with a jolt as he suddenly overheard two women discussing the newspaper headline.

He heard one of them laugh and say, 'I always knew he was one of them!' Jake noticed they were both wearing the same uniform and were obviously employed by the supermarket.

The one who had just been bad mouthing his brother continued. 'Can you believe he was wearing make-up on TV last night?'

Her friend was having none of it. 'Ah don't be like that, Tracy. I quite like him. And they all wear make-up on TV these days.'

Tracy wasn't easily dissuaded. 'Don't give me that! He was really camping it up on there with Julian Clary. A straight man wouldn't act like that!'

'This is 1997, Tracy. We're not living in Victorian England now, you know. You're just jealous cos you know he wouldn't look at you twice. Although didn't you say that you could pull any bloke you fancied?'

'I wouldn't want to pull him! I like my men a lot more masculine than that.'

'Well, I think he's lovely. Leave him alone. You know how the papers like to invent stories.' It was a relief that at least one of the two women was defending Jake's brother.

Jake was tempted to get involved in the conversation, but he thought better of it. It felt quite acceptable to be secretly defensive of Michael, but something else altogether to stand up for him in public. How dare someone else criticise his family though. Sue had often come very close to getting a mouthful from Jake whenever she'd ridiculed his brother, but he had always managed to hold back, fearing her intention was usually to provoke him, especially since she always delivered her taunts with a sickly smile.

Jake was acutely aware that he'd only been happy for the first few months of his marriage to Sue. He struggled now to see the positive things that had once attracted him to his wife. Nowadays, he thought she acted like a spoilt brat most of the time. Her wealthy father owned an extremely successful furniture business and Sue was now also quite rich herself, since her dad had given each of his three children a 24% share in the company. Jake and Sue lived in a large house in Hove, mainly paid for with Sue's money of course, as she was very fond of reminding him. Despite their extravagant lifestyle, Jake was well aware that the money hadn't made either of them very happy. Sue worked long hours for her father and was extremely close to both her parents and her siblings too. In contrast, she always seemed quite pleased that a rift had developed in Jake's own family. When he'd told her that his sister, Alice, had made up lies about him to turn their parents against him, his wife had seemed to take great pleasure in seeing him upset. Jake hadn't been with Sue for very long before he had started to notice her self-centredness.

Giving a very unconvincing smile to the two shop assistants, Jake tossed a copy of the offending newspaper into his shopping basket. He carried on around the store, choosing some milk and a bar of chocolate to secretly eat on his journey home, and then made his way towards the self-service tills at the front of the supermarket.

Having paid for his shopping, Jake headed out into the car park and threw his carrier bag into the boot. He drove an old grey Volvo 850, which at one point had belonged to his father-in-law. All the members of Sue's family renewed their cars each year, and invariably Jake ended up with one of their cast offs. He'd had this car for a couple of years now and even though it wouldn't have

34

been his car of choice, he still enjoyed driving it. He turned the ignition key and the engine started first time, the music from the car's built-in hi-fi system suddenly blaring out and startling him. He hadn't realised just how high he'd turned the volume up on his journey here.

His wife had her own car and didn't have a key to his, so this really did feel like his private domain. It was quite liberating to listen to whatever he wanted on the car's CD player, without having Sue complain about his choice of music. He was currently playing *ABBA Gold*, and 'The Winner Takes It All' was reaching its crescendo. Jake started singing along at the top of his voice as he reversed out of the parking space, and headed for the petrol station on the other side of the car park. As the current track faded, Jake waited for the next song to start. He knew this album off by heart and the next number was one of his favourites - 'Money, Money, Money'. He smiled as he realised just how much he identified with the character portrayed in the song, and wondered if meeting a man with money really would solve all his problems. He shuddered as he imagined his wife's reaction if she knew that he'd had this thought.

Jake pulled up at one of the petrol pumps. Still singing 'Money, Money, Money' in his head, he put ten pounds' worth of petrol into the car's tank and headed over to the kiosk to pay. As he returned to his car, a blue Volkswagen Golf GTI pulled up at the pump next to his and a good-looking, dark-haired guy got out, winking at Jake before heading into the service station shop. Jake blushed, astounded at how much the man looked like Robbie Williams. He was tempted to hang around until the man came back out again, briefly fantasising that they would strike up a conversation. Once again, the thought of the response he'd get from Sue if she ever found out about his gay leanings sent a shiver down his spine, so he jumped back into his car and headed home.

By the time he got back, Sue had fortunately already left for work, so he could sit and read the newspaper article about his brother in peace. He laughed out loud in a couple of places; did anyone really believe the stories these journalists concocted? You would have to have a very vivid imagination to believe that Michael could consume the amount of alcohol they were quoting and still be able to perform so well on stage. Michael had always been teetotal when Jake had known him, so the story sounded extremely dubious.

For obvious reasons, Jake had never actually seen Michael in concert, although he did have a copy of his latest tour video, which he had secretly stashed away from Sue's prying eyes. He had been very keen to see if Michael's stage persona was really all it was cracked up to be, and had covertly watched it one day when Sue had been at work. He'd really enjoyed it and the thought had crossed his mind once again that perhaps he should try to make contact with Michael to see what kind of reception he would get after such a long separation.

When they'd last met, Jake had definitely got the impression that his brother couldn't care less about his family any more. He still felt quite guilty about his own part in their falling out though, since he'd discovered after their split that record royalties really did take time to work their way through the system. He now realised that Michael had probably been telling the truth about having very little disposable cash at the time.

Until now, Jake had always veered against trying to get in touch with his brother again though, the main reason being that if he did, his wife would probably tip off the press and make an embarrassingly big thing of it. Wouldn't she just love to bathe in all the publicity it would cause? She would love nothing more than to be

36

part of Michael's jet-set existence.

Sue was so desperate for fame that when she'd found a couple of adult magazines in one of Jake's old briefcases, she had insisted on him submitting topless photos of her to the 'Readers' Wives' section of one of the publications. Although Jake really didn't want other men to be ogling his wife, he had reluctantly agreed to send the pictures in, in exchange for Sue not confiscating his sleazy collection. Luckily for Jake, Sue hadn't noticed that all the porn magazines she'd found had contained images of naked men as well as women. She had actively encouraged Jake to buy the next few issues, just in case her photo was featured. No surprise really when she therefore went into ecstasy when one of the pictures had made it into print. She'd even taken the magazine into work to show it off to all her work colleagues. How embarrassing was that? Heaven only knew what they would have made of it and Jake was certain that they would now have a very sordid impression of him and his wife.

Fortunately, Sue hadn't yet found out that Jake also had a stash of hidden videos. Soon after moving into their detached home, he had discovered a small ledge up inside the ornamental brick-built chimney in the main lounge. He no longer remembered how he had originally found it, but was fairly confident that Sue would never think to look up there. Jake could only just about reach the concealed shelf, and always managed to graze his arms in the process. He still couldn't believe his luck at having discovered the perfect shelter for hiding anything he didn't want his wife to see. If only the shelf had been wide enough to hide his magazines up there too, then he wouldn't have had to endure Sue's foray into the porn industry.

His wife had found him watching an ABBA

video once and had teased him by saying that two of the gay guys at work were big fans of the group, implying that perhaps Jake was that way inclined too. Since this was the very last thing he wanted her to suspect, he lied that he hadn't actually bought it, but had won it in some random competition in a music magazine. He promised his wife that he would donate it to the local charity shop, although in reality he knew that there was no way that he would be able to part with it - his secret video collection was one of the few things that brought joy to his life now. It had ended up being the first video to make its way up the chimney.

Jake frequently felt the need to escape his mundane existence, although Sue would never understand that of course. The hidden ABBA video had been joined by several others over time, and the most conspicuous of the stash was a gay porn video entitled 'Hard to Please', which he'd secretly bought in Soho on a trip to London a year or so ago. There'd be no way of explaining that one away if Sue ever found it. Until now he was fairly certain that she had no idea about his attraction to men, but the discovery of that particular tape would leave her in no doubt. His brother's tour video was also hidden up the chimney, together with a straight porn movie for good measure, to try to calm Sue's anger if she found his illicit collection. Funnily enough, he'd never even watched that one.

Jake often wondered how he had fallen into this trap; having a wife when he would much rather be in a relationship with a man. Despite the continued, cruel existence of Clause 28, the local government act prohibiting the promotion of homosexuality, he was aware that gay people were becoming much more visible than they had been, say twenty years ago. Yet he still didn't feel able to 'come out' without there being huge repercussions.

Sue had come along when Jake had been at a particularly low point in his life. His parents had recently died and he'd just lost his job. He'd only been in the bar where he'd met her because a friend, whose sofa he'd been sleeping on that particular week, had insisted on taking him out to try to cheer him up. At the time, he'd been bowled over that someone had found him attractive, although now he often wondered why Sue had given him a second glance. On that fateful night, he hadn't even bothered washing, shaving or brushing his hair and he'd been wearing the same clothes for days. Maybe she had seen something in his eyes that had told her that he could easily be controlled.

Looking back, he was certain that his estranged celebrity brother must have been a big pull for her in the beginning. He now regretted having mentioned it to her when they'd first met. She had subsequently suggested he invite his famous sibling along to their wedding, but Jake had refused point-blank. Since then, she had frequently tried to convince Jake that contacting Michael would be a good idea, fantasising that it would inevitably lead to backstage passes, star-studded parties and even more money.

Sue seemed to be able to read Jake like a book and constantly reminded him that she had saved him from destitution. She was definitely an alpha female, both at work and at home: even her father was afraid of her. Her husband certainly was! She would frequently ridicule Jake for not having a job, even though he spent day after day looking for one. Instead of encouraging him and helping to build his confidence, she seemed intent on breaking his already extremely low self-esteem and would often taunt him that one day she'd find herself a better man; a wealthy one perhaps. Little did she know that Jake dreamt of the very same thing for himself.

Things had started to go downhill for Jake whilst he'd been working for a local law firm. The responsibility of the role had weighed very heavily on him and rather than talk about his feelings, he'd bottled everything up. It had all come to a very public head in the middle of a court case where he was representing his company and he had literally crumpled before everyone's eyes. He'd fled from the courtroom a nervous wreck and the case had been adjourned. Jake had never gone back to his job after that. He was certain that sharing the details of this traumatic experience had only added ammunition to Sue's already brimming armoury against him.

Jake got up and walked over to where he had left his jacket and rummaged in one of the inside pockets for a packet of Marlboro and a lighter. Unlocking the French doors, he stepped out onto the patio and lit a cigarette. He had tried so hard to kick what his wife called his 'dirty little habit' many times, but had failed on each occasion. In his younger days, a cigarette would be all it would take to relax him, but now all he felt whenever he smoked was guilt, especially since his wife was always complaining about the cost of him buying them. She was in control of the purse strings around here and she never let him forget it.

A couple of years previously, Jake had briefly worked as a cleaner at a local cinema. He had been made redundant following the arrival of a multiplex on a retail park nearby, spelling disaster for the already struggling, small independent. Jake missed working there, even though Sue would often taunt him that the only work he would be able to get now was as a cleaner. It was yet another thing that spotlighted the difference in the couple's thinking: Jake thought that a cleaner was a very worthy member of society whereas his wife looked down her nose at anyone who didn't earn a significant salary. Jake's current lack of employment certainly wasn't due to laziness; he'd lost count of the number of vacant positions he'd applied for. He sometimes wondered how he managed to keep everything together and was sure that anyone else in his situation would have had a nervous breakdown by now.

Jake's body froze, as he was suddenly aware of someone else in the garden, watching him. He slowly turned his head towards the side gates and his eyes were met by the smiling face of Enrique, the couple's part time Spanish gardener. Jake scoffed at his own cowardice. He was certain that he should have been feeling anger at the unexpected intruder in the garden, rather than fear.

Sue was very proud of the fact that they had a team of workers helping them out at home, with Enrique the gardener being one of what she called their 'house staff'. Jake was often concerned that each of these staff members had a key to the house, or in Enrique's case, a key to the side gates, but Sue always told him to toughen up and act like a real man whenever he voiced his concerns about security with her. Jake was very aware of the fact that Sue had a soft spot for Enrique too, but wouldn't have ever dreamt of confronting her about it.

'Good afternoon,' beamed Enrique, smiling joyfully. Jake tried to act cool and took a slow draw on his cigarette. He hated how cheerful Enrique always was. He also had his doubts about the amount of work the gardener genuinely did for his money and if it was down to Jake, the man would have stopped working for them ages ago. Sue always had the final say though, and Enrique therefore carried on being in their employ.

'I'm here to work in the garden,' Enrique announced in his heavily accented English. Jake had to try very hard not to make a sarcastic comment about it possibly being the first time that Enrique would actually be doing some work. Instead, he found himself smiling back and asking if the guy would like a drink.

'I see Sue in the street. She say she bring me wine when she come home.' Enrique evidently knew her whereabouts better than Jake did, since he hadn't been aware that she was doing a shorter shift at work that day. No sooner had he registered this but Sue appeared. He thought how suspicious it was that Enrique and Sue had arrived in the garden almost simultaneously, but kept this to himself.

'I'll get you that wine', she said to Enrique, with Jake's stomach turning at the fact that she'd spoken to the gardener first. He tried to push his suspicions about Enrique and Sue to the back of his mind, as he had done many times before, but she did tend to make her affections for the young Spaniard very obvious at times. Jake scolded himself for being so mistrusting. What would she see in a handsome, twenty-something guy anyway? Maybe he'd best not go there …

'I'm just going upstairs to change and then I'll pour us all a nice glass of wine,' Sue shouted over her shoulder as she brushed past Jake and headed into the house, snatching the cigarette out of his fingers, running it under the kitchen tap en route and throwing it into the bin. Jake and Enrique looked at each other and there followed an embarrassed silence.

'I'd better let you get on then, Enrique. Looks like there's a lot that needs doing in the garden today. This sunshine is waking everything up.' Jake hoped that Enrique would notice the sarcasm in his voice and get on with doing some work. He was sure that he noticed a look of hurt in Enrique's eyes but he didn't care; the man was here to do a job after all.

With that, Jake walked back into the house and discreetly looked out of the kitchen window to make sure that the gardener wasn't shirking again, or following him into the house to get the wine that Sue had offered.

Enrique was walking across the garden and heading back out to his van to collect his gardening tools, and was removing his T-shirt as he walked. It was a warmish day but hardly the weather for taking your top off, Jake decided. For the first time ever, he was acutely aware of how sexy Enrique was. He couldn't help but notice just how tight the guy's shorts were and he was instantly aware of the response it was creating in his own trousers. Despite himself, Jake now regretted all the negative things he'd said about the gardener in the past and was so glad that his wife hadn't listened to his complaints, but had insisted on keeping the man on instead.

He'd never seen Enrique in this light before - if anything he'd previously found him quite repulsive. But there was something about him today that Jake couldn't quite put his finger on, as much as he would have liked to. Was it that Enrique had recently had his hair trimmed and was now sporting a close-cropped cut? Jake found himself wishing he could run his hands across the gardener's head. Or maybe it was Enrique's tanned, toned physique that was turning him on - he'd never really noticed it before but then he'd never seen Enrique topless previously. Perhaps Enrique did work hard at his gardening after all - you wouldn't get muscles like that from sitting in front of the TV. Jake knew that Enrique liked to visit Brighton Beach whenever he got the chance, and had bumped into him down there on a few occasions. Enrique had always been fully clothed whenever he'd seen him along the seafront, but he couldn't help fantasising that the guy possibly had an all-over tan from visiting the town's famous naturist beach.

Jake stood slightly back from the window so that he couldn't be seen and watched Enrique bring various tools from his van into the garden prior to starting work. He saw him sit down on the low wall surrounding the swimming pool and flex his muscles in the sunshine. Every movement the gardener made just seemed to tease Jake even more and he was so focused on Enrique that he didn't even hear his wife coming down the stairs and walking into the kitchen.

'Checking up on him again, are we?' she asked, making Jake physically jump. He'd have to think fast to explain this one - there was no way she would fail to notice his growing excitement.

'What? Um … Oh no, I didn't even notice him, actually,' he stuttered. 'I was just daydreaming about what you might be changing into on this pleasant, sunny morning, my love.' With that he turned round so that he was facing his wife and as expected, her eyes shot instantly down to his pelvis. He immediately regretted what he had just said.

'Were you now?' she teased. 'Well, we'd better do something about that then, hadn't we?' She took her husband's hand and dragged him towards the staircase. Jake began to panic.

'We can't do that with Enrique in the garden! What if he comes in?' In his fantasy, Jake really hoped that Enrique would. One thing was for certain - it would be Enrique that Jake would be thinking about as his wife had her wicked way.

'He'll be busy for ages yet - and he'll just have to wait for his glass of wine. I've got some pressing business I need to attend to with you first.' Sue gave Jake a mischievous grin as she led him up the stairs.

Ten minutes later, Jake was lying on his back staring at the ceiling and Sue had turned her back on him and was sulking. This wasn't the first time he'd not been able to perform for her.

Chapter 4
Alexandra

As the curtains closed and the audience continued to cheer and scream, Michael found himself at the top of that precarious staircase once again. He was constantly impressed at how such an enormous construction could magically slide back onto stage again at the end of every show. The choreography for his final number concluded with him reaching the summit and shaking a tambourine in the air. His feet were on two different steps, with one empty stair between them. This manoeuvre had always worried him and as soon as he sensed that there was no longer a gap in the curtains, he noisily dropped the tambourine and carefully sat down, by first bending over to put his hands on either side of the top step to steady himself. It was such a relief to have got through the second night's show in Stockholm and to know that he only had one more gig left on this current tour. He looked at the littered stage beneath him and as the cries of the public started to fade, he immediately began to feel the emptiness he always felt after a show. There was always such a stark contrast between being idolised by a capacity audience and then being completely and utterly alone.

He sat there motionless for a while as the crew began to slowly fill the stage, intent as always on deconstructing the set and packing up in record time. Michael always found this disrespectful whilst he was still on the stage, but never mentioned it to anyone, especially not his manager, whom he trusted about as far as he could throw him. It would only end up being on the front page of some stupid tabloid with a headline like 'Star's Brattish Tantrum' or 'Michael's Temper Out of Control Again'. He often wondered how much his manager received in backhanders when he sold these stories to the press.

He decided it was time to head back to his dressing room and really hoped he would get there before anyone else; he hated being watched as he took off his stage clothes and removed his make-up. His manager had no discretion whatsoever and Michael often wondered if he charged his ever-changing entourage extra to watch his client disrobe.

The house lights were now up and the whole stage was a lot brighter, allowing the crew to work safely as they took everything apart, prior to packing it all into trucks for transportation to the next venue. At least Michael felt a bit more confident now that he could see properly to descend the staircase. He carefully made his way to the bottom and cautiously walked across the stage, trying not to step on any of the teddy bears, flowers and various types of underwear that had been thrown at him during his last few numbers. He hurriedly made his exit and the arena manager escorted him down the corridor towards the sanctuary of his dressing room. Unsurprisingly, there was no sign of his bodyguard, Clint. On the way, Michael had to endure the usual hand shaking, ruffling of his hair and mock punching of his upper arms as the stage hands and arena staff congratulated him on yet another great show. He put a fixed grin on his face that he hoped didn't look too much like a grimace. At least here in Stockholm, the backstage staff were a lot more reserved than in some other venues he had played. He'd never forget once being hoisted up and carried along by a team in Rio. It had taken him a couple of weeks to recover from their rough handling.

He ran into his dressing room and slammed the door shut, before locking it behind him. He stood with his back against the door and caught his breath for a few moments. Sliding out of his sequinned jacket, he let it drop to the floor. He had three sets of identical clothes, allowing one set to always be in the process of being cleaned. He found it interesting that his stage clothes would always be collected after he'd left the venue, and a clean set would appear in his next dressing room, ready for the ensuing show, as if by magic. He had absolutely no idea who was responsible for this, but even with Ricky's lacklustre support, the system still seemed to work. In some ways, it felt like being part of the 'Elves and the Shoemaker' fairy tale, with mystery, anonymous pixies secretly working on his costumes behind the scenes.

Michael took a few calming breaths and hurriedly unbuttoned his shirt and flicked off his shoes. He pulled off his socks and undid his trousers, letting them fall to the ground and stepping out of them by taking exaggerated large steps across the room. He scurried towards his Christian Dior dressing gown, which was hanging from a peg on the back of the door. Michael kicked his jacket, trousers, shirt and socks into a pile on one side of the room. It felt quite rebellious to be treating his expensive clothes so carelessly, but that was the kind of mood he always found himself in after a show. He suddenly panicked, realising that his jacket needed to be put onto a hanger so that it wouldn't get creased. It was the only item of clothing not to be cleaned after every show - hardly surprising, considering the cost of it and the fact that he wore it for a total of nine minutes each night.

He knew it would only be a matter of time before

there would be a knock on the door, and his manager would outlandishly appear with another group of sycophants. He'd actually been very lucky the previous night as only a couple of very friendly local celebrities had come to meet him backstage and there had been no sign of his manager at all. Unfortunately, there had been a note waiting for him when he'd arrived here this evening, confirming that Ricky would definitely be making an appearance tonight.

Michael was self-aware enough to realise that this part of his tour routine could sometimes be a guilty pleasure, since he had met several of his own idols this way: Joan Collins, Grace Jones, George Michael, Liza Minnelli, Dusty Springfield - they'd all come to his dressing room to meet him during his career. They had all far exceeded Michael's expectations and had all been absolutely fabulous. Although generally, he had to admit that these amazing people were rare pearls. The majority of his after-show guests were complete losers, and whenever he encountered them, he felt like a caged animal in a travelling circus.

It always amused Michael how most people who came backstage would discreetly observe him in his dressing gown, and inadvertently focus on his exposed chest, naked calves and bare feet whilst they were talking to him. Michael knew exactly what they would be thinking - that he probably wasn't wearing anything underneath. With his stunning good looks, he was sure that this would make the ladies' hearts beat faster, as well as a few of the men. He briefly considered giving tonight's after-show visitors a flash; it would certainly liven up the proceedings - for him, at least. It gave him quite a kick to greet his guests in only his dressing gown, and he felt like a real tease at times. But hey - if you couldn't tease your so-called fans, then there really was no hope. On most occasions, his backstage visitors would have been right with their assumptions, and Michael wouldn't be wearing anything under his robe. But tonight, he was wearing his favourite Jockey briefs - it was cold here in Sweden.

True to form, no sooner had Michael put on his dressing gown than there was a loud knock on the door, making him jump. Suddenly the panic started again. After the deafeningly loud concert, this dressing room seemed so quiet, and the knock on the door was like a sudden clap of thunder. Michael tried to calm himself. Within seconds, there was another, even louder knock and someone rattled the handle of the door. He knew that he had to get his act together, since he had no choice but to put on a good show for his manager's cronies.

Michael tried to take some more calming breaths before reluctantly unlocking the door. In a split second, he was violently pushed out of the way, and in walked his manager, Ricky Dallas, followed by an entourage of about a dozen people. The dressing room here was probably one of the largest Michael had ever occupied, and right now he was glad of that. Ricky was all smiles, acting like the cat that had just got the cream.

Michael sometimes found his manager's behaviour quite embarrassing. Ricky had allegedly been a big star in the 1960s, although nobody, apart from Ricky himself, could remember any of his success. The most perplexing thing of all was that Ricky would often wax lyrical about his past triumphs, and loved to tell stories about how his fans wouldn't let him leave the stage. Michael found it all a bit dismissive, considering how successful he himself was right now, and especially since Ricky implied that his own success had definitely eclipsed Michael's own. Ricky would often brag about how he had made a fortune, although he seemed to have very little to show for it these days. He hadn't aged well either and the excesses of drink and drugs had taken their toll on his appearance.

Ricky was in his element as he approached Michael. 'Great show as always, dear boy,' he gushed. Michael squirmed as he realised that his manager was about to embrace him. Ricky reeked of his usual, very strong, cheap after-shave and Michael always found himself stinking of it for hours, after he'd been subjected to one of Ricky's bear hugs. But now was probably not the right time to address this particular issue, so he just stood there as Ricky threw his arms around him and kissed him forcefully on both cheeks. Michael tried not to make his irritation evident to the other people in the room and shot as genuine a smile as he could muster in their direction.

After what felt like an eternity, Ricky stood back and turned to the assembled crowd. Michael came to the conclusion that his manager looked even more fake tonight than the last time he had seen him. He had obviously dyed his hair again, but not very successfully, since there were evident streak marks running down his face and neck from his hairline. Ricky must have been in front of the sun lamp again too, because he had a very uneven tan. He had bragged to Michael in the past about how he and his wife would often have a 'spa day' at home, where they would replicate all the things you would usually do at an expensive spa. Michael wondered what Ricky did with all the money that he earnt through being his manager, since he seemingly couldn't afford to go to a proper spa. His clothes always looked very old too and sometimes even threadbare. He was sure that Ricky thought that he looked amazing, yet you didn't have to study him for long to see that it was all a very thin disguise. Maybe the very heavy after-shave was also meant to be part of that deception. Michael had frequently seen Ricky take a bottle of cologne out of his bag and spray it liberally across his face and clothes, as if it were some kind of fairy dust that would make him sparkle. It was all quite sad really.

Michael's heart suddenly skipped a beat, since there before him stood the most gorgeous looking woman he had ever seen in his life. He felt his face redden and tried not to stare as his manager continued to mumble something in the direction of the gathered party. There were over a dozen people standing in the room at that particular moment, yet Michael's eyes were fixed on one person only. The young woman gave Michael the sweetest of smiles. He suddenly noticed that his manager had launched into introductions, and Michael hoped that he hadn't missed catching her first name.

Ricky was definitely out to impress this particular group and seemed intent on presenting them all one by one. With an exaggerated air of aplomb, he gently took the first guest by the arm and led them towards Michael. This individual looked very much like Ricky, and Michael wondered at first if it could be his manager's brother. The man enthusiastically shook Michael's hand and in a hushed tone, whispered into his ear that he was the director of his own investment company and would be more than happy to take care of some of Michael's money for him. He had a very distrustful look and Michael was relieved when his manager abruptly led him away and brought the next person forward. Each member of the party shook Michael's hand and congratulated him on his outstanding performance. Ricky seemed to be saving the best looking of the bunch to last, and it felt like torture. Michael wondered if perhaps he was doing this on purpose, since he must have been well aware that Michael would find this particular lady attractive. *After all, who wouldn't?* thought Michael. Eventually, Ricky took the woman by the arm and led her forward.

Michael was trying his best not to make it obvious that he found her so alluring. She really wasn't his usual type at all: he usually went for petite blondes. This beautiful woman was of average height and had long, curly, black hair, with a centre parting. She wore a low-cut, black T-shirt underneath a black, rock chick style leather jacket and black jeans. She was sporting a pair of kitten-heel black boots, which her jeans were tucked into. As she approached, Michael noticed that she was wearing a very subtle, flowery perfume. It was actually quite amazing that he could smell it at all considering Ricky's heavy scent, which had now engulfed the room. The other guests were all wearing coats, since it was freezing outside, yet the only concession this tough cookie of a woman seemed to be making to the cold weather was a long woollen scarf, draped around her neck, and a small raspberry-coloured beret, which she wore set back on her head.

'Michael, this is Alexandra Garbo. She's been dying to meet you!' announced Ricky. The beautiful woman's hand came out towards him and he found himself holding on to it for much longer than he probably should have. Or had things just started to run in slow motion? Michael's mouth opened to speak but instead he made a strange sighing sound, which made the rest of the group laugh and seemed to break the heavy atmosphere at least.

'Garbo? As in Greta Garbo? I'm a big fan of those old black and white movies,' he heard himself mutter.

Alexandra smiled, making her amazing eyes sparkle even more. 'Well done - we are related very distantly. There aren't that many of us Garbos here in

Sweden. I think you'll find I'm not quite as reserved as my namesake though.'

Michael found himself almost purring as he listened to her dulcet tones. He'd always loved the Swedish accent. Alexandra had finally managed to free her hand from his clammy grip, although she didn't seem to be making any effort to return to the rest of the group.

'I've taken the liberty of booking a table for us all at a restaurant nearby,' declared Ricky. 'Perhaps you'd prefer it if we let you finish getting changed and then met us there later?'

Michael would usually be horrified at such an idea and absolutely furious with his manager for arranging such an event without checking with him first. He normally hated attending these after-show dinners with Ricky's associates. He also despised having to walk into restaurants on his own and would always feel everyone's eyes burning into him as he entered the room. But right now, all Michael was interested in was getting to know Alexandra better, and all other thoughts seemed to have vanished from his head. Of course, there would be no guarantee that she would be joining them at the restaurant but Ricky had said 'all of us', so Michael was clinging to the hope that she was. He found himself agreeing in what sounded a bit like a whisper - what had happened to his voice? Within seconds, Ricky started leading the party back out of the room.

It took Michael a moment to come to his senses. 'Don't I need to know which restaurant we're going to and how I'm going to get there?' he cried, as his manager disappeared from view. Ricky popped his head back round the corner of the door and gave Michael the kind of look you would give a child who has just been cheeky to its parent in a room full of strangers.

'I've told your driver where we're going, young

man.' Michael's stomach went over at his manager's dismissive tone, especially in front of the others. 'He's waiting for you at the stage door.' Ricky seemed to linger for a moment or two as his gaze shot between Michael and Alexandra. He had a smug look on his face, aware that there was already some chemistry between them. He finally turned on his heels and continued to lead the rest of the crowd out of the room, and Michael heard him continue with his mindless banter as the group made its way down the corridor and away from Michael's dressing room.

As the last of the party left, Michael was pleased that the object of his affection seemed to be holding back. Michael saw her take a card and pen out of her handbag and then scribble something down on the back of it. He was enchanted as she held the business card out towards him with another sensational smile.

'Here - this is where we're going. It's a fantastic restaurant called Berns,' explained Alexandra, 'so please don't worry.' Michael noticed again what an amazingly cute accent the woman had, obviously Swedish but there seemed to be a hint of American thrown in too. Michael took the card and held it in his hand, staring at it like it was a work of art. He was overjoyed, since at least he now had her phone number.

'It must be difficult for you to move around freely, being such a big star,' consoled Alexandra. 'I can only imagine.'

Michael smiled. 'I've had my moments. I try not to make a big thing of it though, if I can.' At least he had found his voice again.

'The restaurant we're going to was established in the 1800s and it's one of my favourites. I absolutely love it there. It's a hotel too and many famous people have been there in the past. I hope you won't be disappointed

- I helped your manager choose it. I'd like to think the other Swedish diners will leave you alone too. We tend to be a bit more reserved than the rest of the world, here in Sweden.' Michael realised that he was starting to fall for this lady. He was absolutely certain that she was the most beautiful woman he had ever met and he felt that he could happily listen to her voice forever.

'I've heard of it, actually,' said Michael. He hadn't, but wanted to give the impression of being cool and of knowing the Swedish capital better than he did.

'That's amazing! Would it be too forward of me to ask if you'd like me to wait for you, so you don't have to walk into the restaurant alone?' she asked. Michael suddenly had a vision of Alexandra standing there watching him as he shook off his dressing gown and prepared himself for a night on the town. She seemed to read his mind as she added, 'I would wait in the car of course,' and gave him a cheeky wink. Michael was tempted to insist that she stay, as he knew she'd be impressed if she saw the toned body that was lurking beneath his dressing-gown, but decided not to embarrass the woman.

'I'd really love that,' Michael replied. 'It would mean a lot. I don't think Ricky ever thinks of such things, but I really do struggle with making an entrance on my own.'

'It's ironic, isn't it? You can perform in front of thousands of people but it's much harder when you are alone in the real world.' How did she have any idea how he felt? If anyone else had said this, he would have taken an instant dislike to them for making such a sweeping assumption. But when Alexandra spoke about it, it was as if she really did understand.

'You've got it in a nutshell,' beamed Michael.

'I've never experienced it personally, of course,'

---

she confessed. 'But I've worked as a make-up artist for some years now, and from what I'm told, you're not alone in feeling that way.'

Michael felt it was way too soon to ask Alexandra if she'd like to be his make-up artist for the final night of the tour. He wondered if perhaps she was already working for someone else anyway and just had the night off.

'That's comforting to know. Who have you worked for?' he asked.

'This night is all about you, Michael, not me. Maybe I'll tell you another time. Why not get ready and we can speak more at the restaurant.' She really did seem too good to be true. It was so rare to meet someone in the entertainment industry these days who would want to miss the opportunity of blowing their own trumpet.

'That's so kind. I hope you will tell me more about your showbiz experiences later though. I bet you have some amazing stories to tell. I hope we can manage to sit together in the restaurant too.' Was Michael sounding overly keen already? His manager had once told him that he had attachment issues.

'Probably not as wonderful as the stories you will have to tell me. But yes, let's make sure we sit together tonight. Anyway, I'll leave you to get ready.' There was another dazzling smile.

Michael was desperate to keep their conversation going. 'Do you know everyone else in Ricky's party?' he asked.

'No - only Ricky. He's put me forward for jobs before. He invited me along tonight because he knows I'm a big fan of yours. I live in Stockholm and happened to be free this evening so it worked out perfectly.' Michael wondered why Ricky hadn't procured Alexandra to be the make-up artist for this current tour but was very pleased to hear that she was a fan nonetheless.

'That's very sweet of you to say that. I hope you won't be disappointed when you get to know me better. I'm really nothing like the man you saw on stage tonight.'

'That's good to hear. He'd be hard work, I think. I'm sure I would much prefer his down to earth twin brother.' She gave him a very coy look. 'But you both seem to have the same very good looks, so things are already looking quite promising to me.' Michael wasn't sure who was flirting the most - he or Alexandra.

'I'll meet you outside. Actually, I'll wait in the corridor and we can leave together. It's freezing out there tonight. Don't be long now.' Alexandra gave him a little wave as she left the room.

Michael felt as if he had just been hit by a bolt of lightning. He'd never experienced a feeling like this before, and had always ridiculed people who had spoken of love at first sight. This was totally crazy anyway - he didn't know a single thing about this woman, apart from the fact that she was Swedish and worked as a make-up artist. But she seemed very sweet and where was the harm in a bit of flirtatious banter? She would definitely make the rest of the evening much more bearable. Michael really did feel that tonight was going to be very different to one of Ricky's usual boring dinners.

A surge of adrenalin rushed through him, although this time it was pleasurable, rather than being the beginning of yet another panic attack. Before he could stop himself, he found himself dancing on the spot. As he slowly did a mock strip tease and threw his dressing gown onto the floor, his body froze as he spotted that the dressing room door hadn't been closed properly and that a pair of cute, inquisitive, very Swedish eyes were following his every move. Michael blushed but decided to make the most of it, and carried on with his fervid dance.

Chapter 5
BLT

Alice's Jeep sped down the M20 towards Dover, its tyres occasionally skidding on the rain-drenched tarmac as she overtook all the other motorway drivers. Throughout the journey, she frequently commented on how annoying the other motorists were to be abiding by the national speed limit. Her three passengers alternated between frantically staring out of the side windows and glancing at each other; anything to avoid looking ahead to see what might be in their path. Alice's average speed was far exceeding 100 mph. They all knew better than to comment on her reckless driving though; Brian had attempted to do so on a previous trip and had been sent to Coventry for weeks afterwards.

As if to make matters worse, Alice insisted on eating non-stop throughout the journey too. They had only been on the road for just over an hour, but she had already consumed two rounds of cheese and pickle sandwiches, three Mr Kipling Cherry Bakewells, a family sized chocolate bar and a cheese and onion pasty. The fact that Alice was a pescatarian certainly didn't mean that she had a healthy diet. She was washing everything down with a large bottle of cheap supermarket-brand cola. Brian had drawn the short straw and was sitting in the front passenger seat, in charge of passing Alice the food upon request from two large Tupperware boxes she'd prepared earlier. She threw the cola bottle back at him after taking another slug from it and the fizzy liquid splashed onto the new Spice Girls T-shirt he'd bought especially for the trip. He exchanged an angry look with the two passengers on the back seat.

Ironically, compared to Alice's prolific appetite, none of her companions had eaten a single morsel that morning so far. The inhuman noises made by the driver as she belched her way through the entire contents of the food boxes were enough to put the others off from attempting to share any of the produce she had brought along.

'Are you sure we're going to make it to the ferry in time?' asked Brian, the constant worrier of the group, as Alice swerved to avoid yet another car. After a few seconds he realised she hadn't heard him. The car's CD player had been blaring out 70s hits ever since they'd left Brighton. Occasionally, between mouthfuls of food, Alice would throw her left arm out across Brian, as if to silence him, and scream out a handful of lyrics she remembered from one of the songs.

'CAN WE TURN THE MUSIC DOWN A BIT?' screamed Tim, sitting with his ex-partner Louis on the back seat, before adding more quietly, 'I can't hear what anyone is saying.'

Alice grunted in temper and clicked the music off completely. Poor Baccara were cut off in their prime. There was no way they'd be getting that boogie now. Louis and Brian both glared at Tim, who blushed as his guilt suddenly hit home. He found his mouth drying up as he realised that he had now created an excruciating atmosphere and that he was therefore solely responsible for trying to salvage the rest of the journey.

What he hadn't realised was that Alice was on a much shorter fuse than normal that day. The postman had thrust an envelope into her hand as she'd opened the front door to leave home. She'd considered just throwing it onto the doormat at first, thinking she could deal with it when she got back, but then curiosity had got the better of her. She'd torn it open to discover a letter from the authorities, inviting her in for an interview the following week. *What a lot of fuss and nonsense*, was her first thought. She wasn't due for a review of her benefit claims for another nine months, so it had naturally sparked some concern. She knew she'd be able to give an outstanding performance at the interview and would practice with her crutches beforehand, but it didn't stop her dwelling on the impromptu request. No matter how hard she tried to shake it off, the nagging worry wouldn't go away.

Tim racked his brain for a subject that Alice wouldn't be able to resist getting involved in and eventually decided to try to pander to her ego. 'I still can't believe how clever you were to win that competition, Alice. And how kind you were to invite the three of us along to share your prize with you. I've never been to Paris before,' he said, knowing that Alice loved flattery. Louis beamed at him. Despite their break-up a few months previously, Tim and Louis were still the greatest of friends.

The boys all held their breath for a moment but Tim's strategy worked. Alice broke out in a broad smile as she bathed in the glory of having won the 'Trip to Paris' competition in her local newspaper. The prize had originally been for two flight tickets and accommodation in the French capital, but Alice had managed to get the flights converted to a ferry crossing for a car and four passengers instead, lying to the newspaper that she had a fear of flying. The trip would be much more fun with three friends, rather than just one, plus much more advantageous to her financially.

Alice responded to Tim's praise with her typical monosyllabic laugh, which sounded more like a honk than anything else. She looked at him over her shoulder and pulled a face of pure pride. All three of her co-passengers let out a harmonious cry of fear as they noticed that she had taken her eyes off the road, yet again. Alice seemed completely oblivious to the fact that she was meant to be observing what was going on ahead of her on the motorway.

'It wasn't that difficult to answer the questions actually. I know Paris like the back of my hand,' she gloated.

The boys knew all about Alice's many trips to Paris - they'd had to endure her talking about them enough in the past. Alice usually travelled everywhere by plane, which was quite convenient with her living fairly close to London Gatwick airport. The boys had actually been very puzzled as to why she had chosen to travel by road and sea this time, especially since Brian had seen the competition when it had originally appeared in the newspaper, and remembered quite clearly that it had mentioned air travel as part of the prize. Little did they know that Alice had already worked out in her head that this would definitely be a much better option for her; for a start she'd already asked the three boys to pay a token £30 each towards petrol. She'd insisted that the newspaper had only given her enough funds for the ferry crossing, and nothing towards the journey to the port and back, which was why she needed them all to chip in. This was all a complete lie, of course.

Alice had arranged to park her car free of charge at a long-lost penfriend's house to the west of Paris, although she'd told her travelling companions that she would be paying the owners of the property to leave her car there for the weekend. They hadn't been at all surprised to discover that this was yet another cost they needed to contribute to. If the boys had had any sense, they would have realised that they could have each afforded a return plane ticket to Paris for a lot less than the outrageous sum of money that Alice was charging them for this journey to France and back.

'I'm really in awe of you, Alice. I've always wanted to go to Paris and I think it's so impressive that you know the city so well,' enthused Tim from his back seat.

It was quite incredible how Alice, at the age of 26, had already travelled so much. She had clocked up more air miles than anyone else the boys knew, not only in Europe but in America and Australia too. Despite the fact that the three of them worked so hard, none of them ever quite managed to match Alice's extravagant lifestyle or to equal her impressive travel record.

Alice had been in her late teens when they'd first met her and even back then she'd often bragged incessantly about the number of overseas trips she'd been on with her parents. She'd also boasted outlandishly about how rich they were. After her mum and dad had both died, she'd complained to her friends that she'd 'only' inherited their house and that her brothers had shared the rest. This couldn't have been any further from the truth.

Alice seemed to have a bottomless pit of money and spent a fortune on memorabilia by her favourite artists: Erasure, Pet Shop Boys and the Communards, to name but a few. The boys had first made her acquaintance in a gay bar in Brighton, and at the time they'd assumed she was a lesbian. When they'd tried to fix her up with a female friend from their group, Alice had been horrified and had explained that the only reason that she frequented that particular bar was because she felt less intimidated by the men there, unlike at 'straight' venues. Over the years, the boys had discussed amongst themselves whether Alice was in fact asexual, since they'd never known her go on a date with anyone of either sex. It was a subject they'd never been brave enough to broach with her.

'When were you last in Paris?' asked Louis.

'Just a couple of years ago. I went with Nigel. Although the less said about him the better.' The boys had witnessed her latest argument with him at first hand when they'd all been out together a couple of nights previously, and therefore chose not to comment. 'We stayed in his mum's apartment near the Sorbonne,' she continued. Nigel had already told them all about it and they were well aware that Alice hadn't contributed a single penny towards anything on that particular trip.

Yet again, Nigel had been ousted from Alice's circle of friends, after he had suggested that Alice must be illegally claiming benefits. Everyone who'd ever been close to Alice felt the same way as Nigel did about her finances and where she must be getting all her money from, but nobody else had ever dared to vocalise this opinion before.

Alice hadn't worked in all the years the boys had known her, although she claimed she had once been employed as an admin assistant at a local clinic. As if to confirm everyone's suspicions, on the very rare occasion when she bought a round of drinks, she would always raise a toast, smirking 'this one's on the government.' Alice could be quite crass at times and certainly wasn't afraid of hiding the fact that she had lots of disposable cash. The fact that she drove a six-month old Jeep was also testament to that.

All three boys had frequently wondered why they stayed in contact with Alice, since she was often extremely rude to them. They usually concluded that, in some perverse way, she amused them. She was a larger-than-life character who, despite her vicious tongue, was more entertaining than the most hilarious comedy character they'd ever seen on TV. They all enjoyed a good gossip about her behind her back.

The boys screamed as Alice swerved again, narrowly avoiding yet another car.

'April in Paris,' sighed Tim, once they had all recovered.

'You do realise that it's still only March though?' asked Brian, realising that his friend was probably still nervous after his previous faux pas.

Tim blushed. 'Well, it's almost April.' He anxiously laughed and Brian gave him an understanding wink. Alice ignored the comment completely.

'So do you know exactly where we're staying whilst we're in Paris?' Louis was definitely the most excited of the group, and had taken out a Paris map he'd purchased in London before the trip, which he was now perusing.

'The hotel is near the Bastille apparently,' replied Alice. 'It's very central.'

'Isn't that a prison?' asked Tim, sounding concerned.

Louis laughed. 'It was a prison, but I think you'll find it was destroyed during the revolution.' He was tempted to comment that Alice would probably quite happily let the three of them stay free of charge in a prison if it meant that she could still pocket the money they had paid her for their hotel rooms, but bit his tongue instead.

'Hopefully we'll be able to sample the nightlife while we're there as well,' Alice continued. 'I hope you boys have brought enough spending money?'

All three of Alice's passengers had spent hours on the phone to each other before the trip, discussing how much money they should take with them. They had eventually decided to bring along just a handful of francs, and to take their credit cards with them as a back-up, just in case. They'd made a pact not to mention the credit cards to Alice though. Otherwise, she'd be booking tables at the most expensive restaurants in Paris, assuming they would be picking up the bill. Nobody answered Alice's question but they all exchanged a knowing look.

One of the things that annoyed the boys most about Alice was that she had found it absolutely hilarious when she had discovered that some of their other friends occasionally referred to the three of them as BLT, an acronym for a bacon, lettuce and tomato sandwich of course but also, unfortunately, for their combined first names. She had rarely called them anything else since then. Although it had been quite funny the first time they'd heard it, the joke was wearing extremely thin now. They knew that Alice would use the term even more if she knew just how much it annoyed them, which is why they had chosen never to comment on it since. All three of them knew that they would be hearing this acronym many times during their time in Paris.

Keeping just one hand on the steering wheel, Alice reached across and took out a wallet of CDs from the glove compartment. Ignoring the road ahead once more, she flicked through the discs and selected the one she wanted. She ejected the previous one from the car's music system and clumsily put it back with the others, feeding the new disc into the slot. Swerving to avoid a van in her path, she handed the CD wallet to Brian, for him to put back into the glove compartment. The boys were well aware that they wouldn't be hearing any current music - Alice had frequently shared her hatred of anything that had made it into the charts in the last ten years or so. ABBA's 'Summer Night City' began to blare out of the car's speakers, its sudden introduction making them all jump. Tim glanced at Louis and rolled his eyes, mouthing 'More ABBA Gold'. It wasn't that the boys didn't like the Swedish group, in fact all three of them were big fans. It was just that Alice seemed to be stuck in a 70s time-warp.

Due to the volume of the music, not another word was spoken by the travelling companions until they reached Dover. The port seemed very quiet as they approached the ferry terminal, and they were all surprised to get through security and passport control without even having to leave the car. Everything seemed to go very smoothly, apart from Alice accusing Tim of flirting with the port official who had come over to the vehicle to check their documents. This really made the boys laugh, since the man was at least fifty years older than them and looked as if he was on his last legs.

They waited in a queue to board the Sealink ferry for a very short time and Alice was soon instructed to drive her vehicle onto the boat. They were all pleased to get out of the car and hurriedly made their way up the stairs to find a suitable place to sit for the duration of the crossing. Alice wanted to sit as close to the bar as possible and when Tim asked if anyone would like something to drink, Alice shocked everyone by ordering a meal as well. After everything else that she'd consumed on the car journey, the boys were amazed that she would have room for any more food, let alone the large portion of fish and chips she requested. Tim now wished he'd never offered to get drinks, since he found himself paying for Alice's food too. So much for the boys' pact not to fall for Alice's usual trick of getting others to pay.

By the time that Alice had finished her food, Brian was feeling quite poorly. He'd suffered from travel sickness as a child, but had hoped that he'd grown out of it by now. Unfortunately, this wasn't the case. The other two boys did their best to look after him, although Alice made it clear that she thought he was making a terrible fuss about nothing, and even went as far as saying that she thought he was putting the whole thing on, despite his dreadful colour and the fact that he had to run to the toilet every ten minutes or so.

Fortunately for Brian, it wasn't too long before they arrived in Calais, and they were soon driving on very clear French roads towards Paris. It was obvious from the start that Alice wouldn't be making any concession to Brian's fragile state by driving any less erratically. If they thought that her driving had been bad in the United Kingdom, it was far worse in France, where she seemed to pay very little attention to the fact that she was meant to be driving on the right hand side of the road.

Alice had arranged to park her car at a house in Saint-Germain-en-Laye, a town about ten miles to the west of Paris. The lady who lived there, Martine, had once been a pen-pal of Alice's and had been very surprised when she had received a letter from Alice, after such a long break in their correspondence. She assumed this meant they were now going to be in regular contact again, and was looking forward to catching up with her long-lost friend. Little did she know, but Alice was only interested in the free parking and had no intention whatsoever in rekindling their friendship.

Thanks to the very quiet roads, they were soon pulling up outside Martine's house. They were astonished to find that it was a thatched property, and quite English in style. It was fronted by an extremely well-tended garden, with a narrow winding path leading from the pavement to the front door. There was a double fronted garage to the left of the house and Alice parked her Jeep in front of one of the two marine blue garage doors, acting as if she owned the place. They all got out of the car and the boys took their holdalls out of the boot. They had all travelled very lightly, unlike Alice. They wondered how long it would be before she ordered them to retrieve her enormous case.

Martine came rushing out to greet her friend, so excited to be seeing her again. It had been several years since they had last met, on a French exchange trip arranged by their schools. Alice looked at the woman as if she was mad and was visibly disgusted as she was kissed on both cheeks. Georges, Martine's husband, asked Alice in perfect English if she could please park her vehicle in front of the other garage door, so it wouldn't be in the way of them getting in and out with their own car during the foursome's stay in Paris. Alice seemed quite taken aback when he also asked if she could leave her car keys with him, just in case he needed to move her vehicle at some point. Begrudgingly, Alice handed them over.

After some brief introductions, Martine told them that she had prepared some refreshments, but Alice declined the offer - quite rudely the boys thought. Martine looked very hurt that her hospitality was being turned down. Alice was very keen to get away as soon as possible. The last thing she needed was for the couple to mention that she was parking there free of charge, since she'd already collected her travelling companions' contributions towards the non-existent parking costs. The boys were all disappointed, since the French couple seemed so friendly. Brian, in particular, would have given anything to look inside the house, since he took a real interest in property and how houses were presented. He knew better than to press the issue with Alice though, since she was already acting very tetchily. Once Georges and Martine realised that Alice was determined not to enter their house, they instead insisted on driving the Brits to the local RER railway station in their fiery red Renault Espace. The boys noticed that Georges really struggled to get Alice's suitcase out of her boot and into his.

During the short car journey, Martine mentioned that she hoped they'd all be able to spend some time together when the group came back to collect Alice's car, although the response on her friend's face said it all. The boys knew their return visit to Martine and Georges' house would be just as brief as the one they'd just experienced and exchanged embarrassed glances.

They realised just how heavy Alice's enormous suitcase was when they had the job of getting it onto the station platform, and even more so when they arrived at Charles de Gaulle–Étoile station, where they needed to change trains. They decided to share the duty of pulling the case along, although of course its owner made no effort at all to take her turn. Instead, she just shouted at them for going so slowly. The station was extremely busy and Alice acted as if she knew which platform they should be heading for. Brian, who was still feeling quite fragile, was brave enough to stop and check one of the boards displaying the Paris Métro map. He very soon concluded that they were going completely the wrong way and that they needed to turn around and go almost as far back as the platform they'd originally come from. Alice pretended that she'd been telling them that all along and the boys knew better than to disagree.

After two further train changes, they were relieved to make it to their destination station, République, where their hotel was situated. Alice spent the entire journey complaining very loudly about the French and although she was speaking in English, the others still found it very discourteous and truly hoped that nobody nearby could understand her. They got off the train and headed up to ground level.

Tim and Louis made it to street level first, and were standing marvelling at the art deco Métro sign and an ornate lamppost at the top of the stairs when they heard a dreadful crash and a loud cry. They looked back to see Brian spreadeagled, face down on the steps, with Alice's hefty, indestructible Samsonite suitcase lying at the very bottom of the staircase. Alice was standing next to the case and her face was bright red with anger. She was shouting at Brian.

'I knew I shouldn't have left you in charge of my case, you eejit! I really should have known better than to think you were man enough to cope with it. I hope for your sake that you haven't damaged anything inside!'

By this point, Louis and Tim had rushed down to Brian's side and were trying to help him up. He was in shock and there was blood everywhere. They all glared at Alice, who showed no concern whatsoever. Paying no attention at all to the now abandoned suitcase, Brian's two friends helped him up to the top of the stairs. Fortunately, they found themselves standing next to a Holiday Inn hotel and, without even thinking, they dragged him in, hoping that at least there would be somewhere for Brian to briefly sit and recover his senses.

Tim produced some wet wipes from his bag and started to tend to Brian's injuries. He had cut his knee and his nose was bleeding. Tim instructed Brian to pinch his nose whilst he tried to clean him up. A member of the hotel staff came over and asked, in perfect English, if he could be of any assistance. When he found out what had happened, he went and got a first aid box, taking out a large plaster to put on Brian's wounded knee.

Alice had joined them by this point and seemed to be pulling her case behind her as if it weighed very little. She was obviously much stronger than the three boys and was evidently still furious with Brian for losing grip of her precious suitcase and didn't seem to care at all that he was hurt.

'If we don't get a move on, they'll release our hotel rooms to someone else,' she chided.

'I think you're being very unreasonable, Alice,' Louis snapped, without thinking. His two friends looked at him in shock, thinking he must have lost the plot. They would never have dared to say something like this to Alice.

There was a stunned silence and for a brief moment, the boys thought the entire trip might be in jeopardy, judging by the look on Alice's face. They suddenly noticed that she had tears in her eyes though, as she looked at them sheepishly.

'I've only got Brian's interests at heart,' she whined. 'I can't believe you could ever think otherwise. Once we get to the hotel, perhaps he can rest properly. I'm really hurt by your remark, Louis. After everything I've done for you all.'

Brian rushed in to try to save the situation. 'I'm sure I'll be fine after a minute or two, Alice. All three of us are so grateful to you for inviting us along on this trip and can't thank you enough. I'm sorry I lost my grip on your case. I'll be more careful next time.' He was in a lot of pain but knew that he had to ignore that right now.

The hotel staff member asked where they were all staying and cheered them up by saying that it was just a short walk away. With Tim and Louis' support, Brian got back up and after thanking the hotel employee, headed back out onto the street, with Alice following close behind.

'Which one of you is going to look after my case now? Obviously not Brian!' she asked, seemingly having recovered from her very brief moment of empathy. She was surprisingly speechless when all three boys ignored her and carried on walking ahead, in determined solidarity, each of them just taking care of their own piece of luggage. They got to the corner of a very grand square called Place de la République, with Alice now making a loud fuss and huffing and puffing as she pulled her case along behind her. They turned right into a smaller street, as they had been instructed to do by the Holiday Inn employee.

Hôtel Piaf was a vintage establishment, tucked away not far down the road they had taken. It was in a very wide, tall building with five steep steps leading up to the hotel's entrance. As Brian struggled to reach the impressive vintage doors, holding on to a conveniently placed railing on one side, Tim and Louis took charge of Alice's case. Once inside, Alice told the boys to wait in the hotel bar, sauntering off in the direction of the reception desk. Louis, whose parents lived in France and who was fluent in French, chuckled to himself at the thought of how Alice was going to conduct herself whilst attempting to check them all in. He'd have loved to have followed her but decided that it was probably best if he didn't. She had conveniently forgotten about his French language skills and he was quite relieved. Otherwise, she'd have been pushing him forward all weekend to deal with the locals. He'd discussed this with the others before the trip and they had agreed that he was doing the right thing by not mentioning it to Alice.

They made themselves comfortable in the hotel's bar area. It was the first time they'd been alone, without Alice, since they had left Brighton. In whispered tones, in case she suddenly returned, they discussed their plight.

Brian was keen for the three of them to find a different hotel and to continue their holiday without Alice, even if it meant losing money, but the others thought it best to see how the rest of the day panned out, comforting their friend by saying that at least the three of them were in this together. They agreed to do their best to ignore Alice's selfish, bullying behaviour and to try to still have a good time.

It was a few minutes before Alice reappeared, holding up just two key cards. Since there didn't appear to be a barman on duty, the boys hadn't yet managed to get any drinks.

'There's been some kind of mix up with the reservation,' sniggered Alice. The boys noticed that she didn't look at all concerned. 'The newspaper has only booked two rooms - a double room for me and another room with three single beds for you chaps. It looks like the three of you will have to share, but I'm sure you won't mind doing that.'

When the trip had originally been discussed, Brian had revealed to the others that he distinctly remembered that the prize advertised in the newspaper had only included one double room. They were therefore well aware that Alice must be making an additional booking for the extra room herself. They also knew that she would have gone for the cheapest option available, despite charging the boys top dollar for it. Tim took the key card from her and looked at the other two as he raised his eyebrows.

Alice caught sight of this and glared at him. 'Consider yourselves lucky that there was a room available and that I invited you along in the first place. I've got plenty of other friends I could have chosen instead. Anyway, there's no time to worry about it now; we've got to make the most of our time here. So come on, let's get unpacked so we can hit the town.'

The boys wondered who these other imaginary friends of Alice's were, since she hadn't mentioned anyone else to them for a very long time. And at that precise moment, they weren't feeling particularly lucky to have been invited along.

Alice put Tim and Louis in charge of her weighty case again. 'The lift is out of order apparently, and I'm not going to be able to carry this up the stairs,' she explained. Trying to make Brian laugh and raise his spirits, Tim discreetly asked his two friends what Alice might have packed for such a short stay in the French capital, to make the case weigh so much. Neither of them dared to reply, just in case Alice overheard.

Like a small flock of sheep, the three lads followed Alice up the winding staircase to their rooms, with Brian limping slightly and the other two still struggling to handle Alice's enormous suitcase. They reached Alice's room first and Tim and Louis managed to drag the huge case in, leaving it in the middle of the room.

Unsurprisingly, Alice's room was very luxurious with a massive queen-sized bed in the middle and a balcony overlooking the street. The boys looked at each other and smiled, hopeful that their room would be of a similar standard. They didn't manage to linger for long though, with Alice insisting that she wanted to come with them to inspect their accommodation.

They were totally shocked when they reached the top of another narrow staircase and opened the door to their room. It was nothing like Alice's at all. Tucked away in the hotel's attic, it had a threadbare carpet and the bright sunshine was streaming in through the windows and skylight. With the room being in the roof, it had the temperature of a garden shed in summer and was sweltering. It had three of the tiniest beds they had ever seen, crammed closely together, and it appeared that the room hadn't been used or even cleaned for a very long time.

Tim ran his finger along the top of a rickety chest of drawers on one side of the room and was visibly stunned at how thick the dust was. They all noticed that the look on Alice's face was one of amusement rather than concern. As soon as she had contented herself with the dilapidated state of the boys' accommodation, she turned around and headed back towards the door, chuckling to herself.

'I'll give you fifteen minutes to get unpacked,' she shouted over her shoulder. She'd evidently forgotten her comment earlier about Brian needing some time to rest. 'See you back in reception. Then I think you all owe me a tasty meal to thank me for this lovely holiday.'

As Alice disappeared from sight, Tim slammed the door behind her. This prompted raised voices from the adjoining room, informing the boys just how paper-thin the walls were.

Brian sat down on one of the miniscule beds and tears began to roll down his face. It was all too much for him. He was still feeling quite rough after both the ferry crossing and the fall down the stairs, and this awful room was just the last straw. Louis sat down next to him and put his arm around his friend's shoulders in an effort to console him.

Tim just stood there, shaking his head. 'That woman is a first-class bitch and I can't believe that she's duped us yet again!'

Brian began to rock back and forth on the bed in despair as Louis tried to keep his arm around him.

Meanwhile, after closing the door to her own luxurious hotel room, Alice dragged her heavy case from where the boys had left it, leaving tracks and a streak of mud on the plush carpet in its wake. She kicked off her shoes and threw herself backwards onto the massive bed, causing it to shudder in protest. A contorted smile spread across her face.

'This is the life,' she squealed out loud, 'I just know that this is going to be the best holiday ever, despite having to spend it with those eejits.'

Chapter 6
The Griffin Cinema

Jake was sitting at the back of his favourite café on George Street, the main shopping area in Hove. He was enjoying a cup of hot chocolate and a croissant with jam - his weekly treat to try to cheer himself up. He was sick and tired of being out of work. In the beginning, he'd enjoyed the break, but that feeling had started to wear off after a short while. He'd not had a job for such a long time now and couldn't even remember when he had last been called for an interview, despite the fact that he'd applied for so many vacancies. In fact, it sometimes felt as if he was single-handedly keeping the Post Office going, what with all the stamps he'd been buying. As time had moved on, he'd felt his confidence drain even further.

He hadn't set his sights too high, and had even been applying for part-time cleaning jobs over the last couple of months. He'd cleaned at his local cinema previously, and had been given a glowing reference. Jake had to smile at the application form for one of the cleaning jobs though, since it asked for details of other languages spoken. Was it essential to be fluent in French now to be able to clean for a living, he wondered. He couldn't quite get his head around that one. Needless to say, he hadn't got the job anyway.

His daydreams were brought to an abrupt halt by the ringing of his mobile phone. His eyes quickly darted around the café to see if anyone else had heard it. He hated having to carry this thing around with him - it was the size of a brick. He hadn't had it for long and didn't know anyone else who had one yet, apart from most of Sue's snooty work colleagues. It was such a pain having to take it with him wherever he went, but Sue insisted that he never leave the house without it. It always made him feel so pretentious whenever he had to use it. Jake blushed as, one by one, the other customers in the café glanced in his direction. As he frantically felt inside his jacket for the phone, a few of them raised their eyebrows.

Jake was quite dismayed when he didn't answer the call in time. What if it was someone calling him in for an interview? If that were the case, he was hopeful they'd leave him a message. He continued searching for his phone in his jacket, amazed that such a large thing could be so hard to find. He eventually located it deep inside the lining. The material inside one of his pockets had split, probably due to the weight of the bulky device, and it had somehow managed to slip through the hole. It took Jake some time to manoeuvre it back up into his pocket.

He hit the power button and the display screen appeared. One missed call - an unrecognised number. He now had the dilemma of whether to call the number back or not. There was no way that he was going to return the call from here though - there were too many people sitting close by and he didn't want them all knowing his business. He quickly finished his hot chocolate and hurried out onto the crowded street.

He headed for the nearby park, where he knew it would be quieter, and found an unoccupied bench. He took out his phone, which he had very wisely put into the unripped pocket on the other side of his jacket, and called the number back.

A friendly male voice answered after just a couple of rings. 'Griffin Cinema, good morning!'

'Hi! My name is Jake Rimmer and I just had a missed call from you?'

There was a brief pause and a whispered conversation at the other end of the phone. Jake could hear the sound of glasses clinking and jovial conversation in the background. He heard some laughter and hoped it wasn't because of his surname. He didn't think he would ever get used to some people's reaction to it.

'It was my colleague Madeleine who called you, so let me transfer you over to her.' The man sounded quite upbeat and Jake thought he detected a slight Australian twang in his voice. There was a click as the call was put on hold and then the voice of an equally friendly female member of staff came on the line.

'Is that Jake?' the lady asked.

'It is. I just had a missed call from you.'

'That's very kind of you to call me back, Jake. I was given your details by a friend of mine, following a job application you made to her company. I was very impressed that you'd listed a mobile phone number on your CV so I thought I'd see if I could get hold of you on it. Are you still looking for work?'

Jake was a bit taken aback that someone had shared his details without asking his permission, but decided that beggars couldn't be choosers. He was also embarrassed that she now knew that he had a mobile phone. It made him feel such a poser.

'Yes, I am still out of work. Do you have something available then?' Was he sounding desperate?

Madeleine laughed. She sounded nice. 'I'm ringing from a brand-new cinema that's just opened in Lewes. We opened on Friday so I doubt you've heard of us yet. It's called the Griffin Cinema.'

Funny name for a cinema, thought Jake.

———

Madeleine seemed to sense Jake's confusion. 'It's privately owned and is a boutique cinema. I wondered if you'd be interested in coming along to see us, just for an initial chat? Looking at your CV, you could be just the person we're looking for to join our team.'

Jake felt himself blush. What did he have to offer? How come nobody else had looked at his CV and thought this before? He considered that perhaps she'd noticed that he'd cleaned at another cinema, but decided not to draw attention to it, just in case she had another position in mind.

'Are you around this afternoon at all?' asked Madeleine. She was obviously telepathic and seemed to have picked up on the fact that Jake was the anxious type and would try to talk himself out of attending the interview if it was planned too far in advance.

'Yes, I could do that,' replied Jake. 'But can you tell me some more about the job before I drive over there? I'm also a bit concerned that you've been given my details by someone else, without them checking with me first.' Although he was worried that Madeleine might be put off by him being difficult, it just didn't seem right that his CV was seemingly being handed around between potential employers. He realised he could be talking himself out of a job here, but it was a matter of principal.

'Please don't worry,' said Madeleine, crossing her fingers as she prepared to tell a lie, but sounding as if she understood his point of view. 'I was chatting with a friend earlier in the week and she was saying that someone really smart had applied for a job with her company but that the vacancy they'd applied for had already been filled. I told her we were quite desperate to employ someone very quickly and managed to talk her into sharing your CV with me. It's all my fault and I'm really sorry. Why don't you come in to see us and I can show you around and explain everything?' she continued. Jake felt quite guilty now.

What he didn't know was that the person who had shared his CV with Madeleine had done so as a joke, hoping to make her laugh at how badly it had been pulled together. Rather than finding it funny, Madeleine had felt sorry for Jake, since the CV had reminded her very much of her brother, who had also found himself out of work, after previously having had a permanent job in a restaurant in Sydney. Madeleine was a very kind, altruistic person and had selected the majority of her team because she'd felt sorry for them. She wasn't quite sure what the cinema's owner would make of that, but she really didn't need to share this piece of information with them.

'What have you got to lose?' she asked. 'We'll even give you a free drink when you get here. We've got our own car park too, so all it's going to cost you is the petrol.'

This sounded a bit too good to be true, but she was right - what did he have to lose?

'OK, give me the details and I'll be there,' Jake conceded.

'I don't know if you know Lewes at all? We're right at the bottom of the hill, just off the high street, near the big supermarket. Do you know where I mean?'

Jake actually knew Lewes very well. Just thinking of the place gave him quite a buzz. Before meeting Sue, he had spent a lot of time there. He loved the old quirky shops, the castle, the Anne of Cleves House Museum - everything about the place, really.

'Yes, I think I know where that is,' said Jake.

'Can you get here in an hour or so?' asked Madeleine. Jake smiled at how keen she was to see him.

He was sure she'd change her mind very quickly when she met him. He really did need to work on his self-esteem.

He thought about it for a moment and concluded that he had enough time to get home, quickly change and smarten himself up a bit before heading off for the interview. He'd be able to get to Lewes in about twenty minutes in the car.

'I'm sure I can,' he answered.

'Sounds good,' she concluded. 'Just ask for me when you get here. My name is Madeleine.'

'Thanks,' replied Jake. 'I'm looking forward to meeting you.'

'See you soon.' He heard the phone disconnect. There was no going back now.

Jake was gripped by his usual panic. Was Lewes too far to travel for work? Would they want him to work unsociable hours? What would the money be like? He didn't know a single thing about cinemas, apart from how to clean one. And why was Madeleine so keen on meeting him and possibly offering him a job? But since the rest of his day was absolutely clear, he really did have no excuse. Hopefully, he'd earn some extra brownie points from Sue too, who would be impressed that he'd been for an interview, even if he didn't ultimately get the job. With a renewed spring in his step, he made his way back home.

Once there, he did an extremely fast turn-around, putting on his interview suit, splashing his face with some water and brushing his hair. He gave himself a quick squirt of his favourite after-shave, Calvin Klein's CK1, to give himself some confidence. The fragrance had only recently been launched and Sue had bought him a gift set of it for his birthday. He felt quite irresistible when he wore it. He ran out to the car and jumped in, slamming the door shut with a new-found vigour. It was amazing what wearing a suit and putting on a bit of after-shave could do for your mindset.

The journey from Hove to Lewes was a pleasant one and he listened to *ABBA - The Album* on the way, to try to calm his nerves. In the distance, the dazzling sun was reflecting on the surface of the sea, lifting Jake's spirits even further. When one of his favourite ABBA tracks, 'Hole In Your Soul', came on, he couldn't resist cranking the volume up even further. He was totally sung out by the time he neared his destination, and he hoped he wouldn't sound too croaky for his interview.

Arriving in the beautiful market town of Lewes, he turned into the high street and drove along it, remembering earlier, happier times. He knew exactly where the cinema was located from Madeleine's description of it, so he made his way down the hill and turned right.

The cinema was very easy to find, and the car park was virtually empty, so he parked without any problem. He wondered whether punters would be keen enough to make such an effort to travel out to Lewes to see a film though. But then he guessed that the majority of people wouldn't have his driving phobia and Lewes had its own fairly substantial population anyway.

Jake decided he had enough time for a cigarette before going in. He took out a packet of Marlboro from the glove compartment and was disappointed to find the box empty. He tutted to himself. It really wasn't the end of the world though, as he smoked so rarely these days, so much so that he hadn't even thought of buying a new packet. Instead he chose to have a Polo mint. At least he'd have nice fresh breath for the interview.

He was quite intrigued by this new cinema so decided to take a walk around the outside of the very striking building. It was very Art Deco in style and had several golden griffins, perched at regular intervals at first floor level, some of which were currently glinting in the sunshine. They looked very out of place.

There seemed to be two entrances to the cinema, one on each corner, and by discreetly peering inside he noticed that they both led to the same foyer. There were film posters around the outside of the building, advertising what was currently being screened inside. Jake pondered on the fact that going to the cinema was something else that he'd stopped doing since meeting Sue, and this thought made him feel quite depressed.

In an effort to distract himself, he decided to take a closer look at some of the film posters. One of them was for a *Jurassic Park* sequel called *The Lost World*, the title of which seemed to sum his life up completely. What had happened to the easy going, happy-go-lucky boy he'd once been? It really was as if he'd completely lost touch with that world now.

He checked the time on his watch. Still a few minutes to go. Assuming that it would probably look quite good if he arrived early, he took a deep breath and walked in. Madeleine had promised him a free drink after all, and he didn't want to miss out on that.

Once inside, he was immediately impressed by the décor. There was a bar along one side of the room, behind which a member of staff was using a cloth to polish a glass. The barman looked over and smiled at him. He was quite cute, Jake decided. *Easy, Tiger*, he thought to himself. Since the foyer was completely devoid of customers, he felt he had no choice but to walk up to the bar. He noticed that there were black and white photographs of movie stars all around the room, and brown leather chairs and wooden tables scattered about. It couldn't have looked any more stylish.

'Hi there, can I help you?' asked the man behind the bar. Jake thought he detected that very slight Australian accent again and assumed it was the same man who had answered the phone earlier.

'I've come to see Madeleine,' explained Jake. He thought it might sound a bit rude if he mentioned the free drink at this point.

'Oh, you must be Jake,' the guy replied. Jake was a bit taken aback and it must have shown on his face. 'It's OK, Madeleine told me you'd be coming,' explained the barman. 'She said to get you a drink of your choice. What'll it be?'

Jake found himself liking this chap already. 'Could I just have a cup of tea, please?' he asked.

'You're British then?' laughed the man. 'Sure thing. Take a seat and I'll bring it over.'

Jake found himself climbing onto a bar stool next to where he was standing. He did this without thinking and suddenly considered getting down again and taking a seat further away, although perhaps sitting at the bar gave the impression that he was quite friendly.

The barman stopped polishing the glass and held out his hand towards Jake, giving him a big grin. 'I'm Jason by the way. Welcome to the Griffin Cinema.'

Jake shook his hand and then watched him go to the other end of the bar and set about making some tea, eventually bringing it back on a tray. He looked very smart in his tight-fitting white shirt, black trousers and waistcoat. Jake wondered if the guy knew that he was being observed. If he did, it didn't seem to bother him.

Jason slid the tray over towards Jake, and winked. 'I'll go and let Madeleine know that you're here, Mate,' he said. Jake was quite pleased that he'd already achieved 'mate' status with Jason.

Jason vanished, giving Jake the opportunity to

have a better look around the cinema foyer. He already felt quite relaxed here, although it did seem extremely quiet. He assumed there were currently no films being shown.

Whilst waiting for Jason to return, Jake ascertained that there were three screens, since there were large illuminated numbers on the walls at various points, with arrows pointing in different directions. Screen 3 appeared to be upstairs but the other two were on the ground floor. Jake wondered if Madeleine would be giving him a tour whilst he was here. He hoped so. He guessed that would depend on how well the interview went.

Jason reappeared with a 30-something, tall, slim, long-haired, blonde lady who wore a black suit and white blouse - the same monochrome colours as Jason, and obviously the cinema's uniform. Jake assumed this woman was Madeleine. She walked over to the bar, shook Jake by the hand and introduced herself.

'Thanks so much for coming in, Jake. You did that in very good time.' She nodded over to a secluded area in one corner of the foyer. 'Shall we go over there and have a chat? Bring your tea.' Jake wasn't sure whether he'd be able to enjoy his tea now that the interview had seemingly begun. He picked up his tray and followed Madeleine over to one of the tables.

Once they were sitting down, Madeleine explained a bit about the cinema. Apparently, it was privately owned by a local entrepreneur.

'So, tell me about yourself, Jake,' smiled Madeleine. Jake had been dreading this bit. He always thought he came across as quite boring, and never really knew what to say.

'Well, I'm married and I live in Hove,' he began, after a fairly long silence. 'I don't have any children. I've had a few different jobs over the years, but have been out of work for some time now.' Jake didn't feel as if he was selling himself very well.

'Do you like going to the cinema?' asked Madeleine, trying to help him along.

'I love films but don't get the chance to go to the cinema very much these days,' he replied. Maybe he should have pretended that he was an avid cinema goer instead?

'Well, it's nice you've got an interest in movies, at least,' responded Madeleine. 'As I said on the phone, we've only just opened and we're still trying to build our team. From what I read on your CV, I think you'd be really good as one of our front of house staff. That basically means welcoming punters when they arrive and selling them tickets and answering any questions they may have. It would be great if perhaps you could help behind the bar sometimes as well, and of course we'd give you training for that. You'd be showing people to their seats too. We'd also need you to check that the three auditoriums are clean and tidy between movies. That kind of thing, really. How does that sound?'

'It sounds excellent and I have to say I love the look of this place already. It's quite refreshing that it's not like the giant multiplexes I've been to.' Jake was pleased he'd thought of something positive to say. He felt as if he was in a dream and had never known an interview to go quite this well before. He was also relieved not to have been offered a cleaning job.

'It's fab, isn't it?' grinned Madeleine. 'Of course, you'd be on a couple of weeks' trial. Are there any times of day you can't work?' Jake had been expecting this question and had been worrying that he might be landed with unsociable hours.

Madeleine seemed to sense his concern, especially when he didn't reply. 'We can start with some daytime shifts anyway, and then take it from there.' It felt like she was offering him this job on a plate.

'That's brilliant,' Jake beamed. He suddenly realised that working late might be the perfect way to get away from Sue in the evenings too, although he guessed that his wife probably wouldn't like the idea very much. 'When do you want me to start?' he asked, trying not to let the excitement show too much in his voice.

'You could do a couple of hours now, if you have time?' Madeleine suggested. 'Although no problem at all if you need to rush off. I'm sure Jason could show you a few things behind the bar. We already think of him as our very own Tom Cruise, as he mixes a mean cocktail.'

I bet he does, thought Jake.

'I'll need to leave by 4pm, if that's OK?' Jake was a bit worried about heading back home in the rush-hour traffic. He'd have to get over his traffic phobia if he took this job though, especially if he was scheduled to work an array of different shifts.

'That's absolutely fine,' Madeleine replied. 'You didn't even know you'd be working today, did you, so we can hardly say that you can't leave when you want to. Finish your tea and I'll take you on a quick tour of the building. I'll go and share the good news with Jason and ask if he can look after you for a couple of hours. We're not showing any films until later this afternoon, so it doesn't matter that you're not wearing our monochrome colours. Although I have to say, you're looking very smart anyway.' Jake blushed. 'Do you have a white shirt and black trousers you can wear when you're on duty?' Madeleine asked. Jake nodded. 'I'll need to take a few more details from you before you leave, like bank details et cetera, but apart from that we're done. Welcome aboard, Jake!' She stood up and shook his hand again.

Jake beamed. 'Thanks, Madeleine!'

He watched her head towards the bar and speak to Jason, who looked over and gave him a thumbs up. Jake hurriedly poured some by now lukewarm tea into his cup and added some milk before taking a quick slurp. He gave himself an imaginary pat on the back. 'You did good, kid,' he muttered under his breath. He'd certainly be in Sue's good books tonight.

Madeleine came back after a minute or two and invited him to follow her over to the staircase, which led up to the cinema's Screen 3.

'We've got three screens and the one upstairs is the largest,' she explained. 'It has 130 seats. The two screens downstairs have 80 and 60 respectively. Obviously, we show the bigger films in Screen 3.' As they arrived at the top of the stairs, Madeleine pushed some double doors open. The room was dimly lit and Jake thought it interesting that instead of rows of identical cinema seats, this room had rows of sofas and armchairs instead. They all looked new and very comfortable.

'This must have cost a fortune,' he enthused, shaking his head in amazement.

'I think there was no expense spared when this place was kitted out,' explained Madeleine. 'The owner wants to give punters the best experience possible. The old cinema had been virtually abandoned previously, so it took a lot of work to get it back on its feet. For my first few weeks here, I was having to wear a hard hat!'

Jake was quite disappointed that he hadn't been involved at that point. He'd have quite liked pretending to be a member of Village People.

'I don't know if you saw the menus downstairs, but we provide waiter service whilst the films are being shown, in all three screens,' Madeleine explained. 'That's something you could help out with too, actually.'

'I'm more than happy to do that,' replied Jake. 'I hadn't noticed the menus but I was probably too nervous to notice much.' There was something about Madeleine that made Jake feel that he could be honest with her.

'That's understandable. I hope you're going to like it here, Jake.'

They were standing with their backs to the enormous movie screen. Looking out towards all the brightly-coloured seats, Jake decided to ask the question he'd been dying to ask. 'What makes you so keen to give me this job?'

'I know how hard it can be to get work at the moment. Jason is my brother and he was struggling to find work back in Australia, so I think it's a worldwide thing with unemployment right now. He'd been living out there for a while and everything was going well until he was made redundant from the restaurant where he worked. When I got the manager's job here, I asked if he'd be interested in working for me, and he jumped on a flight back to England the very next day. He's still got his British passport so he was able to take the job without any problem. I know he's hardworking and he knows better than to let me down. It seemed the ideal solution. When I read your CV, you reminded me very much of him. You probably shouldn't share my reasoning with anyone else though, as they might think me crazy. There - I've only known you ten minutes and I'm sharing secrets with you already. Just shows you how trustworthy I think you are.' She seemed determined to build his confidence. *If only Sue was like that,* thought Jake. Madeleine seemed very aware, because of her brother he guessed, of how easy it was for your self-esteem to drop after being unemployed for a long period of time.

Jake found himself smiling. 'I don't think you're

crazy. I just think you're a very kind person and I really appreciate it,' he gushed. He found it interesting that Jason was Madeleine's brother and was quite proud of himself for recognising the slight Australian twang earlier. He wondered how long Jason had been living out there to pick up the accent.

Madeleine led Jake out of the room and they made their way back down to the ground floor in silence. She showed him Screen 1, which was just as opulently furnished as the one upstairs. As they crossed the foyer, towards Screen 2, Jake looked over at Jason, who gave him another wink and nodded. Jake decided he was going to like working here.

Chapter 7
Swedish Rhapsody

Michael had never been to Berns restaurant before, but was feeling a bit more confident about going there after Alexandra's recommendation. He remembered from previous visits to Sweden that he would certainly have less hassle from fans here than anywhere else in the world, as long as his so-called *Secret Seven* fans hadn't managed to find out where he was dining. They had set themselves up as an elite group of fans who followed him wherever he went, determined to profess their undying love for him. They thought of themselves as the *crème de la crème* of his admirers, whereas in reality they were just plain annoying. Michael sometimes called them the Enid Blytons, referencing the author of the famous *Secret Seven* series of books, although he'd never dared to call them that to their faces. He found himself constantly trying to outwit them, yet they always seemed to be able to predict his every move and would appear at almost every event - be it an official one or a private function. He often wondered how they managed to afford the soaring costs of air travel to enable them to follow him around the world. On a previous occasion, at a different restaurant in Stockholm, they had waited outside for him whilst he'd been eating. They'd got more raucous by the minute and had eventually started singing a selection of his songs so loudly that the restaurant manager had suggested Michael go out to deal with them. He had done so and signed autographs and posed for photographs, albeit begrudgingly. They had apparently remained outside the restaurant after he'd left through a back door. He really hoped they wouldn't make an appearance tonight.

He did a final check to make sure he'd packed everything into his bag. He often thought that leaving a dressing room was very much like checking out of a hotel room and was glad to see the back of some and would gladly visit others again. Content that he hadn't left anything behind, he walked out of the room and found both his bodyguard and the arena manager waiting for him outside. It was evident by the surly look on Clint's face that he had been waiting for some time. He looked Michael up and down dismissively and continued to chew his gum. It was very tempting to remind him who was paying his wages but instead Michael consoled himself with the fact that there was only one date left on this current tour and then the bodyguard would be out of his life. He would definitely not be employed again.

The arena manager led Michael towards the exit. There was no conversation but Michael knew the format by now and was glad not to have to make small talk. They turned a corner and as they made their way down a rather lengthy corridor, Michael spotted Alexandra waiting at the very end. She gave him a little wave and he smiled and waved back. He'd only known this woman for half an hour or so yet he already felt quite at ease with her, which he took as a very good sign. Maybe it was a bit too early to be building his hopes up like this but right now, she seemed a lot more genuine than most of the other people in his life.

Hopefully, there wouldn't be anyone waiting outside the arena tonight, what with the temperature being so low. In an ideal world, he'd be able to get into the car with Alexandra in peace. In some strange way though, he decided he'd quite like her to see just how popular he was. Maybe a couple of adoring fans waiting for him wouldn't be so bad after all.

When they reached Alexandra, the arena manager pushed the stage door open and stood back to let Clint step outside first. The bodyguard made an overly exaggerated show of checking that everything was safe for them to leave. Michael could see a group of fans waiting by his car, and as the couple walked out, Clint hurried ahead of them and put his arms out wide to stop the fans approaching. Michael recognised a couple of the assembled crowd from a previous occasion, so decided to stop and sign a few things. He was known in fan circles as being very approachable and he hated to disappoint.

Keen to get rid of Clint and feeling fairly safe in the company of his driver and Alexandra, Michael told his bodyguard that he wouldn't be needed any more that evening. It was obvious that the guy couldn't wait to get away as he scurried off without even saying goodbye. *Probably planning on going to some local nightclub to show off his muscles*, thought Michael.

He looked across at Alexandra, who was waiting by the car and was tempted to tell her to get into the vehicle to stay warm, but then selfishly decided not to, so she could witness this very brief fan meeting at close hand.

One of the girls waiting, who was Japanese, asked Michael to sign a CD that he hadn't seen before. He examined it closely. It appeared to be a compilation of his most successful songs in Japan and he was very surprised that he hadn't been aware of its existence until now. He always tried to keep up to date with his own releases around the world.

Michael smiled at the fan. 'This is the first time I've seen this one,' he confessed. She nodded and produced a second, still-sealed copy, from her bag. She handed it to him and in broken English told him it was a gift. Michael was really touched by this gesture and gave a little bow, thanking her sincerely. He carefully signed the open copy for her. Thankfully, the majority of his fans were extremely respectful and made up for the small handful who could be a real pain in the neck. Michael hurriedly put the second CD into his bag and continued signing, making sure he gave the Japanese fan an extra couple of autographs.

Another member of the group, who was Canadian, asked if it was true that Michael's debut album was going to be re-released as a deluxe edition. Michael had recently been informed by the record company that this would be happening the following Christmas, but he thought it best not to confirm this just yet. He gave a very vague response instead. He carried on signing until he knew that everyone had at least one autograph and then walked away, waving goodbye to the assembled group as he went over to join Alexandra.

The driver opened the car door as Michael approached. Alexandra was chatting with the man in Swedish and unbeknown to Michael, was asking him to take them to the restaurant via a scenic route. She was very proud of her home town and wanted to point out some of the most famous Stockholm landmarks to her new-found friend on the way.

As they drove off, Michael shivered as he acclimatised to the warmth of the car. It was so cold out there tonight and he really hoped that Alexandra had been impressed that he had still spent time signing for his fans. He was wearing a coat and a flat cap but was definitely not properly dressed for the sub-zero temperatures in Stockholm tonight. Alexandra seemed quite unfazed by the weather, even though what she was wearing could hardly have been described as winter wear.

'Weren't you cold waiting out there for me?' asked Michael, trying to hide another shiver.

'I guess I'm more used to this weather than you. It's winter right now - so you can expect it to be very cold in Sweden. A lot of people find it depressing but it's actually my favourite time of year. I like how you can go indoors and get snug. We call it *mysa* in Swedish, which roughly translates as 'cosy'. I love to shut the world outside and get all nice and warm,' explained Alexandra.

'That sounds lovely,' responded Michael, genuinely. 'Is it going to be *mysa* in the restaurant tonight then?'

'I'm not sure about that, especially with Ricky around, but I do think you're going to like it there.' Alexandra smiled at Michael.

'I think I will - especially with your company,' he beamed, realising that he was flirting again.

Alexandra leant over and took hold of Michael's arm 'So, tell me - how well do you know Stockholm?' she asked, staring flirtatiously into his eyes.

'I've been here a few times,' he replied, hoping she'd be impressed. 'Although to be honest, I've never really had the chance to look around properly. I've only seen the inside of hotels, restaurants and a couple of concert venues really. I usually just do my show and then fly off again.'

Alexandra smiled at him and seemed pleased with her secret plan. 'Good, because I've asked the driver to take us via a special route to the restaurant so I can point out some of the sights for you. It won't take us very much longer, especially at this time of night. Actually, we can start here.' She pointed out of the car window. 'The area we're now in is called Söder, which was originally quite a working-class district.' Michael really was bowled over by her command of the English language. 'It's now quite a bohemian area,' she continued. 'You can get a great view of the city from up here.'

Michael, who had been gazing at Alexandra rather than out of the window, thought he'd better glance outside, briefly at least. Stockholm really was quite breath-taking. The heavy, newly fallen snow gave the place a fairy-tale atmosphere and with Alexandra at his side, he felt as if he was dreaming.

'So do you live in central Stockholm?' he asked, hoping the answer would be yes. He liked the idea of her living in such an enchanting place.

'When I'm home, yes. I've been quite lucky with work assignments over the last couple of years and although I'm obviously not a recording artist like yourself, it has felt like I've been constantly on tour. I've got an apartment here on Söder, just up there.' She pointed up from her side of the car. 'I don't think I'd want to live anywhere else, apart from in Sweden, although there are also some other lovely places in the world.'

'Have you spent much time in England?' asked Michael.

'Yes, a lot. I studied there after I finished school. But that's for many years ago now.'

Michael realised this was the first mistake he'd heard her make in English. 'You don't say 'for many years ago', just 'many years ago',' he explained. He hoped this came across as helpful rather than as an admonishment.

'Ha! I do know that but I keep forgetting. In Swedish we actually say 'for many years ago' and I often end up doing the same in English. Sorry.'

'Please don't apologise. If I spoke Swedish even a tenth as well as you speak English, I'd be a very happy man. Say something for me in Swedish.'

Alexandra always hated it when someone asked her to do this but how could she refuse such a lovely man?

'*Jag är så glad att vi träffades ikväll,*' she said, giving Michael that corker of a smile again.

'Which means?' asked Michael.

'That I'm so glad we met this evening.'

Michael gave a little laugh. 'Me too. And I can't wait to see Ricky's face when we walk into the restaurant together. I dread to think what he's told you about me.'

'He's not actually told me very much at all, to be honest,' replied Alexandra, not very convincingly. 'He did mention that you're a big ABBA fan though.'

'Isn't everybody?' chuckled Michael.

Alexandra turned away and pointed out of the window again. 'We're just going past the Royal Palace,' she explained. 'Although I doubt we can stop for tea since the king and queen spend most of their time just outside Stockholm. They're a lot more down to earth than your royals, I think.'

Michael looked out at the vast building and thought how lovely it was that it was situated next to the water.

'Over there is the Grand Hotel. Probably the best hotel in Stockholm,' declared Alexandra, pointing in the opposite direction.

'Obviously why I'm booked in there tonight then,' grinned Michael, making Alexandra blush.

'Of course you are. Is it where you always stay when you're in town?'

'It tends to be. I love staying there actually. It's one of my favourite hotels. Have you been there?'

Michael hoped this might come across as an invitation and that if he played his cards right, Alexandra might be joining him there later.

'I've only been for meals in the restaurant,' she confessed, giving him a look which he hoped meant that she had the same agenda. 'We're coming into the main part of the city now.' She leaned forward slightly and said something to the driver in Swedish.

'What was that all about?' asked Michael.

'I've asked him to drive us past Sergels Torg. It looks spectacular at night.'

It was a short drive away and Michael noticed how comfortable he was in Alexandra's company and that whenever there were silences, he didn't feel the need to fill them.

'Here we are - Sergels Torg. I love seeing it at night,' gushed Alexandra.

Michael looked out at a tall, illuminated structure. It looked fairly new. 'What is it then?' he asked.

'Sergels Torg is the name of the square, actually. It's named after a famous sculptor who once lived here. It's quite an important square - the Bank of Sweden has its offices here, one of our biggest department stores is just over there and there's also the City Theatre. This area is known as Norrmalm - it's a very expensive area to live in.'

'Are you charging me for this tour, by the way?' asked Michael, playfully.

'Yes, I'll send you my invoice later. We're not that far from the restaurant now.'

They drove down a long, wide avenue and the driver indicated and turned off the main road, pulling up outside a beautiful, ornate building. Michael admired the row of stunning arched windows all along its façade. There was a covered-in balcony that appeared to be part of the restaurant, running along the entire front of the building. Everything was illuminated in gold and it looked a bit like an enchanted palace. It was evident from the signage that it was a hotel as well as a restaurant and despite the time of night, it looked very busy inside. Michael panicked that perhaps it might not be quite as safe as Alexandra had implied, although he was relieved that he couldn't spot any fans waiting outside at least.

As if sensing his concern, she tightened her grip on his arm. 'It'll be OK. I promise,' she said. With the best will in the world, Michael knew she couldn't really promise that, but hoped she was right. The driver came round and opened the door for the couple to get out. Grabbing his rucksack which was lying by his feet, Michael hopped out, holding out his hand to help Alexandra as she also climbed out of the same side as him. They both thanked the driver, who confirmed he'd be waiting for them outside, whenever they were ready to leave. *So at least there's an escape plan if I need it*, thought Michael.

Alexandra led Michael by the hand towards the restaurant and they climbed the marble steps leading up to its entrance. Once inside, the maitre d' instantly recognised Michael and greeted the couple, taking Michael's coat and Alexandra's jacket, beret and scarf. He then showed them to their table.

The restaurant felt warm and welcoming as they walked through it. Michael spotted a few people check him out as he walked past, but was relieved that nobody seemed to be making any effort to approach him. The candlelight gave a golden glow to the room and Michael could already hear Ricky's booming voice, holding court with his other guests. Fortunately, when they got to the table, there were two empty seats next to each other, on the opposite side of the table to Ricky. The maitre d' pulled out one of the chairs for Alexandra to sit down and once she was seated, did the same for Michael. *So far, so good*, thought Michael.

They were given menus and Michael suddenly noticed that the other diners at their table had already finished their main courses. He thought this quite rude, since it hadn't taken him that long to get changed and they'd all known he was on his way. They'd probably been encouraged to do so by Ricky.

'Are you hungry?' he whispered to Alexandra.

'A little,' she replied. 'I might just have a couple of starters.' Michael decided to let her do the ordering.

Ricky, who had earlier ordered champagne for everyone, instructed the waiter to pour a glass each for the two new arrivals.

'I propose a toast!' he declared. 'To my favourite client, Michael, and … his friend!' It was so obvious that Ricky couldn't remember Alexandra's name, even though he did seem to look very pleased with himself for having introduced the couple. Everyone around the table held up their glasses towards Michael and Alexandra and they raised theirs in return, although neither of them put the glasses to their lips.

'What would you really like to drink?' asked Michael, as a protest against Ricky's attempt to force the champagne on them. It was obviously too much to expect his manager to remember that his 'favourite client' was teetotal.

'Just some still water will be fine for me,' responded Alexandra. 'I don't actually drink alcohol.'

'Me neither,' confessed Michael. 'Although I know it's not very rock and roll. I hope that doesn't disappoint you.'

'Good for you. I think that's great. No wonder you look so fit and healthy,' enthused Alexandra, slightly provocatively, Michael decided.

They mutually agreed to share four starters and Alexandra did the ordering.

'You two seem to be getting along very well,' Ricky slurred loudly across the table. He had evidently already had more than enough to drink. *How embarrassing*, thought Michael. He shot Ricky a fake grin, before looking away and continuing his conversation with Alexandra.

'So, tell me the names of some of the stars you've worked with over the years,' Michael coaxed.

'I'm not naming any names - I'm far too discreet for that. But I'm happy to tell you some stories,' she replied, coyly. Michael pulled a disappointed face.

'Not even for you, my darling,' she added. Just hearing her use this word of endearment towards him made Michael feel all warm inside. She seemed to sense this and gave him a cheeky smile as she continued. 'I think one of the funniest situations I've been in was when I was working with an Italian artist quite recently. I don't think you'll be very familiar with the Italian pop scene, so it's probably safe for me to tell you this story.'

Michael shook his head. 'You'd be surprised. I really like European pop music, although to be honest, I don't actually know that many Italian singers.'

Alexandra lowered her voice. 'He was very vain to say the least and would arrive backstage every evening with a full face of make-up, although he always insisted that he wasn't wearing any. I had to be very creative and discreetly remove his existing make-up, zone by zone, before adding my own.' Michael pulled a face of mock disbelief. 'This happened night after night,' she continued. 'The other funny thing was that he obviously coloured his hair too, but not very well, since there were always streaks of dye running down the back of his neck, where he hadn't wiped it off when he'd applied it.'

'Makes me think of Ricky,' said Michael, nodding over towards his manager.

'Precisely!' chuckled Alexandra. 'I've noticed that with him too'.

'So what did you do about that?' asked Michael.

'I would always put make up on his neck to try to hide it. He must have known what I was doing but never said a word,' replied Alexandra, shaking her head.

'He sounds like a real ego-maniac,' laughed Michael. 'I hope I'm never like that.' Alexandra licked her finger and slowly ran it down Michael's cheek as he attempted to take a sip of his drink.

'No make-up there,' she announced, causing Michael to accidentally spit out some water as he guffawed.

'That was chancy,' he commented, 'I could have still been wearing my stage make-up.'

'And if I hadn't spotted that, then I wouldn't be very good at my job, would I?' winked Alexandra. 'I assume you removed it after the show? You may be one of the top pop stars on the planet but already I get the impression you're actually very down to earth.'

'I try to be. That's something I got from my parents, actually. They were both very grounded. I do look after myself and enjoy the good things in life but I'm just a human being after all. My mum and dad taught me that whatever your position in life, nobody is better than anyone else. And I truly believe that. That's probably why Ricky annoys me so much. He's so full of himself sometimes.'

'Sometimes?' questioned Alexandra, chuckling and looking across in Ricky's direction. 'I've yet to see him when he's not showing off.' They obviously both trusted each other enough already to be able to make such comments. Sensing that he was being spoken about and assuming that whatever was being said was complimentary, Ricky looked over and raised his glass in their direction.

'Up yours, you old bastard!' toasted Michael, just loudly enough for Alexandra to hear. She burst out laughing and tried to pretend that she had choked on her drink. Ricky didn't seem to notice anything untoward in his drunken state.

'I like a man who's a bit cheeky. Just so you know,' confessed Alexandra.

'That's so good to hear,' replied Michael. 'I can be very cheeky when I want to be.' He tried to give Alexandra a seductive look but failed miserably, which resulted in them both dissolving into fits of giggles. Some of the other guests at the table looked at them disapprovingly.

'Miserable bunch of losers,' whispered Michael into Alexandra's ear. She nodded in agreement. Michael took hold of her hand under the table and squeezed it. She gave him the sweetest smile in response.

Although Michael was feeling extremely relaxed, he noticed that he still jumped whenever anyone walked by or came anywhere near their table. He was convinced that he wouldn't be able to get through the whole evening without somebody bothering him for an autograph.

Alexandra sensed this. 'Relax, baby,' she whispered, the candles from the table reflecting in her eyes. She really was having a great influence on him.

Their food arrived: spicy prawns, deep-fried cauliflower, salmon skewers and tofu with black beans. The waiter also brought some other dishes including rice, and various sauces.

'You chose well,' said Michael, tucking in.

'I'm sure I read somewhere that you're a

pescatarian, like me,' responded Alexandra. 'Anyway, it's not hard to choose good food when you're dining here.'

Michael came to the conclusion that Alexandra had been right with her raving review of the place. There was such a gorgeous aroma coming from the food and it tasted out of this world.

'And what I'm really pleased about is that absolutely nobody has bothered me so far,' confessed Michael. 'That's unheard of these days.'

Alexandra looked chuffed. 'I told you so. Actually, I went round to all the tables when we arrived and asked people to leave you alone. Didn't you notice?' Michael laughed again and hoped that this idyll would last for the rest of the evening.

They carried on eating in virtual silence, occasionally pulling faces of ecstasy at each other, prompted by the deliciousness of the food.

'So, who do you have back in England? Have you got a big family?' asked Alexandra, between mouthfuls.

'I've just got one brother and one sister but I don't have any contact with either of them now.' Michael always found the situation with his siblings so painful that he usually tried to blank it out completely. He didn't know Alexandra well enough to share that yet though. His little sister Eva suddenly crossed his mind too, making him feel even sadder.

'I'm really sorry to hear that,' Alexandra sighed, sounding genuinely concerned. 'What happened?'

'Don't think me rude but I'd rather not talk about it.' Michael thought it best to change the topic of conversation, as he was afraid he'd get emotional if he opened that particular can of worms right now. Whenever he was away from home, his estrangement from Alice and Jake seemed to hit him even harder. He was feeling quite homesick tonight, even though Stockholm and Alexandra were both doing their best to make him feel very welcome. Sensing that he should at least offer something else in response, he added, 'I do have a couple of people who live on the grounds of my house though, and they're very much like my family.'

'Friends, lodgers or servants?' asked Alexandra, in all seriousness.

Michael pulled a face. 'I hope they don't think of themselves as servants. I do refer to them as my staff though and they are on the payroll, but they're my friends too. I'd be lost without them. Ted drives me around when I'm in the UK and looks after the house and gardens. His wife, Krystal, does the cleaning and cooks my meals. They live in their own house next door to mine. You'd like Krystal - she's a qualified hairdresser and came over from Germany about twenty years ago. She refuses to do my hair though, as she's always scared I'll ask her to come on tour with me and she's afraid of flying. I really miss them when I'm away from home and they really do feel more like family than staff these days. We often eat our meals together. Ted is a qualified accountant and used to work for the BBC so he's therefore good at advising me if Ricky is ripping me off too, which he usually is.' He suddenly realised that he'd shared a lot more than he usually would with someone he had only just met. He was definitely falling under this woman's spell.

'That sounds very grand having another house in your grounds,' Alexandra commented.

'Actually, I have a question for you, Alexandra. Are you working with anyone at the moment?' Michael hoped she might realise that he was deliberately changing the subject. Fortunately, Alexandra picked up on this and decided not to proceed with her questioning.

'I'm not. My next assignment starts next week in New York. I'm with that particular client for a few weeks and then I've decided to take some time off.' Michael already knew better than to ask who she'd be working for in America. Possessively, he made a mental note to check out who was touring the US at that time, especially since he now knew that they were kicking-off their tour in New York.

'So - cheeky question,' continued Michael. 'Are you free tomorrow night to come and help me get ready for my concert in Paris? Thanks to Ricky, I don't have anyone to help me before the show. It's the last night of the tour and there'll be a party afterwards, where I'd love you to be my guest, if you're available?'

'Luckily for you - and me - I have nothing in my calendar tomorrow, so I'd love to help and I'd be happy to do it free of charge.'

'I think I can afford to pay you,' insisted Michael. 'Ricky is tight, as you know, but I'd even pay you with my own money, if necessary.'

'I know, but it will be a pleasure to be there with you. Plus it's just one night, so it really doesn't matter.'

'Actually, let's not tell Ricky,' suggested Michael. 'He'll be at the party for sure but he often doesn't bother coming to the gig beforehand. That's been my usual experience with him, anyway. I think he likes to go straight to the party, so he can welcome everyone as they arrive. He'll be in his element, acting as if he's the star of the show.'

'That's not very nice of him. He's meant to be your manager and should therefore always be there supporting you.' Alexandra was quite shocked, even though she knew what Ricky was like.

'That may well be the case, but you know him,' responded Michael.

People were preparing to leave the table. Being his usual well-mannered self, Michael stood up and waited for each of them to come over to say goodbye, cringing slightly as some of them gave Alexandra a knowing look, as if to imply that she'd got lucky tonight. Michael was certain that both he and Alexandra had made an equal amount of effort that evening and despite what the other guests might be thinking, she didn't strike him as a gold digger.

Once everyone else had gone and they were left alone at the table with Ricky, Michael realised that he was now responsible for settling the bill and getting his manager out of the restaurant. Ricky looked as if he had taken root. Michael had been watching him and had noticed that he hadn't made any effort at all to say goodbye to any of the guests, but had just sat there in a drunken stupor.

'Have you got a car outside?' Michael shouted across the table. Ricky shrugged his shoulders and shook his head. This wasn't the first time that Michael had found himself playing a game of role reversal with his manager. He called the maitre d' over and politely asked if he could book a taxi to take Ricky back. If Michael had been on his own, he'd have let Ricky share his car, especially since he knew they were staying at the same hotel. But there was no way that he was going to let his useless manager spoil what remained of his evening with Alexandra. He was relieved when the maitre d' explained that a car was already waiting outside for Ricky. Without saying anything further to Michael, the guy called a waiter over and they both lifted the intoxicated diner from his seat and carried him out of the restaurant, much to the amusement of some of the other diners. Michael sometimes wondered exactly what he paid Ricky for - he seemed to cause embarrassment wherever he went.

Michael had enjoyed the scenic journey to the restaurant so much earlier that he was now thinking that it might be a good idea to continue their tour of the city before going back to the hotel. It would also mean that Ricky would be well and truly ensconced in his room by the time they got there.

After a few minutes, the maitre d' returned and explained to Michael that Ricky had given him his credit card when he'd arrived, so he would use that to take payment for the meal. Michael thanked him for the great food and complimented him on the restaurant's décor and found himself apologising yet again for Ricky's appalling behaviour. The maitre d' asked if he could give the credit card to Michael for safe keeping once he'd taken payment.

Alexandra had been watching the proceedings, visibly impressed. 'You're amazing!' she commented. 'I can't imagine many artists dealing with that the way you just did.'

'Just doing my job - not!' chuckled Michael. 'Is Madam ready to leave this establishment?'

The Maitre d' handed Ricky's credit card to Michael as they made their way out of the restaurant. They headed towards the waiting car, hand in hand, and a couple of press photographers approached and started taking pictures. Rather than trying to stop them, Michael decided to go with the flow and just smiled in their direction. He wasn't sure where this relationship was heading, but after such a relaxing evening, he really didn't care who knew how happy he was.

The driver held open the car door for them to climb in and Michael asked if he'd be able to drive them around Stockholm a bit more before taking them back to the hotel. The guy nodded and Alexandra said something to him in Swedish.

As soon as they started their journey, she apologised for bringing up the subject of Michael's family earlier, since she hadn't meant to upset him.

'It's not a problem. I try not to think about it, let alone talk about it, but you weren't to know that,' he explained.

'Well, remember I'm here if ever you do need to talk.' Alexandra really was a very special lady. 'Don't take this the wrong way,' she continued, 'but I won't stay with you tonight. I know I'm making a big assumption here but I wanted to avoid any embarrassment later.'

Michael was a bit taken aback. 'That's OK. Any particular reason?' Was he sounding a bit too predatory? It suddenly dawned on him that she'd probably been giving the driver her address earlier.

'I'm really enjoying getting to know you but I'd like us to take things slowly. I'd hate for us to have one explosive night together and then drift apart.'

'Of course that's OK!' Michael tried very hard to hide his disappointment. 'You're still coming to Paris with me, I hope?'

'I sure am. When do you leave Stockholm?' At least Alexandra was still sounding keen.

'Tomorrow, very early afternoon. Why don't you join me for brunch at the hotel first?'

'I'd absolutely love that. 10.30am OK?' She nodded and gave him a big grin.

'Perfect!' They'd just arrived outside Alexandra's flat and she kissed him gently on the cheek. 'Thanks for understanding.' She got out of the car and he watched her walking up the stairs to her apartment block. As she was about to go in, she turned and gave him a wave and a big, beaming smile.

As the taxi drove off, Michael noticed that the

radio was playing softly in the background. He hadn't been aware of it before but it was now very prominent in the quietness of the car. Jackie Wilson's 'I Get The Sweetest Feeling' was playing. As he listened to the lyrics, Michael thought that the words described exactly how he was feeling at that precise moment.

Alexandra closed the door to her one-bedroomed apartment and wondered how things had ever got this crazy. She'd accepted this assignment to help her out of her current financial state but what she hadn't anticipated was to have genuine feelings emerge for Michael. His public persona had always repulsed her, yet here she was, feeling sorry for the man and beginning to fall in love with him. That had definitely not been on the cards, but there was no going back now. She'd already accepted an advance on this piece of work and couldn't see any other way of paying off her debts. She'd not worked for months and since her parents had been killed in that horrific car crash, her life had turned upside down. She hated having to lie to Michael but there was no other way. Ricky had introduced her to him for a reason and it was essential she got the necessary information out of him. He was nothing more than a deluded pop star after all, and she really did need to pull herself together and stop herself from getting any more emotionally involved than she already was.

Chapter 8
Respite

Alice was leading her fellow travellers a merry dance in Paris. They had been 'out on the town', as she liked to call it, on their first night in the French capital and despite the boys' best intentions, she had managed to fleece them good and proper. She had primed them well over the years and knew exactly which buttons to push to make them feel indebted to her. On this occasion it was for facilitating the trip to Paris. All their cash had gone and Alice had somehow become aware of their plans to use their credit cards in an emergency. She, of course, had decided that she was that emergency. Before leaving Brighton, she'd already planned that she would be spending very little of her own money whilst in Paris.

They had got back to the hotel very late. On returning to their almost uninhabitable room, the boys had spent a long time agonising over what to do about the situation, and had found it impossible to sleep in their rough beds. In the end, at about 5am, Louis had suggested that he go down to reception to see if he could get them moved to a different room. They had noticed that the hotel was exceptionally quiet when they'd returned from their night out - especially for a city centre hotel in a European capital. Louis was hopeful that there might at least be one vacant room they'd be able to move to, since the one they were currently in really was unbearable. He was totally shocked at what he discovered when he spoke with the member of staff on duty at reception, who greeted him in impeccable

English when he walked up to the desk. Although he was a fluent French speaker, he decided not to trump her by insisting that they speak French. He enquired about their reservation and explained that they weren't at all happy with their room.

'Funnily enough, I was on duty when your colleague phoned a few weeks back to make the booking,' she commented. 'I remember the conversation very well because of how bizarre it was. Your friend told me that her three travelling companions wanted the cheapest room available and seemed shocked at the rate I quoted for one of our basic shared rooms. The budget she mentioned was way below the price of a three-person room anywhere in Paris, so my only option was to offer her the room you are in now. It's one we rarely use and on the odd occasion that we do, it's usually for a member of staff who, for one reason or other, isn't able to get home. We do indeed have other rooms available, but they are of course at a higher rate. The hotel is actually quite empty right now.'

Although he was well aware of Alice's devious ways, this revelation knocked Louis for six. He was furious, and knew that his two friends would be too. When the receptionist told him the amount Alice had paid for their current room, he was in total disbelief, since she was charging them three times that price. He knew there was no way they could stay where they were, so readily agreed to one of the alternatives that was being offered. He reserved the new room by using his credit card and commended the receptionist on her flawless English.

She laughed, 'I'm not sure I can accept that compliment to be honest, because my mother is English, but thank you. My name's Katherine by the way.' She held out her hand, which Louis shook amicably.

He suddenly had an idea; a way for the boys to get their own back on Alice. Perhaps they could be just as scheming as their fair-weather friend.

'Actually, would I be able to ask you a big favour?' he asked Katherine.

'That depends. What do you have in mind?' she asked, giving him a very friendly smile.

'It's a bit cheeky but as you've probably guessed, the lady, and I use that term loosely, who made the booking for us is a bit of a monster,' Louis explained. 'Could I leave a letter here for her?' he asked. 'I'm thinking that my two pals and I could play a little trick on her and not let her know initially that we've moved. We've arranged for her to come to collect us from our current room later this morning and when she gets no response, she will no doubt come down to reception, to see if you're aware of where we are. This is where the letter comes in.'

'Do I need to know what will be in this letter or is it best I don't?' asked Katherine.

'Might be best if we don't involve you too much, if that's OK. You'd already be doing us a massive favour by handing it over,' Louis grinned.

'Of course - in fact, I'd probably prefer it that way,' replied Katherine. 'I'm on duty now until 10am, so it's more than likely it'll be me she sees when she comes down.'

'Even better,' smiled Louis. 'I'll go and get us moved into our new room and will bring the letter down once we've decided exactly what we're going to say. By the way, do you have an envelope and some paper?'

Katherine looked under the reception desk and found a couple of sheets of headed hotel paper and an envelope which she handed to Louis. 'Good luck with whatever you come up with. Actually, let me just check something,' she added, as she tapped away on the computer. 'Yes, I can do that,' she muttered to herself, before looking up at Louis. 'I'm going to refund the cost of the original room you were in and add it as a credit on your new room. Does that sound OK?'

Louis thanked her profusely. She gave him a new key card and he rushed back upstairs to tell Brian and Tim the good news. He knew that they would be just as livid as him at Alice's despicable behaviour. His head was spinning through lack of sleep anyway and processing the news of Alice's deception was almost sending him into orbit.

Instead of going straight back to his friends, Louis decided to check out the new room en route. He was astounded at what he found. Katherine had booked them into to a deluxe room, even though the price she was charging was for a regular one. It was quite a relief to find someone so kind and helpful - a total contrast to Alice with her underhand tactics. This new room was outstanding and was more like a suite than a regular hotel room. It was far superior to the one Alice was in. He was tempted to go straight back down to reception to thank Katherine again but decided to wait until he returned with the letter. It felt like he was floating on air as he returned to Brian and Tim. When he got there, he found them sitting on their beds, still looking extremely stressed.

'Pack your bags, Guys, we're moving,' he announced with glee. 'You're never going to believe where we're going.'

'Packing won't be hard, since we haven't unpacked yet,' commented Tim. 'How have you managed to get us moved?'

Louis explained everything as the three of them quickly gathered up their stuff and ran out of the dilapidated room.

'This is incredible!' gasped Brian, when they got to their new accommodation, 'Alice is going to be so jealous.'

'I don't think we should tell her we've moved. I think we should play her at her own game,' suggested Louis. None of them could believe how Alice had gone out of her way to make such a cheap booking for them and Tim shared how he didn't think he'd ever be able to face her again without saying something.

'She's a bitch!' concluded Brian, 'and that's putting it mildly. I wish we could think of a way of getting back at her somehow.'

'I've got an idea, actually,' confessed Louis. 'The lady on reception has said she's happy for me to leave a letter with her for Alice, who is bound to go down there when she finds we're not in our original room. I know this is really bad, but I thought we could leave her a note saying we've had to take Brian to the hospital following his fall. It would explain why we're nowhere to be seen. Or do you think that's going a bit too far?'

'I don't think anything would be going too far, after what she's done to us,' replied Tim. 'Right now, we all need a break from that awful woman. I don't know about you two, but I could do with some sleep before we go out. Alice won't know where we are, so we'll get some peace. Come to think of it, we could even spend the whole day in Paris without her. After all, she'll think we're at the hospital.' He beamed at his friends.

'That's a fab idea! Come on, let's write this letter.' Louis sat down at an ornate desk, in front of a large window with a stunning view over Parisian rooftops. With the help of the other two, he composed what could be taken as a hurried note to Alice, saying how Brian had become very ill during the night, and that they'd had to call an ambulance. They were giggling as they put the letter together. Revenge was going to be so sweet.

Once it was finished, Louis took the letter straight down to reception and left it with Katherine, asking at the same time if they could be left undisturbed in their new room for a few hours so they could catch up on their sleep. Louis also explained how touched they were with the fantastic upgrade Katherine had given them.

She was very modest with her response. 'It's the least I could do,' she said. 'Good luck and I really hope you enjoy the rest of your trip.' With that, Louis went back up to the others and they rather belatedly got ready for bed. The three of them eventually fell asleep after chatting excitedly about how furious Alice was going to be with them and what a wonderful day they were going to have in Paris without her.

Two hours later, Alice was lying in bed, enjoying the Parisian sunshine streaming in through her window. It had taken her a minute or two to realise where she was when she'd first woken up and when she did, a smile had spread across her face. She adored Paris.

Alice remembered a family holiday she'd spent here as a child. One of the cassettes the family had loved listening to in the car was ABBA's *Super Trouper* album, and one song in particular reminded her of that particular holiday. It was called 'Our Last Summer', and was about a couple's romantic trip to Paris. As the family had walked around the French capital, they'd sung some of the lyrics out loud in all the appropriate places around the city. The song was playing in her head right now and it brought back such happy memories.

She jumped out of bed and went into the bathroom, splashing her face with some water. Once she'd brushed her teeth, she tugged off the oversized T-shirt she'd slept in and put the previous day's clothes back on. What was the point of creating extra washing for when she got back home? There really was no time to waste - Paris was waiting! She grabbed her rucksack and headed up to the boys to wake them.

Alice knocked on what she believed to be their door for several minutes. Eventually someone from a neighbouring room came out and angrily shouted something at her in French. Alice swore back in English and then stormed off to the breakfast room, assuming the boys had already gone downstairs. Why could they never follow such simple instructions? There was no sign of them in the restaurant though and Alice was getting more furious by the minute. She returned to their room once again and this time, used both fists to knock even louder. The door shook and at one point she was concerned she might break it down. She knew the boys were lazy but how could they possibly sleep through her loud knocking? Fortunately, the man in the next room didn't make a second appearance. She eventually gave up and marched down to reception.

A young couple was in the middle of checking in, but this was of no concern to Alice. She went straight up to the desk and shouted at the woman on duty, ordering her to hand over a spare key to her travelling companions' room. Katherine just glared at her. After her conversation with Louis earlier, she wasn't at all surprised by Alice's rudeness. Apologising to the two guests she was in the process of helping, she handed Alice the envelope that Louis had left, whilst giving the impertinent woman her best sickly smile. Alice snatched the letter and looked very confused.

As she skulked away, she tore open the envelope and read its contents. She shook her head in disbelief.

How pathetic that the boys had decided to take Brian to the hospital. He was such a wimp. All he'd done was fall down the stairs. Well, they could waste their time at the hospital if they wanted to. She was going to have some breakfast and then enjoy her time in this marvellous city.

A few hours after finally settling down, Brian was wide awake again and lying in his wonderfully comfortable hotel bed, staring up at the ceiling and thinking of all the places he'd like to visit whilst here in Paris. He just needed his two friends to wake up. In an effort to stir them, he went into the bathroom and had a shower. It was such a relief to have nothing more than a few grazes and some aching muscles after his fall the previous day. He put on some clean underwear and wrapped a towel around his waist. As he came back out, Tim yawned loudly and stretched his arms up towards the ceiling. He swung his legs round so he could sit upright on the side of the bed and smiled widely at Brian.

'We're in Paris!' he exclaimed. 'And if I'm not mistaken, we seem to have shaken Alice off for a few hours too.'

Louis let out a loud cheer, signalling that he was now also awake.

'So, what are we doing here then?' asked Brian, as he finished getting dressed in the semi-darkened room. 'I'm ready! You two need to shake your arses! Let's get out of here!'

Tim and Louis took it in turns to shower at breakneck speed.

Brian thought it was interesting how some people might think that the gay community was made up of identical clones. Whilst his roommates were getting ready, he contemplated how he and his two friends couldn't be more different from each other if they tried.

He himself was probably the fittest of the trio: he went to the gym most mornings before work and was also a keen runner. If the three of them ever went out together, he liked to think that he was the one who would turn the most heads, with his toned muscles always on show through his tight-fitting vest tops. He often wore his long, dirty blond hair in a pony tail. He had once proudly been mistaken for Johnny Depp in a nightclub. OK, it had been quite dark in the club, but he had happily accepted the compliment.

He looked across at Tim and felt quite sorry for him with his extremely small, skinny frame - even his XS clothes seemed to hang off him and he'd once confessed to his friends that he usually bought women's jeans because they fitted him better. Tim had short dyed blond hair and was the only one of the three who people often guessed was gay. He was, quite rightly, very proud of that fact. Neither Brian nor Louis did anything to try to hide their sexuality, yet they seemed to get a lot more attention from the females than Tim.

Brian chuckled to himself as he suddenly realised you could line the three of them up in size order, as Louis was definitely right in the middle, build-wise, of his two friends. He was also the one who was most interested in fashion and would usually spend what remained of his wages on clothes each month, after setting aside enough funds for the essentials. Oddly, he'd packed surprisingly little for this trip to Paris and hadn't expressed any interest at all in buying any clothes whilst here. With Alice ripping the three of them off, the poor guy probably had no money left to even consider it. It was a shame though, with Paris being one of the fashion capitals of the world.

The room soon smelt like a perfume shop with the various shower gels and aftershaves that the boys had used. Brian was actually quite impressed that his friends had managed to get ready in just twenty minutes - definitely a record for them.

They were all starving after having unintentionally missed breakfast. They left their room and as they made their way out of the hotel, Louis checked to see if Katherine was still on duty at the reception desk, hoping he'd be able to tell her again how much they loved their new room. He couldn't see her though, so hurried out to join his two friends who had already gone outside. They guessed that the hotel restaurant would now be closed but were excited to look for somewhere else to eat in the big city.

The sun was shining brightly as they made their way towards the Métro station, all three of them excited to soon be exploring the city without Alice. Brian in particular was as animated as a child, as he enthused about seeing the Eiffel Tower and maybe even going to the Louvre. They took the number 9 Métro train westbound, and sat huddled together, pawing over a map of Paris and working out their itinerary for the day.

They got off the train at Trocadéro and rushed back up to ground level to get their first glimpse of the Eiffel Tower. They gasped in unison, much to the amusement of the vendor on a crêpe stall next to them. The three boys each decided to order one, eagerly watching as the mixture was poured onto the hot plate and levelled out with a small spreader. Brian's was ready first, a chocolate one, and he tucked into it noisily. The others wanted lemon and sugar on theirs. Tim paid for them all with some francs he'd managed to keep hidden from Alice the night before.

Once they'd finished their crêpes, they ran down towards the Eiffel Tower, delighted to be so free and easy in the French capital. They knew that today could have been very different if they'd been spending it with Alice, although none of them dared mention her name, in case it might somehow make her appear.

They chose not to go to the top of the Eiffel Tower as the queue to the summit was quite long, but contented themselves with taking photos of each other from its base and subsequently from the Champ de Mars, the big open green space behind the famous Parisian landmark.

Needing something more to eat than just a crêpe, they retraced their steps to Trocadéro station and crossed the road towards a row of cafés and restaurants. They noticed the first of many posters around Paris advertising a concert Alice's estranged brother was giving at the Zénith Arena.

'Wouldn't it be funny if Alice bumped into him whilst we're here?' commented Brian. 'I'd love to witness that reunion! Sparks would fly!'

Tim wasn't so sure. 'I doubt Michael would want to re-establish contact with his crazy sister. After all, would you?' They all chuckled.

'She's still family though, isn't she?' contributed Louis, pensively. 'Blood is thicker than water, as they say.'

They all pondered on this as they approached one of the cafés, which had an impressive display of baguettes on show in its window. After checking with a waiter inside that it would be OK to pay with a credit card, Brian announced that he would be treating the others to lunch. They took their seats and ordered sandwiches and hot drinks.

Both Brian and Tim were constantly impressed that Louis was fluent in French. His parents had lived in France for many years and as a child, he had always spent his school holidays with them. For the rest of the time he had carried on living with his maternal grandparents in England. But having spent such long holidays in France during his formative years, he had picked up the language fairly effortlessly. His friends listened to him placing their order and bantering with the waiter in French. Brian remarked to Tim how much lovelier a *chocolat chaud* sounded to a plain old hot chocolate.

'Do you know what they call them in German?' asked Tim, who had also been brought up bilingual by his mother, Krystal.

'No idea,' laughed Brian.

'A *Schokobrötchen*,' smiled Tim. Although he'd heard people say that the German language could sound quite harsh, he'd always found it quite beautiful. It probably depended on who was speaking it, to be honest.

Once they had finished their food, they decided to take the same Métro line as before, just two stops back this time to Champs-Élysées. Emerging from the station, they stopped to admire the Arc de Triomphe in the distance. They bought some chocolate from one of the shops along the famous avenue and scoffed the lot between them as they made their way towards the impressive arch.

Brian had mentioned many times that morning that he'd like to go to the Louvre to see the Mona Lisa, although the others were concerned that they hadn't booked in advance. Brian was so insistent that the other two eventually gave in, knowing how much it would mean to him. They turned round and strolled all the way down the long avenue towards the famous art museum, passing yet more posters advertising Michael Hambelton's upcoming show. They took a few snaps of themselves in front of one of the posters.

'We'll have to hide these pictures from Alice

when we get back home,' commented Tim. 'She'll be furious that we paid them any attention.'

They soon found themselves in the Tuileries Gardens, where they stopped to watch children sailing little boats on the man-made circular ponds. Everything seemed so much different here compared to Brighton. Even the sand on the floor made it feel more exotic than the paved streets back home. Walking further into the gardens, they reached the impressive Arc de Triomphe du Carrousel, a smaller version of the Arc de Triomphe. Brian informed them that it had been built so that Napoleon, who was very short sighted, could look out of his window at the Louvre Palace and imagine that he was seeing the larger version of the arch in the far distance.

The boys soon spotted the large glass pyramid in front of the Louvre, which they all found quite stunning. Brian had been dreaming of visiting this place for years and explained to his two friends that when the pyramid had first been built, it had attracted as much criticism as praise. All three of them thought it struck a great contrast to the museum behind it. They sat on the tiles around the edge of the water surrounding the pyramid and Brian put his hands in and wiggled his fingers. He really couldn't believe that he had finally made it to this iconic spot.

After a couple of minutes sitting in the warm sunshine, Tim asked the question that Louis had also been pondering. 'So how do we get into the Louvre?'

Brian, who had been watching people going in and out, smiled. 'Through the glass pyramid! Just over there!' The other two looked in the direction that he was pointing and the penny dropped. There was a constant flow of people coming in and out of two revolving doors.

'Come on then!' declared Tim. 'We've come all this way - let's go in!'

They made their way to the entrance and went

down the escalator inside. Fortunately, they discovered that it was possible to buy a day ticket, so Brian treated the others to the entrance fee, for being kind enough to pander to his constant badgering about wanting to visit the museum.

'I wouldn't fancy your credit card bill when you get back!' exclaimed Tim. 'It's very kind of you, Brian, but you don't have to pay for us all the time. It's my turn next.'

There were two exhibits that Brian really wanted to see: the Mona Lisa and the Venus de Milo. Both were very easy to find and upon entering the room containing the Mona Lisa, they noticed there was a very large group of people gathered in front of Leonardo da Vinci's stunning masterpiece. Brian and Louis stood at the back of the assembled crowd, waiting their turn to get to the front to see the artwork close up. They were suddenly aware that Tim was nowhere to be seen and assumed that he had gone off to find the toilet. When their turn came to admire the iconic painting, they commented on how much smaller it was than they had imagined. After a minute or so, they walked away and found Tim, looking at a painting on the wall directly facing the Mona Lisa.

'What's he up to?' asked Brian, as they approached.

Tim smiled, 'I decided that this poor painting probably gets ignored because of its location. Everyone comes to see the Mona Lisa and is oblivious to what's facing it.'

'What is it?' asked Brian.

Louis read from the display card, ''The Wedding Feast at Cana by Paolo Veronese.' It's a beautiful painting and you're right, it's not in the best position here. Everyone does come into this room just to see the Mona Lisa. Well spotted, Tim!'

They found the Venus de Milo and also admired several other exhibits on the way, and visited the museum shop, each buying a handful of postcards. Brian also purchased a poster of the Mona Lisa.

'You'll have to hide that if Alice spots us coming back into the hotel,' advised Tim. 'She thinks we've spent the day at the hospital, remember?'

Brian already had a plan. 'I'll just say that I was discharged from the hospital after a couple of hours and I felt a lot brighter, so we decided to go to the Louvre. Anyway, Alice is hardly going to be sitting at the hotel waiting for us, is she?'

'Let's hope not!' shivered Tim exaggeratedly.

They took the escalator out of the Louvre and walked the fairly short distance to Notre Dame Cathedral. They'd had a fantastic day so far and the beautiful weather just added to it.

Upon reaching the cathedral, they decided not to go in but to sit on one of the benches around the square in front of it, so they could admire the impressive medieval construction in all its glory.

'I can't believe what a great day we're having without Alice,' sighed Brian. 'She's going to be furious with us but I don't care. It's made me decide I'm not going to follow her stupid rules any more. I'm not scared of her and I've had enough of her being such a cow to us. I think it's time we started standing up for ourselves.'

'Good luck with that!' laughed Tim. 'With that attitude you might find yourself being left behind in France!'

'To be honest, that would be the very worst-case scenario though, right?' persisted Brian. 'She couldn't do anything more than that, could she? I've been thinking - she needs us a lot more than we need her. I don't believe she's got any other friends left, apart from us. She has no contact with either of her brothers and doesn't have any other family, as far as I know. If she chooses to stop seeing us, then she's pretty much on her own.'

'That may be true, but who's going to tell her about this new strategy of yours?' asked Tim.

'I will!' Brian declared, quite decisively. 'But it would be good to know that you're both in agreement with me.'

'Of course we are!' confirmed Louis. 'When exactly are you planning this big showdown? I want a ringside seat!'

'Tonight! There's no time like the present. As soon as we see her back at the hotel, I'm going to tell her we want a word with her in our room. The room we've had to move to because the original one she booked for us was so bad. We can use that as an example of how terribly she treats us sometimes.'

'I think we should find somewhere for dinner and drinks to give us some Dutch courage first, don't you?' Tim sounded quite sceptical about Brian's plan. He'd been having similar thoughts for some time and his friend was right - they really did need to stand up to that awful woman. But there was a very big difference between thinking it and putting it into action. They decided to rest for a few more minutes, making the most of the warm early evening sunshine and the awe-inspiring view of Notre Dame. This trip to Paris was turning out to be quite life-affirming.

Chapter 9
Flowers

Jake couldn't remember when he'd last been so buzzing with excitement. In a matter of a few hours, his self-esteem had shot right through the roof and he was enjoying every single minute of his new job at the Griffin Cinema. Madeleine seemed to be the perfect boss and it was hard to comprehend that she had contacted him about this job without him even applying for it.

He'd popped into her office a couple of times during the afternoon: once to give her his bank details and another to agree a shift pattern. To say that she was flexible was something of an understatement as she was very relaxed about the times that he could or couldn't work. She just kept saying how pleased she was to have him on board.

She invited him to come back the following day for a special team building event, where everyone would get to the chance to meet each other. It would also be the perfect opportunity for them to cover off all the necessary policies and procedures together as a team. Jake thought this sounded quite exciting and wondered whether he would like the other members of staff. He was also really pleased when Madeleine told him he'd be able to claim the hours for the team event on his time sheet. They had agreed that for now he would have a flexible contract, just until he'd completed his probation period, to make sure that both he and Madeleine were satisfied that this job was right for him. She handed him a £20 note as an advance on his salary and insisted that he tell her if he needed any more money in the interim, since payday was still a couple of weeks way. He had to pinch himself to make sure he wasn't dreaming.

Madeleine's brother, Jason, didn't disappoint either. Jake loved his new colleague's bubbly personality and his cheeky sense of humour. His jaw ached from laughing so much during the couple of hours they spent working together. Jason had been instructed by his sister to show Jake the ropes behind the bar. When Jake had heard Madeleine use that expression, his vivid imagination had conjured up an image of Jason tying him up, although sadly that hadn't happened.

It was obvious that Jason had been working as a barman for several years, since he knew the names of every cocktail. He made Jake giggle by mentioning the rudest cocktail names he could think of and by confessing that he had a penchant for 'Sex on the Beach' and a 'Slow Screw'. He had a wicked glint in his eye when he asked Jake to name his favourites. Jake couldn't answer for laughing so much. At one point Madeleine came out of her office to see what all the noise was but just smiled when she saw that the two men were getting on so well.

Jake asked Jason where he was living, since Madeleine had said that he'd only been back in the country for a short time, and Jake was impressed to discover that Jason had sorted out his living arrangements in the UK before he'd even left Australia. Jason seemed really pleased with himself as he told Jake that he was staying, free of charge, at a cousin's house on the banks of the River Ouse, nearby. It was a large, detached, thatched property which had once belonged to a local duke. Jason's cousin sometimes worked in America, which was where she currently was, and as a result, Jason also got to use her black Jaguar XJR while she was away. Jake was no expert in cars but Jason made it sound very flashy and super sexy.

In turn, Jason asked his new colleague lots of questions too, but Jake found himself not wanting to divulge very much, since the thought of his wife, his home and everything else in his life made him feel quite sad and certainly sounded a lot duller than Jason's exciting set-up.

Jake replied with a casual, 'I'm married and live in Hove,' and changed the subject quickly, asking Jason where in Sydney he'd been living, even though he himself had absolutely no knowledge whatsoever of the Australian city. He chose not to admit this to his new friend.

Jason wasn't going to be fobbed off that easily. 'You don't sound too happy with your situation, my friend. Don't get me wrong but I got the feeling you batted for the other team. Maybe I shouldn't say this but you remind me of some of my gay mates back in Oz.' Jake wondered if this was the perfect opportunity to be honest with both himself and Jason and reveal that he was more interested in men than women. It felt like such a big thing though and he wasn't sure this was the right moment, especially since, although he was really enjoying Jason's company, he had only known the guy for a couple of hours. Instead, he just smiled awkwardly, making them both feel quite uncomfortable and creating an embarrassing silence.

There was so much more that Jake wanted to know about Jason, with his sexuality being at the very top of that list. But since Jake hadn't been prepared to share much about himself, it somehow felt inappropriate to probe too much, so he drew an imaginary line in the sand instead.

Jason persisted with his questioning though and

was keen to know if Jake had ever been to Australia. He hadn't, but admitted that it was definitely one of the places he'd like to visit. He decided to impress Jason with his knowledge of Aussie music instead and started waxing lyrical about Crowded House, John Farnham and Kylie Minogue, amongst others. He also confessed how much he loved Olivia Newton-John, who, although born in the UK, he'd always thought of as Australian.

'You're not doing much to convince me that you're not gay!' laughed Jason. 'I think Kylie and Livvy have a fair few gay fans.' Jake wondered how he knew this. Was it because he liked them too and was gay himself? How he wished he could ask the question directly, but for now he would just have to live in hope. He found himself blushing slightly and hoped that Jason wouldn't notice.

Jake looked at the clock and was surprised to find that it was almost 4pm. Since he wanted to try to avoid the rush-hour traffic on his return journey to Hove, he decided it was time to finish for the day. Madeleine had already said that she was more than happy for him to leave whenever it suited him and had told him several times how grateful she was that he'd stayed, considering he'd only come in for an interview originally. Jake was really pleased he'd made the extra effort. He said goodbye to Jason, shaking hands and adding that he'd see him the following day at the team meeting. He then stuck his head round Madeleine's open door to thank her once again for giving him this amazing opportunity.

'You've really made my day,' she responded. 'I'm over the moon that you and Jason are getting on so well too. I think our team is going to be brilliant! I really appreciate you coming in today, Jake!'

As he left the cinema, Jake felt like he was floating on air. He couldn't wait to tell Sue that after what felt like an eternity, he finally had a job. Not only that, but one that he thought he was really going to love.

When he got to the car park, there was only one other vehicle there. He wondered where Jason had parked the flashy car he'd mentioned. Maybe there was a staff car park he didn't know about. He made a mental note to ask about it the following day.

The sun was still shining brightly, lifting Jake's mood even further. It was exceptionally good weather for the time of year and he wondered if this was a sign of a good summer to come. He had a feeling that this year, things were going to be very different to previous summers, and he fantasized about being on the beach with Jason and being invited to barbecues at his house.

As he drove out of the car park, with Robbie Williams' *Life Thru A Lens* album blaring out from his car stereo, he felt on top of the world. It felt so good to be back in one of his favourite towns and as he drove past the castle he realised that he had a massive smile on his face. He couldn't wait to explore the place again during his breaks at the cinema. He loved the fact that the town even had its own currency, the 'Lewes pound', which could be spent in the local shops, alongside pounds sterling.

He sang along at the top of his voice to 'Let Me Entertain You', and was amazed that his usual panic about getting stuck in rush-hour traffic hadn't raised its ugly head. He couldn't remember when he had last felt this happy. Sue's anticipated pride in him for getting this job was going to boost him even more. He decided he was going to stop off on his way home and buy her some flowers.

He walked into the supermarket feeling like he'd just won the lottery and it felt really good to be able to look at the CDs in the music section and know that he could afford to buy one without thinking twice. A large free-standing display board promoting his brother Michael's latest album caught Jake's eye and he couldn't help but smile. If only he could share the good news about his new job with Michael. It was at times like these that he missed him the most. He picked up a copy of one of the CDs from the display and examined it closely, reading the track listing on the back. He decided to buy it and proudly carried it around the store in his hand. He knew that Sue wouldn't be home for some time yet, so he made the decision to drive the long way home so he could listen to Michael's album in peace. He wouldn't dare mention the purchase to his wife, since she'd only say it was a waste of money and would probably find a few other negative things to throw in about his brother too, as per usual. She was so ambivalent at times: one minute wanting to meet Michael and running him down the next. Jake had learnt to avoid mentioning him whenever possible. There seemed to be an ever-growing list of things that he avoided talking with his wife about.

When Jake had married Sue, she had demanded that he change his surname to hers, rather than follow the tradition of the wife taking the husband's name. He'd therefore become Jake Rimmer following the wedding, with Sue maintaining that hers was a much rarer surname than his. As if to clinch the deal, she'd told him that if he persisted in keeping his own name, then it would mean the end of her particular line of Rimmers. Jake found it interesting that Sue's brother-in-law seemingly hadn't been asked to do the same thing. He consoled himself with the knowledge that if Michael had any children, then they would be continuing the Hambelton name. One positive thing about changing his name to Rimmer was that he hadn't been hassled by the press about his famous brother since.

Before leaving the supermarket, Jake chose some red roses for Sue and then went to one of the tills to pay for his shopping. Fortunately the cashier wasn't the chatty type and just pulled a disgruntled face when Jake smiled at her. He didn't care though - he simply couldn't wait to get back to his car and listen to his brother's new album.

As always, he struggled to remove the cellophane wrapper from around the CD but eventually succeeded and slid the disc into the music player.

The album was called *Kaleidoscope*, and the first track, which was entitled 'A Fool's Garden', opened with a beautiful orchestral piece which sounded very lush. He sat there motionless, unable to drive away, caught up in the magic of the music. He picked up the CD case and inspected the booklet. He noticed that Michael had written all the tracks on the album himself and Jake couldn't help but feel a surge of pride. It really was a good thing that Sue wasn't here right now as she'd be far from impressed.

As the second track, the title track, began to play, Jake pulled away and headed towards the seafront. He was definitely not going home until he'd finished listening to this album. Sue wouldn't be back yet anyway, so there really was no rush.

Several tracks later, he turned right at the roundabout in front of the Palace Pier and drove along the promenade towards Hove. Neither the screeching seagulls nor the crawling traffic seemed to be bothering him today.

Jake suddenly spotted Enrique, dressed up to the nines in a smart black suit, black shirt and silver tie, walking along the pavement. He watched the Spaniard cross the road in the direction of the Grand Hotel. The gardener was completely oblivious to Jake's presence and marched up to the hotel's entrance, looking like he didn't have a care in the world. Maybe one of Enrique's other clients was treating him to a meal, pondered Jake. Either that or he was earning a lot more money from his gardening than one would expect. He certainly charged Jake and Sue a tidy sum for the work he did for them.

As Jake headed in the direction of home, the CD was just reaching its crescendo. *Perfect timing*, he thought. He had absolutely loved it and was glad to have had the opportunity to listen to it without Sue making scathing remarks. He decided to leave the CD in the car.

He parked on the drive and went indoors. There was a light flashing on the answering machine and so he pushed the button to listen to the message, instantly recognising his wife's voice.

'*Oh hello - it's me! I forgot to mention that I've got to work late tonight. It's month end and we're going to be here until very late. We've ordered pizzas in so you'll have to fend for yourself for dinner.*' Jake was taken aback by the abruptness of Sue's tone. No sign of any endearment at all. He felt the excitement about his new job begin to drain away. He'd imagined them having a celebratory meal together when she got home.

He took the roses he'd bought for his wife into the kitchen and found a vase to put them in. He left them in their cellophane wrapper. Sue would enjoy arranging them later - it had been a long time since he'd bought her flowers. He ran upstairs to change out of his suit and came back down to prepare some food. Sue mentioning pizza had made him fancy it too, and luckily for him there was a good selection of them in the freezer.

Rather than setting the table just for himself, he decided to eat the pizza off a wooden chopping board, which he would usually never dare to do if Sue was around. Once cooked, he divided the pizza into four and took it into the lounge. He turned on the TV and started to eat the pizza with his fingers. It felt quite rebellious to be eating like this - Sue would call him a slob if she could see him now and would be furious, especially since he sat watching *Neighbours* and *Coronation Street*. Sue would never allow him to watch soaps when she was home.

He suddenly noticed that it had got dark, so he turned on a couple of lamps and then took the now empty chopping board back into the kitchen, hitting the switch with his elbow to turn the light on in there too. He carefully put the evidence of his meal into the dishwasher. He wondered when Sue would be home and whether he should call her to check that she was alright. He concluded that he was worrying unnecessarily and was certain that if he called her, she'd probably only have a go at him for disturbing her. He went to the freezer and took out a Cornetto, throwing its wrapper into the bin before returning to the lounge. He plonked himself down in front of the TV again. He wished he had some idea about when Sue would be back so he'd know whether or not there was enough time to watch his brother's tour video again. He decided against it. It was OK during the daytime when he could be certain that Sue was safely occupied at work, but there was no knowing when she might suddenly march in tonight.

His anxiety soon got the better of him and he eventually called Sue's mobile phone. There was no answer and he chose not to leave a message. Hopefully, she'd notice the missed call though and would ring him back to let him know that all was well. Time dragged on and it was not until 10:43 that he heard the sound of a car door slamming and his wife's key turning in the lock. Sue seemed surprised to find him still up when she put her head round the living room door.

'I was getting worried about you,' confessed Jake, smiling.

'I'm a grown woman so why would you worry about me? I left you a message - didn't you get it?' She seemed angry with him. She was obviously tired after working so late so Jake decided not to react.

'I did get it and tried to call you a couple of hours ago.' Jake was trying to sound as calm as he could but inside, he was fuming. Sue disappeared back into the hallway and he then heard her footsteps on the tiled kitchen floor, followed by the sound of the back door slamming. Curiosity soon got the better of him, so he decided to join her in the kitchen. He really wanted her to calm down so he could tell her his good news about the job. Also, she must have found her lovely flowers by now.

Jake was shocked to find that the flowers had vanished. He walked past his wife and looked out of the kitchen window into the darkness. He could just about see that she had put the vase of flowers on the garden table.

'Why have you put your flowers out there?' he asked, confused. 'There's a frost forecast tonight.'

'Oh, they'll be alright,' she barked. He suddenly noticed his wife's alcohol breath. Since she'd said they were having pizza delivered to the office, he guessed that someone must have brought some drinks in too.

'How was month-end? All finished?' he asked, trying to show an interest.

Sue roared with laughter. 'As if you'd know anything about that! Have you enjoyed your day of leisure, husband dearest?' she slurred. 'And why have you bought me flowers? Have you got something to feel guilty about?'

Jake decided to play his trump card. 'Actually,

I've got some very good news to share with you. I've got a job!'

Sue looked at him in disgust. 'Oh really? Who's been mad enough to employ you then?'

Jake decided to ignore her offhand manner. She'd been drinking, after all. Although she was often mean to him, she wasn't usually this bad. He suddenly remembered a previous occasion when she'd had too much to drink and had managed to drive her car into a ditch. The car was a complete right-off, but Sue had somehow managed to climb out of the vehicle unscathed. She had vowed never to drink so much ever again and had always kept her promise, until now it seemed. But at least she had got home safely this time.

'I've got a job in a new cinema in Lewes,' he proudly announced, hoping this might snap her out of her awful mood.

'What - as a cleaner again?' she chuckled. 'I just can't wait to tell my friends that my husband has got a school leaver's job!'

Jake was horrified at Sue's response to his news. 'It's not a cleaning job!' Jake thought it best not to mention that keeping the cinema tidy would be one of his duties. 'I'm going to be one of their front of house staff. I didn't even apply for it. I guess I was … head hunted.'

'You only get head hunted for top jobs, Jake, not for menial jobs in cinemas!' Sue scoffed.

Jake decided that this was going nowhere and didn't want to say anything he'd regret in the morning.

'Would you like a hot drink?' he asked, trying his best to keep his cool.

'I'll make my own drink, thanks. I don't need a school boy making it for me!' She looked him up and down and roared with laughter again.

'Did you drive home?' he asked.

'No, I flew back. Of course, I drove home - how else would I have got here?'

'OK, I'm just concerned. I can tell you've had a drink.' He instantly regretted saying this.

'And who wouldn't have a drink, married to you? You're a loser, do you know that?' Sue shook the kettle to make sure there was enough water in it and put it back into its cradle, flicking the switch to turn it on.

Jake thought it best to shut the conversation down completely. He was so angry with his wife, but was certain that it was the drink that was making her act this way.

'I'm going to bed now. See you when you come up,' he said, trying to keep his voice measured.

'You're not sleeping with me tonight!' Sue sneered. 'You can use one of the spare rooms. Oh - and are you going to your little job again tomorrow or have you worn yourself out for the rest of your life now?' She was really going for the jugular this evening.

'I'm going to work tomorrow, yes. I really enjoyed it there today and there's so much to learn. I'm meeting the rest of the team in the morning. I'm really looking forward to it.'

Sue mimicked his voice, 'I'm really looking forward to it.' She gurned at him and turned to continue making her drink.

Jake tried to hide the hot tears that were welling in his eyes. How could Sue be so horrible, even if she had been drinking? He said no more but went upstairs and chose to sleep in the bedroom that was furthest away from the room where they usually slept together. He knew from previous occasions how loudly Sue snored when she'd had a drink and he really needed to get a good night's sleep before going back into work the next day. It wouldn't look very good if he arrived at the cinema looking like he'd had a night on the tiles. He sat on the bed in stunned silence, the only light in the room coming from the street lamp outside. The true extent of his broken relationship with Sue suddenly hit him. He knew that things couldn't carry on like this but had absolutely no idea how to unpick it all.

He pulled the curtains and then turned the bedside light on. Undressing down to his briefs and T-shirt, he climbed into bed. His head was spinning and he wasn't sure how long it would take him to drift off. He switched the lamp off and tried to get comfortable. He lay there for at least half an hour with the events of the day running around his head: the excitement of his new job and meeting Jason, but sadly, also Sue's unforgivable behaviour. He listened out for her coming upstairs but was fast asleep long before she did.

Chapter 10
Betrayal

If Michael was ever asked in interviews to choose his favourite city, he would always say Paris. He'd arrived in the French capital earlier that day and, as always, had been like an excited child looking out of the limousine windows on his journey from Charles de Gaulle airport to his hotel. He'd soon spotted both the Sacré Coeur and the Eiffel Tower as he neared the city.

Sadly, whenever he came here for a concert or promotion nowadays, it felt like he was viewing Paris from a goldfish bowl, since there was never any time for him to actually enjoy the city. Even if he did have some time to himself, there was no point going out, since he'd undoubtably be mobbed. He'd tried to disguise himself in the past but with very limited success. The last time he'd tried it had been in Madrid, where he'd donned large black sunglasses and a beanie hat. His disguise had failed within minutes and he'd frantically thrown himself into the back of a passing taxi, begging the driver to take him back to the hotel. Annoyingly, even the cabbie had asked for an autograph. Michael realised afterwards that wearing a woolly hat at the height of summer probably hadn't been a great strategy; even if he hadn't been famous, he would have drawn attention.

He was currently having a half-hour break in his room at the famous George V Hotel. When he'd arrived in the French capital early that afternoon, he'd been driven straight to the concert venue for a sound check. Michael hated the pandemonium surrounding these things, with dozens of people running around doing last minute preparations for the show. It was always such a relief when it was over.

He'd spent the last couple of hours doing press interviews in his suite and had met umpteen journalists, in what had felt like an endless stream. Each of them had had a ten-minute slot with him and they had been wheeled in one after the other. There had been little time for pleasantries.

Michael had been growing increasingly tired of the usual questions he was always asked: Did he have a girlfriend? What was his favourite colour? Did he have any pets? Did he have a favourite food? What was his favourite animal? He wondered how many times his answers to these questions had made it into print and whether it gave the impression that he had a very shallow personality. He didn't really expect to be asked anything political or about his religious views but something outside of the usual boring questions would at least make things a bit more interesting, both for him and the readers.

During today's round of interviews, he'd really clicked with a journalist called Jacques, who represented a leading French music magazine and was the only person to actually show an interest in the person behind the Michael Hambelton mask. Although it was a bit of an unusual situation, Michael somehow felt that he could trust this guy and decided to take a chance on enlisting his help. He'd been told that one of the best cheese shops in Paris was the Fromagerie Beaufoy, on the Boulevard Saint-Germain, and he would often fantasize about visiting the store. Michael knew that there'd be no chance of him being able to go there himself without being recognised, so at the end of the interview, he asked Jacques if he would be prepared to help him with an undercover mission. He was delighted when the Frenchman readily accepted. Michael always carried some local currency, in case of an emergency, and had two hundred-franc notes in his wallet, which he gave to Jacques. Michael asked if he'd be able to visit Fromagerie Beaufoy for him and buy a selection of cheeses. They obviously needed to be ones which would travel well. Michael had been well aware that he may never see his money again and that the journalist could just choose to mention the strange request as an aside in his article. He was therefore overjoyed when he subsequently got a call from hotel reception to say that a package had been delivered for him and asking if it was ok to bring it up to his room. It was obvious from the contents of the bag that Jacques had spent far more on the cheeses than the amount of money that Michael had given him and he was really touched. He'd make sure to send a thank you note to the guy once he was back home and was pleased that he'd remembered to ask for the man's business card. Krystal would be as excited as he was with this cheese stash. She was just as obsessed with trying new cheeses as Michael was.

Michael was feeling totally drained. He had a TV recording lined up for the following morning and regretted having agreed to do it now, especially since he also had tonight's concert to get through. As usual, too much had been crammed into his packed schedule. He tried to console himself with the fact that he always found TV studios a lot more entertaining than interviews with journalists. He loved observing the lights, cameras and people rushing about. He sometimes got the opportunity to perform a song or two as well, which he really enjoyed, even if it was generally to playback. Michael was always proud of how proficient he was at lip synching and unlike some performers, he always tried to give the impression that he was actually singing live. He'd seen one of his contemporaries on TV recently who was singing about two feet away from the microphone. How could anyone be expected to believe that that was a live performance?

His thoughts suddenly turned to Alexandra and how much he was looking forward to seeing her. He'd hoped that she'd have been here by now, since they'd agreed that she would travel with him from the hotel to the concert venue. He guessed it wasn't her fault for being late though - you were always in the hands of air traffic control when you travelled by plane. All it took was for your flight to be delayed and your whole schedule could fall apart. He had originally suggested that she take the same flight as him from Stockholm to Paris but she'd explained that she had some family issues to attend to before joining him. She'd already told him that both her parents were dead so he wasn't quite sure who she was referring to, but had decided not to probe too much, since the last thing he wanted was for her to start questioning him about his own family situation again.

Michael knew that Alexandra had a mobile phone and was tempted to call her on it to see where she was, but then had second thoughts. If her flight had been delayed, she'd be stressed enough anyway, without him hassling her further. Even if she did arrive late or didn't show up at all, he knew he'd still be able to cope. He'd looked after himself at the last few gigs after all.

Frustratingly, he'd slept really badly the previous night. He'd had a repetitive dream that he couldn't shake off. In it, his car was driving him round and round the Arc de Triomphe and he kept seeing the faces of his parents and siblings appearing through the car window. He'd had this dream before but not for a very long time.

Alexandra's questions about his family had definitely stirred things up.

He really had to make the most of this very brief break and was currently resting on the enormous hotel bed. This European tour had taken its toll on him. He was so relieved that tonight's show was the very last one. It was at the legendary Zénith Arena and he'd been told that it was a 7,000-seater.

On Michael's journey from the airport into the city earlier, he'd been driven past the impressive, almost complete, Stade de France, which was opening the following year. It was being built to host the World Cup, which France was about to host. Michael had heard that the venue would double up as a concert venue too, with an audience capacity of 80,000, and he couldn't wait to play there, hopefully on his next tour. He was currently on an arena tour but there were already discussions about his next outing and whether it should be limited to stadiums only. It would mean fewer shows, since he'd be able to play to a lot more people in far less time. After having just played 56 dates, he knew that anything less would feel like a real luxury.

Michael stretched out on the bed and the next thing he knew someone was knocking loudly on his door. He glanced at the time on the digital bedside clock and realised that he must've dozed off. He jumped up, pulled himself together and in blind panic, ran over to look through the spy hole to see who it was. It was such a relief when it turned out to be Alexandra. He opened the door and they embraced.

'I fell asleep!' he confessed frantically, con-cerned that he might now be running late. He kicked the door shut.

'I think you've still got a few minutes left before you need to leave, so don't worry,' she consoled. 'Sorry

I'm late. My flight was delayed.'

'I thought as much,' sighed Michael. 'But thank heavens you're here, Alexandra! I hadn't booked a wake-up call with reception as I didn't intend to fall asleep. There would have been pandemonium if I'd not arrived in time for the show!'

'I'm certain that someone would have woken you. Clint is loitering outside in the corridor and I'm sure he would have knocked if you'd not appeared.'

'I don't know about that,' laughed Michael. 'I think he'd absolutely love it if something went wrong. He makes it fairly obvious that he should be the star around here. He rarely talks to me these days but when we were on better terms, he told me all about his dreams of becoming a professional actor.'

'I think you just rub each other up the wrong way,' suggested Alexandra. 'Anyway, your driver would have come up to look for you if you'd not come down.' Michael loved her logic. She tightened her hug on him, to show her support.

'Would you like a quick drink or something else?' asked Michael, realising that this sounded quite suggestive. He wasn't sure they'd have time for the 'something else' right now, even if she agreed.

'It's OK, I've got my water,' replied Alexandra, She held up a half empty bottle of Evian. 'Are you ready?'

Everything that Michael needed would have already been delivered to the venue, so he quickly paid a final visit to the bathroom and grabbed his ever-faithful rucksack as he headed for the door, with Alexandra following close behind. Ricky had once referred to Michael's rucksack as his 'teddy bear', since he never went anywhere without it. Little did his manager know that it contained several things which could help Michael to relax if the need arose.

The couple left the hotel room, hand in hand, with Clint sulking behind them as they walked down the corridor and took the lift down to reception. Not a single word was spoken. As they came out of the lift, Michael noticed a few heads turn, but before anyone could approach him, he rushed towards the hotel exit, pulling Alexandra behind him. He spotted his designated driver, Jules, who had been appointed to look after him during his stay in Paris. The handsome Frenchman gave Michael a salute and as they made their way towards the car, Michael spotted a handful of photographers waiting outside. There were a few fans waiting too but Michael really didn't have time to stop on this occasion. It was also pouring with rain, and there was nowhere to shelter. Although he did feel quite sorry for the people who had been waiting, he told himself that he'd not asked them to turn up, so shouldn't feel guilty. Luckily, there was no sign of the *Secret Seven* fans, as they were always a lot pushier than the others and would have no doubt jeered at him for not stopping.

Fortunately, the car had blacked out windows and once Jules had the couple safely ensconced on the back seat, he took his position behind the steering wheel. Clint climbed into the front passenger seat and the car slowly pulled away. The radio was playing softly and Michael smiled when he noticed that ABBA's 'Voulez-Vous' was coming out of the speakers. *How French*, he thought.

As they made their way from the hotel to the concert venue, they drove down the Champs-Élysées. At one point, Michael did a double take as he caught sight of a lady who looked very much like his sister, Alice. She was carrying two Virgin Megastore bags and was accompanied by three men. He briefly considered asking his driver to pull over, before realising that there was nowhere for them to stop. There were double parked cars all along both sides of the avenue and no room at all for any more.

Because the traffic was going so slowly, he was able to observe the mysterious woman quite closely and concluded that it was either Alice or the most perfect doppelganger he'd ever seen. He was momentarily tempted to jump out as he watched her turn into a side street. She seemed to wave her carrier bags in his direction and shout something. It really did look so much like her but what on earth would she be doing in Paris?

'Are you alright?' asked Alexandra.

Michael had to think fast, since he really didn't want her to go chasing after this woman, whether it was Alice or not. She had already been asking far too many questions about his siblings. He also wondered what he would say to Alice if he came face to face with her, and what kind of a reception he would get.

'I thought I saw a friend walking along the pavement,' was the best he could come up with. 'How's everything at home?' he asked, hoping it wouldn't be too obvious that he was frantically trying to change the subject.

'Yes fine, thanks,' she responded. When she didn't elaborate further he decided not to push it. He smiled to himself, realising that neither of them seemed willing to elaborate on their family situations. As if reading his thoughts, Alexandra asked him yet again about his brother and sister. If there was one thing that niggled him about her, it was that she just didn't seem prepared to stop probing him about this. He was sure it came from a good place though, so he tried his hardest not to be angry with her. She was probably just intrigued.

'I promise I'll tell you one day, just not now,

OK?' She looked a bit taken aback so he pulled her close to try to console her. 'It's still very painful for me,' he tried to explain. Luckily, she let the subject drop again and so they continued on their journey in silence.

As the car arrived at the arena, Michael observed the hullabaloo outside through the blacked-out windows. A seemingly endless queue of people was waiting to get inside whilst others were loitering by burger vans and makeshift merchandise stalls. There were various TV crews dotted around and a journalist from the BBC was so engrossed in his reporting that he accidentally stepped backwards into the path of their vehicle. Michael was certain he'd never seen anyone jump quite so high as Jules sounded the very loud car horn. The guy leapt to safety, glaring at the imperceptible passengers inside as he did so. Michael thought it was a shame that the viewers would probably never get to see that particular piece of footage, as entertaining as it was.

They made their way down the side of the arena, and Michael spotted a large group of fans waiting outside the entry gates, which had just been opened to allow his car to drive through. Security officers were holding the fans back. Michael told the driver to stop briefly and then noticed through the tinted glass that his *Secret Seven* fans were amongst those waiting. He opened his blacked-out side window about an inch and as he did so, an album cover and autograph book were poked through the gap. He looked at Alexandra and pulled a face.

'It's your fault for stopping,' she laughingly chastised him. Clint gave him an admonishing look from the front seat.

Michael unzipped the side of his rucksack and took out a pen. He started signing the things that were being posted in. Inquisitive eyes were trying to peer through the gap. He signed about a dozen pieces, thrusting everything back out towards the fans afterwards. After about a minute, he started to close the window again, being careful not to trap any of the merchandise and, more importantly, fingers. He told the driver to proceed through the open gates.

They drove past gigantic lorries and it seemed like there were roadies everywhere. Once parked up close to the venue, they got out and were immediately shown to Michael's dressing room. Clint, in his own little world as always, caught sight of a couple of the backing musicians and went off in their direction.

'Thank heavens we've got rid of him,' chuckled Michael. 'He's got the personality of a dried prune. It wouldn't be so bad if he at least tried to be friendly.'

'You really don't like him, do you?' asked Alexandra.

Michael seemed to ponder on this before replying. 'I don't think it's that I don't like him. I just struggle with him a bit. I find him a bit odd, to be honest. When I first met him, do you know how he introduced himself?'

'Tell me,' chuckled Alexandra, raising her eyebrows.

'He said, 'I'm as flinty and steely as Mr Eastwood, my namesake, and you'll soon realise that I'm the strong, silent type.'' Michael tried to hide a brewing smile.

'Sounds like the perfect character type for a bodyguard then,' commented Alexandra.

'Perhaps - if it were true. The first few times he was accompanying me, I couldn't shut him up. He even had the nerve to ask if I could give him some introductions to help him with his acting career.'

'And did you?' asked Alexandra.

'I told him I'd have a think. After a few days he

stopped talking to me for some reason, so that made my mind up and I decided not to introduce him to anyone.'

'Maybe that's why he's sulking with you?' suggested Alexandra.

'Well, it's not very professional, is it? He won't get very far in this industry with that attitude.'

'So, what's your usual routine for getting ready?' asked Alexandra, growing tired of his bitchiness. 'You told me not to bring any products, because you like to use your own.'

Michael felt slightly embarrassed. 'I have to be careful what I use on my skin as I get an allergic reaction to some creams and potions, which is why I like to use my own box of tried and tested products.' He pointed to a dented old metal tool box which had been left on top of the dressing table in front of the mirror. 'Everything you need should be in there.'

He looked around the room and recognised it from a previous visit. It had been redecorated since the last time he'd been there though and he quite liked the sage green on the walls. He made a mental note to ask Ted if he could have the main bedroom in his house painted the same colour.

'Great! Well take a seat and let's make a start,' grinned Alexandra, walking over to the box and opening it up to examine what it contained. Michael took his seat and watched her as she selected a few items. She asked him if he'd mind getting into the dressing gown that was neatly folded on the table next to the box, to avoid getting make-up on his clothes. He suddenly felt very shy, and so hurriedly undressed and managed to get into the robe before Alexandra returned from the bathroom with a towel.

'That was quick!' she commented as he sat down. She put the towel under his chin in preparation for applying the make-up. She set about her task like a true professional and Michael realised that he'd forgotten how lovely it was to have someone else take care of him, rather than doing it all himself. They chatted as she worked, with her occasionally telling Michael to stop talking so she could work around his mouth. He found the whole experience quite erotic and wondered if she felt the same. She would occasionally smile, which he took as a good sign.

In an attempt to keep Michael from talking too much and to entertain him, Alexandra said she'd tell him about some strange customs she believed were unique to the Swedes.

'I don't know if you know this already, but if you give someone flowers in Sweden, it's considered very rude to present them wrapped in paper. So, if you're invited to someone's house, you have to take the wrapping off before you knock on the door and then hand over the flowers, sometimes dripping, to your host,' she explained.

'What do you do with the paper then?' asked Michael, trying to speak without opening his mouth too widely.

'You give that to the person separately,' laughed Alexandra. 'I told you it was a strange custom. Another funny tradition we have is to wake someone very early on the morning of their birthday with a cake.' She stepped back to examine her work so far and seemed satisfied. 'I mean like 6am or something,' she continued. 'It's quite sweet when you're a child but wears a bit thin when you're older. I thought when I first moved into my own place that I'd escape this strange tradition but then my friends turned up outside my bedroom window at dawn and almost woke the entire neighbourhood with their singing.' Michael tried his best to smile at her with his eyes, since she was working on his lips again.

'What else can I think of to tell you?' she pondered. 'Oh, I know … Ricky would be considered very rude in Sweden as we don't think very much of people who are too loud. I think he breaks every rule, in fact,' she commented. 'We prefer people to be respectful and speak quietly. Like I'm doing now, actually.' She gave him another of her knockout smiles.

Michael sensed he was allowed to speak again and asked if she'd always lived in Stockholm. He'd obviously spoken too soon though.

'Please keep your face still as I haven't finished. Yes, I have always lived there. My parents both had Swedish roots but my mum was born and raised in Texas. Her parents had moved out there from Sweden in the 1940s and my grandfather had quite a successful matchstick company in America. My mum met my dad when he was in the US studying and the rest is history, as they say. She moved to Stockholm with him when he finished his studies. My maternal grandparents used to visit Sweden quite frequently for business anyway, so they didn't mind too much, since they knew they would still see a lot of her. My dad was originally from Jönköping, in the south of Sweden, but when they came over as a couple, they decided to settle in Stockholm. Jönköping is the match capital of Sweden, by the way.' Michael found this interesting but regretted that he'd managed to somehow bring the conversation back to families, which was the last thing he'd intended to do. Fortunately, he was still under strict instructions not to move his face and therefore couldn't speak, so didn't feel entirely responsible for the short silence that ensued.

Alexandra continued with her work until she was done. 'There - you look amazing, even if I say so myself! Look!' She carefully removed the towel and stood back.

Michael looked at himself in the dressing room mirror. She really had done a much better job than he ever could. He beamed at her and thanked her, putting his hand against his chest to emphasize his gratitude. 'I can see why you're in such high demand with my peers in the music industry.' He noticed Alexandra blush slightly.

'What do you like to do with your hair? Do you normally put anything on it? It's very short.' She ran her hand gently over his scalp and he felt a sensual shiver trickle down his spine. 'I didn't see any hair products in your box of tricks,' she queried.

'Don't laugh! I usually just put some glitter spray on it,' he chuckled. 'There should be a can of it in the box.' Michael shielded his eyes as Alexandra gave his hair a quick squirt.

'Phew! That stuff smells toxic!' Alexandra commented.

'It probably is,' replied Michael. 'I have to get my kicks somehow.'

'Now your clothes,' directed Alexandra. 'Although you can probably manage to get into those yourself, I imagine.'

Michael seductively peeled off his dressing gown - he was wearing his underpants at least - and walked over to the clothes rack, choosing tonight's first outfit and slowly putting it on. He was feeling much more comfortable with Alexandra again now and hoped she'd be impressed to see that he was in such great shape. As he started to silently run through the set list in his head, he realised he'd been ignoring her by doing so. 'I'm so sorry - just trying to get into the zone,' he explained.

She laughed. 'Don't worry - I'll be here ready and waiting when you rush back between songs to change. Are the clothes in the right order on the rail there?'

Michael checked and they were.

Now that he was finally ready, he admired himself in the mirror and did an elaborate twirl in front of Alexandra, who started clapping and cheering. Michael did an exaggerated bow and asked if she'd like a drink. He poured her some sparkling water from one of the bottles that had been left for him and they joked about sitting there drinking water when most pop stars would probably be knocking back the champagne by now.

'I've been thinking about what you told me the other day about not being able to go out without being recognised,' said Alexandra. 'I might be able to help you with that. I did a course in transformational make-up once and although I'm not suggesting you go out looking like a monster from outer space, I'm sure I could make you look very different to how you do now. Even you wouldn't recognise yourself!'

Michael wasn't convinced but didn't want to burst her bubble. 'That would be awesome!' he beamed. 'I really appreciate the help you've given me tonight.'

'My pleasure,' was her response as she took his hand and gently kissed it, so as not to disturb the masterpiece she'd created on his face.

They continued chatting, hardly noticing the fifteen-minute call. Eventually, the dreaded final knock came for Michael to head towards the stage. Alexandra gave Michael a high five and told him to break a leg.

'That's the right thing to say before a show, I believe?' she asked. Michael nodded and did a little bow. He blew her a kiss and opened the door, allowing the rumble from the full-to-capacity arena to grow louder in the room. The noise was quickly muffled again as he closed it shut behind him, giving her a final nervous wave as he left. Alexandra hurried over and locked it. She sat down in the seat that had just been occupied by

Michael and listened to the sounds coming from outside. Within a couple of minutes, she heard the music strike up and a loud cheer as Michael was revealed on stage.

She looked around the room and exhaled. She was very uncomfortable with what she was about to do but knew she had no choice. She was meant to have made this call way before now but this was the first opportunity she'd had since arriving in Paris.

She walked over to her bag, which was perched on the table next to Michael's make-up box, and took out her mobile phone. Returning to the seat, she stared at the screen for what felt like an eternity before mustering up the courage to make the call. She selected a number from her contacts and put the phone to her ear, listening to the ring tone and dreading the person at the other end picking up. It was a very long time before the call was answered and when it was, her heart sank.

'Hi it's Alexandra,' she said, nervously. There was a long silence.

'I'm very sorry,' she continued. 'I've not had the chance to call you before now but just to confirm, I've arrived in Paris.'

She could tell by the response from the other person that they were extremely angry with her.

'Nothing to report yet but I'm still trying. He's obviously very upset about it all,' she explained. This conversation was going far worse than she had anticipated. 'Listen, I'm sure I'll be able to get all the information you need if you just give me some more time.'

Alexandra listened to another angry outburst and tried not to let the fear show in her voice as she replied. 'I know you have a deadline but I can hardly force him to talk.' The other person was just shouting abuse now.

'I appreciate you can't pay me any more money

158

until I deliver the goods. As I said, I just need some more time …' She was cut off mid-sentence by yet more yelling.

'No, I can't go back to England with him, you know that. I'm getting married in Stockholm on Saturday. I have explained all of this before.' Alexandra was so tempted to hang up but knew that it would only make matters worse.

'Look - I assure you - I'll go to visit him once the wedding is over. My future husband won't be impressed if I cancel, so it's very difficult for me, but I do desperately need your money.' She wished she hadn't had to disclose this last bit, since it made her feel very vulnerable, but she really was relying on these funds.

There was a loud click indicating that the other person had hung up. Alexandra glared at her phone for a moment before turning it off and angrily throwing it onto the floor. She sat with her head in her hands as tears started to roll down her face.

Chapter 11
Homeward Bound

Unbeknown to Alice, the boys were sleeping quite soundly in their newly-appointed room as she stormed out of the hotel, after having read their note. Incredibly, Louis and Tim had fooled her into thinking that they had taken Brian to the hospital. She was furious. She was so blinded by fury in fact, that she marched all the way to the local Métro station before remembering that breakfast at the hotel was included in the price of her room. Angrily, she did an about turn and retraced her steps.

By the time she got back, the dining room was extremely busy and she struggled to find somewhere to sit. A continental breakfast was all that was available, which Alice hated. She'd have much preferred a full English, especially since, as usual, she was starving. She examined the food that was laid out in abundance on three tables along one side of the room. What Alice really fancied was some proper toast - the brioche bread on offer just didn't hit the spot. She approached one of the waiting staff and demanded very loudly that he fetch some proper sliced bread. After lots of gesticulating, he eventually understood her and explained in broken English that they only had what was on display. It went completely over his head when Alice very loudly launched into the virtues of a Mothers Pride loaf.

She finally settled for a croissant, which she heavy-handedly fed into the toasting machine at one end of the table, ignoring the sign next to it, which stated very clearly in English amongst other languages, that it was only suitable for the sliced brioche. Within seconds, her croissant got stuck inside the machine and caught fire. The other diners gasped as Alice frantically tried to fish it out with a metal knife. One of them rushed over to intervene and to try to stop Alice electrocuting herself. Rather than being grateful, Alice just glared at him and stood back, abandoning the situation completely as the man sensibly unplugged the toaster and succeeded in putting the fire out. *Stupid foreigners*, thought Alice. *That would never have happened with English bread.* She hastily tore a few hunks off a giant baguette and put them onto a plate, together with some *pains au chocolat.* She also helped herself to some cheese and a few of the small packs of butter and jam that were on display. Depositing everything on her table, she then returned to the breakfast bar, and picked up one of the large cereal bowls. She filled it with a mixture of muesli and cornflakes, before topping it off with what was left of a jug of milk.

Some of the other diners observed her in amusement as she noisily started to consume everything. Although she wasn't at all keen on this French food, it didn't stop her from eating every morsel. She paid one final visit to the breakfast bar and unashamedly took a few more pastries for a mid-morning snack. She'd paid for this food after all. She wrapped them up in a serviette, threw them into her rucksack, and stormed out of the hotel.

Alice took a train towards Montmartre, looking very disapprovingly at the other passengers. They all looked very different to her. Once there, she huffed and puffed her way up the steep hill to the Sacré Coeur, and then rested on a bench for a bit as she tried to get her breath back.

161

Walking around the Place du Tertre, she was asked by several artists in English if she'd like them to sketch her. *What a ludicrous concept*, she thought, swearing at them as she walked away. She dreaded to think how much they would charge her for this privilege. She was also bemused at how they all assumed she was English. She was wearing her favourite blue and white Brighton and Hove Albion football top but surely that didn't prove anything. She'd been a big fan of the south coast team since her father had first taken her to one of their matches. The shirt was looking quite threadbare now but she still loved it. She hadn't originally intended to wear it for more than one day, but it was still fairly clean, and so she'd decided that there was no point in dirtying something else, just for the sake of it.

She sat outside a pavement café and enjoyed a *chocolat chaud* in the morning sun. She retrieved the pastries she'd packed earlier and started tucking into them. The proprietor of the café came out and tried to explain to her that she wasn't allowed to eat her own food here. She ignored him, pretending not to understand, and finished eating them anyway, throwing the serviette they had been wrapped in onto the table. She paid what she thought was an extortionate amount for the hot drink and started to make her way back down the hill.

There were so many reminders of her brother, Michael, in this city right now. She'd passed several posters advertising a concert he was giving in Paris, and found it very strange that he should be here at the same time as her. She half smiled as she wondered how he might react if she turned up unannounced at the stage door, demanding to see him. It was extremely tempting, but the fear of him rejecting her was far too great for her to consider actually doing it. It would be so simple for him to put things right. All he had to do was apologise

162

for not having got back in touch and for the selfish way in which he'd walked out of her life.

Alice did have a very strange thought that perhaps she might randomly bump into Michael in Paris, but then chuckled at the realisation that a global superstar wouldn't be walking the same streets as her. Her brother would probably be swanning around in a fancy limousine instead.

After a while, she turned a corner and noticed a *fromagerie* on the other side of the road. Her French was pretty non-existent, but even she knew that this was a cheese shop. She remembered that Michael had been obsessed with the stuff when he was younger and had even asked for a mountain of cheese instead of a birthday cake once, on his fourteenth birthday. Alice was able to recall the memory like it was yesterday.

In an effort to shake her brother out of her head, she took a train back to the centre of town and found an Irish pub where she enjoyed a couple of pints of Guinness. She chatted with some other English-speaking tourists who were also taking refuge there. They all agreed that it wasn't worth visiting a French restaurant for lunch and that the menu on offer here was much more appealing. Alice ordered a shepherd's pie, which looked delicious and came with buttered vegetables. She consumed the meal whilst sitting at the bar and once she'd finished, she ordered yet another glass of the smooth Irish stout. The barman made a joke about her knocking them back a bit fast. Alice just glared at him.

Whether it was the effect of the Guinness or the fact that she was feeling truly relaxed for once, but it suddenly dawned on her that glaring at people was something she seemed to be doing a lot lately. Looking back, she wondered if some kind of depression had descended on her, turning her into a dark shadow of her former self. This realisation hit hard and made her feel quite dizzy. She put her hands onto the bar to steady herself. The old Alice wouldn't have been so harsh with everyone around her but it seemed to have become her *modus operandi* nowadays. What had happened to the cheerful, happy-go-lucky girl she used to be?

When her parents had died, initially Alice had thought that she was dealing with the grief quite well. Her neighbours and the friends she'd had at the time had all rallied round, frequently bringing in cooked meals and phoning to ask how she was. Sadly, it was only a matter of time before all of that stopped. People began to get on with their own lives and expected her to do the same. That's when the real grief had started to kick in. Alice very soon became resentful and envious of everyone else around her. They all seemed very content with their happy little families and at times it felt as if she was the only person in the world who'd be coming home to an empty house. Over time, her bitterness towards everyone had just intensified. She never considered telling anyone how bad she felt and therefore, as a result, instead of treating her with compassion and understanding, they stopped having contact with her altogether.

Alice realised she had to get a grip. It was very unlike her to be maudlin like this. She reminded herself of all the good things in her life and top of that list was of course her exciting new venture. She'd invested in the revival of a derelict cinema, which was being managed by a young woman with lots of cinema experience. Alice was paying the girl a pittance and was looking forward to making a surprise visit to the cinema as soon as she got back from Paris. Although the woman seemed very willing and able, Alice didn't trust her, and had even been contemplating threatening to sack her. She hadn't actually done anything wrong but Alice liked to keep people on their toes. She loved the feeling of power, even though it did nothing to combat her ever-deepening feeling of loneliness.

Alice's knew that her three travelling companions on this trip to Paris were the only friends she had left now and she was suddenly ashamed at how badly she had been treating them. She wondered why they had even stayed in contact with her, considering her abysmal behaviour towards them. If she wasn't careful, she realised she'd be losing their friendship too and that was the last thing she wanted. Alice knew that she had to make amends somehow, but how could she do that without it being cringingly embarrassing? She had to change this victim mentality and to start treating others, especially Brian, Louis and Tim, with a bit more respect. She resolved to make a start later that day and hoped that her friends wouldn't makes it too difficult for her. Alice had found a restaurant discount voucher in her hotel room that morning. She would offer to buy the boys dinner that evening and with 50% off both food and drink, she'd be able to cheaply repay them for their friendship and start to make amends. She was well aware of how sentimental they got about these kinds of things.

Tears started to stream down her face and she decided to move from the bar to an empty table where she couldn't be so easily seen. It felt like all the sadness, all the loneliness and all the twisted emotions were suddenly coming to the surface. She sat there, lost in her thoughts, for a couple of hours, reflecting on the misery of her current life and ordering a few more drinks in the process.

She thought again about the letter that had arrived just before she'd left home, inviting her to come in for an interview with the benefits office. It had been playing on her mind ever since. What if her time was up, and the authorities had finally caught up with her? She shook her head to try to think more clearly. She'd outwitted the powers that be many times before, and was certain that she could do it again. It was just a matter of sharpening her resolve.

Realising that the drink in front of her wasn't the answer, she hurriedly dried her tears and paid the bill, trying her hardest not to let the barman see her sorrowful face. She even bit her tongue and stopped herself complaining about the extortionate cost of the food and drink. Looking at her watch, she couldn't believe it was already almost 5pm. Had she really been wallowing in self-pity all afternoon?

The voucher that Alice had found was for a restaurant in the first *arrondissement* of Paris, right in the centre of the city. She was now determined to make a reservation there for later. With a dizzy head, she left the Irish pub and made her way towards the nearest Métro station.

Paris was a big city and she wasn't quite sure how she was going to find her friends. The chances were slim, but she could at least try. Alice had had a mobile phone for some time now, and found it very annoying that virtually nobody else she knew had one. It would have made things so much easier if one of the boys had one. She'd not even bothered to bring her phone out with her today - what would have been the point of carrying it around all day with no opportunity to use it?

Getting off the train at the appropriate stop, she walked along the Seine, browsing some of the second-hand books and vintage magazines for sale on the riverside stalls along the way. *Ridiculous prices for a load of old tat*, she thought, before reprimanding herself and fixing a false grin on her face.

As Alice approached Notre Dame Cathedral, she did a double take as she noticed her three friends sitting on a bench, with their backs to her. She decided to creep up on them and was astounded when she got close enough to hear their conversation. They were complaining about her, and it appeared they had made a pact to confront her later. She went cold whilst listening to their spiteful banter and stood there in disbelief. She knew she'd been difficult with them but had she really been that bad?

After a minute or two, she couldn't listen to their catty remarks any longer, and decided to make herself known, walking round to the front of the bench as the three boys froze in shock.

'I've just been listening to you. Is that what you really think of me?' she asked. 'And I have to say that you don't look like you've been to the hospital, Brian!'

Brian tried to hold on to his earlier resolve. 'I'm feeling a lot better now and thanks to these two guys, I've managed to see something of Paris today too. And where have you been, Alice? Not stalking us all afternoon, I hope?' He was feeling exceptionally brave now but wasn't quite sure how long it would last.

Alice wasn't prepared to change the subject. 'You do realise that I put a lot of effort into arranging this trip? None of you were forced into coming away with me, you know.' She looked like she was about to burst into tears and Brian suddenly felt very embarrassed. She was evidently still managing to push the appropriate buttons to make them all feel bad.

'We do know that, Alice, and we appreciate it,' said Louis, trying to calm the waters. 'Poor Brian here was in a lot of pain earlier, but fortunately he's much improved now. Tim and I have done our best to help rally him and we're glad you're here to help us look after him now.' He wasn't quite sure whether Alice had any heart strings to pull on but it was certainly worth a try.

Alice seemed to soften, remembering her plan to be kinder towards her three friends. 'That's good to hear,' she replied. 'Unless you've already made other plans, I've found a lovely restaurant for tonight, just on the other side of the Seine, over there.' She pointed in the direction she assumed the restaurant to be in. 'I can of course go there on my own, but I was planning on asking for a table for four.'

And expect us to pay, thought all three boys, simultaneously.

She astounded them though. 'Perhaps you'd let me buy you all dinner tonight? It must be my turn?' The boys looked at each other, wondering if perhaps it was Alice who should have been taken to the hospital earlier, since she was acting completely out of character.

'That would be lovely, Alice,' said Brian. 'There's nothing I'd like more and it's very kind of you, isn't it boys?' The other two nodded in disbelief.

Like little chicks following their mother, the three boys walked behind Alice as they headed off to find the restaurant. It was called *Le Gros Gourmand* which made Louis laugh. He would later tell his friends that in English this meant 'The Large Greedy Person', which was a perfect description of Alice. It soon became apparent, however, why Alice had offered to pay for their meal. Not only did the restaurant have a fixed-price, very limited menu but they noticed Alice hand over a voucher to the waiter when they arrived. Much to her chagrin, he announced very loudly in impeccable English that their meal tonight would therefore be half price. The boys concluded that they shouldn't have expected anything less.

They all enjoyed the food, even though the

portions were very small and there wasn't much of a choice. The dessert menu arrived and Alice excitedly told the waiter that she was pleased that it included her absolute favourite - *crème caramel*. He smiled and went into the kitchen, returning with a large washing-up bowl sized dish of it. He laughed and as a joke, he put the whole bowl down in front of Alice as he went to get the boys' desserts, and to fetch a smaller dish to serve Alice's pudding into. He was shocked when he returned to find Alice voraciously tucking into the contents of the enormous bowl. There was no way that he would be able to serve any of it to anyone else now, but realised that the mistake had been his and not hers. He shared a Gallic shrug with the boys as he put their desserts down in front of them.

Alice was in her element. 'I can't believe he's given me the whole bowlful!' None of the boys thought it a good idea to try to explain to Alice that this had obviously not been the waiter's intention.

Their conversation was suddenly interrupted by the sound of a commotion outside and they noticed that it had started to rain, very heavily. People were rushing past, trying to get to their destinations without getting drenched. The waiter hurried over to close the doors, hoping to prevent the rain flooding into the restaurant. There hadn't been a cloud in the sky when Alice and the boys had arrived and they all hoped the storm would end just as quickly as it had begun. Unfortunately, it didn't and it was still pouring down when the time came for them to leave.

They ran to the nearest Métro station and were wet through by the time they got there. They all found it hilarious though, and were all in fits of giggles as they went down the station steps, even Alice. Despite gasping for breath, she was the first to arrive on the relevant

169

platform.

Tim whispered into Brian's ear. 'She's definitely a lot fitter than the rest of us! I wonder what the benefits office would make of that?' His friend shrugged.

It was still absolutely teeming down when they got back to République and they were all totally drenched by the time they reached the hotel. Alice was still being very jovial with them and rather than question her new amenable behaviour, the boys decided to just go with the flow. Brian chose not to act on his earlier plans to confront her, especially since she was now very tipsy and would have just laughed at anything he had to say. Instead, they said their goodbyes at her hotel room door.

Alice informed the boys that they needed to be packed and in the breakfast room by 8am the following morning. She suggested they leave their luggage at reception before heading out for their last day in Paris. Their ferry was booked for 11pm and they needed to leave the city by 7pm. Brian expressed his concern that they may not have enough time to get to the port in time, especially since they needed to take the RER back to Georges and Martine's house and then drive from there to Calais. Alice dismissed this with a flick of her hand. At first Brian thought she was going to hit him and flinched to get out of her way, which made Alice roar with laughter.

'See you all in the morning, BLT!' she smirked. The boys all squirmed at her use of their initials. She stumbled into her room and slammed the door shut in their faces.

'Goodnight and good riddance to you too, Alice!' exclaimed Brian, quite loudly. At that moment, he really didn't care if she heard him.

The boys went to their room and spent an hour or so happily chatting about the wonderful day they'd had and joking about Alice and her funny behaviour. They eventually got to sleep, each dreaming about a different aspect of their trip so far.

By the time Alice appeared the following morning, the boys had already checked out and had handed their luggage in for safekeeping at reception. They were waiting for her in the breakfast room and had been reminiscing about old times and how they'd first met. As students, they'd all worked together for American Express in Brighton. Brian still worked for the them in their HR department. Tim and Louis were now qualified accountants. They had dated for a while and had even once rented a flat together in Seaford. It didn't take them long to realise that they made much better friends than lovers though, and even now, they had an extremely strong bond. A lot of people assumed they were still together, because of their incredible closeness.

By deliberately checking out earlier, the boys hoped that Alice wouldn't discover that they'd changed rooms. All three of them had already had their breakfast by the time she appeared and cringed at Alice's behaviour as they watched her devour enough food for at least three people. They pretended to be deaf when she suggested they make a snack for later, although it didn't stop her filling her own rucksack with an ample selection from the breakfast bar.

Alice's suitcase still needed to be brought down from her room and she requested the boys come with her to help, as she wouldn't be able to manage it on her own. They looked at each other and inwardly groaned. They doubted that she had even bothered to open the case at all during the trip, since she had worn the same clothes throughout their stay. They hoped she'd had a shower at some point at least, and imagined that she wouldn't have been able to resist using the free toiletries provided by the hotel.

Alice had always been a tomboy and they had never known her ever wear a single speck of make-up. Her ginger hair was cut quite short in what she described as a 'pixie cut', and the boys often wondered if she chose this style because it made her look even more boyish.

Once Alice's case was safely ensconced at reception, they left the hotel and decided to spend the day along the Champs-Élysées, where they could do some last-minute shopping.

They started their day at the Place de la Concorde, which Brian explained had once been called Place de la Révolution, and had been the site of the infamous guillotine. This had been where both Louis XVI and Marie Antoinette had lost their heads. Looking at the beautiful square now, it was hard to imagine that it had once been the scene of such gruesome events.

They soon reached the shops and Alice was keen to buy some CDs in the Virgin Megastore. The boys said they'd like to buy some aftershave from one of the shops they'd passed the previous day too, a few doors down from the music emporium.

Once inside the music store, Alice acted like a thing possessed, filling one of the store's shopping baskets until it was overflowing. The boys were waiting for her by the tills and couldn't believe how much she was about to spend. In hushed tones they had a conversation about where she got all her money from.

'I'm sure it's tax payers' money she's spending,' spat Brian. 'It really shouldn't be allowed. Someone needs to report her. It's just not right.'

'I thought Nigel was planning on telling the authorities about her?' questioned Tim.

'I stupidly talked him out of it again,' confessed

Brian. 'Although I wish I hadn't now.' Brian recalled all the effort Nigel had put into researching who he needed to contact. 'I told him he wouldn't want it on his conscience if she got sent to jail,' he said, regretfully. 'He still tries to have a discreet go at her whenever he can though. He told me last week that he'd bought a copy of the 'Mr Greedy' book and anonymously sent it to her in the post, with a note saying that he'd seen the book and thought of her. She's not mentioned it but I bet she knows it was from him.'

'Unless she thinks it's from one of us?' chuckled Louis.

'Doesn't she have any shame?' asked Tim, as he caught sight of Alice grabbing yet more CDs from the shelves. 'She seems really brazen about flaunting the amount of disposable cash she's got. The most frustrating thing is that I know several people who are in really poor health who have applied for benefits but have been refused. If Alice is really getting all this money from the state then she must be telling some massive lies to the authorities. She's much fitter than all three of us put together. That money should be going to the people who deserve it.'

'I've made my mind up to do something about it when we get back,' resolved Brian.

'I'll support you with that!' declared Tim, and Louis determinedly nodded his head in agreement too.

Alice suddenly appeared in front of them, having now paid for her purchases at the till. The boys' conversation came to an abrupt end. Alice looked very satisfied with herself as she proudly held up her carrier bags.

'Happy now, Alice?' asked Brian, giving his other two friends a knowing look. She ignored him completely.

173

There was a big display for Michael Hambelton's latest album to one side of the shop's entrance and as they left, Brian wondered how Alice must be feeling, with her brother's face blatantly staring at her. Nothing was said though and they walked out of the store and strolled towards a fragrance shop, further down the street.

Each of the boys bought a bottle of eau de cologne as Alice looked on, impatiently. She really couldn't see the point of them buying these fancy scents, when she had never worn perfume in her life.

'I hope you've still got enough money left to buy me a meal after wasting your money on that rubbish!' she chastened.

Brian was still feeling quite empowered. 'We're all spent up, Alice!' he consoled. 'Looks like we'll be going Dutch.' She glared at him and marched out of the *parfumerie*, with the three boys following close behind.

They called in at a few other shops along the Champs-Élysées, with the boys trying desperately not to get separated from each other. None of them wanted to get stuck on their own with Alice, since conversation with her on a one-to-one basis was so painful sometimes and would usually descend into childish banter.

She insisted that they stop off at McDonalds for a snack, since she wanted to see if their menu was any different from the branches in the UK. The boys were astounded when she managed to find room for a Big Mac and fries, even though it wasn't that long since she'd gorged herself on the hotel's abundant breakfast. They just settled for coffees.

Brian suggested they visit Le Petit Palais on the other side of the road - an art museum he had heard good reports about. Alice, who had never been interested in the arts, insisted on sitting on a bench outside whilst the boys went in. She reminded them of their decision to have a proper meal together before leaving the city, which made the boys smile, since none of them had actually agreed to this. It was a shame though, since it meant that Brian and his two friends had to rush around the exhibition, rather than taking the time to enjoy it.

When they came back out, they noticed that Alice was eating yet again, having started on the feast she'd helped herself to from the breakfast table that morning. They joined her on the long bench and sat there for a while, trying not to focus on her noisy open-mouthed munching.

'Where are we going to eat later?' asked Louis, winking at the others.

'I'm sure we'll find somewhere,' responded Alice, between mouthfuls. She didn't seem to be in any particular hurry to get going.

'Does anyone need to do any more shopping?' asked Tim.

'I want to buy some food for the car journey back home,' advised Alice. 'Hopefully I can find some normal stuff. I'm not keen on this French rubbish.' She looked at what was left of a croissant she'd been eating and threw it onto the sandy path in front of her. A couple of pigeons swooped down to devour it.

Alice finally stood up and they got on their way. It didn't take them long to find a small supermarket down a side street. Alice spent almost half an hour selecting what she thought was suitable food and the boys ignored her as she very loudly complained about some of the French products.

Once back outside, they continued further down the same street and stopped to browse a menu outside a restaurant. Alice marched straight in - not at all interested in the boys' opinions about the food choices - and asked in English for a table for four. The restaurant looked fairly empty, with just one loved-up couple sat by the window. Brian discretely commented to his two friends that the lack of customers might not be a good sign, but since none of them was intending to eat very much, they chose not to say anything. Menus were given out and there was lots of chat about what to have. The boys were still full from breakfast, so decided on omelettes, with Alice surprising nobody by ordering *steak frites*. She also asked for a bottle of red wine for them to share and the waiter brought a carafe of water too, which is what the boys drank. Before heading out that morning, they had planned to have an ice cream before leaving town, so none of them wanted a dessert.

As Alice finished off a third glass of wine, she asked for the bill, with the others wondering who she would be expecting to pick up the tab. Surprisingly, she went along with Tim's suggestion to go Dutch. Brian dared to ask if she would still be within the legal limit to drive after having drunk so much, which was met by yet another of her glares. All three boys were concerned though - it was a long journey back to Brighton, and her driving was perilous enough anyway, even without her being under the influence of so much alcohol.

Whilst waiting for the waiter to bring the bill, Alice noticed that the restaurant was playing a French version of ABBA's 'The Winner Takes It All', which, according to Louis, was by a French singer called Mireille Matthieu and was called 'Bravo Tu As Gagné'. Although Alice was a very big fan of the Swedish supergroup, she had never heard this version of their song before.

It was trying to rain again by the time they got back to the Champs-Élysées. Despite this, they found a stall selling ice creams and the boys each chose a plain vanilla cornet. Alice didn't want to be left out and asked for a double scoop of melon flavoured ice cream on a chocolate coated cone, which the others thought sounded quite sickly.

'You'll go pop, Alice!' Brian joked. 'I don't know where you put all this food.'

'I think you'll find that you'll be the one going pop when I leave you behind in Paris,' snapped Alice, as she loudly slurped at her ice cream.

The boys had been nervously looking at their watches for the last hour or so and wondering if perhaps they should be heading back to the hotel to collect their luggage. Alice was getting more and more annoyed with them for wasting her precious time in Paris by worrying about the time schedule.

They took a final stroll towards the Arc de Triomphe and Tim commented on how busy the traffic was now - it was crawling along. He told Alice that it was a good thing they'd parked outside the city and she looked quite chuffed with herself for having come up with such a great idea.

As they were about to turn down a side street, Brian noticed a flashy car with blacked out windows, stuck in the jam. He joked with Alice that her brother might be inside. She glanced towards the car, proudly holding up her stash from the Virgin Megastore.

'Well if it is him, I haven't bought any of his awful music!' she shouted. The boys looked at each other and cringed.

It seemed quite obvious to the others that Alice was dragging her heels on purpose, but she eventually relented and agreed that they could now leave the city centre. They took the relevant trains to get them back to République. It felt a lot longer than just two days ago since they'd first emerged from the station.

There was a queue at reception when they got back to the hotel but Alice still marched straight up to the desk, announcing that they needed to collect their luggage. Louis was disappointed that it wasn't Katherine on duty as he would have liked to have discreetly thanked her once again for helping them with their upgrade. The man on duty looked quite taken aback by Alice's offhand manner, but handed her a key and pointed towards a door behind him, which had a cartoon picture of a suitcase on it. The boys quickly found their bags and dragged Alice's heavy Samsonite case out. Unsurprisingly, she just stood there impatiently watching them and then tossed the key back to the receptionist, not bothering to lock the door behind her. The key landed on the floor and Alice cackled loudly as the four of them headed out onto the street. It was raining, yet again.

Tim had got the short straw this time with Alice's enormous case, although the boys quietly told him not to worry as they'd all be taking it in turns. Alice had decided not to pack her purchases from the Virgin Megastore into her case, and proudly swung the carrier bags of CDs beside her as she walked along in the rain. She'd put the food she'd bought into her rucksack for easy access later.

Once they got back to the station, feeling wet and miserable, they boarded a Métro train to take them to Charles de Gaulle Étoile, via a station called Concorde. The boys were glad they only had to change trains once more, since the weight of Alice's case was making the journey quite unbearable. They were relieved when they eventually boarded the final RER train.

They got a taxi from the train station to Georges and Martine's house, which Brian somehow ended up paying for. The taxi driver charged them extra for Alice's heavy case, which he had great difficulty getting into his boot.

Alice was surprised to find her car in the same spot where she'd left it. She'd imagined the reason why Georges had asked for her keys was so he could use her vehicle whilst she was busy in the city, but she now had her doubts. She had wisely made a note of the mileage before handing him the keys. If Georges hadn't used the car, then he had missed a trick. If she'd have had the chance to use someone's else's car without telling them, she'd have certainly done so.

Yet again, they were invited in for some refreshments but Alice refused, explaining that they needed to leave immediately in case there was traffic on the way to the port. As much as the three boys would have loved to have gone in, they were quite concerned now in case they missed their ferry. They were booked on the 11pm crossing and it was already fast approaching 8.30pm. Martine looked quite distraught that Alice had turned down her invitation for a second time, since this meant that they had hardly spent any time together at all. So much for this being a rekindling of their friendship. Her heart sank as it dawned on her that perhaps Alice had been using her all along, just to get free parking during her stay in Paris. She vowed to never respond to this rude Englishwoman ever again.

Georges handed Alice back her keys and helped Brian to lift Alice's case into the back of her vehicle. As they were about to say their goodbyes, Alice's mobile phone started to ring and she hurriedly grabbed it from her rucksack, handling it like a hot potato that might burn her fingers. She looked at the screen and her face reddened. The boys had never seen her like this before. Telling them that it was the hospital calling, she quickly scurried down the road, disappearing from view behind a parked van so she could take the call.

Brian asked his two friends in hushed tones whether Alice had mentioned anything about hospital visits before and they shook their heads. They all stood there in the dark like lemons, with Georges and Martine wondering whether they should wait for Alice to return or go back inside. Luckily for them, the three boys were polite enough to engage them in conversation while they waited.

To try to ease the atmosphere, Louis decided to chat to the couple briefly in French, explaining how rude he found Alice and his reasons for not reminding her of his language skills during their stay in Paris. They both laughed, obviously having already got the measure of Alice. Martine told him how disappointed she was that her former pen-pal had snubbed her by not wanting to spend any time with her and her husband. She now felt totally used.

Furious with the caller for ringing at such an inopportune moment, Alice dealt with the call in her usual brusque manner. Aware that she might possibly be overheard by the group assembled by her car, she tried to keep her voice down, but couldn't help but lose her temper on a couple of occasions. She was beyond frustrated that the person on the other end of the line didn't seem to be taking things as seriously as they should be. Alice finished the call by shouting loudly down the phone and hanging up.

She glared at the screen and became even angrier when she noticed that she'd had a couple of missed calls from the hopeless woman at the cinema earlier in the day too. Why was that stupid girl phoning her every five minutes? She'd been employed to do a job and Alice didn't want to hear about every single thing that she did. She'd certainly be getting her marching orders when Alice paid her a surprise visit later in the week.

Martine, Georges and the boys had all been trying to listen in to Alice's side of the call, but hadn't managed to catch very much, apart from a few profanities here and there. The boys questioned her about it when she returned but she just shook her head and explained that it had been a doctor checking on her current medication. They all looked at each other, in total shock that someone would shout at a medical professional in such a rude manner. Plus, in all the years the boys had known Alice, they'd never seen her take a single pill, so it was all quite puzzling.

'Get in the car, BLT!' she ordered, and everyone apart from Alice said goodbye to Martine and Georges. Alice ignored them completely and just climbed into the driver's seat. Without even a wave, she drove off down the street. The boys' relief was palpable when they arrived at the port in time to catch their ferry.

Unsurprisingly, even more food was consumed by Alice on the ferry crossing back to the UK, along with several fizzy drinks.

The traffic on the French side of the channel had been fairly light, but coming out of Dover it was a lot heavier, despite the late hour. At least it kept Alice's speed in check. For some strange reason, she resisted playing loud music on the journey home, which was a relief to her fellow passengers, even if completely out of character. They all noticed that she seemed unusually reserved and they couldn't help but wonder if the phone call she'd taken earlier had involved bad news.

The traffic eventually cleared and despite the heavy rain, they were soon racing back towards Brighton. At one point, Brian dared to suggest that it might be a good idea if Alice were to slow down, what with it being dark and the road conditions being so treacherous. Rather than heed his warning, she just pushed her foot further down onto the accelerator pedal instead.

Alice had bought some French doughnuts - *beignets* as the French called them - which she'd started munching on as soon as they'd left Dover. Once she'd finished them, she started on the rest of the food she'd bought in Paris: several bars of chocolate, a large bag of crisps and various packets of sweets. Oblivious to the concern of her travelling companions about her ability to eat and drive at the same time, she noisily made her way through all the unhealthy snacks as her Jeep thundered along the middle lane of the M25, reaching speeds way above 100mph. She was making no concession at all to the wet roads or the fact that the street lights on this section of the motorway were out.

All three boys suddenly spotted a blue juggernaut ahead, going much slower than they were in the inside lane. They saw its indicators begin to flash, showing that it was about to pull out in front of them. Alice was so busy enjoying her food that she didn't notice this at all.

Chapter 12
Team Building

Jake woke up feeling as if he hadn't slept at all. He'd had a dreadful night and had tossed and turned with bad dreams involving his wife mocking him about his new job. Each time he'd roused, Sue's loud snoring down the hallway reminded him of the terrible way that she had spoken to him the night before. He really hoped he wouldn't appear too shattered when he arrived at the cinema later that morning and did very briefly consider calling in sick, before realising that this wouldn't look very professional on his second day. He also had a really good feeling about this new job and if he were honest, he didn't want to miss the opportunity of seeing Jason again either.

He slowly put one leg out of bed and then mustered up the energy to get the rest of himself out from under the duvet too, creeping into the room where his wife was still sleeping to collect some clean clothes. Fortunately, one of the sliding wardrobe doors had been left open and so he quietly lifted out the hangers carrying his suit and a white shirt without waking her. He carefully rummaged through a bedside drawer to find a clean T-shirt, pants and socks. Sue was completely unaware of his presence and carried on making a deafening noise with her snoring.

He headed downstairs, manoeuvring as carefully as possible to avoid the particular steps which he knew creaked. He took everything into the shower room and put his clean underwear onto a chair, hanging the other items of clothing in the door frame. Fortunately, the house was so large that he was fairly certain that the noise from the shower wouldn't disturb Sue. Their bedroom was on the other side of the house anyway, and to make doubly certain that she didn't hear him getting ready, he'd closed the kitchen door as he'd walked through. He took off the garments he'd slept in and threw them onto the floor, before turning on the shower and stepping under the warm water.

He tried to let the jets of water shake off his tiredness and his low mood. He really hoped that Sue wouldn't surface until after he'd left for work. With a bit of luck, she'd be in a better mood when he got back tonight. As he showered, he found himself thinking about Jason and wondered what he would be doing at that precise moment. How could this guy have made such a big impression on him after just one meeting? It made him realise just how needy he was feeling. Jake turned off the water and jumped out of the shower cubicle, drying himself and imagining Jason's hands instead of the towel caressing his body. Once dressed, he picked up his dirty clothes from the floor and put them into the washing machine in the utility room, together with his wet towel, before heading into the kitchen to fix some breakfast. He decided he'd have muesli so tipped a generous portion, much more than Sue would think he should have, into a bowl and added some milk whilst he waited for the kettle to boil for his tea.

The curtains were still closed at the far end of the enormous lounge when he walked in. Realising that the sound of the curtains opening might wake his wife in the room above, he chose to sit at the dining table in semi-darkness to eat his breakfast. He was ahead of schedule but couldn't wait to get out of the house, as the last thing he wanted was another confrontation with Sue. He hurriedly put the first mouthful of muesli into his mouth and almost choked when a voice from the other end of the room suddenly broke the silence.

'Creeping around this morning, are we?' asked Sue. He'd been completely oblivious to the fact that she was now up and was sitting on the sofa, waiting for him to appear.

'You nearly gave me a heart attack! What are you doing there?' He tried to soften his tone. 'How are you feeling this morning?' His heart was beating nineteen to the dozen.

She ignored his question. 'I really do need to talk to you before you go off to this tin pot job of yours.' She was obviously hungover and still in a lousy mood. He knew the best thing to do was to not respond, so chose to ignore the comment and slowly put down the spoon. He really didn't fancy his breakfast at all now.

'I've been thinking,' she continued. 'Now that you're earning your own money, you won't be needing me to transfer your monthly allowance into your account anymore. It's about time you became self-sufficient. I'll get onto the bank this morning.'

'I'm not going to be earning that much money, Sue,' he replied, frantically. 'Please don't do this. Plus, you know my MOT and service are due next week and there's hardly anything in my account as it is.' How he wished he could tell her what to do with her money. Even in the dim light he could tell that she was smirking at him. He hated having to beg but she was always very fond of making him do just that. He knew there'd be no chance of her changing her mind this morning though, and he just hoped that by the evening she would have calmed down enough to come to her senses.

He got up and almost ran back into the kitchen, tipping all his soggy, uneaten muesli into the bin. He put the used bowl, spoons and mug into the dishwasher. He could imagine the fuss Sue would make if he left them out for her to clear.

Jake hesitated before putting his head round the door to say goodbye, but knew that it wouldn't be in his best interests not to.

'See you later!' he said, as cheerfully as he could.

She glared at him. 'I've not finished with you yet so don't go sneaking off! I need to speak with you about the terrible job you've been doing of cleaning this house.' They had a cleaner who came in on Fridays but during the rest of the week, Jake did his best to keep everything spick and span. 'I've been leaving some traps for you Jake, and you've missed every single one of them.'

'What do you mean, 'traps'?' he couldn't help asking. What spiteful depths had she sunk to now?

'I left some confetti from inside the hole punch under the desk, some biscuit crumbs on top of a few picture frames, that kind of thing. You missed them all.' The tone in her voice reminded him of the very critical, bullying boss he'd had at the law firm.

Jake still somehow found the strength not to react. He grabbed his keys and walked towards the front door. He lifted his jacket from the coat rail and stepped outside, slamming the door shut behind him and fighting back the overwhelming desire to burst into tears. He jumped into his car, refusing to look back, just in case Sue had followed him outside. He was glad he had a half-hour journey ahead of him, because at least it would give him time to calm down before arriving at work.

Suddenly realising that he'd left his bag in the hallway, containing his mobile phone amongst other things, he briefly considered going back indoors. The only person who ever called him on that stupid device, apart from the one call he'd had from Madeleine, was Sue. Well, she could take a running jump today. If she needed anything from him then she'd have to wait until later.

He'd barely eaten anything - half a spoonful of muesli wasn't going to sustain him until lunch - so he decided to drive into Lewes and find somewhere that served a proper breakfast. He had almost an hour and a half before he needed to be at work so there was more than enough time. He felt the pocket of his trousers and was relieved to find that he had remembered to pick up his wallet. As he turned on the music system in his car, Michael's voice blared out of the speakers. Jake's first reaction was to turn it down in case his wife heard it inside the house. He promptly decided that at this moment in time, he really didn't care if she did.

'Oh Michael!' he sighed out loud. 'If only you were here now.' Tears began to stream down his cheeks. He put on his seatbelt and as he did so, he noticed that Sue's car wasn't in its usual spot on the driveway and was, in fact, nowhere to be seen. So, she'd been lying about driving home last night. Probably a good thing since she'd obviously not been in any fit state to do so. It made him wonder just how often she'd lied to him in the past and it suddenly hit him that his relationship with his wife was completely irreparable now. She only really spoke to him these days if she had something nasty to say and they lived very separate lives. But did he actually have the strength to do something about it? He started to really sob. He knew that he needed to get away quickly, so indicated and headed off.

His brother's voice seemed to be consoling him from the car speakers. The songs on this album were even more beautiful on second hearing and Jake resolved to listen to it again on his journey home that afternoon.

He had regained his composure by the time he reached Lewes. He parked in the cinema car park and even though it was still very early, was surprised that his was the only car there. Looking at his watch, he thought it was quite possible that nobody else had arrived at work yet. Although he had only started working at the cinema the day before, he already felt a sense of belonging and this thought lightened his mood as he walked the five minutes or so up the hill towards the town centre.

He found a quaint little café that had an extensive breakfast menu advertised outside and went in. Jake had secretly hoped that perhaps he'd bump into Jason on his walk into town but unfortunately, there was no sign of him. Smiling to himself, he realised he was getting a bit obsessed with this man. Jake ordered a cooked vegetarian breakfast and a large mug of tea, and sat listening to the friendly banter at the tables around him. The gentle sound of the breakfast show that was coming from the café's radio added to the cosy feel of the place. The fact that one of the songs they played was ABBA's 'Chiquitita' just seemed to confirm to Jake that all was not lost. He thought how appropriate the lyrics were and would have given anything to be able to have a face-to-face with the ABBA girls, to tell them about everything that had happened and how he was feeling. He was certain that they'd understand and would have some good advice to give him.

He felt a lot chirpier by the time he'd had something to eat and gave the waiter a sunny smile as he paid the bill. He headed back out onto the street with a new-found spring in his step. He was still half an hour early but at least it would make him look keen.

As he pushed his way through the cinema doors, he was astounded to find that the place was now buzzing with staff and very unlike how it had been the previous day. Jason was behind the bar again, now joined by two other young men. One of them had a shaved head and looked like he spent a lot of time at the gym and the other one looked a bit like a young Elvis Presley, complete with quiff. Jason spotted his new friend coming in and gave him a salute before whispering into the muscular guy's ear. Jake suddenly felt very jealous and wondered what had been said. Since the other man didn't look in Jake's direction, he guessed that it had probably not been about him.

Madeleine appeared from her office, carrying a large cardboard box. She spotted Jake and came over, kissing him on both cheeks whilst balancing the package in her hands. He asked if she needed any help and she hesitated but then agreed, telling him to follow her. He took the box and they went upstairs, where she led him into a room he'd not seen the day before. There was a large oval table in the middle, surrounded by chairs, and a screen that had been pulled down at the front of the room. Jake noticed that an overhead slide was being projected onto the screen, showing the agenda for the day. He was glad that he'd offered to help his new boss now, since he'd have hopefully earnt a couple of extra brownie points by doing so.

Madeleine asked him if he'd mind emptying the contents of the box and putting one of everything in front of each seat: a notepad, a sealed pack of Post-it notes, a biro and a felt-tip pen. Feeling quite intrigued, he decided not to ask any questions but just did as he was told. He suddenly felt like the teacher's pet but was proud of it and thought it showed what a great relationship he already had with Madeleine. The two of them chatted away although Jake chose not to tell Madeleine about the disastrous evening he'd had.

Once everything was set up, they made their way

back downstairs. Jake went up to the bar and Jason gave him a high five, asking what he'd like to drink. He went for a cup of tea again, since everyone else seemed to be drinking hot beverages. He watched his friend preparing his drink.

'Do you never drink anything else? asked Jason, teasingly. 'Because if that's the case, there goes my plan to get you drunk.' Jake tried to think of a funny retort but failed. He was tempted to ask Jason what he had in mind once he'd got him drunk but bit his tongue. Just as his tea was ready, Madeleine appeared on the staircase and got everyone's attention. She instructed them all to follow her upstairs, adding that they could bring their drinks with them. There was a real buzz in the air and Jake could tell that he wasn't the only one who was excited about working here.

They all went upstairs, exchanging polite smiles and pleasantries on the way. Jake held back slightly, and was pleased when Jason and one of the other guys from behind the bar caught up with him. He hoped that maybe this meant that he'd be sitting next to Jason for the meeting. He was right, and as they took their seats, Jason introduced him to the muscular guy, whose name was Pierre and who came from Martinique in the French West Indies.

Interrupting their chit chat, Madeleine welcomed them all to the team event. She went through the morning's agenda and asked if there were any questions. There weren't, so she began her presentation, asking the Elvis lookalike, who had just joined them and whose name was Roger, to dim the lights. He was jangling a large set of keys and Jake assumed he must have been locking the cinema doors before coming up.

Everything seemed so new and intriguing. They were told that the refurbishment of the building had been commissioned by the new mystery owner. Somebody asked whether Madeleine could tell them who it was but she just smiled and explained that unfortunately her lips were sealed.

Everyone was asked if they could take it in turns to stand up and introduce themselves and Jake cringed at the thought. But he really didn't want to look unfriendly, so was instead very brief, just saying his name and that he lived in Hove. As he sat down, Jason winked at him. 'Forgotten the wife this time then, Mate?' he whispered, which made Jake blush.

Once the introductions were over, Madeleine proposed an ice breaker, in the form of a cinema quiz, so that everyone could get to know each other a bit better. She told them all to get into teams of three and Jake was pleased to find himself with Jason and Pierre, although doubted that he himself would know any of the answers. He surprised himself though and miraculously, their team won. They were awarded a bottle of champagne, which Jason took and put under his chair.

'We'll have that later!' he grinned, giving Jake a wink, which created all sorts of weird and wonderful ideas in his mind. He found Pierre very friendly too and wondered if he'd be joining Jason and himself for the drink later. Part of him hoped not.

They were shown some short video clips about health and safety, and Madeleine handed round some printed documents for them all to read and sign. A few of the other staff had been making notes in the pads they'd been given and Jake decided to do the same - if only so it would look good. Jason playfully jolted his arm at one point. Jake noticed that his new friend wasn't bothering to write anything down himself. *No need to impress your sister*, thought Jake. He had listened to Jason and Madeleine chatting away the previous day and had envied their easy banter. If only he had that kind of relationship with his own sister.

Madeleine went through some other important policies and procedures with the team and Jake found himself impressed at how skilfully she skipped between the overhead slides. The significance of the felt-tip pens soon became clear, as they had to take it in turns to draw an image of another member of the team on a flip chart, which Madeleine had wheeled out. Jake thought this might be quite tricky, since most of them had only just met each other. There was therefore a lot of pointing and nervous laughter as everyone tried to remember each other's names.

It was pretty obvious who Jake would draw. He had always been very good at art at school and created an impressive, very recognisable caricature of Jason.

'Masterpiece!' shouted the barman when the drawing was finished, causing Jake to blush from ear to ear. As he returned to his seat, his new friend noticed this and patted him on the leg.

'You've got a real talent there!' he chirped. 'I might ask Madeleine if I can take the picture home to frame.' Jake sensed himself go even redder.

Returning to her presentation, Madeleine showed them a slide with everyone's roles within the team. Jake was surprised at how many duties there were, although Madeleine did explain that there would be a lot of crossing over of responsibilities with them being a fairly small group. She enthused about how proud she was of her new team and was certain that everyone would work very well together.

Jake found himself daydreaming at one point, looking around the room at the people present. He was aware that his poor night's sleep was beginning to catch up on him. Hopefully, Sue would be at work when he got back, if she'd not been too hungover to go in. It would be great if he could have forty winks before she came home.

He zoned back in to Madeleine's presentation just in time to hear her announce that the team event had now come to an end. Everyone began to leave the room and most people said goodbye to Jake before departing. He watched Jason put his jacket back on and check his watch.

'I've got a doctor's appointment I need to get to,' he told Jake.

'I hope it's not anything serious?' asked Jake, before realising that perhaps he hadn't known the guy long enough to ask this.

'Just need to register with a new doctor,' replied Jason, laughing. 'I hope he's got warm hands.' Jake felt himself blush again and quickly looked away, trying to hide his embarrassment. He was glad that Jason hadn't mentioned any more about drinking the champagne that they'd won earlier though, as it would have definitely sent Jake to sleep, which wouldn't have done much for his kudos. Jason gave him a quick hug and Jake noticed his wonderful aftershave and hoped that it would linger on his clothes for a while.

They slowly made their way downstairs and Madeleine came over to say goodbye. She asked Jason if he could quickly pop into the office before leaving. Jake made his way out to the car park. A few of the other staff were out there chatting, but Jake just waved at them as he drove off.

He decided to go straight home since he could feel a headache coming on - probably caused by his lack of sleep - and didn't even listen to any music on the journey.

When he got back, there was still no sign of Sue's

car but he was surprised to see Enrique's van on the driveway. He wasn't aware that the gardener was due for a visit. The side gates were open so Jake walked round to the back garden, expecting to find Enrique skiving again. He was nowhere to be seen, although the sliding doors into the house were slightly open. This puzzled Jake since Enrique only had a key to the garden gate and not to the house. It dawned on him that this probably meant that Sue hadn't actually gone to work after all, and his heart sank.

He slid the door open further and crept into the house, wondering what was going on. There was nobody downstairs but he could hear music playing upstairs. As he stood listening in the hallway, he noticed a receipt on the console table. He couldn't help put pick it up to examine it. It was for a room at the Grand Hotel in Brighton and his mind flashed back to when he had spotted Enrique on his way there the previous day. He couldn't believe how blatantly the receipt had been left out for him to see, and it left no doubt in his mind that there was definitely something going on between his wife and the gardener.

He quietly made his way up the stairs and noticed that the music was coming from the main bedroom. He suddenly heard his wife's voice, although she wasn't talking, but was instead making very loud sounds of ecstasy. Jake felt himself freeze and for a brief moment he didn't know what to do. Something drove him forward though, and he slowly pushed the bedroom door open.

What he saw was a complete shock to him yet also confirmation of what he'd been suspecting for some time. He could see the back of the gardener, naked on the bed, thrusting into Sue, whose face was obscured by Enrique's head at first but came into view as Jake walked further into the room.

It took a moment or two for his wife to register that he was there, at which point she started to scream, 'GET OUT! GET OUT!'

At first Jake wondered if she was addressing Enrique or himself. He suddenly felt quite peculiar. His body was very hot and clammy and a tightness, which quickly turned into a sharp pain, erupted in his chest. Everything began to go fuzzy and he felt himself fall to the floor.

Chapter 13
Flying

Michael had had a fear of flying for some time now. When his music career had first taken off, he'd disliked air travel but he wouldn't have labelled it as something he was afraid of. But after some very scary flights, where he'd actually feared for his life, he now hated it more than ever. He still carried on doing it though, because there really was no other feasible option. He'd hoped that over time, facing his phobia would make it go away, but this had unfortunately not happened. To make matters worse, whenever he was airborne, he would stupidly torture himself with memories of previous bad flights, which would only make him feel worse.

His thought process usually started with him going back to the worst flight he'd ever experienced, when he was touring the US two years previously and was travelling from New York to Boston. At the time, he'd been shocked that the flight had actually gone ahead, since the weather conditions had been atrocious. The taxi journey from the hotel to the airport had been bad enough, with buffeting winds and torrential rain making it hard for the chauffeur to steer safely through the city streets towards the airport. Once there, Michael had genuinely expected to see that all flights had been cancelled but, worryingly, this hadn't been the case. When he'd reached the departure lounge, it was obvious that the other passengers were concerned too. He'd still anticipated an announcement to come through at any moment, saying that the flight was definitely not going ahead.

Waiting to board the plane, he'd stared in horror through the lounge window at the tempest raging outside. He'd been travelling with a Swedish bodyguard, Rickard, on that occasion and to give the guy his due, he'd done his best to try to keep Michael calm.

Unsurprisingly, it had been the bumpiest take-off he'd ever experienced. Within minutes it had felt like the plane was being thrown about in the air. Michael had dug his nails into the arms of his seat and had silently prayed for his life. He could hear people crying and then ultimately screaming following an announcement from the pilot that they were right in the middle of a violent tornado. Michael had let out an involuntary guffaw at that point - talk about stating the obvious. The aircraft had already been tossing around in the eye of the storm for a good five minutes by then. There had been no further communication from the cockpit after that and it had truly felt like he was in the middle of the worst nightmare ever. The lights had flashed on and off a few times before they were plunged into total darkness and the plane suddenly started to plummet towards the earth. It was just like one of those Hollywood movies, complete with the roaring sound of an aircraft about to crash. Even Michael's bodyguard, who had been trying his hardest to play it cool, was making whimpering sounds by that point and was crossing himself.

Somehow, at the eleventh hour, the pilot had managed to regain control and they had slowly begun to ascend again. The lights had come back on. There had eventually been a further announcement that they were diverting to Manchester, New Hampshire. This hadn't helped Michael's fear at all, since he wasn't sure where this was in relation to their original destination. Twenty minutes later, when they miraculously landed and everyone gave a round of applause, Michael offered up a prayer of thanks. He had gone to a Church of England school as a child and had been a Christian ever since, but it was at times like this that his faith was strongest. Michael had initially vowed that he would never fly again but had then realised that unless he intended to spend the rest of his life in America, he had no choice but to face at least one more flight. On his return journey back to the UK, everything had of course gone without incident.

Whenever he was flying, Michael tried very hard to counteract his negative thoughts with memories of better flights. He remembered one trip, when he was travelling from Stockholm Arlanda to London Heathrow, which had been the best flight he'd ever experienced. He had boarded the aircraft to find that it was a much bigger plane than the usual standard Airbus used for flights within Europe. At first, he'd panicked that he'd got on the wrong plane, but then a member of the crew had explained to him that this larger jet was needed in London, and instead of flying there empty, it had been designated to their flight. There had therefore been far less passengers on board than the plane was designed for, and the journey had been so smooth that Michael had even been brave enough to take a walk down the aisle to the toilet at one point - something he never did on a flight.

Prior to any long journey, Michael's strategy was always to reduce his water intake for twenty-four hours, to ensure that he wouldn't need to use the facilities during the journey. Although he knew this was bad for his health, his fear of being trapped in a plane and being so frozen with fear that he would be unable to go to the loo, far outweighed this. For the same reason he always refused food and drink on board and really envied other passengers who seemed to act quite normally and enjoyed getting sozzled whilst airborne. Michael never drank alcohol anyway, as he was always afraid of being out of control. So when friends suggested he have a couple of drinks to calm his nerves before a flight, he just looked at them as if they were crazy.

Michael had discussed his fear of flying with a long line of therapists over the years but none of them had managed to make him feel any better about it. He still hoped that one day, someone would come up with a magic cure. Until then, he just carried on suffering.

It was such a shame that he had to fly so much, but he knew that it was part of the job. He had once considered investing in his own bespoke jet, thinking it might make things easier, but had changed his mind when he'd subsequently been invited to fly on a friend's private plane. He had very quickly discovered that journeys on smaller aircraft were even bumpier than on commercial ones. He had even contemplated travelling around Europe by road, on a customised tour bus, but that felt even scarier than getting on a plane. The thought of endless hours being cooped up in a coach, travelling at high speed up and down motorways, wasn't appealing at all. So, because of this, he continued to fly around the world, albeit under duress.

As usual, Michael was travelling with his bodyguard today. They had hardly spoken so far this afternoon and within a few minutes of taking off, Clint was already napping. Michael wondered how the guy could claim to be protecting him when he was asleep, although at least it meant that there was no need to make awkward small talk. If he had been awake, Clint would have definitely been more interested in flexing his muscles for the crew anyway.

Michael always flew first or business class

whenever possible. It usually gave him the luxury of being seated at the front of the aircraft and, once everyone was settled, autograph hunters from economy weren't normally able to reach him. Fortunately, the cabin crew on most flights tended to be quite territorial and were very strict about keeping the hoi polloi away from the passengers who had paid a lot more for their seats. Unfortunately, Michael still sometimes had people bother him. To try to avoid this, his usual stance was to wear the very obvious disguise of a flat cap and sunglasses, which he kept on for the duration of the flight.

To help him cope with his fear, Michael always travelled with a selection of distractions in his rucksack. The most important of these, of course, was his Sony Walkman. His favourite song to listen to onboard a plane was 'Eagle', the lead track on *ABBA - The Album*, and he'd already listened to it twice through his headphones today. He couldn't think of a more appropriate flying song and the lyrics were very apt when you were in the air. He always had a book to read too, currently Sebastian Faulks' *Birdsong*. He'd just read a couple of chapters of that and was now trying to distract himself by listing in a notebook all the things he wanted to do during his upcoming time off. It was so hard to focus through this terrible fear though.

Michael had originally planned to be travelling back to London by Eurostar, and had been furious with Ricky when he'd discovered that he'd been booked onto a flight instead. He immediately tried to reserve himself a ticket on the train, only to discover that all seats were fully booked. It seemed to compound Michael's fear even further, knowing that there had actually been an alternative to being on this flight. To make matters even worse, Michael was travelling on his least favourite airline, one which he'd previously vowed never to fly with again.

It would have helped if he'd been travelling with someone nice today - for one thing, people seemed less likely to disturb you if they could see you were occupied with someone else. This wasn't guaranteed, of course, but if you chose well, then your travelling companion could keep you so engaged that time would seem to pass so much faster. Clint was definitely not playing that part today.

Michael had really hoped to be flying with Alexandra today, but she had acted very strangely the previous evening and hadn't even attended the after-show party in Paris. The weirdest thing of all was that even Ricky hadn't made an appearance. He'd not seen either of them after the concert and Alexandra had messaged to say that she wasn't feeling well and had gone to bed. There had been no response to any of his subsequent texts. Although Michael had only known her for a couple of days, his intuition told him that something was wrong. It was such a shame because he'd had such high hopes for this new relationship. Her behaviour last night had left him feeling like he had invested far too much far too soon, as usual.

Michael looked out of the plane window and could just about make out the English Channel below, barely visible through the white clouds. He often compared his loneliness to being lost at sea, flailing about in the water and struggling to stay afloat, desperate to be rescued. Instead of driftwood, he would often metaphorically find himself grabbing hold of someone nearby, in the vain hope that they would save him. This either resulted in him scaring the other person off completely or with them ultimately using his desperation as a weapon against him.

When he'd left the hotel earlier, there had been a lot more journalists waiting outside than usual, but he'd managed to dodge them. It was obviously a very slow news day if they were reporting on the end of his current tour. A couple had tried to approach him at the airport too, but surprisingly, Clint had succeeded in stopping them from getting too close.

One of the crew had clocked Michael when he'd boarded the plane and had given him a smug look of recognition. Michael guessed that the guy had spotted his name on the passenger list earlier. Annoyingly, he noticed this same steward whispering to the other crew members before take-off and one by one, they had all looked across in his direction. They'd stared at him throughout the flight like he was a monkey at the zoo and had been so unprofessional that Michael had yet again made a mental note to absolutely refuse to travel with this particular airline in the future. He thought he'd already made this perfectly clear to Ricky previously, yet somehow that message hadn't made it through to the company who booked Michael's travel.

He glanced at his Emporio Armani watch - a gift from his parents on his eighteenth birthday - and was relieved to see that the flight was almost over. He'd somehow forgotten that he was in the air for a few moments. Michael liked it when he got lost in daydreams whilst flying. To be honest, today's journey hadn't been too bad at all.

It was comforting to know that he'd soon be back on the ground again and on his way home. The best thing of all was that he had nothing in his diary for the next ten days. This tour had been hard work, to put it lightly, and he felt completely burnt out. He desperately needed some time to relax and recharge his batteries.

He knew that Ted would be on his way to collect

---

him by now. He found this such a relief and couldn't wait to catch up with both of his house staff. They were certainly a lot more than just employees; in fact they were amongst his closest friends these days and he tended to spend a lot of time with them when he was at home. He'd met the couple when they'd lived next door to him at a previous property and he'd been impressed at their discretion and unpretentiousness even then. They'd been completely unfazed about living next door to a famous pop star and Michael had felt very relaxed in their company from the word go. He trusted them completely. When he'd purchased Greengage Farm, he'd asked them to come and work for him and they'd moved into an adjacent property in the grounds. Although he sometimes felt guilty that they often ended up being on call 24/7 when he was home, he consoled himself with the knowledge that at least they had their own house to live in and that they were free to do whatever they pleased when he was away. He wasn't sure they made the most of that free time though, since Ted always ensured that both properties and the communal grounds were kept in excellent order and Michael knew that a lot of that maintenance work would take place whilst he was out of town. Krystal would usually do a deep clean of both properties while he was away too. He was absolutely certain that neither of them would be putting their feet up during his absences. Michael had had many conversations with Krystal about this in the past, to check that she and her husband were still happy with the arrangement. She had explained that because she was such a home bird, the current set-up suited her perfectly. He chose not to push her on what Ted's viewpoint was.

Greengage Farm was situated near Arundel, a market town in West Sussex, although sadly, Michael had only ever been into the town centre once. He had

203

been seriously impressed with the medieval castle and cathedral but had caused such a commotion by being there that he had never chanced it again. Visitors would often wax lyrical about the place and he truly hoped that one day he'd be able to return. How he hated living in this goldfish bowl.

He'd had both properties on his estate extensively refurbished before moving in and there was still quite a hefty mortgage outstanding. Although he'd had the means to purchase the estate outright at the time, his accountant had suggested taking out a mortgage for tax reasons.

The main house had all the usual rooms you'd expect to find in a property of its kind, but also had a recording studio, an indoor swimming pool and, even though Michael shamefully never used it, a gym. There was a large orangery in the grounds too, which was used for entertaining purposes, for functions of more than a dozen people. Krystal usually did all the cooking but outside caterers were employed for larger events. The estate encompassed several acres, including a large wooded area and several fields. Ted headed up a team of gardeners who worked all year round to keep the grounds in optimum shape. Both main properties were tastefully decorated and furnished.

Breaking Michael's reverie, the pilot announced that they were about to make their descent. This was music to Michael's ears and he truly couldn't wait to get home. Just the thought of it put a big smile on his face. He knew that Krystal would have been up very early that morning giving his house a final spruce and to start preparing a welcome home meal for him. Ted would have polished the car and had a quick walk around the terrace and parterre to make sure that everything was shipshape.

What Michael didn't know was that before leaving for the airport that morning, Ted had noticed on the security cameras that there was already a worryingly large crowd of people gathering at the end of the driveway. This wasn't unusual - there would often be fans waiting and it had even been known for some of them to erect tents on the other side of the road, intent on camping out to catch a glimpse of or even meet their idol.

Ted always dreaded having to drive through large groups of people in case someone got hurt. Some of the fans seemed to have no concept whatsoever of how dangerous it was to throw themselves in front of a moving car. He remembered that an obsessed fan had even put their baby in the path of the vehicle once, thinking that it was a sure-fire way to make Michael get out. Fortunately, another fan had had more sense and had quickly pulled the baby to safety, much to the annoyance of its mother.

Michael's car had blacked-out windows so it was impossible to see who was inside, which sometimes made the situation even more frustrating for Ted, if he was alone in the vehicle at the time. There would still be the usual hysteria with fans surrounding the car, even though their hero wasn't inside. Ted was often tempted to drive out with the windows wide open on those occasions, to show that he was the only person in the car. But he'd never chanced it - knowing his luck, some of the fans would try to climb inside.

Occasionally, if the number of people outside the property got too large, Ted would ask a local security firm to send a team out to deal with the crowd. Ted had made one of those calls this morning. With the professionals in place, he hoped that everything would be under control by the time he got back with Michael.

He got into the car and triggered the electric gates

to open. So far so good. It had been known for the press and fans to make their way all the way down the drive and to be waiting on the other side of the gates, even though they were trespassing on private property by doing so. Fortunately for Ted, today they all seemed to be taking note of the invisible line drawn between the narrow lane and Michael's driveway.

Ted slowly made his way through the gates and down the drive. As he did so, he observed the crowd waiting in the distance, noticing that there were a lot of photographers in attendance today. This was quite puzzling, since it was quite rare to see the press outside the house, unless there was a particularly unsavoury headline about Michael on the front pages that day. Perhaps the paparazzi just wanted some shots of Michael returning home after his record-breaking world tour. It did seem a bit bizarre though - hadn't they had ample opportunity to take photos of him on stage over the last few months? Ted took everything in his stride these days though and tried not to overthink it. His job was to get his boss home safely and that was exactly what he intended to do. He tried to ignore the noise of the baying crowd as he carefully manoeuvred the car through them.

Michael was relieved when the pilot safely landed the aircraft and as it taxied along to its allocated gate, he whispered a silent prayer. Clint made an overly exaggerated performance of yawning and stretching his pumped-up arms into the air. Michael chose to ignore him. He truly hoped he'd never have to meet the guy again after today.

Even before the announcement was made that the plane's doors were open, the other business class passengers were already on their feet and blocking the aisle. Michael's usual stance was to wait until everyone else in his section of the plane had disembarked and then make a mad dash for the exit at the very last minute. By doing so, he could usually escape before the tourist class passengers appeared.

He was really dreading that one of the cabin crew might pounce on him for an autograph or a photograph as he tried to get off the plane today, especially after the way they'd been observing him during the flight. He'd experienced this in the past and today's ensemble looked very much like they might have this in mind.

The pilot advised everyone that the doors were now open but Michael remained in his seat, as he watched the handful of other business class passengers make their way off the aircraft. Quickly grabbing his rucksack from under his seat, Michael crossed his fingers and took the opportunity to stand up, rush past Clint and swiftly make his way off the plane. It took his bodyguard a good minute or so to catch up with him. Michael knew that it was the guy's responsibility to get him safely out of the airport terminal, but he really didn't care about that right now. Although he knew it was extremely rude, Michael couldn't even be bothered to say goodbye to him. He did wonder if perhaps Clint was expecting some kind of tip, in which case he was going to be sorely disappointed.

Michael speedily cleared both passport control and customs via the airport's VIP services. He knew that it certainly helped matters that he travelled with just hand luggage. His suitcases tended to be dispatched from his hotel by courier to save him the hassle of checking them in and then collecting them from the baggage carousel upon arrival. He was always impressed that his luggage would often arrive back at his house before he did and he had never yet had anything get lost or damaged. He'd heard so many stories of cases arriving at destination airports in a terrible state or even sometimes not arriving at all. Having just hand luggage also meant that he could quickly navigate through the airport's VIP services with less chance of being recognised.

He briefly stopped off at the airport toilets and locked himself in a cubicle, pulling out a full bottle of Evian water from his rucksack and guzzling it down to try to replenish his low fluid levels. He had a headache and knew that he must be extremely dehydrated. He threw the empty bottle back into his bag and left the cubicle, finding it hugely embarrassing to find Clint lingering outside the toilet door.

Michael pushed past him and rushed out towards the terminal doors. Fortunately, he found Ted waiting outside. He looked very professional in his chauffeur's uniform, standing by the car and waiting for his boss to emerge. Ted hurriedly opened the back door for Michael to jump inside. There were no further sightings of Clint and within seconds Michael was being driven out of the airport complex and was heading home.

During the journey, Ted broke the news that there had been a large crowd waiting outside the house that morning and that he had called the security firm to come out to deal with it. They were both bemused as to why so many people would be waiting there that day.

Michael and Ted chatted amicably on their journey home. Ted wanted to hear all the gossip about the tour and what Michael's manager had been up to during that time. The guy did have something of a reputation amongst Michael's inner circle.

Michael decided to tell Ted about Alexandra and how disappointed he had been that she hadn't travelled back with him today. He really hoped he'd hear from her again but wasn't convinced. After her strange behaviour the previous evening, part of him wondered why he was bothering with this relationship at all.

He suddenly remembered the stash of cheese he had tucked away in his bag. Ted agreed that Krystal would be very keen to sample it. She shared Michael's obsession with cheese and there were even plans afoot to convert one of the outbuildings into a cheese dairy. They'd had someone come out to the house the previous year to show them how to make cheese and it hadn't seemed as difficult as they had first imagined. Michael's dream was to one day have his own brand of cheese for sale in the shops.

When they were almost home, Michael shuffled across to the middle of the back seat, so he could get a better view out of the front windscreen as they approached home. His heart sank when he saw that there was still a very large crowd of people waiting in the lane, mainly made up of the press. He was relieved that Ted had alerted the security company, since it looked like they had come out in force and had installed barriers to hold everyone back. Fortunately, a safe gap had been left for the vehicle to drive through.

Michael was puzzled though: why were there reporters here today when he'd been doing press interviews throughout his tour. He didn't think that him arriving back home would warrant news coverage. There was no rhyme or reason to it, and Michael found it incredible how stories about musicians could make the headlines for days on end. He vividly remembered the furore Take That had caused when they had announced that they were breaking up. Although it was no doubt worthy of coverage, somehow it had eclipsed all other news headlines for several days.

Ted slowly drove the car between the rowdy throng. As they passed, Michael distinctly heard one of the reporters shouting at the top of his voice. 'Do you have any comment to make about your sister?' he asked.

Once they were safely through the security gates, Michael spotted his two blue-grey Maltese cats, Tobias and Othello, sitting next to each other on the low brick wall surrounding the parterre. True to form, as Michael got out of the car, Tobias jumped down and started to run towards him, whilst Othello sauntered much more slowly in his direction. Michael crouched down to make a fuss of his beloved pets, relieved that they still remembered him, despite him having been away for so long.

The journalist's words were still echoing around Michael's head. What had the guy been referring to? Had Alice concocted yet another fake story about her estranged brother? And if so, what had she come up with this time? Would she ever stop telling these terrible lies about him? It was so hard to believe that his sister could really hate him so much. It was at times like these that he was truly glad that she was no longer in his life.

Chapter 14
Survivors

Following the crash, whilst still trapped in the upturned vehicle, Tim had drifted in and out of consciousness. He felt totally numb and had no idea at all where he was. He could hear what was going on around him though, which reassuringly confirmed that he was still very much in the land of the living. There had been the sound of sirens and subsequently a medical team attending to him, but it had been so frustrating not being able to communicate with the ambulance crew. He'd found it impossible to lift his eyelids or to find the strength to open his mouth to speak and had had no choice but to just let everything happen around him. From what he could deduce from overheard conversations, he'd been in a car accident, although he couldn't remember a single thing about it. He did, however, have very vivid memories of a recent trip to Paris with three of his friends that kept going round inside his head. He knew that Alice had driven them there, but he couldn't fathom out whether this trip had taken place recently or in the distant past. He tried his hardest not to think too much; the only part of his body where he seemed to have any feeling coming back was in his head and it was so painful. He'd never had a headache like it before. It made everything such a jumble. His brain seemed intent on playing a slide show of his previous life experiences. He wondered if this was what people meant when they talked about your whole life flashing before you as you were dying.

After a while, Tim realised that he was now

tucked up in a hospital bed. It was comforting to hear the nurses talking about his ongoing treatment. He very quickly ascertained from their chatter that he had a drip going into his arm, although he couldn't actually feel it.

Brian had remained conscious both during and after the accident. He had initially been in unbearable pain with his neck and left arm, which had been bent at a very odd angle. He was relieved when the emergency services had arrived. When he was first brought into hospital, he had been given an anaesthetic to allow the surgeons to reset his arm, which had apparently been broken in two places. He was extremely thankful to have survived the crash and to know that his two closest friends were still alive too. Like them, he was now sporting a very uncomfortable neck collar to support one of the injuries he'd sustained as a result of the crash. His face was bandaged up too, which felt very odd. He remembered everything that had happened on their journey home from Paris. As a result, he had already been briefly interviewed by the police.

Poor Louis was also in a bad way, with whiplash and several broken ribs. He was currently fast asleep, pumped full of pain killers and totally oblivious to what was going on around him.

Brian had noticed that the minute hand on the clock on the hospital wall moved forward five minutes at a time, which he found quite unnerving. The first time he'd spotted it, he'd thought he was going crazy. Nothing seemed normal anymore and time certainly wasn't moving at its usual pace. Propped up in bed, he was feeling a lot more comfortable than he had done a few hours previously. He was amazed at how quickly he seemed to be improving. Those drugs were obviously working their magic.

He looked across at Tim and Louis, who were

212

both out for the count on the other side of the ward. They both had intravenous drips going into them and at first, Brian had wondered if they were in comas. Although the medical team were very limited with the information they were prepared to share with him, he'd been assured that his friends were just sleeping, partly as a result of the trauma they'd sustained but also because of the medication going into them.

One of the nurses had taken Brian for a brief walk down the corridor earlier, and he had seen his reflection in the mirror. He'd concluded that the bandages around his head made him look a bit like the Invisible Man, whom he'd seen in an old black and white movie once. If he remembered the film correctly, you'd only been able to see the Invisible Man because he'd been all bandaged up.

He had asked the team looking after him for news of Alice. She'd been the driver of the vehicle they'd been travelling in after all, and he couldn't stop thinking about her erratic driving and how she had constantly stuffed her face with food throughout the journey, frequently taking her eyes off the road. As usual, she'd refused to wear her seat belt, so he knew she would have probably come off far worse than him and his two friends.

Just before the crash, Brian clearly remembered seeing a huge juggernaut ahead of them and then chillingly realising that Alice hadn't spotted it. At the very last moment, he had screamed and she had swerved to avoid the lorry. Their vehicle had sped off the motorway at terrific speed and smashed through the metal barrier along the side of the road, causing the car to somersault into the field beyond. Brian definitely blamed Alice for the accident, although he'd not yet mentioned this to anyone. When he'd been interviewed by the police an hour or so previously, he had been very economical with the truth and had pretended that he didn't remember every single detail of the events that were now firmly imprinted on his brain. He'd also failed to mention that he'd watched Alice consume enough wine in Paris to be over the limit. Surely, blood tests would reveal that anyway.

Brian really wanted to be able to talk things though with Louis and Tim, before revealing anything further to the authorities. He could always blame temporary amnesia if they subsequently decided to divulge more. He'd overheard one of the nurses saying that nobody else, apart from the occupants of the vehicle they had been travelling in, had been injured in the crash, but he still didn't want to get Alice into any more trouble than necessary. He was trying his hardest not to think of the consequences if Alice hadn't swerved to avoid the lorry.

He knew that he had to stop interrogating the hospital staff about Alice as it was very obvious from their responses that they were getting extremely frustrated with him. He even wondered whether the staff on the various wards communicated with each other, in which case the nurses on his ward might be completely oblivious to Alice's condition. He'd been so desperate for information earlier that he had asked James, one of the friendlier nurses and the one who Brian thought might be the most conspiratorial, if he would escort him down to the female ward to see Alice. This had been met with a very icy glare, followed by a well-rehearsed statement that this was completely out of the question. Brian hoped that sometime soon he might be able to sneak down to Alice's ward unaccompanied, but did realise that with his head currently covered in dressings and his arm in plaster, he'd be easily spotted. The nurses seemed to be watching him like hawks too, so there was little chance of him getting away with an undercover mission right now.

He had noticed a woman in her late twenties visiting Tim earlier. She'd sat by his friend's bedside, occasionally holding his hand. Brian had tried to smile at her when she'd looked over but she hadn't spotted this. Hardly surprising really with him looking like he'd done ten rounds with Mike Tyson. Annoyingly, he was being assessed by a doctor when Tim's visitor had been in too. He was determined to catch her attention if she came in again. He was curious to know who she was and he also wanted her to know that he was a close friend of Tim's. If she did come back, Brian had already decided that he wouldn't tell her much about the accident - just the same information that he'd given the police. He really did want to discuss everything with his two friends before revealing anything more.

It felt funny when he tried to eat. His face was covered in bruises and the stitches and bandages pulled at his skin. His neck brace was quite uncomfortable too but at least he was able to feed himself with the hand of his good arm. On the bright side, the intravenous drip that had initially been going into him when he'd first come in had now been removed and he was on pain relief tablets instead.

When James, who was already his preferred nurse, had escorted him down the corridor to the patients' lounge earlier, Brian had noticed that the other patients in there were old men and were all sleeping. The television in the room was tuned in to a children's channel, which probably didn't do much to stimulate the room's occupants. He had told James that he'd prefer to be taken back to his side ward instead.

Brian's family lived in Scotland and on his brief outing down the corridor earlier, he'd managed to speak to his mum on the payphone to tell her what had happened. She'd promised she'd be down to see him at the weekend. His dad had died a couple of years previously and he knew that his mum worked long hours at the local supermarket to support herself and his two younger brothers, so he felt guilty to be adding even more stress to her life. He'd tried to talk her out of it, but being such a wonderful mother, she had kept insisting that she wanted to visit him, especially after what he had been through. Brian ultimately won though, and he made a promise to visit his family as soon as he could. In the meantime, they could keep in touch by phone. Whenever they saw each other, it tended to be Brian who made the journey up to Scotland and his mum had only been down to Brighton once in the five years he'd lived there. He really hoped that he would look better than the currently did when he went to visit her, since she would be shocked to see him in his present state. He half wished he'd not seen his reflection in the mirror earlier.

Brian had been wondering if anyone else he knew was aware that he was in hospital and made a mental note to phone a couple of his friends, whose numbers he was sure he remembered, once he was feeling a bit brighter. It was a shame that he was in hospital in Crawley rather than Brighton, since this would make it much harder for them to visit, although it was only a forty-minute journey by car, so still possible for them to come and see him.

Looking across at his friend Louis, Brian thought it was sad that the poor guy probably wouldn't be having any family visit him during his hospital stay. His parents lived in France and he rarely saw them. They were avid Francophiles, hence why they'd named their only son after the multitude of French kings, and had bought a bargain-priced chateau in the Loire Valley when Louis was just five years old. It sounded as if they'd had no problem leaving their only son in the custody of his maternal grandparents when they'd left the UK, using the excuse that they still wanted him to be educated in England. He'd spent summer, Christmas and Easter holidays in France though, basically being used as an unpaid child labourer. As an adult, he'd chosen not to visit them very often. He always spoke very highly of all four of his grandparents, who had now all died sadly, but rarely mentioned his mum and dad, which spoke volumes. Brian wondered if Louis' parents had been notified that their son had been involved in an accident, and guessed that even if they had, there would still be little chance of them crossing the Channel to visit their only child.

Brian was currently sitting in the armchair next to his bed and the nurses had put a trolley table in front of him, so he could eat his lunch. He'd chosen quiche and salad, followed by jelly and fruit with cream. He was amazed that the hospital kitchen catered so well for their vegetarian patients, of which he was one. He was also impressed that he'd adapted so well to eating with just one hand.

He was just finishing his dessert when Tim's mystery visitor appeared again. Brian froze as he was about to take his last mouthful of jelly. He was quite concerned though, as her face looked so pale and sad. Visiting hours didn't begin until 2pm and it wasn't even one o'clock yet. His heart sank as he considered that she may have only been allowed in early because there was a serious problem with Tim.

Gulping down the last bit of jelly, Brian pushed the dessert bowl to one side. He watched the visitor tidying the bedside cabinet next to Tim's bed. Hopefully this was a good sign. She surely wouldn't be doing this if she'd been told that he was on his last legs. Brian was

217

determined to speak with her today, but since she'd only just arrived, he decided to wait a few minutes. He watched her sit down next to Tim and take hold of his hand. She started speaking to him quietly, but Brian couldn't hear what was being said. Sadly, there seemed to be no response from Tim.

Brian eventually took the plunge and cleared his throat very loudly, hoping it would get the woman's attention. She briefly glanced around the room and caught sight of him looking across at her. He raised his good hand in her direction and she gave him a little wave back. He was relieved when she got up and started walking towards him.

'How are you?' she asked.

He laughed. 'I've been better. How's Tim?'

The visitor looked surprised, 'Oh! You know my brother?'

'Ah, so that's who you are!' exclaimed Brian. 'Yes, I've been friends with Tim for years. We used to work together.'

'With Louis too?' she asked.

Brian tried to nod but failed miserably due to his neck brace.

'Yes, I'm good friends with Louis too. I don't know if you realise, but he's in the bed next to your brother. The three of us were in the same crash.' He suddenly wondered if Tim's sister knew they'd been in an accident but then realised that she must do. Why else would she think her brother was in here?

'I just hope they both wake up soon because it's quite lonely in here,' he confided, trying to make light of the situation, hoping it might make her feel a bit better about her brother's condition.

'I've been told that sleeping is good for him,' she said, looking concerned.

'They told me that too. Apparently, he's not in a coma or anything," said Brian.

'They're pumping quite strong pain killers into him via the drip. Let's hope that's what's knocking him out. I'm Pippa, by the way.' She held out her hand and Brian shook it awkwardly.

'And I'm the Invisible Man,' he responded. He guessed from her expression that she hadn't seen the film. 'Sorry - I've decided I look a bit like the character in that movie.'

'Nice to meet you, Invisible Man,' she chuckled. 'Do you remember a lot about the accident?'

Brian chose to proceed with caution. 'I remember the journey and seeing a juggernaut in front of us,' he offered, hoping this wouldn't prompt too many further questions, but guessing that it no doubt would. 'My real name is Brian,' he added.

Pippa looked at the remnants of Brian's lunch in front of him. 'I hope I'm not disturbing you whilst you're eating?" she asked.

'No, I've finished,' he responded, pushing the suspended table to one side with his leg. 'Hospital food isn't as bad as they say, you know. It's much better than these scratchy pyjamas they've given me to wear.'

'Why aren't you wearing your own clothes?' asked Pippa.

'Chance would be a fine thing,' grumbled Brian. 'I've been told our luggage is probably still in the boot of the Jeep at the compound, where it was taken after the crash. I've got no idea when we'll get it. We were on our way back from Paris. Did you already know that?'

'Yes, Tim told me about Alice winning the competition in the newspaper,' said Pippa. Brian was relieved that she knew that much at least. 'I know all about that terrible woman,' she continued. 'Tim has told me so many stories about her. I hope she's not to blame for the accident.'

'I don't know who was to blame.' Brian needed to steer the conversation away from Alice fast. 'We had a great time in Paris. It's a shame it ended like this, although hopefully all four of us will be OK, eventually.'

'Do you know if Alice survived the crash?' asked Pippa.

'They won't tell me anything about her, unfortunately. I assume she must be injured too since she was dri…,' he stopped mid-sentence, realising the mistake he'd just made. He wouldn't usually be that stupid. He guessed it must be his fragile state that had loosened his tongue. Although he could tell from Pippa's expression that she had guessed as much anyway.

'Tim didn't tell me how you were getting to Paris. I'm not surprised that she was driving you there though. I bet she was charging you all a fortune for the privilege too? If she's left my brother with any long lasting health conditions, then she'll have me to answer to!' she spat.

Just at that moment, a noise started to come from Tim's bed and Pippa ran across to him.

'He's waking up!' she shouted. Brian stood up to join her but then decided to observe the proceedings from across the room. Pippa looked down at her brother, who was lying there with his eyes open, staring up at her. He was moving his mouth and trying to lick his lips.

Pippa took a glass of water from the bedside cabinet and, realising that she wouldn't be able to get her brother to drink any of it without drowning him, she put her fingers into the glass and rubbed them over his lips in an effort to moisten them. Brian thought how practical this was.

'What's happened?' asked Tim in a very faint voice.

'You're in hospital,' explained Pippa. 'Your friend Brian is over there and Louis too.'

'We were in a crash coming back from Paris,' Brian shouted across the ward. 'Do you remember that?' Tim looked at his sister and tried to nod.

'Can I sit up?' he asked.

'I don't know if you're allowed to. Don't move! I'll fetch a nurse,' instructed Pippa, as she headed out of the ward.

'I remember the crash,' said Tim, croakily raising his voice, hoping that Brian could hear him. 'Alice didn't see that lorry, did she?' he asked.

'I don't think so,' responded Brian, hoping that nobody was listening to their conversation. 'But thank God we're still alive. I'm not saying too much about the accident to anyone until we find out what's happened to Alice. I keep asking how she is but they won't tell me anything.' Brian was so pleased to be able to finally speak with his friend and hoped that Tim would go along with his strategy of not getting Alice into any more trouble than necessary.

Pippa soon came back with a nurse in tow. She proceeded to ask Tim some questions about how he felt, as she set about doing some medical checks. She requested that Pippa leave them alone for a few minutes as she pulled a screen around the bed.

There was suddenly a noise coming from Louis' bed too. It was hardly surprising with all the commotion going on that he had woken up as well. Pippa hurried over and found him also lying there with his eyes wide open, starring at the ceiling, just like her brother had been.

'Hello Louis. I'm Tim's sister, Pippa,' she explained, wanting to take Louis by the hand but then deciding not to touch him, in case there were injuries that she wasn't aware of.

'Hi, Buddy. I'm here too!' shouted Brian, getting up and heading over towards his friend.

'There's a nurse with Tim, so hang on in there and I'm sure they can sort you out as well,' Pippa suggested. 'Seems the three of you are very lucky indeed.'

Louis sighed. 'Although I don't feel very lucky, lying here,' he mumbled. 'I feel so tired.'

'You're probably full of morphine,' suggested Brian. 'Don't panic! I'm sure you'll be fighting fit in no time.' He only hoped he was right.

Another nurse hurried into the room and saw that Louis was now conscious too. Pippa and Brian were sent away, to give her some room to work. Brian went to sit on his bed and Pippa followed him. They watched as a screen was pulled around Louis too and listened to the activity going on around the two beds.

'I might go down to the female ward and give Alice a piece of my mind!' exclaimed Pippa. Brian was aware that as keen as he was for news of their crazy friend, Tim's sister marching onto Alice's ward and shouting at her probably wouldn't help matters.

'Wait and see what they're doing with Tim first,' he diplomatically advised.

A third nurse appeared and went behind Louis' screen. After a while, both screens were pulled back to reveal Tim and Louis sitting up. The three boys waved at each other. Just one nurse now remained and was trying to make Louis more comfortable. Pippa rushed over to speak with her brother and Brian could tell from his facial expression that he wasn't too happy with what she was saying. He heard Pippa raise her voice, to let her brother know that there was no point disagreeing with her.

'I know you've not had any contact with them for years,' Brian heard Pippa say, 'but they really do need to know. They're your parents, after all.' She seemed to suddenly realise that she'd been shouting and lowered her voice. Brian therefore didn't catch the rest of the conversation.

A very tall, 20-something, fairly good-looking blond guy walked onto their little ward.

'Would anyone like to request a song for us to play on hospital radio?" he asked. Pippa shook her head, but Brian suddenly had a plan.

'I would!' he declared.

The young man came over and looked very keen as he stood there, poised with his pen and pad in hand.

'What would you like us to play and who is it for?' he asked.

'Can you play a song for our friend, Alice, who I'm hoping is on the female ward?' Brian asked quietly. 'I've been trying to get a message to her but have been failing miserably. It might be nice if she hears a song that we've requested for her.' Brian thought this might be the perfect way for them to let her know that they were all OK. 'But how will she know to listen?' he asked, realising that he hadn't even been aware that there was a hospital radio station until now.

'Well, I'm currently going round the wards to let everyone know how they can tune in. There are some headphones hanging up behind your bed.' He seemed so excited that somebody was actually asking for a request that he didn't elaborate further. 'Anything in particular you'd like us to play?' he asked.

It didn't take Brian long to come up with something. 'Can you play 'Waterloo' by ABBA?' he asked. 'She's a big fan of their music. And can you say it's from Brian, Louis and Tim. Maybe add that perhaps we should have taken the Eurostar from London Waterloo to Paris. She'll understand that and hopefully it will make her smile.' He was hoping it might appeal to her very warped sense of humour.

The guy noted everything down. 'I'm sure we can do that,' he smiled. Without saying another word, he turned on his heels and walked away, bumping into a male nurse who was on his way in. At first Brian thought the guy was coming to do further checks on Tim and Louis, but then realised that he was heading in his direction. The young man's badge advised that he was 'HCA J. Meadows'. He proceeded to pull a screen around Brian's bed.

'I just need to check your temperature, blood pressure and stuff,' he advised. 'How are you feeling?'

'Not too bad,' Brian replied, 'I'm not really in any pain.' He was really hoping that he'd be sent home soon and even though he was sure that this guy probably wouldn't have the necessary authority to discharge him, it surely wouldn't do any harm to get him on his side. He decided to try his best to charm him. 'That's an interesting name, Mr Nurse. What does the HCA stand for?' he asked.

'Don't let the nurses over there hear you calling me that. They've told me I'm the lowest of the low in their eyes because I'm just a healthcare assistant. They only give me the basic stuff to do around here, although don't worry, I am qualified. I'm not just some stranger who has wandered in off the street.' Brian looked at him and smiled. 'Terrible news about your friend,' the guy continued in a very quiet voice, as he stuck a thermometer under Brian's tongue. 'I hope it wasn't too much of a shock for you when you found out. Must've been terrible to be in the crash with her. It's a miracle you three boys survived, considering the fact that she didn't.'

Brian went cold. He snatched the thermometer back out of his mouth with his good hand, causing the healthcare assistant to snap at him sternly.

'What do you think you're doing?' he asked.

Brian did momentarily consider acting as if he already knew about Alice, but was well aware that he wasn't a very good actor and doubted he would be able to carry it off.

'Is she really dead?' he asked, catching his breath.

The medical assistant tutted and wrestled the thermometer out of Brian's hand, putting it back under his tongue. He looked very serious.

'I'm surprised you didn't already know. Surely someone must have told you.' Brian couldn't believe how bluntly the man had delivered the news but guessed that if you worked in a hospital then this was probably something you dealt with on a daily basis. He was still struggling to get his head around the awful news.

Oblivious to this, the guy went on, seemingly enjoying a good gossip. 'I think the police will be speaking with you at some point,' he said with some authority. Brian chose not to tell him that they'd already interviewed him once. 'It's bound to be in all of tomorrow's papers,' he continued. 'I don't think they've revealed that she had other people in the car with her yet though, which might give you and your friends a chance to recover a bit before the news hounds start bothering you.'

It was slowly dawning on Brian just how lucky the three of them really were to have survived the crash. Thank heavens he and his two friends had been wearing seatbelts, unlike Alice, bless her soul.

As soon as the medical assistant had pulled back

the screen and left, Brian started crying, wondering how on earth he was going to break the news to the other two.

He also needed to get a message to that radio station guy to cancel the song he had just requested for Alice. It seemed very inappropriate now, with Alice having finally met her Waterloo.

Chapter 15
Brighton General

In Brighton, Jake had woken up on a hospital trolley and had initially wondered where he was, since the last thing he could remember was the sight of his wife in bed with another man. He'd noticed the sharp clinical smell entering his nose even before he'd opened his eyes and it reminded him of the medical room at his old school. He'd spent many an hour in there as a child, faking symptoms such as a headache or an upset stomach, to get him out of PE and games. The couch in that room had definitely been a lot more comfortable than this hospital trolley. He was aware that he wasn't wearing any shoes but this didn't stop him climbing off and wandering out of an open door, finding himself in the car park.

Jake's sudden appearance sent the hospital porter, who was having a sneaky cigarette outside, into turmoil. He'd been instructed to wheel the patient into an observation ward and since his charge had been unconscious at the time, had been certain that he'd get away with a very quick break. The last thing he'd expected was for the patient to suddenly attempt to escape. He frantically threw his cigarette onto the floor, stamping it out. He quickly ran over and tried to usher Jake back inside. The poor guy was already in his boss's bad books and the last thing he needed was to be caught shirking his duties yet again.

Having had a phobia of hospitals since he was a child, Jake tried his hardest to free himself from the porter's persuasive grip. Even when the man tried to calm him down by saying that he'd probably be able to go home very soon, Jake still demanded that he have his shoes back so he could leave immediately. At that very moment, a handsome, dark-haired doctor appeared and came over to see what all the fuss was about. He had the bluest eyes Jake had ever seen and looked like he'd stepped out of a hospital soap opera on TV. His American accent added to this illusion as he demanded to know what was going on.

'It's very kind of this man to be looking after me but I'm quite well enough to go home now,' insisted Jake. 'If I could just have my shoes back then I won't take up any more of your precious time.'

The doctor had obviously experienced this kind of anxious behaviour before.

'Perhaps you'll let me be the judge of that, Sir. We just need to run a few more tests before we release you.' His use of the word 'release' made Jake panic even more, since he now felt as if he was under arrest. 'Just come this way,' continued the doctor and Jake found himself reluctantly following him as if the guy were the Pied Piper of Hamelin. Had he been hypnotised by the man's blue eyes or was it because he really was feeling quite unwell? There was a part of him that wondered if perhaps be should be checked out by this medical professional after all.

They entered a long ward with rows of empty beds on both sides, prompting Jake to wonder where all the patients had gone.

The doctor seemed to sense his concern. 'We use this room for day patients,' he explained. 'They've all gone now, so you've got the ward to yourself.'

He asked Jake to remove his jacket and sit on one of the beds and did some basic checks whilst asking exactly what had happened. There was no reaction from him whatsoever when Jake told him about walking in on Sue and Enrique. The guy seemed completely unfazed and Jake wondered if perhaps he was used to hearing all sorts of kitchen sink dramas.

The doctor asked Jake to strip to the waist and lie down on the bed. Jake wished he'd stuck with the healthy eating regime he had started recently, since he knew he didn't look particularly attractive with his top off. But he had no choice - this wasn't the right time to start acting coy. As he was undoing the buttons of his shirt, the porter reappeared with his shoes. Jake had the sudden urge to try to escape again, but since the doctor had blocked him in with a trolley full of machinery, and was setting everything up to run some checks, he thought this might not be a very good idea. With his heart beating - he wished he could calm it down in case it gave an untrue indication of his state of health - he settled onto the bed.

The clinician listened to Jake's heart, took his blood pressure and did a few other checks. He then started to stick pads to various points on Jake's torso. As he was leaning over him, Jake noticed the doctor's name badge and smiled to himself.

'Dr Carrington,' he read out loud. No wonder the man looked like he'd once been a member of the *Dynasty* cast. Jake watched as the doctor attached cables to each of the pads and explained how an electrocardiogram worked. He tried to pacify Jake by saying that it was a simple and useful test to record the rhythm, rate and electrical activity of his heart. He told Jake to try to relax as much as possible, which was no easy feat with such a good-looking doctor standing over him. He was pleasantly surprised that the test only lasted a matter of minutes and was relieved when the pads were all removed. He quite enjoyed the experience of the doctor's fingers occasionally making contact with his skin but flinched each time the sticky pads pulled at his chest hairs.

The medic explained that the tests he had done so far didn't reveal anything untoward, but to be absolutely certain, he wanted to do some further investigations. He told Jake that he'd be arranging some blood tests too and would like to keep him in overnight for observation. The doctor was hopeful that Jake would be able to go home the following morning and suggested that Jake's blood pressure may have dropped as a result of the shock he'd had, and that perhaps this is what had caused him to black out.

A nurse appeared on the other side of the bed with a further trolley and Dr Carrington explained that she would be taking the blood samples. Jake was petrified of needles so immediately looked the other way. He desperately tried to think of something to distract himself. It occurred to him that he didn't know where he would be going when he was finally allowed to leave. The harsh realisation that he wouldn't want to be sleeping under the same roof as his wife any more almost made him forget the fact that the nurse now had a needle in his arm. Perhaps he'd have to check into a hotel or maybe Sue would have arrived at the hospital by then, begging for his forgiveness, although he really couldn't see it. Even if she did, he realised that as far as he was concerned, their relationship was over. It had been dragging on for far too long anyway. It really was about time that he accepted his attraction to men and if this current episode should be teaching him anything at all, it was that life was too short to be living a lie. This last week had been a real whirlwind, what with getting the job at the cinema, finding his wife being unfaithful to him and then, as a result, ending up in hospital. He really

230

needed to see this as a fresh start. Perhaps everything had happened for a reason.

Snapping Jake back into the present, the nurse handed him a couple of pills and a glass of water. He swallowed them down without even thinking to ask what they were. She smiled at him, prompting Jake to realise that he couldn't remember the last time that someone had taken care of him. Tears began to well in his eyes. He bit his lip, telling himself that he was probably feeling this way because of the shock he'd had. The nurse settled him down and even pulled a sheet and blanket over him. She then left, explaining that the doctor would be back to see him again shortly.

Jake decided to try to relax. There was no way that he would agree to spend the night here, but he may as well make the most of the surprisingly comfortable bed and pillow whilst waiting for the doctor to return.

When Jake opened his eyes again, the ward was crowded with other patients. Confused, he looked at his watch and discovered that it was almost 9am. How had he managed to sleep through the noise of all these people arriving? He was generally a very light sleeper and to have slept so deeply was very unlike him. He felt embarrassed and hoped he hadn't been snoring.

He was busting for the loo, so threw the bedding aside and sat on the side of the bed. His head was spinning and he cautiously looked around. He really hoped the staff wouldn't stop him walking to the toilet and insist on him using a bottle instead. Trying to give the impression that he was totally fine, he got up and discreetly headed towards the end of the ward. As he got there, he glanced out of the window and blinked several times in disbelief when he caught sight of Jason in the car park. Jake decided that it must be some kind of hallucination, caused by his current state of health. What would Jason be doing here, after all?

When he came back out of the toilet, he considered making a run for it, but since he hadn't thought to put his shoes back on or to retrieve his jacket, he changed his mind. He decided instead to go back to his bed, and nodded sheepishly at some of the other patients on his way. They all seemed to be in hospital gowns and Jake felt like a dirty stop out, in his crumpled suit trousers and shirt. He wondered what time they'd had to arrive for their procedures. They all looked quite settled, as if they had been there for some time.

Jake's bed was at the far end of the ward and when he got there, he glanced up and spotted Jason again, this time chatting with one of the nurses. She pointed in Jake's direction and Jason started to head towards him. He was glad the guy hadn't arrived whilst the doctor had been doing his tests the previous evening, since Jason looked a lot fitter than him and he'd have been ashamed to be seen topless, looking so out of condition. He was really pleased to see a familiar face, even though in reality he hardly knew this guy.

'What are you doing here?' Jake asked, probably smiling a bit too widely and sounding much more excited than you'd expect someone to be when they're on a hospital bed and greeting a new work colleague.

'I saw you through the window and wondered what was going on,' explained Jason. 'I thought I'd come and find you. What on earth has happened?'

Jake decided to be completely honest with Jason and told him how he'd walked in on Sue and Enrique and how his marriage had been a sham for a very long time. He asked Jason if he remembered when they'd been working in the cinema and he had assumed that Jake was gay.

Jason nodded. 'It just seemed pretty obvious to me from everything you said, but I hope I didn't speak out of turn.'

'Well you were actually quite right,' Jake confessed. 'I am gay and I'm not keeping quiet about it any longer. I'm officially appointing you the first person I'm coming out to, so consider yourself honoured.'

His friend smiled but didn't say any more. Jake had been hoping that perhaps there would be a similar revelation from Jason at that point, but it wasn't forthcoming. After a very long silence, Jake asked what Jason was doing at the hospital anyway.

'Pierre had a procedure yesterday and I've come to pick him up, although I'm very early,' explained Jason. 'I expected the traffic to be a lot worse.' Jake chose not to ask what Pierre had had done, just in case it was something embarrassing. He couldn't help but wonder what Jason's relationship was with the French guy for him to go out of his way to come to the hospital to collect him so early in the morning.

'I really didn't intend to stay here overnight,' explained Jake. 'Hospitals make me feel quite ill.' They both giggled at the irony of what he had just said. Jake found it such a relief to be able to laugh.

'They probably gave you something to make you sleep,' suggested Jason. Jake suddenly remembered the pills he'd been given by the nurse after she'd taken his bloods. He now wished he'd asked her what they were.

There was a very loud commotion and Jake noticed two nurses trying to stop Sue from marching onto the ward, with Enrique in hot pursuit. She shook the medical staff off and headed towards Jake. She didn't look like she'd come to see how he was.

In a matter of seconds, she was stood over his bed, glaring at him.

'Still pretending to be ill, are we?' she barked. 'Nobody's going to fall for that one.' Enrique was standing a couple of metres back, looking quite awkward.

'Thanks for coming in the ambulance with me last night,' spat Jake. 'Not!'

'Anyone in their right mind could tell that you faked that faint,' Sue chuckled. 'Why the hospital is wasting their time with you is a mystery to me. I could have told them you were just being a drama queen, as per usual!'

'You know that isn't true.' Jake wasn't sure why he was trying to reason with her but this had been his stance for so long now that it was just second nature. Suddenly he saw red though. 'That must have been a shock, when I walked in on you.' He couldn't help it. She couldn't just get away with this; he had to confront her, even though he knew it wouldn't get him anywhere. How stupid had she and Enrique been to not make sure that the house was secure before having some afternoon delight?

Sue roared with laughter. 'Don't you realise we did that deliberately, you idiotic little man?' she spat. 'We've never been very discreet, but you've always been far too stupid to notice. I bet you loved seeing Enrique's naked bum!'

Jake felt himself blush and looked timidly at Jason. He now couldn't decide whether she had really wanted him to find her and Enrique in bed together or whether she was just trying to make it look that way to save face.

'Anyway, as you know, I've found a real man now and won't be needing you anymore,' she taunted. 'I'll arrange for your things to be delivered to you if you give me your forwarding address.'

Jake was shocked at how venomous Sue was being and found himself stammering. 'That house is half mine you know. You can't just throw me out!'

'Well, I'll let you into a little secret, my darling.' Jake noted the sarcasm in his wife's voice. 'The house is and always has been in my dad's name, so don't go thinking you're going to get half of it. My family has got a great legal team too, and they'll make sure you don't get anything else out of me either.'

Sue suddenly turned her attention to Jason. 'Who's this loser then - your boyfriend?' she asked. 'Does he know yet just how useless you are in bed?' Jake glanced around the room and noticed that all the other patients were enjoying the impromptu performance. There wasn't a single one of them who wasn't gawping at the events unfolding around his bed. It appeared that even the nurses on the ward had been turned to stone, as they stood there with their mouths wide open, observing the proceedings.

Jason came to Jake's defence. 'I'm not, but if I were, I'd be very proud of it! Sounds to me like you're doing my friend here a big favour. I think he's better off without a bitch like you.'

He may as well have slapped Sue across the face, judging by the look his statement prompted. She turned on her heels and, without another word, flounced back out of the ward with Enrique in tow, leaving Jake and Jason staring after them.

'Oh and by the way,' Sue shouted over her shoulder. 'Enrique spotted you ogling him from your car the other day when he was on his way to meet me at the Grand Hotel. You pervert!' She did a sinister laugh, which was cut short as she tripped herself up on a loose shoelace. Jake was disappointed that she somehow managed to save herself from falling flat on her face.

'Nice lady,' chuckled Jason sarcastically. 'Why on earth did you marry that?'

'Good question,' replied Jake. He looked at the nurses and the other patients in the room, who were still staring. 'That's it guys, the show is over now!' he declared, doing a mock bow from his bed before promptly bursting into tears.

'Hey come on - look on the bright side. You're a free man now!' consoled his new friend, sitting on the bed and putting his arm around him. 'You're young - you're good looking - the world is your oyster! 'So Many Men, So Little Time', as the title of the song goes.'

It didn't quite feel like that right now but Jake appreciated the support and knew that Jason did have a point. He couldn't help but wonder how Jason knew the song he'd mentioned though, since it hadn't been a mainstream hit in the UK and he was only aware of it because it appeared on a compilation CD of gay club hits that he had stashed away in his car. Perhaps it had been a major hit in Australia whilst Jason had been living out there.

'It doesn't solve the problem of where I'm going to live though, does it?' asked Jake, concerned that he was now technically homeless.

'Don't be daft! You can stay at mine!' Jason was smiling as if he always had the solution to everything. He was sitting so close that Jake was very tempted to kiss him. But this probably wasn't the right time or place for that and he really didn't want to freak Jason out.

Jake remembered that Jason had told him about the amazing house where he was currently living and part of him couldn't wait to see it, although it still felt beyond generous that such a new friend was inviting him to stay. Jake certainly didn't fancy staying on his own in a hotel right now, and it would be nice to have someone else around, especially if that someone were Jason.

'Are you sure?' he asked, giving the guy the opportunity to back out if he was now thinking that he'd been a bit hasty with his offer.

'Wouldn't have suggested it if I wasn't. When are you allowed to leave?' Jason asked.

'Well, I guess the doctor has to see me first but I'm hoping I'll be able to leave after that.' Jake really did want to get out of here as soon as possible.

'I'll go and find out what's going on then,' suggested Jason. 'If I can vouch for you, perhaps they'll let you go sooner. Have you had anything to eat?'

'I'm bloody starving!' confessed Jake. 'I didn't have any dinner last night and I don't think the breakfast trolley visits this ward, what with it being used just for day cases. Unless I slept through it, of course.' He tried to give Jason his best 'little boy lost' look.

'Well you can have something to eat at my place.' Before Jake could protest, Jason went over to speak with one of the nursing staff. The two of them left the ward and it wasn't long before Dr Carrington reappeared with Jason following close behind. The doctor looked very tired and Jake wondered if he was still on duty from the previous evening.

'You can't go home yet, I'm afraid,' he advised, looking very angry. 'We've admitted you for the time being. It's essential we keep an eye on you for at least twenty-four hours.'

'I'm not staying!' Jake protested. 'You've not found anything wrong with me, after all.' He was determined not to spend a moment longer under this roof. 'And I'm not impressed that you gave me sleeping pills! That was very underhand of you!'

'We didn't give you sleeping pills,' the doctor explained. 'You had a couple of Valium, which I think was quite appropriate considering how anxious you were.'

'That's just as bad! You can't go drugging your patients, willy-nilly!' He did wonder if perhaps he was putting on a bit of a show for Jason, who was quietly observing what was going on.

'As I already told you, it's quite possible that you blacked out because of your blood pressure dropping,' explained the doctor. 'But that doesn't mean we shouldn't proceed with caution.'

'Well, I don't want to stay here and I didn't agree to being admitted. Please do what you have to do and then I'm leaving.'

'If you go now, you'll need to sign a form, discharging yourself. That will mean that you're excusing us from our duty of care and if anything happens to you, then you'll be entirely responsible,' explained Dr Carrington, evidently not very impressed with Jake's behaviour.

'I don't care!' exclaimed Jake. 'Fetch the form!'

'If that's the decision you've made, then I'll get it.' The doctor shook his head and left.

When he was out of sight, Jason voiced his concern. 'Are you really sure about this, Mate?'

'You heard him! It was probably the shock that made me black out. I'll be fine. Are you sure I can stay at yours though?' Jake thought he'd better check again as he really didn't want to end up out on the street.

'Of course. Where are your things?' asked Jason, looking around.

'I don't have anything apart from the clothes I'm wearing. I'll have to deal with that later.' This prompted him to think about his secret video stash, hidden up the chimney at home. He hoped that at some point, Sue would let him into the house, preferably alone, so he could retrieve it. He smiled to himself that this seemed to be the only thing he was concerned about getting back. It wouldn't really matter now if Sue found his videos, although he didn't want to give her the satisfaction.

They sat in silence as they waited for the doctor to return. Jake was certain that the medic was taking his time on purpose. He eventually reappeared and checked Jake's temperature and blood pressure again whilst glaring at him.

'Your blood pressure is extremely high,' the medic announced.

'I'm not surprised. It's your fault for stressing me out by trying to keep me her,' Jake snapped. He tried to remove the inflatable cuff from around his arm but the doctor intervened, carefully unwrapping it himself. He left the room again and returned with a discharge form for Jake to sign.

'You do realise this is an important statement you're making?' he reiterated. 'We would still prefer to keep you in for a bit longer to make sure there's nothing seriously wrong with you.' He was obviously not taking Jake's decision lightly.

Jake had made his mind up though. 'I'm sorry but I really don't like hospitals and I think it would do me more harm than good to stay.'

'I still think you're being very foolish,' chided the doctor. 'I'll be sending a full report to your GP in due course, so please make sure you contact him.' He looked at Jason. 'Promise me you'll keep an eye on him.' Jason nodded, feeling like he was being judged too.

Jake hurriedly signed the form and the doctor took it away.

'Come on then - get me out of here!' he exclaimed, climbing off the bed and putting his shoes on. He grabbed his jacket and headed for the door. He was still feeling very light headed but he wasn't going to admit that to anyone, especially not the doctor.

When they reached the hospital foyer, Jason reminded Jake that he was actually here to collect Pierre, so left him sitting in the waiting area whilst he went off to find his other friend. He couldn't have been gone any longer than two minutes before he reappeared. Pierre was with him and held out his hand. Jake quite liked how these foreigners had a habit of shaking hands.

'How are you feeling, Pierre?' he asked. The guy didn't elaborate on what he'd had done but explained that he was on painkillers and was pleased that the procedure was over. There was an embarrassed silence and Jake wondered if he should perhaps be filling it. But he was feeling quite sorry for himself and really didn't have the strength or the inclination to do so. He realised that he had absolutely no empathy for anyone else right now.

'Let's get you two home!' declared Jason. The thought that he now lived at Jason's, albeit temporarily, gave Jake a warm glow.

They reached the car park with Jake keenly looking out for the flashy black Jaguar XJR that Jason had told him about. He was shocked when his friend walked over to a battered, old, lime green Ford Cortina and opened the passenger door for one of them to get in.

'Where's your Jag? asked Jake.

Jason looked a bit shame-faced. 'Oh, it's had to go in for a service. I'll have it back in a couple of days.' Jake noticed Jason glance at Pierre, who was looking a bit confused.

Jake watched Pierre throw his overnight bag into the boot before climbing into the back seat, and waited for Jason to take his place at the wheel. Only then did Jake climb into the front passenger seat and slam the door. After a few attempts, the car started and in a cloud of black smoke, they kangarooed out of the car park.

They made small talk in the car, mainly with Jake asking the other two questions. Although not feeling brilliant, he was elated to be out of the hospital. Pierre seemed an interesting chap and had a cute accent. Jake remembered that he hailed from Martinique in the French West Indies.

They very soon reached Pierre's place and once they'd said goodbye to him, they continued their journey to Jason's. Jake couldn't wait to see this flashy house that belonged to Jason's cousin. If he remembered correctly, it was a detached, thatched property on the banks of the River Ouse, that had once belonged to a local duke. *What a great start to this new chapter of my life*, he thought.

After another short drive, Jake was mystified when they pulled up outside a row of terraced houses. They were nowhere near the area Jason had originally mentioned but were instead in a road near Preston Park, Brighton's largest park.

Jake was totally confused. 'What are we doing here?' he asked.

Jason looked embarrassed again, but didn't say a word. Instead, he got out of the car and Jake followed him, slamming the car door behind him a bit more forcefully than he'd intended. They made their way towards one of the houses and Jason opened the front door, which led into a tiny lounge. He told his friend to take a seat and asked what he'd like to drink. Once again, Jake asked for a tea.

Curiosity got the better of him though, and so he followed Jason into the kitchen. As he watched his friend fill the kettle, he found he had no option but to ask what was going on. This was meant to be fresh start in his life after all and he was tired of secrets and lies.

'What's all this about, Jason?' he asked, trying not to sound too accusatory.

His friend avoided making eye contact with him at first, but eventually turned round and replied in a voice that was much quieter than usual. 'Well, I didn't expect you to ever come to my house, did I?' He sounded quite ashamed. 'I was just bigging things up a bit. Surely you do that kind of thing sometimes too?'

Looking around, Jake thought the house was perfectly fine and knew that he wouldn't have a problem living there. It was actually quite sweet that Jason had been trying to impress him though, even if it had been with lies.

'Honestly, this is fantastic. You really don't have to pretend to be something you're not because you're great as you are.' Jake wondered what else Jason might be concealing about himself. 'Promise me that you won't ever do that again,' he continued, realising that he was sounding a bit bossy. 'Sorry - I'm not telling you what to do, but this really is …,' he tried to think of the right word but all he could come up with was, '…lovely.'

Jason smiled at him. 'Thanks, Mate. I guess I was just trying to make you like me.'

'Of course I like you!' exclaimed Jake. He really wanted to give the guy a big hug but wasn't sure how it would go down now that they were alone. 'Actually, do you have some tissues and some paracetamol?' he asked.

'I know where some are!' said Jason. He remembered seeing a box of tissues that his cousin had left on the coffee table in the lounge and was glad to have an excuse to briefly leave the room. He was happy to be helping Jake but was feeling slightly out of his depth. He really wasn't used to dealing with men who were in touch with their feelings, unless they were drunk. He'd seen a box of painkillers in the kitchen cupboard, so went back to retrieve them. He put both boxes down in front of Jake, who was now sat at the kitchen table.

'Here. I'll get you some water,' he offered, relieved to have something else to do and standing at the sink for much longer than he needed to, trying to gather his thoughts as he slowly filled a glass.

Jake blew his nose and gave his friend a forced smile as he handed him the water.

'Would you like something to eat now?" asked Jason.

'Have you got any pizza?' asked Jake. 'I seem to be living on the stuff recently but it's what I really fancy.'

'Bit early for pizza but if that's what you want, then sure!' Jason got up and did a big stretch. Jake couldn't help but admire the exposed gap between his T-shirt and jeans.

'Actually, it's good you asked for pizza because I haven't got much else, apart from that and some salad,' laughed Jason as he reached over the kitchen worktop and flicked a switch to turn the radio on. Surprisingly, classical music came out of the speaker.

'Didn't think you'd listen to this kind of thing,' commented Jake.

Jason sighed. 'I find it very relaxing. I used to listen to it when I lived in Australia, so it reminds me of being back there.'

'How long were you living there?' asked Jake.

'I went out there when I left school, basically,' replied Jason. 'It's funny because I don't have any Australian blood in my veins at all, but it definitely feels like home.'

'It does make more sense now, how you managed to pick up the accent, if you were out there for so long,' said Jake. He watched his friend take a pizza out of the

243

freezer, unwrap it and place it onto a baking tray before putting it in the oven. He then got a bag of prepared leaves out of the fridge and put them into a bowl. He cut up some tomatoes, a cucumber and some peppers too. It was quite therapeutic watching him at work.

'Can I do anything?' asked Jake.

'Nope! You can just make sure you eat a lot of it. You need building up, my friend.' Jason really was being so sweet.

Conversation flowed effortlessly. Jason commented on how convenient it was that neither of them had been scheduled to work at the cinema that morning.

Jake asked what it was like living in Australia. He had never heard Jason sound so animated as when he spoke about Sydney and was tempted to ask why he had decided to come back to Britain if he loved Australia so much. Although Madeleine had already mentioned to Jake that Jason had been struggling to find work out there, so he thought it best not to question him any further. Jason got out some plates, knives and forks and set the table.

'Food must be ready!' he said, after a short while. The oven door was opened and the pizza was slid onto a wooden chopping board and cut into six with a pizza wheel. He smiled at Jake as he put the pizza in the middle of the table. 'You look quite pale, so eat up!' He went back over to the worktop to fetch the bowl of salad. 'What are you drinking? I've got some Coke or do you want a tinnie?'

'Can I just have some more water, if that's OK?' asked Jake. 'You don't have to wait on me, by the way, I can get that.' He was suddenly feeling quite dizzy, but didn't want Jason to know that.

'Don't fancy a can of the hard stuff then?' joked Jason. Jake wondered if perhaps he was trying to relax him with the offer of a beer. He didn't tend to drink alcohol and wanted to keep his wits about him anyway, just in case he took a turn for the worse. He was also a bit concerned that drinking one of Jason's 'tinnies' might make him feel even more tearful than he already was.

Jake got up and refilled his glass from the tap. Whilst doing so, he heard Jason get up and go to the fridge to fetch himself a can of lager. Samuel Barber's 'Adagio for Strings' started playing on the radio, and the sadness of the piece instantly pulled at Jake's heartstrings. He sat down again, and everything seemed to suddenly catch up with him. Tears started to stream down his face.

'What up, Mate? It's all going to be alright, I promise!' Jason crouched down in front of his friend, taking his hands in his own. 'I bet the results will be back from the hospital before you know it and they'll find nothing wrong. That was a terrible shock, what you experienced yesterday with that awful wife of yours, but believe me, you're better off without her.' Jason was trying his hardest to put a positive spin on things.

'I know and I'm really sorry,' responded Jake. 'It's not fair that you've ended up stuck with me though. You've only known me five minutes. To be honest, I think it's not just what happened with Sue and Enrique. I think this has all been building up for a long time now.'

'Firstly, I'm not stuck with you,' Jason chided. 'Life gets like that sometimes so don't beat yourself up for feeling the way you do.' He paused briefly and looked very seriously at Jake. 'I had quite a tough time in Australia when I first went down there,' he continued. 'Don't tell Madeleine any of this. I pretended to her that everything was fine and dandy, so she wouldn't worry. In the end I paid to see a counsellor and he really sorted me out. I wish I'd done it years before. Everyone should try it!'

'Funnily enough, I've been thinking about doing that,' confessed Jake. Jason was still holding his hands and it felt good.

'Then why don't you just do it? I'll help you find someone. It can be our little secret, if you like.' Jason wasn't doing anything to dispel the huge crush that Jake was developing on him. 'What do you say?' he asked.

Jake smiled and nodded. 'I'd like that,' he said. 'I really would.'

Chapter 16
Ceefax

Michael felt bad for not lingering any longer with his two cats, Tobias and Othello, on the terrace, but he really needed to get indoors to check Ceefax. He truly didn't know what he would do without the BBC's teletext information service. It was his one-stop shop for everything, including his latest chart positions and news coverage of his media campaigns.

The journalist outside had asked him for a comment about his sister and he couldn't even let himself imagine the latest story she had fabricated. She must have already amassed a small fortune, with all the lies she'd sold to the newspapers about him. Some of them had been quite funny actually, and he did sometimes think that at least she kept his name in people's minds. If he'd had to pay for the media-spin she'd created around him in recent years, it would have easily gone into six figures. He had often wondered what her true motives were. Was it purely financial or was there perhaps something else driving her to drag his name through the mud? It was quite ironic, since they shared the same surname, so ultimately she was slandering her own name too.

It was tragic to think that his relationship with his sister had come to this though; they'd been really close as children but with each new story that Alice concocted, she pushed the chances of a reconciliation even further away. He hadn't consciously done anything to upset her, apart from become famous and wealthy.

As he walked into the house, he spotted Krystal, as she appeared through the door at the far end of the room, having seen the car pulling up outside. She'd spent the last couple of hours preparing a welcome home brunch for him and the smells coming from the Aga instantly made Michael's mouth water. Krystal gave him the biggest hug.

He suddenly remembered that he'd brought something back from Paris to share with her. He put his rucksack on the floor, opened it and took out the package from the Parisian cheese shop, handing it to her and explaining how he'd managed to get hold of the goods inside. As he'd expected, she was over the moon with the purchase and suggested they try some of it later. Ted didn't share their passion for cheese and just observed them both, bemused.

'I need to check Ceefax,' Michael said. 'Looks like Alice may have been up to her old tricks again.' He hurried towards the lounge.

Ted noticed the confused look on his wife's face. 'As we drove in, a reporter asked Michael if he had any comment to make about his sister,' he explained. She shook her head as she knew just how hurtful Alice's lies could be.

'She must have sold another one of her stories,' she said, sadly. 'Poor chap! I wonder if she'll ever stop? She must have a very vivid imagination to come up with all these untruths.'

'From what Michael has said in the past, she wasn't very imaginative as a child. I do wonder if someone else is putting her up to all of this,' suggested Ted.

'I feel so sorry for Michael though,' sighed Krystal. 'Alice is a crazy woman and it's a terrible way to treat a family member, isn't it? It's unacceptable, even if they are estranged.' As she said this, she thought that it may have come across as a bit accusatory towards her husband, who had lost contact with both his brother and sister years ago and hadn't made any effort since then to salvage either of those relationships. It also pained her that they had lost touch with their only son too, after Ted had ousted him a few years earlier. Whether or not her husband had noticed the parallel in what she had just said, he remained silent, although he did look slightly uncomfortable.

'I'm just going over to our house to change out of this uniform,' said Ted. Michael was a stickler for making sure that his driver always looked the part whenever he was being chauffeured around.

Once her husband had gone, Krystal went to check on Michael. She was as intrigued as he was about this new story that Alice had made up. She walked into the lounge and noticed that Ceefax was showing on the TV screen and that the radio was on. At first, she thought that Michael had already left the room, but then she suddenly spotted him on the floor in the corner. He was kneeling down and was rocking backwards and forwards. Initially, she wondered if he'd had a fall as he seemed to be in a very odd position. She hurried over to him and was dismayed to discover that he was quietly sobbing. She crouched down on the floor in front of him, genuinely concerned.

'Michael, what's wrong?' she asked as she put her arms around him. He desperately clung on to her and she gently patted his back but said nothing. She knew him well enough to realise that he would start talking in his own time.

The only sound in the room was coming from Radio 5 Live, playing in the corner. Krystal's hearing suddenly tuned into the broadcast:

'The accident happened in the early hours of this morning on the M25, near the junction with the M23, and it's believed that Alice Hambelton's car went out of control and crashed through the motorway barrier, somersaulting into a nearby field, killing the driver instantly. Miss Hambelton, who was the estranged sister of pop singer Michael Hambelton, lived in the Brighton area. There have been reports that there were passengers in the car, but this hasn't yet been confirmed. If there were, they're not expected to have survived. Fortunately, no other vehicles were involved in the accident and a post mortem will confirm whether or not the driver had been drinking. A lorry driver, who observed Ms Hambelton's car careering off the motorway in his mirror, spoke to us about the incident...'

Krystal listened as the juggernaut driver talked about what he'd witnessed the previous night. Apparently, nobody else had seen what had happened, which was surprising since it was Krystal's belief that the M25 was busy every moment of the day and night. Michael had often referred to it as London's biggest car park, because of the amount of time he'd spent stuck in traffic jams on it. Krystal froze as she tried to imagine how Michael must be feeling. They'd had many conversations in the past about his sister and although Alice had caused her brother so much distress, Krystal knew that he would still be devastated by the news.

'You poor boy,' she heard herself say. 'It's OK, it's OK.' As the words left her mouth, she realised this was a really stupid thing to say, since it was far from OK. She found herself rocking in synch with Michael as she continued to pat his back, not knowing what else to do. Michael slowly raised his head and looked straight at her. His eyes were red and tears were streaming down his face. She offered him a half smile to try to raise his

250

spirits.

'I'm so sorry,' she said gently. Michael struggled to get up, awkwardly pulling Krystal up with him.

'I know she wasn't very nice to me in recent years, but she was still my sister,' he sobbed. 'I'll never ever see her again now.' The tears came even stronger and Krystal tightened her grip on him, stroking his back with her right hand. 'Why did she have to be so horrible?' he continued. 'We could have still been friends. I didn't ever stop loving her, you know.'

'Of course, you didn't,' consoled Krystal. 'I'm sure she knows that now.'

Michael suddenly stopped crying as if he'd had an idea. 'Do you think my brother knows what's happened? I don't even know how to contact him.' With that, he started sobbing again.

Ted appeared in the doorway and stopped in his tracks when he saw what was going on in the room. He gave Krystal a confused look and she tried to discreetly nod towards the radio, where the news story was still playing out. Ted stared into mid-air as he listened to the events being reported. Krystal mouthed that he should turn the volume down, and then nodded back towards the door. Fortunately, Ted understood her sign language and did as he was told. He knew he was useless in these situations so he adjusted the radio volume and left the room. He went into the kitchen, deciding to pour strong drinks for the three of them. It was a bit early for alcohol but today was an exception. Michael had had a massive shock, Krystal was struggling to calm the situation down and he himself had had to drive through a wild mob. He made three Whisky Macs and drank his own straight down, taking the other two into the lounge.

He found his wife and Michael still locked in a tight embrace. Michael noticed Ted coming in and glared at him as he approached, taking the drink that was being offered. He took it to the sofa and sat with his eyes fixed on the Ceefax page on the TV screen. Krystal sat next to him, gently placing her hand on his arm. She knew there wasn't anything else she could do right now, apart from be there for him.

'Shouldn't I have been informed about this before it went public?' Michael asked. 'And won't I have to make a statement to the press?'

'I think it's up to you,' Krystal responded. 'Do whatever you think is best. But don't rush into anything.'

'But the news hounds will stay outside until they get what they want, won't they?' said Michael, concerned. 'They're like a pack of wolves.'

Krystal really did feel so sorry for him. She knew that he must be exhausted after the extensive tour he'd just completed and this news about his sister had obviously knocked him for six.

'That's up to them,' she consoled, trying to be helpful. 'We could always send Ted out to say you're not making a statement yet. That might get rid of a few of them, at least.' She looked over at her husband, who didn't look too impressed with the idea. Fortunately, Michael didn't notice.

'Would you mind, Ted?' asked Michael, whilst still staring at the television screen. Ted looked at his wife and raised his eyebrows. He hated it when she put him forward for difficult tasks.

Michael finally took a sip of the drink that Ted had given him and grimaced when he realised that it was alcoholic. Krystal smiled to herself. Would Ted ever remember that Michael was teetotal?

'If you want me to go out there to speak with them, then of course I will,' said Ted, slightly begrudgingly, his wife thought.

'Maybe think about it for a moment or two first, Michael' suggested Krystal, trying to save face with her husband. 'This is such a massive shock for you and you've got to make yourself the priority here.'

She was very mindful of the brunch that was probably spoiling in the kitchen but wasn't sure if it would be appropriate to mention it. She really didn't want the food to be wasted and was sure that a good meal might help Michael to regain his strength a little right now. She finally decided to be brave enough to address the issue.

'It's completely fine if you don't want to do this, but the meal I've made for you is going to burn if I don't dish it up soon. Why don't we have something to eat?' She was relieved when he nodded. He got up and followed her into the kitchen. Ted tagged along, feeling like a spare part.

'I think it would be good if Ted could go and speak with the journalists outside,' decided Michael.

Ted hesitatingly went out but was back within a minute or two.

'What did they say?' asked Michael.

'Not much,' replied Ted. He didn't think it a good idea to tell Michael that a couple of the journalists had actually been quite rude to him. He sat down, sliding over a magazine that was in the middle of the table. He pulled it onto his lap when he noticed that Michael was on the cover.

'It's OK, I know I'm in that magazine,' guffawed Michael, as he fetched a tissue from the worktop to dry his eyes and blow his nose. 'I'm sorry about making such a fuss. I didn't realise that Alice's death would have such an impact on me.'

He went to the fridge and poured himself an orange juice. He'd left the whisky that Ted had given him in the lounge. He looked at Krystal and guessed that she must have abandoned her drink too, so offered her some juice, which she declined. She was too busy dishing up their half burnt food.

'She's your sister, Michael, so I'm not surprised at all that this has affected you so badly,' Krystal consoled. 'Blood is thicker than water, as they say.' Again, she wondered if Ted might think she was indirectly having a go at him for his fractured family ties. She was relieved when he didn't respond. She noticed that he now had his head in the magazine, and as she went over to the table, she couldn't resist snatching it away from him.

Michael took the empty seat next to Ted as Krystal proceeded to bring several delicious looking dishes over to the table. She'd prepared home-made vegetarian sausages, her own version of Spanish baked eggs, hash browns, mushrooms and toast as well as her signature baked beans. She placed a warmed plate in front of each of them and sat down herself, waiting for Michael to serve himself first. She noticed that although he had stopped crying, he was still looking very distressed. His eyes were extremely red.

'I wonder if there's anything I need to do? We were a very small family after all, and there's only me and my brother now,' sighed Michael. 'It makes you realise that these family rifts are pathetic really. Although I don't think there's any way that Alice would have let me back into her life, no matter what I did.'

The buzzer sounded on the main gates, making them all jump. Ted went to investigate what was going on. He had considered disconnecting the device earlier, to stop any journalists annoyingly pushing it, but was relieved that he hadn't when he saw who it was.

'The police are here, Michael,' he called.

Half an hour or so later, Michael asked Ted if he could show the police off the property. Once he'd said goodbye to them at the door, Michael went back into the kitchen.

'Well that wasn't as bad as I expected,' he confessed to Krystal. His friend just smiled at him, not knowing quite what to say. 'They came to tell me the news about Alice,' he continued. 'They also apologised that they didn't get to me before all the news coverage kicked off. I guess they still had a duty to advise her next of kin.'

'That's the trouble nowadays, isn't it? News travels so fast.' Krystal got up and walked over to Michael and lovingly squeezed his shoulder.

'I'm OK!' he insisted. 'But thanks for being there. I'm sure you know how much I appreciate it. I'm now wondering how on earth I can trace my brother.'

His brain must be spinning like a whirling dervish, thought Krystal.

'Why don't you try to have a rest?' she suggested. 'You really don't have to make any decisions immediately.'

'But I don't want to shirk my responsibilities,' responded Michael.

'Nobody can accuse you of that, Michael,' consoled Ted, who had just come back in. 'I think Krystal is right. Don't rush into anything. There's nothing you can do to bring your sister back.'

Once again, Krystal realised how tactless her husband could be sometimes. She looked at Michael, who half smiled at her, as if to say that he was used to Ted and his blunt comments.

'I think I will go for that lie down,' sighed Michael.

'We can try that cheese you brought back from Paris later,' suggested Krystal, hoping this might interest

Michael and take his mind off things briefly. 'Oh, and I've put all your post in the office for when you feel up to it,' she added.

The noise of a phone ringing shattered the stillness of the room.

'Is that yours?' asked Krystal. 'It's like Piccadilly Circus in here today,' she added under her breath to Ted, as Michael rushed off to find his bag. He found it on the floor by the entrance and fumbled frantically inside for his mobile. He got to it just as it stopped ringing and was surprised to see that he'd had a missed call from Alexandra. He stood there for a few seconds, trying to gather his thoughts, before heading back into the kitchen.

'That was someone I met in Sweden,' he explained to Krystal. 'She's a make-up artist who's been working with me recently.' He knew that he was stretching the truth a bit but since he'd already had a conversation with Ted in the car about Alexandra, he didn't have the energy to go through it all again for Krystal's benefit. Hopefully her husband would bring her up to speed when Michael had left the room.

He was keen to call Alexandra back and wanted to do this without being overheard. 'Thanks for the lovely meal, Krystal. It's good to be back.' As he said this he wondered if it really was. He wished he could turn the clock back just twenty-four hours and still be in Paris, where he would at least be able to see Alexandra face-to-face, rather than having to speak with her over the phone. It would also mean that Alice would still be alive.

'You know where we are if you need us,' replied Krystal, as Michael headed back out of the room. She could tell he was in a hurry to phone this mystery woman back.

Michael had hit the 'call back' button even before he'd reached his bedroom and was relieved when

Alexandra answered after just one ring.

'I didn't think I'd ever hear from you again,' he found himself gushing.

'I'm so sorry, Michael. So absolutely sorry,' she replied, sounding like she had also been crying. 'I understand if you'd rather not hear from me again.'

'Don't be daft. Why wouldn't I want to hear from you? The after-show party wasn't the same without you.' Michael was trying to keep himself in check and didn't want to sound too desperate but that was exactly how he was feeling right now, especially after hearing the news about Alice.

There was a pause before Alexandra responded, 'I lied to you, Michael. I lied about so many things.' Her voice was breaking as she spoke.

Michael went cold. This really was the last thing he needed right now. 'What are you talking about?' he asked. 'It's OK if you told a little white lie to get out of the party. I would have probably done the same myself if I could have.' He had the nasty feeling that this was about much more than just ducking out of a party.

'If you hate me once I've told you everything, I'll understand,' continued Alexandra. 'But I've decided you have to know the truth. I shouldn't have even started this stupid mission.'

'What mission? You're worrying me now.' His heart sank.

'I don't even know where to start.' Michael could hear that Alexandra was struggling to speak through her tears.

'The beginning is always a good place,' he advised, stating the obvious as he plonked himself down on the bed.

'Well, I've not been earning much money lately and Ricky told me he had a plan for me to boost my income.' Michael's stomach went over at the mention of his manager's name. He should have guessed that Ricky would be involved in this somehow. Alexandra had been part of his manager's entourage when he'd first met her, after all.

'That's when he put me in touch with your sister,' she continued. Michael truly couldn't believe what he was hearing.

'Alice? Where does she come into this?' Michael was feeling quite defensive now. His sister had only just died and he didn't want to hear anything negative about her, despite the fact that he knew how problematic she had been.

'She was in touch with Ricky because of an in-depth book she was working on about your childhood.' Alexandra seemed to pause so that Michael could take in what she had just said. 'When I first spoke with her, she told me you were always cruel to her and your other siblings when you were kids,' she continued. 'She wanted me to find out what you had to say about that, amongst other things.' She waited for a response from Michael but when she didn't get one, she elaborated further. 'Do you remember that I was always asking questions about your family? I can't believe I even considered helping her now and I feel so bad. I really like you, in fact I more than like you, and I've come to the conclusion that I can't carry on lying to you and have to tell you the truth.' Michael was sitting there in silence, absolutely shocked at what he'd just been told. Had Alice really planned such a malicious book?

'Did you ever meet her?' he asked, not sure if he really wanted to know the answer.

'No, I never met her - we just spoke on the phone,' explained Alexandra. Michael was relieved to hear this and inwardly sighed. 'The last time was just after you went on stage in Paris,' Alexandra went on. 'Remember I was in your dressing room? I was meant to have phoned her before then, but I'd been avoiding it. I called her as soon as you left the room, and weirdly enough, she was in Paris too. I don't actually know why.'

The police had already informed Michael that Alice had been on her way back from Paris when the accident had happened. But he was puzzled as to why she had been there at the same time as him and had even considered that she may have been stalking him.

'She was pressurising me to get information out of you,' Alexandra continued. 'I did try to get you to talk about your feelings for your brother and sisters, but you kept changing the subject. And I'm so pleased about that now because I wasn't able to tell her anything. I'm really sorry to hear what's happened to your sister, but she really wasn't a very nice person.'

Alice had been a real thorn in Michael's side in recent years, but there was obviously a lot more to her hatred of him than he could have ever imagined. He had such mixed-up feelings about his sister now and concluded that he probably did need to hear everything that Alexandra had to say.

'So, what's made you change your mind?' he asked. 'I'm not giving you any money, if that's what you think.' The idea came to him that perhaps, now that Alice was dead, Alexandra was expecting him to help her out financially instead.

'I don't want your money. Just your forgiveness,' Alexandra sobbed. 'But if that's not possible, I'll just say goodbye. I've got something else to tell you too. I was meant to be getting married at the weekend but I couldn't go through with it.'

'Married?' Michael was just as shocked by this as he had been about Alexandra working for Alice. The blows seemed to just keep on coming. 'So why were you flirting with me, giving me the impression that you were interested in me in Stockholm and Paris?'

'Believe me, most of that was genuine. The marriage wasn't. I was marrying a man who Ricky introduced me to, just for money. I was so desperate, Michael. I still am. Ricky isn't a very nice man. I know you already know that but he's a lot worse than you can even imagine. He was encouraging me to help a fugitive get a Swedish passport, in exchange for a large sum of money. At the time, I guess I was so needy that I didn't see any other way forward. But I've realised now that there's more to life than money. And you're the first person I've had strong feelings for in a very long time.'

Michael considered confessing that he'd felt the same way about her. Although he wasn't actually sure how he truly feeling about Alexandra now.

'I think I'd best go,' she concluded, after a long silence. 'But I'm glad you know the truth now.'

'No! Don't go!' he heard himself say. 'Does Ricky know that you're confessing to all of this?' he asked.

'I tried to phone him earlier to tell him what I was planning to do but he's not answering. I've been sitting here for the last hour or so, wondering whether or not to phone you. But then I saw the news about your sister and decided to make the call.' Michael guessed that it must have taken a lot for Alexandra to contact him.

'I do appreciate you calling,' he said, rather half-heartedly.

He could hear that Alexandra was still crying at the other end of the phone. 'Oh Michael, thank you. I truly am so, so sorry about all of this.' There was part of Michael that wished he could just put his arms around her and tell her it was all going to be alright, but he wasn't actually sure that it was.

There was a brief pause before Alexandra snapped him out of his daydream. 'I really am going now. You must be shattered. If you do want to call me again sometime, it would be lovely to hear from you.'

There was so much more that he wanted to ask but she was right, he was absolutely exhausted and they could talk again later.

'I will definitely be in touch very, very soon,' he said. 'And I really do appreciate you calling, although I think we've still got a lot to discuss.'

'Agreed,' replied Alexandra. 'Thank you for taking this so well. It's far more than I expected, believe me.'

'Goodbye, Alexandra,' Michael said, before hanging up.

Michael was totally devastated and had absolutely no idea what to do next or who he could trust now. He'd known that Ricky was hard work and completely unreliable but what Alexandra had just told him was something else altogether. He even found himself questioning Krystal's seemingly loyal friendship. He couldn't wait to discuss all of this with his current therapist, although his next appointment wasn't for another ten days.

How he wished he could somehow speak with his brother Jake. He was the only family he had left now, after all.

He lay on the bed, replaying everything in his mind. It wasn't long before he was asleep.

Chapter 17
Bubble

The previous day had been incredibly traumatic for the three boys. Firstly, the healthcare assistant had brutally broken the news about Alice to Brian, who had subsequently found it almost impossible to share the revelation with his two friends. They were still trying to process the news when two police officers had entered the ward and asked if they could interview the three of them.

Prior to their arrival, Brian had been discussing with his two friends whether he should report the healthcare assistant for being so loose-tongued. They had talked him out of it, since it wouldn't change the situation and certainly wouldn't bring Alice back. This stance quickly changed when the police started their questioning, since the boys had no choice but to reveal that they already knew that their friend was dead. All three of them had decided that honesty was the best policy now and even though they knew that their revelation would get the nurse into trouble, they really had no choice. They hoped that he might still keep his job, although agreed that he should be reprimanded.

Brian was extremely nervous when the police had reappeared, since he knew that he had been very economical with the truth when he had been interviewed by them previously. Alice was now dead though, so there was no point in trying to protect her by pretending that she hadn't been driving recklessly. It had come as a huge relief when the officers had been very empathetic and had even apologised for disturbing the boys when they were still very much recovering from their ordeal. It was hoped that further questioning wouldn't be necessary.

James had brought them a copy of that day's newspaper and they had all gathered together to pore over it. Louis had broken down in tears when he'd read the headline about Alice, and this had set the others off too. Seeing it in print somehow brought it home to them just how lucky they were to have survived such a horrific crash. They were relieved that there was no mention of the three of them in the news report, although it did say that it was believed that Alice had been travelling with passengers. They were very aware that their anonymity might now be very short lived.

Tim had been pondering on his sister's suggestion to tell their parents about the accident. The last time he'd been in contact with them had been four years previously, when he'd come out to them as a gay man. He'd anticipated them being quite shocked, but hadn't expected his father's aggression, grabbing him by the scruff of the neck and throwing him out of the house, telling him to never darken their doorstep again.

Tim had very soon realised that he was surrounded by people who cared for him though, and subsequently sofa surfed for a week or so, before eventually moving in with Louis. Initially, they had been just friends but a romance had soon blossomed.

Despite the fact that he hadn't seen his mother or father since then, Tim had kept in regular contact with his sister. He'd specifically asked her not to share anything about his new life with their parents and had insisted that she shouldn't tell him anything about their lives either. She had faithfully kept her word to him and Tim hoped that she had been keeping the other side of the bargain too.

Although he had originally hoped that his dad would somehow see sense and suggest a reconciliation, this had never happened. He had actually expected better of his mother too and thought she could have at least stayed in contact with him discreetly, without his father knowing. This parental neglect had hit him hard. As time had gone on, the split had become even more entrenched. He couldn't imagine the situation ever changing now, although the accident had made him start to re-evaluate everything in his life. His initial shock at Pippa's suggestion, that she could try to build a bridge between him and his parents, wasn't now as outlandish as it would have been just a week ago. He was considering speaking with his sister later, and tentatively giving her permission to tell their mum and dad about his current situation.

Earlier on, whilst sitting in the day room watching TV, the boys had noticed a suspicious looking man making his way down the corridor outside. He looked as if he had stepped out of a 1930s movie, complete with a sharply cut grey suit and matching wide-brimmed Fedora hat. The three of them looked at each other and Brian pulled a puzzled face. Perhaps the guy was visiting one of the other patients, further down the ward, they concluded. As he went past, Louis commented to the others that he was probably only in his twenties, although he looked much older from a distance. A couple of minutes later, they saw him being frog-marched out of the ward by two of the medical staff, one of whom was James. He came into the lounge on his return, looking very pleased with himself.

'You boys had a very narrow escape there,' he declared. 'Did you see that odd looking man we just threw out?' The boys nodded. 'Well, he was a journalist and he was looking for the three of you. Word is out apparently, so I'm afraid to say that your bubble has now been burst.'

'We thought he looked a bit suspicious,' commented Tim.

'It's only big news because your friend Alice had a famous brother,' said James, stating the obvious.

Brian chuckled. 'Yes, we do realise that. Although she was already estranged from him when we came along. So we've never met him,' he clarified.

'I quite like his music, actually,' confessed James. 'I'll have to keep in touch with you when you leave here, in case you meet him at Alice's funeral. You could get me an autograph.'

The boys laughed nervously, sharing the same thought, that it probably wouldn't be a suitable place for autograph requests.

Once James was out of earshot, Brian addressed his two friends, sounding more than a little concerned. Fortunately, there was nobody else around.

'I wonder if they'll find out about Alice's fraudulent benefit claims?' he asked. 'We did talk about reporting her so many times, didn't we? It seems crazy now that we didn't actually do it.' He sounded like he really needed confirmation that none of the blame lay at his door.

'To be honest, I sometimes thought the whole benefit thing was a big joke to her,' shared Tim. 'Although she never actually confirmed to us that she was claiming anything, did she?'

'Well, she certainly gave us enough hints,' admitted Louis. 'Like you, I feel really bad now that we didn't do anything about it, especially since we definitely had our suspicions.'

'Yes, but we didn't know for sure,' snapped Brian. 'She was intolerable at times and all three of us certainly questioned our friendship with her.'

'I don't know what to think now though,' sighed Tim. 'She was always ripping us off, so maybe it was in her nature. It obviously wasn't just a case of defrauding the state.'

'Do you remember that we were talking about reporting her whilst we were in Paris?' asked Brian. 'I was going to discuss it with Nigel when we got back. I guess it's too late for that now.'

'On a positive note, we never benefitted from any of her ill-gotten gains, so I'm sure we're not in any trouble,' commented Tim. 'We always paid our way. Usually, we paid many times over for anything we did with her. She charged us all a small fortune for that trip to France.'

'We could actually fill many newspaper columns with our stories about her,' joked Louis. 'Although I for one wouldn't want to do that.'

'You're right, we'd probably make a fortune if we did though!' chuckled Brian.

'She was a terrible friend!' reflected Tim, looking up at the ceiling, 'Sorry, if you're up there listening, Alice, but you really were.'

'I think we only kept in touch with her because we found her amusing,' suggested Louis. 'That's how I felt, anyway. Although, it's actually not that funny now.'

'I wonder if the police will want to question us further though, if it comes out that she was a benefit cheat?' asked Brian, still sounding very concerned.

'Well, they're welcome to,' exclaimed Louis. 'We weren't involved in any of her shenanigans, so we're not guilty of anything. All we can say is that we had our suspicions.'

'Typical Alice, though,' added Tim. 'Even though she's dead, it still feels like she's causing us problems.'

They continued discussing their options for dealing with the press, concluding that they should try to find a legal representative and issue a joint statement. Tim mentioned that his sister was married to a solicitor who would hopefully know somebody suitable. They decided they would ask her later. Brian and Louis told Tim how much they liked Pippa.

They were quite enjoying being alone in their four-bed side room away from the rest of the patients on the ward, and hoped it would stay that way until they went home. They sometimes fantasized about who the ideal fourth occupant of their little ward would be, with Brian choosing Brad Pitt, Louis waxing lyrical about Tom Cruise and Tim hoping it would be Bruce Willis. It was funny how they each had a different type. Although, in the real world, they all agreed that personality was probably the most important thing in a relationship. It was one thing lusting after a good-looking movie star but once you'd grown tired of his good looks, you couldn't be certain of much else. Not that they could ever imagine Brad, Tom or Bruce not having sparkling personalities. They admitted that they were all very jealous types too and wouldn't take kindly to hundreds of adoring fans waiting outside for their beaux, either. This led them to wonder what it must be like to be Alice's brother, Michael, since he would have undoubtedly experienced the worst side of fandom. It was funny how Alice had been so against him and none of them could understand why, since the press generally portrayed him as quite a nice guy. The only negative things they had ever read about him were the revelations that Alice had confessed to them that she'd made up. They all agreed that if they had a celebrity brother, they'd go out of their way to be friends with him. Imagine the amazing parties you might get invited to and the famous people you'd be able to meet.

They sat on plastic chairs around the spare bed to play cards. It wasn't the best card table, but it sufficed. Brian seemed to be managing quite well with his arm in a sling, keeping his cards face down on the bed and lifting them one by one with his good hand. They were so engrossed in their game that they hardly noticed that the shady journalist from earlier was back again. He looked at the three of them and was about to walk in when James, together with one of his colleagues, came rushing down the corridor to expel the man again. The boys realised that they needed to act quickly and get their joint statement out there as soon as possible. Pippa appeared just as the guy was being dragged out and gave him a funny look as he was jostled past her. He was being quite vocal about being manhandled. She gave the boys a shrug as she walked in.

'Who's that weirdo?' she asked, which made them all laugh.

'He's a journalist,' Tim explained to his sister. 'He's trying to get to us for a statement. We need to ask if you know anyone in the legal profession who could help us draft a press release.' Brian smiled to himself at how direct Tim was with his sister. They were obviously very close and Tim knew that she wouldn't take offence that there had been no polite greeting before he'd rushed in to ask for help.

Pippa chuckled. 'Well, I probably do know someone but he's actually a good friend of our parents so I'm not sure how you'd feel about that. Ranj has known him for years. Ranj is my husband, by the way,' she clarified for the benefit of Brian and Louis. She kissed all three of them on the cheek. 'I was thinking of telling mum and dad about your accident later,' she continued, deciding to strike while the iron was hot.

There was no response from her brother, who just looked down. His two friends chose not to comment and there followed an awkward silence. Tim sat there silently contemplating what his sister had just said. He couldn't quite bring himself to admit that he had already started to come round to the idea of trying to re-establish contact with their parents.

Pippa sensed this and changed the subject. 'So how are you all feeling today?' She fetched a chair and joined them around the spare bed.

'We're all getting very tired of our Elizabethan collars,' commented Brian, referring to their neck braces. He gently wiggled his head from side to side. He was sure he had a bit more flexibility today. They'd spoken with the medical team and it looked like the whiplash wasn't something that was going to linger for too long. 'Hopefully they'll be off soon,' he said to Pippa, who looked a bit shocked. 'The collars I mean, not our heads,' he laughed. 'They're talking about us going home.'

Pippa looked at Tim. 'Would you like to stay with us for a while?'

'Aww that's so kind, Pippa, but we've been discussing the three of us moving in together for a bit. You wouldn't mind, would you? Brian says we could stay with him.'

'Of course not! I just wouldn't want you to be on your own.' Pippa loved how her brother had such close friends. 'In fact, the hospital might insist on you not being on your own for a while. But remember the offer of staying with us is always there. We've actually got room for all three of you, in fact.'

Tim smiled at his sister and touched her hand. 'Thanks, Sis!' The other two gave her big grins.

'What game are you playing?' she asked.

'It's a version of poker that Brian has taught us

since we've been in here. James, one of the nurses, lent us the cards. We tried to talk him into playing strip poker with us but he wasn't very keen.' Tim hoped this would make his sister laugh but she looked quite taken aback.

'Really?' she asked.

'He's joking!' laughed Brian. 'It's just Tim's vivid imagination running away with him.'

Out of nowhere and taking his sister by surprise with this new enthusiasm, Tim started asking questions about their parents. She found it very encouraging though and caught Brian's eye. He raised his eyebrows, to signify that he thought the same. Pippa decided to respond positively and only hoped that if Tim agreed to a reunion, that both he and their parents would act like grown-ups. She knew their mother would do anything to be back in touch with her long-lost son, but wasn't quite certain just yet how their father would react. He was the one who had caused the problem in the first place, after all.

'They live near Arundel now,' Pippa announced. 'I don't think you know that, Tim. They've got a house on someone else's grounds,' she continued. She wasn't sure whether this was the right moment to mention that they were working for Michael Hambelton.

'They used to have their own house in Goring-by-Sea,' queried Tim. 'You didn't tell me that they had moved.'

Pippa chose to ignore his remark. He'd made it very clear that he didn't want to know anything about their parents after their fall-out.

'They were given a house to live in by their current employer,' she explained. 'They rent out the house in Goring now.'

'That sounds intriguing,' exclaimed Louis, without thinking. He'd made a conscious decision to not get involved in Tim's family conflict, but hadn't been able to resist commenting.

Tim actually sounded very interested too. 'Who are they working for then?' he asked. 'Mum had a job at the local school when they threw me out and Dad was doing odd jobs for people in the neighbourhood.'

'So, here's the exciting part,' continued Pippa, crossing her fingers under the chair. She decided it was now or never. 'Mum and Dad are now working for … fanfare … Michael Hambelton!'

The three boys stared at her in total disbelief.

'Alice's brother?' clarified Tim, thinking he must have misheard.

'Yep! I've wanted to tell you ever since they started working for him. But you've always been so adamant about not wanting to know anything about them, so I was afraid to mention it,' confessed Pippa. 'Especially since you were friends with Michael's sister. I decided it was probably best for everyone involved if you didn't know, as it might have put you in a very awkward position.'

'I think I'd have done the same,' confessed Brian, reassuring her. 'It would have put you in a very difficult situation, Tim, if Alice had known that your parents worked for her brother. She'd have never stopped pestering you. But we don't have to worry about that now.' He was trying his very best to put a positive spin on things. 'So, Pippa, have you met him?' he asked.

'I've only actually met him once,' she admitted, sounding slightly disappointed that she couldn't claim that they were best buddies. 'He's away a lot, either touring or doing promotional work. I've been to their new house loads though, and Mum and Dad get lots of free time when he's out of town. The set-up seems to work very well for them all.'

'What's he like then?' asked Tim, deciding that there was no point in being angry with his sister for not telling him about this before. 'Is he as horrible as Alice used to say?' It felt so strange to be talking about her in the past tense.

'He was very down to earth when I met him. We all had dinner together - me, Ranj, Mum, Dad and Michael. He spent most of the time asking questions about us actually. I felt a bit sorry for him, to be honest. Mum says he gets very lonely. It must be hard for him to meet genuine people, being in the public eye.'

'Not sure I would have much pity for him with all that money,' commented Tim.

'But money isn't everything, is it?' noted Louis, now also feeling sorry for Michael after hearing what Pippa had just said. Tim shot his friend one of his disapproving looks.

'I can't believe that Mum and Dad work for someone famous!' Tim grinned, after a while. 'What exactly do they do for him then?'

'Mum is a kind of housekeeper and cook. Dad does odd jobs and doubles up as a chauffeur. I think he heads up a gardening team to look after the grounds too.'

'I bet they've met a lot of other celebrities whilst they've been working for him, haven't they?' asked Louis.

'Not that many, actually,' replied Pippa. 'I guess Michael must know a lot of other famous people but I don't think he's a big fan of hob-knobbing with the stars, judging by what Mum says.'

'He sounds a bit strange,' pondered Tim. 'If I were in his shoes, I'd be milking it for all it was worth.'

'But we're not all like that, Tim, and I admire him for not being so shallow,' commented Brian. He was still trying to fight Pippa's corner. 'So, if Tim were to get back in contact with his parents, do you think Louis and I would be able to wangle an invite to Michael's house too?' He was really trying his hardest to sell the idea to Tim.

'Who knows?' continued Pippa. 'But I think we need to take this a step at a time, don't you, Tim? Will you let me speak with Mum and Dad? I'm sure they'd love to see you.'

'Well, I know Mum would, but I'm not sure about Dad. But yes, you can try. I'm not holding my breath though.' Pippa could hear the trepidation in her brother's voice, but she took his agreement as a massive step in the right direction.

'Leave it with me,' she said. 'I'll see what I can do.'

'Don't force it. If they'd prefer to leave things the way they are, then that's fine with me. And I'm not meeting them unless they're prepared to accept me for who I am, especially Dad.'

Pippa knew that her brother was not planning on making this easy for either her or their parents.

'I don't think anyone would expect you to compromise who you are,' she said, really hoping that this would be the case, especially with their father. 'Time is a great healer though, so let's hope we've all moved on since that awful incident when Dad kicked you out.'

'Yes, let's hope so,' spat Tim.

Brian caught Pippa's eye and gave her a wink. How exciting that one of his best friends had parents who worked for a global superstar. And what a coincidence that it happened to be Alice's estranged brother. He could only imagine Alice's face if she were here with them right now. Fortunately for all of them, she wasn't.

Chapter 18
Chez Jason

Jake had at least had the chance to freshen up and put clean underwear on now. He'd borrowed some boxers, socks and a T-shirt from Jason, although it felt really odd to be wearing his friend's clothes.

'Are you working today, Jason?' he asked, as he walked into the lounge.

'Yes, but I've spoken with Maddy. I'd promised her I'd do an extra shift later to help sort some stock out, but she's said there's no rush. You really don't have to go in today, by the way. I've explained everything to her. I hope you don't mind.' Jason had obviously chatted with his sister whilst Jake had been in the bathroom. He certainly hadn't wasted any time. 'I thought it was the right thing to do,' Jason continued, now realising that perhaps he should have checked that it was OK with his friend first.

Jake was actually quite relieved that Jason had done this. He'd unloaded so much onto the poor guy earlier so it was nice that he'd had someone to talk to afterwards.

'I'd still like to come in today,' decided Jake. 'I don't think it'll do me much good sitting round here moping all day. And I don't have anywhere else to go.'

'Course! As long as you're sure. I need to take a quick shower first though. I left home so early this morning to pick Pierre up, and didn't have the chance to get ready properly,' said Jason. 'Make yourself a coffee and when I'm ready we'll go to the cinema then.'

Jake watched Jason leave the room and listened to the sound of him having a shower. He tried his hardest not to imagine the scene in the bathroom. Once he heard Jason coming back downstairs, he went into the kitchen and started to wash up the remnants of their pizza brunch.

'You don't have to do that,' said Jason.

'Well, you're not waiting on me whilst I'm staying here,' insisted Jake. He carried on washing up, wondering how long Jason's hospitality would last.

'Still sure you want to come into work today?' asked Jason. Jake was so deep in thought that he didn't immediately respond. 'Cat got your tongue?' joked Jason, which at least broke Jake's silence and made him laugh.

'Of course I am!' replied Jake.

Once they were in the car, Jake was pleased when Jason left the radio on, although he noticed him turn the volume down so they could still chat. Jake smiled when he heard that ABBA's 'Fernando' was playing. It brought back some happy childhood memories.

'This song reminds me of my time in Australia too,' commented Jason.

'How come?' asked Jake. 'You do realise that they're Swedish, not Australian?' he joked.

'Very funny,' laughed Jason. 'I had a friend in Sydney who was a very big ABBA fan. He sat on your side of the church, funnily enough.'

'You'll have to introduce me,' chuckled Jake. 'I quite like the idea of a hunky Aussie surfer.'

'He's one of the nicest people I've ever met, actually,' continued Jason, choosing to ignore Jake's comment. 'He once told me that this song was the longest running No. 1 single ever down there at the time. ABBA were massive in Australia in the 70s, apparently.'

'That's incredible,' said Jake.

'He also told me that more people tuned in to the TV coverage of them arriving in Australia than watched the moon landing,' continued Jason.

'Is that so?' commented Jake, sounding impressed at Jason's knowledge. He noticed again how easy the conversation was between the two of them. It certainly felt like they'd been friends for a lot longer than a couple of days. 'I really wouldn't have put you down as an ABBA fan.'

'There's a lot you don't know about me,' chuckled Jason. 'And you should never judge a book by its cover.'

'It's a very nice cover, I have to say,' teased Jake. 'If I saw it on a bookshelf, I'd certainly buy it.' He looked at Jason, expecting a reaction, and was disappointed when he didn't get one.

They pulled up in the cinema car park and got out. As they started to walk towards the building, Jason stopped Jake in his tracks.

'You're a great guy!' he announced. 'Make sure you always remember that.' He gave him a big hug. It meant the world to Jake to know that he had his friend's support. Yet again though, he found himself questioning Jason's true feelings for him.

When they walked into the cinema, the foyer was fairly quiet, so they headed straight for the office, finding Madeleine with her head in her hands, looking very stressed. She glanced up at them and tried to give them as genuine a smile as she could muster. She stood up and walked over, squeezing her brother's arm and then hugging Jake.

'I'm so sorry to hear about everything that's happened. How are you feeling?' she asked. 'Are you sure you're OK to come in today?'

'I think it will help me a lot, just being here,' confessed Jake. 'More than being on my own, anyway.'

'Do whatever is best for you,' replied Madeleine. 'If you feel like you need to leave at any point, just say.' She looked at her brother and frowned. 'Actually, could the two of you take a seat for a minute.' She went back to her side of the desk and simultaneously, all three of them sat down, which prompted a smile all round.

'What's going on, Sis?' asked Jason.

'I'm sorry to add to your woes,' she explained. 'I'm just a bit concerned. I can't get hold of my boss at head office. It's all a bit odd. I've left a message and she usually gets back to me straight away. In fact, I've tried several times now, but she's not returning my calls.'

Jake thought that he should have known that this job was too good to be true. 'Maybe she's just busy - in a meeting perhaps?' he offered.

'Considering we're her only cinema, it just seems a bit strange. Apart from this woman there's also a man I've spoken to called Ricky and I can't get hold of him either. I have to say, I've always found them both a bit odd. I'm not panicking yet, just a little concerned.'

'I bet she'll call any minute now,' said Jason, trying to make his sister feel better.

She wasn't convinced. 'I'm just not getting a good feeling about this. Please don't mention it to any of the other staff, but I wanted to share it with you. Jake - would you like to work with me in the office today?' She hoped it wasn't too obvious that she wanted to keep an eye on him. Selfishly, she also knew that it might distract her for a couple of hours too.

'I'd love to!' Jake felt like he'd suddenly got a promotion. 'Actually, I've got a favour to ask Jason,' he said sheepishly, looking at his friend. 'Would you be able to give me a lift to my house later, if it's OK with

277

Madeleine? I need to collect some things and I think my wi…,' he stopped himself mid-sentence, realising that he wasn't quite sure what Sue was to him anymore. 'My soon to be ex-wife,' he corrected, 'should be at work by then. I really don't want to bump into her.'

Jason smiled. 'Course, Mate! As long as that's OK with Maddy?' He looked at his sister who nodded. 'I met her at the hospital, actually,' he commented. 'She's a nutter! Oh, sorry Jake!'

Jake laughed. 'You're right - she is.' He glanced over at Madeleine. 'She thought Jason was my boyfriend.' He blushed as he wondered if his boss had also heard the news about him coming out.

Madeleine read his mind and nodded. 'It's OK, Jason told me all about that too. I'm really pleased for you. Well done!' He truly hoped that all future coming out conversations would go as well as this.

Jason stood up, saying that he needed to make sure that everything was organised behind the bar. Jake was now left alone with Madeleine. She seemed such a lovely lady and the thought of spending some time with her actually gave him a warm, fuzzy feeling. The next hour or so sped by with the two of them chatting away.

Jake found it quite therapeutic as he told Madeleine how he'd been struggling with his sexuality. At one point, he suddenly wondered if he was over sharing. His boss seemed very cool with it all though. She couldn't believe the stories he told her about Sue. He realised he should have done something about the situation a long time ago.

There had been no return call from the woman at head office still, and Jake could tell that Madeleine's concern was growing.

Jason eventually stuck his head round the door and asked Jake if he was ready. Pierre and some of the other staff had now arrived, so Madeleine told them not to rush back. She realised it might take some time to collect Jake's stuff.

'I know it's a bit late for lunch, but maybe you could get me something to eat whilst you're out, to save me buying food here?' she asked, putting on a forced smile as they left the office. Jason could tell that she was trying to hide just how worried she was.

Jake was keen to collect his things and, especially, to rescue his hidden stash of videos. The last thing he wanted was Sue to find them. He didn't mention it to Jason, but he was absolutely petrified that he might come face to face with his estranged wife during their mission. She rarely came home from work in the daytime so it was quite unlikely, but the chance was still there. He also wondered if perhaps she might have changed the locks, in which case he didn't know what he would do.

Fortunately for him, once they arrived at the house, there was no sign of Sue's car on the driveway. He truly hoped she had gone to work. His own vehicle was still parked outside, where he'd left it.

'Are you going to collect your car while we're here?' asked Jason.

'I don't think there's any point,' sighed Jake. 'It's registered in Sue's name anyway, so I'll just take my things out of it and then leave it here. It'll save me a lot of hassle in the long run.'

'But how will you get around?' asked Jason.

'Well, for now I've got a handsome chauffeur,' laughed Jake, trying his best not to ponder too much on Jason's question. 'Come on, let's get this mission over with!' He asked Jason to come into the house with him, thinking that the presence of his friend might give him some extra courage. He was relieved when his door key turned the lock without any issue.

Jake ran upstairs, instructing Jason to follow him. Looking around as he climbed the stairs, he realised that everything here just reminded him of Sue. He ran into one of the spare bedrooms and pulled down two suitcases from on top of the wardrobe, dragging them both behind him into the main bedroom. Jason just stood on the landing, looking around in awe.

'Nice house!' he commented.

'Can't wait to get out of it, to be honest!' said Jake, nervously. 'Come on - help me get all my clothes from the wardrobe. I'm not sure where I'm going to store them all yet, but I'm not intending to come back here again after today.'

He lifted down all the hangers on his side of the wardrobe and threw everything onto the bed. He asked Jason if he would mind taking the clothes off the hangers and packing everything into the cases, whilst he headed downstairs.

Determined to rescue his video collection, he almost fell as he ran down the stairs. Grabbing a large carrier bag from the kitchen cupboard, he made his way into the lounge. The house no longer felt like home. He was sure he could smell Sue's perfume in the air and wondered how recently she had gone out. He fell to his knees, carefully feeling inside the chimney breast and pulling out his secret stash. He chucked all the videos into the plastic bag and then headed out into the hallway, dropping his rescued treasure by the front door.

When he got back upstairs, Jason was just packing the last couple of items into the second case and Jake was relieved to see that there was still room left for his underwear. He opened the drawers of the bedside cabinet and scooped up handfuls of T-shirts, pants and socks and put them on top of the neatly packed clothes. He zipped up both cases and, leaving the wardrobe doors and bedside drawers wide open and the hangers all over the floor, asked Jason to carry one of the cases downstairs as he took the other.

Jake's coat was hanging on a hook at the bottom of the stairs and he decided to take it with him. As he put it on, he sensed the weight of his mobile phone in one of the pockets. He asked Jason whether he thought he should leave it behind, since it had always felt like a tracking device, with Sue being able to contact him on it at any moment.

'I'd take it!' Jason advised. 'At least for now. You could let me make a few calls to Australia on it, if your wife is still paying the bill!'

'Can you imagine?' chuckled Jake. He was grateful to his friend for lightning the tone.

Jake opened the front door and swung the first case outside, before picking up the bag of videos. He waited for Jason to walk out with the second case and slammed the door shut.

'Is all of this going to fit in your car?' asked Jake as they made their way down the path, realising that he probably should have thought about this before.

'Yeah, that car is like a TARDIS,' laughed Jason.

Fortunately, there was easily room for the cases and bag in the back of the vehicle and Jake quickly ran over to his own car and grabbed a few things out of the glove compartment, including a handful of CDs. He ejected Michael's album from the music system and put it into its case. He threw it all into an empty carrier bag he found behind the passenger seat and took it with him.

The two of them jumped into Jason's car, with Jake being super vigilant, afraid that Sue might appear at any moment. Jason put his foot down on the accelerator and the car screeched out of the road in a cloud of smoke, making them both roar with laughter.

'That's the way to make an exit,' giggled Jake. 'She'll be furious when she gets home and sees that I've been back to get my things.'

'Hope so,' nodded Jason. 'I still think you need to try to make a claim on that house, even though she says it belongs to her dad.'

'I'll need to find a solicitor at some point but that can wait,' said Jake.

He took the weighty mobile phone out of his jacket pocket and looked at the screen. 'I've had a few missed calls from Sue,' he told Jason. 'Well, she can take a running jump. She obviously didn't realise I didn't have my phone with me, stupid cow!'

'That's the spirit!' chuckled Jason, as Jake threw the mobile device into the footwell in front of him.

'Hey! Be careful you don't break it!' Jason chided, half joking. 'That was a fun outing, wasn't it? You OK if we take your stuff back to mine when we finish work later? I know Madeleine is my sister but I really don't want her to think we're taking liberties.'

'That's fine,' confirmed Jake. 'Let's just hope nobody breaks into the car because they'll be shocked to find my porn stash!'

'You're obsessed with that bloody porn of yours!' laughed Jason. 'Anyone would think you're frustrated!'

'What if I am?' chuckled Jake. 'What are you going to do about it?' He tried to tickle his friend in the ribs. He was feeling so liberated now that he had managed to rescue all his stuff from the house.

'Hey! I'm driving! And don't touch what you can't afford!' Jason was trying to act stern but had a big smile on his face. 'I'm going to stop off to get some fish and chips. I promised Madeleine I'd bring her back something to eat and that's what I really fancy. If you're good, I'll treat you to some too.'

'I'm still full from the pizza earlier,' replied Jake. 'Have you really got room for fish and chips already?'

'I'm a growing boy!' snapped Jason, trying his best to sound hurt. He pulled up outside a parade of shops and jumped out.

Jake stayed in the car and watched his friend go into the fish and chip shop. Jason had left the radio on and Jake sat there listening to 'If I Can't Have You,' by Yvonne Elliman. He made a mental note to ask Jason if he knew that the Bee Gees had written the song for ABBA to record, although they had declined the offer because they only ever recorded their own material.

As Jason was coming out of the shop and heading back towards the car, the radio station's hourly news bulletin began and Jake froze as he heard the main headline.

'Following the death of pop star Michael Hambelton's estranged sister, Alice Hambelton, there has still been no statement from her brother . . .'

Jake felt as if he'd been ricocheted backwards down a long tunnel, although he was conscious of Jason getting back into the car and then chatting away in the background. His ears were whistling as he struggled to listen to the rest of the news story. He hoped he wasn't going to black out again, as this was exactly how he had felt when he'd found Sue in bed with Enrique.

Jason noticed that his friend had gone very quiet and turned to look at him. 'Are you OK?' he asked.

Jake shook his head. He truly hoped it was just the shock that was making him feel this way. He did wonder if perhaps he should have followed the doctor's advice and stayed in hospital after all. Poor Jason was completely ignorant of what Jake had just heard and the fact that it had contained such devastating news.

283

Jake suddenly felt completely and utterly alone and the thought hit him that, in a way, he had lost both his wife and sister in a matter of hours. He was glad that Jason hadn't started the car up yet but was fiddling in the bag of food he'd just bought.

As Jason handed Jake the hot package to look after, he noticed Jake's face. 'What up, Mate?' he asked. 'It's all going to be alright, I promise!' Jake wondered if he should tell Jason about his sister. He was still struggling to process the news himself.

'You'll be right as rain in no time, I promise,' continued Jason. 'You're better off without that terrible woman you were married to.' He was trying his hardest to put a positive spin on things and obviously had no idea that his friend's current sorrow wasn't solely due to his health scare or his failed marriage.

'It's not that,' said Jake, beginning to cry. 'Did you just hear about the car crash on the news?' The hot food was beginning to burn his hands through the paper, so he put the bag down next to his feet.

Jason looked a bit non-plussed. 'Sorry, I wasn't really listening.'

'There was a car accident on the motorway and someone was killed,' Jake tried to explain.

'Things like that happen every day,' Jason consoled. 'You can't let it get to you. You're obviously feeling very low at the moment, after everything that's happened. Come on, cheer up.'

Jake gave an involuntary hoot. 'The person who died was my sister!'

'What are you talking about? How do you know that?' Jason was looking a bit awkward, and was beginning to wonder if he Jake was losing the plot.

'They mentioned her name - Alice Hambelton.' Saying her name out loud just seemed to make Jake feel even more emotional.

'Hambelton? Don't I know that name?' Jason was sounding more curious now.

'Yep! Michael Hambelton! He's my brother!' Jake spluttered.

There was a long silence, with Jason finding it almost impossible to comprehend what he had just been told. 'Why didn't you mention this before?' he eventually asked. 'Does Madeleine know? I'm surprised you have to work if your brother is such a famous pop star!'

'We're no longer in touch,' confessed Jake between sobs. 'There was a family fall-out. It's a very long story and it all seems so ridiculous now!' He took a deep gasp of air.

Jason really didn't know what to do. He was wondering if perhaps he should call in reinforcements to deal with the situation. But who could he call? Jake's wife obviously wasn't an option. He secretly wished that his friend had stayed in the hospital now, although he couldn't vocalise that, of course. He just carried on sitting there, hoping that Jake would calm down very soon. Jason chided himself for thinking that very soon his fish and chips would be cold. He was aware that it must be a massive shock to hear about your sister's death in a radio broadcast, even if you had lost touch with her. He couldn't begin to imagine how he would feel if it were Madeleine.

'Do you have any more paracetamol?' asked Jake, suddenly.

'I don't think you should take any more just yet,' replied Jason, realising that it hadn't been that long since Jake had taken the last lot.

'I've got such a headache,' said Jake. He truly wished he could speak with Michael. They were the only two left now that both their parents and their two sisters were gone. But how easy would it be to make contact with such a massive star? Would his brother want to hear from him, anyway? He liked to think that he would since Michael had always been a kind person. Celebrity couldn't have changed him that much, surely.

Jake sat there, staring into space. He wanted to be able to close his eyes and then wake up in a world where recent events hadn't happened. It felt like his whole life had fallen apart in just a matter of hours.

He cautiously looked at his friend, sitting next to him. Where would he be if it wasn't for Jason? The poor man was probably thinking that he really had bitten off far more than he could chew.

'Do you want me to take you back to mine instead of going to the cinema?' asked Jason. 'I'm sure Madeleine will understand if I explain. I'll still go in though, if it's alright with you?'

'I'd really appreciate that,' Jake replied. He tried to give Jason a hug, which wasn't easy when they were sat in a car with seat belts on. 'I don't know what I'd do without you.'

'Well, you don't have to wonder because I'm here.' Jason started up the car.

On the way back to Jason's, Jake found himself recounting everything about the family feud and how hurt he'd been when his sister had managed to turn their parents against him. He hadn't had any contact with her since their mum and dad had died. Jake was really surprised at how quickly he was calming down and that he could now talk about it all without getting too upset. He told Jason how he'd ended up being estranged from his brother too and that, looking back, it was probably all just a big misunderstanding. Jason continued to drive in silence, listening as the story unfolded. He guessed that

Jake's brain must be completely frazzled.

'I'm sure Alice used to steal from us when we were kids too,' Jake disclosed, shaking his head. 'Michael and I always had money going missing from our room, although she always denied that it had anything to do with her of course, and we never told Mum and Dad.'

'That's terrible!' exclaimed Jason, quite shocked. 'You've had some unbelievable people in your life, what with that awful wife and your crazy sister.'

'I'm sure they'll drag my brother through the mud too, even though he wasn't in touch with Alice anymore either, as far as I know,' Jake sighed. 'I guess it'll sell more papers by mentioning his name.'

'It certainly wouldn't be such big news without him,' agreed Jason. 'But how come you've got a different surname to Michael?'

'I'm sure you can guess whose doing that was!' said Jake. 'Sue insisted I take on her name when we got married. I can't believe I agreed to it now. If she hears the news about my sister, it'll probably set her off again,' he laughed. 'I really hope she won't contact the press - it's the sort of thing she would do. She'd love to have her photo on the front pages.'

'Well, let's hope that doesn't happen then,' agreed Jason.

Jake's mobile phone suddenly started ringing. The two of them glanced at each other and both had the same thought: that it could be Sue.

'I'm not going to answer it,' announced Jake.

'You don't know for sure that it's her,' said Jason. 'Maybe you'd best check.'

Jake picked his phone up and looked at the screen.

'It's an unrecognised number,' he announced,

looking quite concerned.

'Answer it!' advised Jason, not sure whether this was good advice or not.

With that, Jake hit the 'accept' button and put the device to his ear. 'Hello!' he declared.

Jake looked at Jason. 'It's the police!' he mouthed.

Out of curtesy, Jason had pulled up along the side of the road when Jake had taken the call. He'd felt it only right to turn off the engine, to give his friend some peace and quiet so that he could concentrate.

'Phew! I'm glad they didn't ask me to go into the station or anything,' said Jake, as he hung up. 'Apparently they've been trying to contact me at home.'

'Are you alright?' asked Jason.

'I think so,' replied Jake. 'I feel like I'm in some crazy movie at the moment with all these recent events. You heard my side of the call, anyway. They just wanted to tell me about Alice. They were being quite insistent about seeing me face to face at first, until they realised that I already knew.'

'I suppose it's their usual procedure,' said Jason. 'I wouldn't fancy their job, having to break bad news to people. And that's not even the worst part of their job, is it?'

'I'm definitely going to try to contact my brother,' Jake suddenly declared. 'There's no point waiting. I know which record company he's with. If I phone their offices and explain the situation, surely they'll be able to help me?'

'As long as you can get through. I bet they've got the world and his wife trying to get a quote from Michael Hambelton at the moment.' Having said this, Jason instantly regretted it, since he thought it sounded a bit negative. He wished his friend all the luck in the world with getting back in touch with his brother.

'Well, I've got to try,' Jake resolved. 'Even if I have to sit there for the rest of my life trying to get through, I'm not giving up!'

Jason selfishly hoped that his fish and chips weren't going to end up in the bin.

Chapter 19
Press Release

Michael had had a restless night and had tossed and turned for what felt like an eternity. Eventually, he decided to get up. It was still dark outside but he really needed to draft a press release about Alice. This had been playing on his mind for hours, and at least by doing so, he would be able to tick it off his to do list, even though he had absolutely no idea what he should say.

He put on his dressing gown and made his way across the landing, looking at the clock on the office wall as he flicked the light on. It was 5am, far too early to be up and about. His body and mind were shattered, but he couldn't rest any longer. Gathering the latest sheets of paper that had been spat out of the fax machine, he shuffled through them, nonchalantly glancing at the latest sales figures that had been sent in from around the world. He yawned loudly and sat down, taking a pen and some paper out of the drawer. He sat there pondering on exactly what to say, with all the words that had been whirling around his head all night deserting him completely.

His thirst soon got the better of him, and so he headed down to the kitchen to make a cup of tea. It felt strange to be in the house on his own, even though his cats were with him. The first couple of days at home after returning from a tour were always a bit surreal. He knew that Ted and Krystal were next door, so it wasn't as if he was the only human in his little corner of the world. At least he didn't have to worry about making a noise and waking anyone up.

Whilst waiting for the kettle to boil, he went to check the security camera to see if there were still people at the end of the drive. Even though it was dark, he could still make out several cars parked on the verges on either side of the country lane. His stomach went over. *Another good reason to get that press release out there*, he thought.

He made his tea and went back upstairs. He struggled to find the right words but eventually managed to pull something together. He planned on calling his record company as soon as their offices opened, to dictate what he'd written. It was at times like these that his frustration with his manager really got to him, but he knew better than to try to get Ricky involved. He felt quite exposed, having to speak with the press department directly, but there was no point stressing about that right now. There were far more important things to deal with.

He heard footsteps coming up the stairs and turned to find Krystal standing in the doorway, cradling a mug of coffee. He told her about the press release and how he'd been agonising over it all night. She understood totally and patted him on the shoulder, to show her support. She went back downstairs to start preparing some breakfast, prompting Michael to realise just how hungry he was.

At 9 o'clock, after two more cups of tea, Michael finally made the call. He initially got put through to the wrong department, but eventually reached the right person and carefully dictated his initial draft. The PR officer suggested making a couple of tweaks, which Michael was more than happy to do, but there was nothing major that needed changing. The essence of the statement wasn't altered and overall, Michael was pleased with what he'd written. He now couldn't wait for it to be released. Hopefully, he would then be left alone. In a way, this felt like the first step in moving forward after the loss of his sister. As Michael put the phone down, he felt an instant sense of relief.

He went to check the security camera once again and noted just how obsessed he was getting with it. There was now an even bigger crowd outside and he truly hoped that very soon, everyone would move on. The PR officer had agreed to issue the press statement immediately and Michael hoped she would be true to her word. He went back to his desk and reread the final annotated statement:

'It is never easy to express a sense of loss, especially when it is for a member of one's own close family, even if, for reasons I am choosing not to address here, it is somebody one has lost touch with. The initial shock of my sister's death has been succeeded by a mixture of other feelings, including disbelief, regret and sadness. I would like to ask you to give me space to grieve and to respect my sister's memory. May she rest in peace. No further comment will be made.'

He stayed in his office for a while, reflecting on recent events. It had been a crazy couple of days. He thought of happier times when he'd been a kid and didn't have a care in the world. He smiled when he thought of his younger self, his brother Jake and their two sisters, Alice and Eve, and how they used to love pretending to be ABBA. It was hard to believe that both sisters were now gone. Yet Jake must surely still be out there somewhere and Michael made a lightning bolt decision to track his brother down as soon as possible.

It was ridiculous that he couldn't even remember Jake's new surname, although he knew for sure that he had chosen to take on his wife's family name when he had married. Michael had been quite hurt when his brother had given up the Hambelton name, although none of that mattered now. So much time had been lost, and there was no point focussing on the past as it couldn't be changed. He needed to think of the future. At least with the tour over, he had time to try to pull his life back together. This would have been far worse if it had happened mid-tour.

Michael thought about Alexandra and realised how relieved he had been to hear from her the previous day. Her revelations had come as a total shock to him though, and it was almost incomprehensible that she had been part of Alice's plan to try to bring him down. He was still struggling to understand how Alexandra had got involved, even though she'd explained that at the time, she could see no other way to get out of debt. He tried to convince himself that she must be a good person deep down to ultimately not go through with the plan. Michael was usually a really good judge of character and hoped that this wasn't one of the rare occasions when he was wrong. It had actually been music to his ears when Alexandra had admitted that she had feelings for him too. This was a fledgling romance, but he couldn't remember the last time he had felt this deeply about anyone. He remembered how he'd had butterflies in his stomach the moment they had met. There had been times in his recent past when he'd doubted that he would ever be able to feel that way about someone, ever again.

He concluded that he had two very important missions today, the first of which was to track down his long-lost brother. He wasn't quite sure how he would go about that yet. Secondly, he needed to have a very frank conversation with his manager. Although Alexandra had said that she'd been trying to contact Ricky without success, Michael really did need to speak with the guy to hear his side of the story. It was very tempting to just send a text message, as, like Michael, he also had a mobile phone, but it just didn't seem right somehow. They needed to have a proper conversation. He had witnessed the guy becoming increasingly strange over the last couple of years, but surely there must be a very good reason why Ricky had joined forces with Alice to work on her book. He had tried guessing what the man's motives were but he knew there was only one way to find out the truth. He resolved to have breakfast and to then get ready, before attempting to make contact with both Jake and Ricky.

He went back into the bedroom and made a fuss of his two cats, who were still lying on the bed, looking very content. He loved how the three of them always bonded again so quickly when he returned after a long absence. The cats had spent the night on his bed and it had been comforting to know that they were there.

Othello and Tobias simultaneously jumped off the bed, sensing quite rightly that he was getting ready to leave the room. He would have his shower later, since he could already smell the delicious aroma of Krystal's cooking coming up from the kitchen.

He went downstairs with his two cats behind him. Ted had often commented that their devotion to Michael was because he spoilt them rotten when he was home, with tinned tuna and a variety of cat treats, but Michael knew that his relationship with his pets went far deeper than that. Ted could he quite heartless at times.

Truth be told, Michael preferred to spend time on his own with Krystal, without her husband present. There seemed to be no limit to their topics of conversation and she felt like a real soulmate. They could chat away for hours and she was probably his only true confidante these days. Ted was a nice guy and Michael found it easy to chat with him when they were in the car together, but he could be a bit blokey at times. Michael could have done with one of those great Krystal chats today but when he walked into the kitchen, Ted was already sitting at the table with a newspaper open. He looked up and smiled but then carried on reading the football pages he was seemingly so engrossed in.

'Anything about my sister on the front page?' Michael asked. He saw Ted stash the newspaper away, before reluctantly handing it over when he realised that Michael was still waiting for a response.

Michael glanced at the headline and gasped. 'Star's benefit cheat millionaire sister,' it read. He scanned the article, in total disbelief.

'Do you think this is true?' he asked, looking from Ted to Krystal and back again.

'Who knows,' commented Krystal, who had read the article earlier. 'You know what these journalists are like. I can't imagine it being quite as bad as they're saying.'

'I really hope not,' replied Michael. 'There are some really slanderous things they're saying here and I can't believe they've put a picture of me on the front page, rather than Alice.'

'Ready for breakfast?' asked Krystal, trying to change the subject. She glared at her husband, angry at him for not hiding the newspaper away, like she had suggested before Michael had come down.

'I'm not sure I'm still hungry after reading that,' Michael confessed.

'Come on, it's not going to help matters if you don't eat,' consoled Krystal. 'Even if it is true about Alice, there isn't much you can do about it and anyone in their right mind will realise that it's no reflection on you.'

'But it is in a way,' snapped Michael. 'It doesn't

make me look very good, does it? If she's been defrauding the state, then some of the mud is bound to stick to me.'

Krystal stopped what she was doing and glared at him, looking quite perplexed. 'So are we going to waste this meal I've made for us then?'

'I'm sorry, Krys. Breakfast would be lovely,' Michael replied, realising that she really did have his best interests at heart.

'Take a seat then!' Krystal nodded. 'You can then decide what to do, if anything, afterwards.'

He sat down and started to read the front page article properly. He guessed that Krystal was probably right; he hadn't had any contact with his sister for years, so how on earth could he be responsible for anything she had done?

Whilst waiting for Krystal to plate up, Michael fetched some cat treats for Othello and Tobias, who sat patiently as he fed each of them in turn.

Just as the meal was ready, the house phone started ringing and as usual, Krystal answered it. It was very rare that Ted would make any effort to answer the phone and this annoyed his wife at times. He was always very keen to listen in to her conversations though.

Krystal put her hand over the mouth piece as she whispered to Michael. 'It's someone from the record company for you.'

'Who is it? Is it the PR department?' he asked.

'It sounds like that weird man who you were trying to avoid once before.' *It's a good thing she's whispering*, thought Michael. 'Do you want me to take his number and say you'll call him back?' she asked. Michael knew that Krystal wouldn't appreciate him postponing breakfast any further. He agreed and watched her write down the caller's name and number before hanging up.

'Did he give any indication as to what it might be about?' Michael asked, as Krystal handed him the piece of paper. She shook her head.

'They might want a further statement about Alice,' pondered Michael, now deeply regretting that he hadn't just taken the call.

'That wouldn't surprise me at all,' commented Ted. As usual, Krystal felt her husband was wading in about something that didn't actually have anything to do with him.

'I'm sorry I didn't probe any deeper,' Krystal added. She wondered if Michael would now be thinking that she was useless for not having asked for more information, but in her experience, the caller wouldn't have told her much more anyway, even if she'd asked. She was always mindful that she and her husband needed to remember their place.

She was surprised when Michael didn't even look at the piece of paper, but just folded it and put it in his dressing-gown pocket. They hurriedly ate their breakfast whilst making awkward small talk, all three of them avoiding any reference to Alice. Michael knew that it would have been very different if Ted hadn't been there.

Krystal only ate a single piece of toast but Michael chose not to comment. Maybe she was on a diet again. Although he thought she was in great shape, she seemed obsessed with trying every diet on the market and he had lost count of the number of times she'd rejoined both Weight Watchers and Slimming World.

Once Michael had finished his breakfast, he thanked Krystal and even gave her a peck on the check as he headed back upstairs to get ready.

He returned fifteen minutes later, wearing a smart pair of blue jeans and a red Calvin Klein sweatshirt. He liked to be stylish, even when dressing down at home. He had nothing on his feet, which was the norm for him when he was trying to relax. Othello and Tobias had snuggled up in their baskets in the corner of the kitchen, having installed themselves there when their preferred human had left the room. They knew him well enough to know that he wouldn't be giving them any more treats until later.

Michael was holding the piece of paper that Krystal had given him. He told her that he recognised the name of the caller now and that it definitely was the strange man he'd spoken with on a previous occasion. This particular record company executive always came across as a bit star struck whenever he spoke with Michael, which was always very amusing.

He decided to call the number back from the telephone in the lounge but before doing so, he asked the couple about their plans for the day. Ted was intending to work in the garden after dropping his wife into town to run some errands, although they both admitted that neither of them were looking forward to facing the crowd outside as they drove out. Michael had just checked the security camera yet again and noticed that the mob had grown even bigger, which was unnerving, considering that he thought the press release should have gone out by now.

Michael felt a brief shudder of fear at the thought of being left alone in the house when Ted and Krystal went out. He consoled himself with the fact that there were panic buttons all around the house and that the security fence around the perimeter of the property was regularly maintained. He had a sudden change of heart about making the call in the lounge, within earshot of Ted and Krystal, deciding to use the phone upstairs instead.

'Are you going out soon?' he asked Krystal.

'We'll be a while yet,' she commented. 'Do you need anything from us before we go?'

'No, but thanks for checking.' With that Michael headed upstairs and went into his office.

Earlier that morning he had hurriedly cleared his desk, carefully sliding all the post that had come in whilst he'd been away to one side. He knew that a lot of it would be fan mail from people who had somehow managed to find out his home address. It was very hit and miss these days as to whether or not they got a response. He'd made the decision some time ago not to respond to any fan mail that came to the house, but sometimes, if the letters were touching enough, he would make an exception. Otherwise, items were returned without a signature, with a letter enclosed clearly stating that Michael didn't sign any more. This wasn't technically true of course and he sometimes felt mean, but he knew it was probably for the best.

Michael noticed that, as usual, his incoming mail had been divided into two piles, with elastic bands around each bundle. Krystal was always very methodical at handling his post. One fairly substantial stack, with the envelopes all addressed to him, would most certainly be fan mail. The letters in the second group were addressed to Nicola Beth Hammel, a pseudonym Michael used for his anonymous charity donations. Even before becoming famous, he had tried to do his bit to support his favourite charities and this generosity had been ramped up when the big money had started to come in. He remembered just how long it had taken him to create this anagram of his own name and was still quite proud of himself for having created such a clever alias. He knew that some of the letters addressed to Nicola would contain requests for yet more funds, so he wasn't in a hurry to open them.

There'd also be statements from the various charities, which he would just hand straight over to his accountant.

Michael sat down and picked up the phone. This was going to be an interesting call and he hoped that the record company executive wasn't going to be too gushing this time. After a couple of rings, the man answered and once he realised it was Michael, he went into his usual sycophantic spiel. Although it was entertaining to listen to, time was of the essence here and Michael had other more important things to do. He eventually managed to halt the guy's boring monologue to ask why he had called the house earlier. This seemed to prompt shock on the other end of the phone, as the man was obviously hoping for a nice, long chat, as if they were best buddies.

'Well, there's been a call into the office from someone who claims to be your brother,' he eventually conceded, sounding very pleased with himself for having such interesting information to impart. 'We've not been able to verify him but he's being quite insistent. We wondered if you'd like us to have him checked out further for you?'

Michael couldn't believe what he was hearing. Although it could be a crank who'd made the call, he had to give this person a chance. Having decided earlier that morning that he would do everything in his power to make contact with his long-lost brother, if this caller was genuine then it would certainly make things a lot easier.

The man from the record company was still nattering on at the other end of the phone.

Michael interrupted him again. 'Has he left a phone number?'

Once again, the guy sounded extremely shocked that Michael was being so direct and obviously not up for some friendly banter.

There was another long silence before the executive replied. 'He has, so should we give him a call for you and see what he's about?' he asked.

'Could you just give me the number, please?' If the person who had made the call was really genuine, then Michael wanted to be the one to speak with him. He would also be the only one who could recognise Jake's voice after all, so there was no point giving someone else the task.

'I think we should make some enquiries for you first though,' continued the annoying man, trying his best to sound insistent.

'I just told you to give me the number.' Michael was beginning to get quite angry with this guy now.

The man hesitated again before finally giving in, with Michael quickly writing down the number. He repeated it back to verify that he had got it right.

'Thanks,' snapped Michael, before hanging up. He really didn't care if the other guy thought him rude.

He sat there for a while, just staring at the number. What would he say to Jake if it really was him? What kind of reception would he get? They'd parted on such terrible terms. He concluded that this was ridiculous - their sister had just died and they really should be united in their grief. Jake was his brother and if this phone number was really his, then he was obviously just as keen as Michael to get back in touch.

The thought did cross his mind that perhaps his brother was hoping to get money out of him again, but right now he would accept rc-cstablishing contact with Jake on almost any terms. He wouldn't share that particular piece of information though - not just yet anyway. He suddenly felt very emotional as he picked up the receiver and started to dial the number.

A very familiar voice answered. He knew instantly that it was his brother.

'Jake! It's Michael!' His voice broke and he started shaking with emotion. He could hear Jake on the other end of the phone, who, judging by the noises coming down the line, was just as overcome as Michael.

'I've missed you so much!' Jake eventually managed to blurt out.

'You too! You know about Alice?' Michael realised that this was a very stupid question. Unless Jake had been living on another planet, then of course he knew.

'Yes, yes, but it's been so long since I was in touch with her. I can't believe the things they're now saying about her. Why did we let all this happen?' sobbed Jake.

'I don't know but listen, we can't change anything with Alice now,' Michael replied through his tears. 'Are you still in the Brighton area? I need to see you. I'm in Arundel. Can you get here? Are you working?' Michael thought he sounded like some kind of machine, firing question after question, and thought it might be a great idea for a song.

Jake laughed, although it came out as a bit of a snort. 'Yes, I'm down in Hove. Things have fallen apart for me a bit lately. I had a funny turn and got carted off to hospital. I'm OK now though.' He hoped that he was, anyway. 'I broke up with my wife a few days ago too, because I caught her in bed with another man. I've just started working in a cinema this week but I'm off today.' Jake realised that it sounded a bit like the news headlines.

Michael really felt for his brother. 'I hope this doesn't sound too pretentious but I could send a car to pick you up,' he begged. 'You could be here in an hour or so.' He was already beside himself with excitement.

'Do that!' declared Jake. 'I'll give you my

address and I like the idea of a car collecting me, actually. How the other half lives.' He suddenly backtracked. 'Not that I want anything from you, Michael! I just want you back in my life.'

Michael was really touched. 'Don't worry about all that. Let's have a good old catch-up when you get here. I can't believe this!' He grabbed a pen and wrote down the address that Jake gave him onto the back of one of the envelopes on his desk.

'Why did it take Alice dying for us to get back in touch?' he asked.

'Just send the car. I'll be waiting,' gushed Jake. 'Let's not waste another second!'

'OK, Brother,' Michael replied, 'I haven't been able to say that for a very long time and it feels so good. See you very soon then. I've missed you, Jake!'

'I've missed you too!' Jake sounded like he was still crying.

As he hung up, Michael heard his mobile phone ringing. He hadn't actually realised that he'd left it on and was relieved that nobody had called him during the night and disturbed his fractured sleep even further. He found the phone in the bedroom, on the dressing table, where he had left it the previous night. It was still ringing when he got to it and he recognised Alexandra's number on the screen immediately. This was turning out to be quite a morning. It was nice that she was phoning so early in the day though. She was obviously still as keen as he was. Although he still had some nagging doubts about whether or not he could trust her now, he quickly answered.

'Hello!' he said, trying to keep his voice calm.

'Not too early I hope?' asked Alexandra.

'I've been up for hours.' He couldn't hide his excitement, 'I've just spoken with my long-lost brother and he's on his way here!'

'What? That's crazy! I'm so pleased for you! Although it makes me think that maybe I shouldn't ask the question I was about to ask.'

'What question?' asked Michael.

'I was going to ask whether it would be OK for me to come over to see you, but seriously, you need some time alone with your brother.' Alexandra sounded a bit disappointed.

Michael's head was all over the place but he had to give her another chance, especially since she had been so honest with him during their previous call.

'Of course you can!' he heard himself say. 'But aren't you meant to be travelling to New York this week?'

Alexandra took a few moments to answer. 'That wasn't quite true. I just said that to try to put some distance between us.' *Another lie*, thought Michael. It threw yet more doubt into his mind. When would these untruths stop?

'That was before I realised exactly how I feel about you,' Alexandra continued. 'I promise I've not lied to you about anything else.' Michael hoped that she really was telling the truth this time. She certainly knew how to push all the right buttons. 'How long is your brother staying?' she asked.

'I don't know how long he's coming for. It might be a couple of hours or a few days.' Michael's mind was a whirl and for a brief moment he wasn't absolutely certain that he did want Alexandra to come over, especially with Jake on his way too. He concluded that perhaps it was perfect timing after all. There seemed to be so much change in the air, so why not add Alexandra to the mix too.

'The fact that my brother is coming doesn't stop

you coming too,' he heard himself say.

'Are you sure? There's a flight from Stockholm to London that I could get early this afternoon. I've checked and there's space on it,' advised Alexandra.

'Take it!' Michael replied immediately. 'Let me know what time you're landing and I'll send my driver to pick you up.'

'It's a SAS flight that gets into Gatwick at 16:12. Is that OK?' Alexandra was a bit concerned that she was putting too much onto Michael when his priority today should definitely be the reunion with his brother.

Michael was trying to calculate times in his head and thought how busy Ted was going to be, what with collecting Jake and then picking Alexandra up from the airport too. But hey - that was his job, after all.

'Yes that's fine,' he agreed. 'Please forgive me though, because I've got to go. I haven't even sent Ted to pick Jake up yet!' Michael couldn't believe the day he was having.

They said their goodbyes and hung up. The conversation had certainly been a lot more upbeat than the one they'd had the previous day.

Hurrying back downstairs, Michael found the kitchen empty, although the radio had been left on. Quite fittingly, ABBA's 'Dancing Queen' was playing, making him feel quite jubilant with its euphoric chorus. The prospect of a reunion with his brother later and then seeing Alexandra again suddenly hit him. He ran out of the house, before realising that it was pouring down with rain. The water felt quite cleansing though, as if it was washing away the sadness and loneliness of his old life. He did a little dance and spun round with his arms out wide. Krystal did a double take as she opened the front door of her and Ted's house, finding Michael dancing in the rain. He saw her and burst into tears. But for once, they were tears of joy.

'Today is the best day of my life!' he declared, with Krystal looking at him like he had lost the plot. He started revisiting one of the dance routines from his recent tour. 'Who says dreams can't come true?' he shouted.

Once he'd calmed down, Michael explained everything about the two phone calls, and Krystal realised that her plans for the day would have to be shelved, what with Ted now needed for driving. She gave her boss a hug, despite the fact that he had now ruined her day and was soaking wet.

Michael knew that it was early days with both Jake and Alexandra, but he really did have such high hopes. There would undoubtedly be more revelations to come out about Alice too, but he had to try to forget that for now. He resolved to never let his current bubble of happiness burst.

Chapter 20
Breakthrough

Pippa had been really busy between hospital visits. She'd even been to the C&A clothing store and bought the boys some clothes for when they could eventually go home, although she'd had to guess their sizes. When she next visited the ward, she had a carrier bag for each of them. She had also bought a marker pen, realising that they'd need to write their names on the garments, so that the hospital laundry would know who to return them to if they were sent to be washed.

'At last, we can get out of these hospital pyjamas!' cheered Brian. Although the sizing was a bit hit and miss, the three friends were really touched by Pippa's kindness. She had really gone out of her way to help them.

To the huge relief of all three of them, Pippa had spoken with her solicitor husband, Ranj, the previous day and he had arranged for a colleague of his to come in to see the boys earlier that morning, to help them draft a statement to go out to the press. They had decided that they wanted it to be respectful towards Alice without making it look like they had been too involved with her, especially with the latest scandalous revelations. The legal representative had also offered to contact the police on their behalf, since it wouldn't do any harm to make it clear that the boys had been oblivious to Alice's fraudulent activities. They hoped this would mean that they wouldn't need to be interviewed further.

The boys were now quite nervous, knowing that

their statement would be issued imminently, and discussed this with Pippa when she came in.

'Can you honestly tell me that you didn't realise what she was up to?' she questioned.

'We did wonder,' replied Tim, 'but we didn't know for sure and definitely not to the extent that the papers are saying. Do you remember our friend Nigel?' he asked. Pippa nodded her head. 'Well, he decided to have it out with Alice recently and accused her of fraud, which didn't go down too well, as I'm sure you can imagine. He threatened to go to the authorities, but we stupidly talked him out of it.'

'That wasn't very clever then, was it?' chastised Pippa.

'But then, as I explained, we didn't know anything for certain. We're still in touch with Nigel, even though Alice had more or less banned us from ever speaking with him again. Unfortunately, we've not had the chance to speak with him since the accident, but it wouldn't surprise me if he wasn't already in contact with the newspapers. In a way, as long as he doesn't mention us, it might be a good thing, since then they'd get the story they're looking for and might leave us alone completely.'

Pippa still couldn't understand how her brother had been so gullible. 'But wasn't it fairly obvious what she was up to? I think it makes the situation so much worse that she was apparently already a very wealthy woman when she started making those benefit claims. She certainly wasn't in need financially. She sounds appalling and I know from things you've told me in the past just how badly she treated the three of you. It's hard to believe that you kept putting up with her despicable behaviour.'

'I think in the beginning we just found it funny,'

explained Brian, desperately trying to fight their corner. 'It would give us something to laugh about afterwards and we always used to share her latest antics with Nigel when we saw him. But she definitely got worse as time went on. The way she acted in Paris was completely unacceptable.'

'I think we did find her amusing, as strange as it may sound,' confessed Tim. 'She would sometimes say that the government was paying for her drinks if we ever went out, but when we questioned her about it she would just laugh. To be honest, I think she only invited us along on the trip to Paris so she could make money out of us. And Brian is right - she was a real monster while we were there. We had a conversation amongst ourselves during the trip and made a pact to discuss it with Nigel when we got back and to encourage him to report her. We were even considering doing it ourselves. She did always seem to have a lot of money all the time, despite the fact that she never went to work. Looking back now, it was more than suspicious, especially since she told us many times that she didn't inherit anything from her parents, apart from their house.'

'That was a big fat lie though, wasn't it?' declared Pippa. 'They're saying that her parents left her a small fortune.' She was still finding it all very hard to comprehend.

'We had no idea about that,' insisted her brother. 'Or at least she never mentioned it to us.'

'Let's hope for your sakes that the newspapers will be happy just speaking with Nigel then, if he agrees,' continued Pippa. She wasn't saying anything to make the boys feel any better about the situation and her brother knew why. In his heart he knew they'd all been idiots and as usual, his sister was seeing things from a much more logical perspective.

'In a strange way, us being in here for a few days has probably done us all a big favour,' commented Brian. 'Being out of general circulation has at least meant that we've not been easily accessible.'

'I agree but your safe little bubble isn't going to last forever,' warned Pippa.

Tim had always loved his sister's direct way of viewing things, although she could often be quite frustrating. But at least he always knew exactly where he stood with her and never had to worry that she was telling him something just to make him feel better. In some situations, like this one for instance, he sometimes wished she would.

Louis had been sitting there in silence, listening to the conversation. 'I do think Alice has taught us all something,' he suddenly said. 'We need to respect ourselves more and not let anyone put us down like that again. It's quite shameful how we let her get away with so much.'

Pippa looked at her brother with a glint in her eye. 'Anyway, I've got some big news for you.'

'You're not pregnant?' laughed Tim. He'd had many conversations with his sister in the past about this and had told her that she was now solely responsible for providing grandchildren.

'No, dear. I've told you we don't want children.' She hesitated a bit before continuing. 'I've had a discussion with Mum and Dad about you,' she confessed.

Tim's heart sank. He had indeed agreed that she could speak with their parents, but he hadn't expected it to happen quite so soon. He still felt so much anger towards his dad.

'Well, they'd like to come and see you!' Pippa declared. 'Understandably, they were totally shocked when I told them what had happened to you and it took a lot of persuading to stop them from driving here straight away!'

'What? Dad as well?' Tim was struggling to believe what he was hearing. 'He does know that nothing has changed about my sexuality, doesn't he?'

Pippa hadn't actually broached that particular subject when she'd spoken with their parents on the phone the previous evening, but she had had conversations with their mother about it in the past and had been told that their father did now regret having acted the way he had.

She crossed her fingers under her chair as she responded. 'Yes, he knows that. They're just really concerned about you.'

Tim glanced at his two friends who looked like they were waiting for a positive reaction.

When it wasn't forthcoming, Brian decided to step in and fill the awkward silence. 'I think that's great news, don't you, Tim?'

'It is, as long as my dad doesn't make a scene here in the hospital. None of us needs that right now,' Tim replied, looking rather concerned.

'I don't think that's going to happen,' snapped Pippa, sincerely hoping that it wouldn't. 'Have they mentioned when you might be discharged yet? Mum was asking if they could come in tomorrow. Do you think you'll still be in here then?'

That was certainly a lot sooner than Tim had imagined. 'Can't they wait a couple of weeks before we set a meeting up?'

Pippa glared at him. 'If Dad is making the effort to come and see you, don't you think you could at least try to make an effort too?' She noticed that Tim now had tears in his eyes. 'I'm not sure you're ever going to get an apology out of him,' she continued. 'I know that what he did was wrong but I'm trying my best to get you guys back together. You could have died in that accident, Tim. Can't you try to give Dad a chance?'

'Like he did me, you mean?' her brother snarled, prompting a gasp from Brian. 'I'm sorry,' Tim continued, 'I'm still so annoyed with him.'

Pippa looked at Brian who gave her a conspirational look. His own father had died several years previously and he knew that he would give anything for his dad to be able to come in to see him right now.

'That's settled then. I'll bring them in with me tomorrow,' Pippa concluded, obviously not prepared to take no for an answer. 'Try to meet them half way if you can, Tim.'

'Maybe. But they'd better be nice to me,' he replied, avoiding making eye contact with her. This was seemingly not going to be as easy as Pippa had imagined.

When she had initially spoken with their parents and told them about Tim's accident, it was true that they had wanted to jump in the car and drive to the hospital immediately. Pippa was aware that this wouldn't have gone down very well with Tim and knew that she needed to proceed cautiously with her brother. The last thing she wanted was for Tim to kick their father out of the hospital in a similar fashion to how he himself had been evicted from the family home a few years previously. She knew she had to stage manage things carefully and felt that the best way to do this was to accompany their parents when they came in.

Since working for Michael Hambelton, their dad had obviously seen a lot more of the world and had presumedly met lots of other gay people too, realising that they were no different to anyone else. She was certain that his original, unacceptable behaviour towards

Tim had come from a place of ignorance. Although this didn't justify how he had acted, she had tried her hardest to see things from his point of view.

She'd promised their parents that she would call them back that evening, just to confirm that it would be alright for them to come and visit Tim. She resolved to have a private conversation with their mum at the same time, so she could at least test the water about their father's current view on Tim's sexuality. It was very convenient at times that she and her brother had been brought up bilingual by their German mother, especially when they needed to have private conversations that they really didn't want their father to understand.

'So, who's up for a game of cards then?' asked Brian. He smiled at Pippa and she was grateful to him for trying to break the awkward atmosphere that had descended on them. She also appreciated the moral support she felt he was sending her way. It was such a relief to know that there was at least one other person on her side.

Chapter 21
Angie Baby

Jake couldn't ever remember feeling quite as excited as he currently was. He was going to see his brother again - his pop star brother! He felt as if he was floating on air. Sue would be furious if she knew. But since he'd managed to avoid her since she'd made a big scene at the hospital, why should he care what she might think?

Although he hadn't been in touch with his brother for such a long time, Jake hadn't stopped worshiping him from afar. He laughed out loud when he remembered buying Michael's latest tour video and watching it a few times in secret, whilst Sue had been out. It was as if his brother had become his guilty pleasure. But hopefully, that was all about to change and he didn't care who knew.

Jake thought it quite funny the things that popped into his head sometimes. He suddenly imagined himself in a limousine with Michael, driving past his old marital home, with Sue standing outside with her mouth wide open in disbelief as she spotted them going by. He truly hoped that might actually happen one day - it would be so satisfying to see the look on her face. Deep down, he knew that she was extremely jealous of Michael's celebrity lifestyle and he wasn't sure how she would cope with the knowledge that Jake might now become part of it.

Despite their stupid family dispute, Jake could already tell from the very brief telephone conversation that he'd had with Michael that everything was going to be alright between them. It was true what they said about blood being thicker than water.

Jake was currently alone at Jason's house, waiting for Michael's car to come to fetch him. He had cheekily tuned the radio away from the classical station it had been on to a local pop station instead. Gina G's 'Ooh Aah … Just A Little Bit' was playing. It was such a joyous song and Jake couldn't help but turn it up and bop around the room to it. The thought did cross his mind that he couldn't actually be very ill if he was able to dance around so frantically. Gina G's anthem reminded him that he'd really wanted to watch the Eurovision Song Contest in recent years but Sue had forbidden it. He suddenly realised that he'd now be able to watch whatever he wanted on TV: soaps, music programmes, even men's swimming.

The intrusive sound of his mobile phone ringing broke into his daydream. He was in such a trance that it took a few seconds for it to dawn on him what it was. He wished now that he'd left it behind at the house, since he had never wanted to have the stupid thing anyway. His heart sank as he wondered if it might be Sue calling. He was currently on cloud nine and the last thing he needed was for her to spoil things.

He searched for the phone, half hoping that it might stop ringing before he got to it. It did, but then suddenly started playing its monophonic tune again. As was often the case, he found it in his jacket pocket and he briefly stared at the screen, slightly perplexed. It was yet another number he didn't recognise.

'Hello?' he answered, nervously.

'Is that Mr Rimmer?' asked a man's voice.

'Yes. Who is this?' He truly hoped it wasn't a journalist trying to get a quote about Alice.

'It's Dr Russell from the local practice. Can you

hear me?'

Jake realised that the radio was still blaring.

'Hold on a moment,' he replied, going and turning the music down. He ran back to the phone. 'Sorry about that.'

'That's better,' said the caller. 'As I said, it's Dr Russell. I've been trying to contact you on your home number.' Jake recognised the medic's voice now, from the couple of times they'd met in the past. He sounded very warm and friendly - exactly how you would expect an old-school doctor to sound. 'I noticed we also had another number for you. Is it one of those new-fangled mobile things?'

Jake confessed. 'Yes it is. Actually, my wife and I have split up.' He was surprised at how quickly the statement had slipped out.

'I'm really sorry to hear that,' consoled the doctor, sounding slightly taken aback.

'Please don't be! To be honest, things haven't been good between us for a long time.' Jake decided that the doctor may as well know the truth. 'I found her in bed with another man and that made me faint, I think.'

The doctor wondered if Jake was expecting him to offer some free counselling, which he would normally happily do, if he wasn't so pushed for time.

'I've just got the results back from your hospital tests,' the GP explained. 'Would you be able to make an appointment to come in to discuss them with me?'

Jake's heart sank. With his new found happiness he didn't need any bad news right now. 'Can't you give me the results over the phone?' he asked. 'I'm not quite sure when I'll next be in the vicinity.' It dawned on him that the world was his oyster now. Plus, he knew it was virtually impossible to get an appointment at the surgery these days anyway.

'I'm afraid not. I'd really like to see you.' The doctor wasn't doing anything to allay Jake's concerns about the results.

'Is that because it's something serious?' Jake asked, half wishing he hadn't.

The doctor seemed to soften, hearing the concern in Jake's voice. 'It's not serious at all,' he clarified. 'I don't usually make a habit of giving results over the phone, that's all.' He paused for a moment, deep in thought. 'But considering your current situation, I'm prepared to make an exception. Especially since there's really nothing to worry about. After what you just told me about the shock you had, it's quite possible that your blood pressure dipped, which may have been why you fainted. From the results I have here, I can't see anything wrong at all, which is very good news.'

Jake couldn't believe what he was hearing and did a little dance on the spot. Gina G seemed to be really happy for him too as she continued to give a little bit more on the radio, albeit much quieter now.

'Oh, thank you, Doctor! That's amazing news!' Jake gasped.

'You've obviously been through a tough time and I'm so sorry to hear that,' the medic continued. 'How are you coping? Perhaps you could still try to find the time to come in to see me at some point so we can have a chat? It doesn't have to be this week, just sometime in the future.'

What a kind man, thought Jake. 'I'm actually not doing too badly, thanks,' he clarified. 'I've got some good people around me now, and they're all supporting me.' He thought of Jason, Madeleine and even, hopefully, his brother.

'That's very good to hear. But as I said, please do come to see me when you can. You know where we are, don't you?'

'Yes, of course. I'm so grateful to you for giving me the results over the phone too.' Jake hoped the medic appreciated just how appreciative he was.

'You're more than welcome. Please take good care of yourself,' the doctor concluded.

Just as they hung up, the house phone started ringing.

'It's a hive of activity here today!' Jake said out loud, as he threw the mobile phone onto the sofa and lifted the receiver of Jason's landline, shouting a much louder greeting into it than he had intended.

'Is Jason there?' asked a female voice. Jake noticed she had an Australian accent.

'No, he's at work at the moment. Can I help? I'm his housemate.' *What was it today with these mystery callers?* he thought.

'He never told me he had a housemate. He said he lived alone,' questioned the girl on the other end of the phone. Jake was a bit bemused. Who was this woman to have an opinion on who lived with Jason?

'And you are?' he asked.

'I'm Angie, his girlfriend!' came the response. Jake felt like someone had punched him in the stomach. Jason's girlfriend? She had never been mentioned in conversations previously. In fact, Jake had definitely got the impression that his new-found friend was young, free and single. He had even fooled himself into thinking that Jason had been flirting with him on more than one occasion. As his head flooded with disappointment, he heard a key in the door and in walked the man in question. Jake glared at him, and held out the receiver.

'I believe this is for you,' he snapped, piercing his lips and sounding very accusatory.

Jason looked at him, confused. Jake promptly

318

handed him the phone and stormed out of the room. He knew he needed to calm himself down, so went into the kitchen and took a seat at the table. He really didn't want the excitement of his impending meeting with Michael to evaporate.

Jake reminded himself just how much positivity there currently was in his life. He couldn't let this one thing derail him. Having the opportunity to reunite with his brother was really beyond his wildest dreams and he was truly relieved at the news he'd just been given by the doctor too. But it did feel like Jason had been leading him on at times - or was that all in Jake's imagination? He could hear his friend talking on the phone in the other room but couldn't quite make out what was being said, apart from occasionally hearing the word 'baby'. He recognised the flirting tone - Jason had used it often enough on him. Jake was fuming now. Eventually the call ended and Jason came into the kitchen to join him, looking shamefaced.

'Are you alright?' he asked, taking the chair next to Jake.

'So … Angie? You conveniently didn't mention her before,' snapped Jake, realising that he was sounding extremely possessive.

'I'm sorry, Jake. Maybe I played this wrong but I really didn't want to hurt your feelings. I felt you needed a friend right now and I got the feeling from the start that you kind of liked me. I didn't mean to lead you on, I hope you can believe that. You're such a great guy and …'

Jake broke him off mid-sentence. 'It's OK, you don't have to explain,' he said. 'Maybe I misread things. It's my own stupid fault. Why would you be interested in me anyway?' It was starting to dawn on him just how genuine Jason was and that it was actually quite sweet that he'd gone along with Jake's crush, to try to make him feel better.

'Come on, don't be like that.' Jason gave him one of his cute smiles. They had always melted Jake's heart previously and this one was no exception.

'If it's any consolation,' continued Jason, 'if I were gay, I'd jump at the chance of being with you. Oh and by the way, Pierre at the cinema has got the hots for you.' Jason put his hands up. 'Truth be told, I really enjoyed the attention you were giving me. There - I've said it now!'

Jake hadn't ever thought of Pierre like that. He didn't even know the man very well and had only met him a couple of times.

'Brotherly hug?' suggested Jason. 'Just to show that there's no hard feelings.'

Jake found it impossible to resist - he knew from recent experience that his friend really did give good hugs. They got to their feet and embraced. Jake took in the aroma of Jason's aftershave again and wished things could have been different. *If only this Angie woman wasn't on the scene*, he thought to himself. Jason had obviously not wasted any time in getting involved with someone, since he'd only been back from Australia a short while. But then he was such a good looking, sweet guy, so was bound to have been snapped up quickly. Jake was quite disappointed when the hug eventually ended.

'So who is Angie?' he asked, trying his hardest not to sound bitter.

Jason sighed. 'She's a girl I met back in Australia.'

'So did she follow you here?' Jake concluded that she must be really keen to travel half way across the world to get her man.

'She was planning a trip to visit her family here anyway. It was just coincidental that she happened to be here at the same time as me.' Jason shrugged. It obviously didn't seem a big deal to him.

Coming to his senses and realising he had bigger fish to fry, it suddenly hit Jake that he'd not told Jason about his calls with both Michael and the doctor.

'Anyway, you're not going to believe this. I've got some big news to tell you. I still can't believe it myself!' he declared. 'I'm waiting for a car to pick me up to take me to see my brother!'

'How come? I know you said you were going to try to get in touch with him but …' Jason looked quite taken aback.

'I know! I phoned the record company this morning and the next thing I knew Michael phoned me! He's sending a car to take me to his house. I'm so excited!' Jake threw his arms around Jason again, making his friend laugh.

When Jake eventually stepped back, he remembered his other news too. 'Oh, and the doctor phoned too. They can't find anything wrong with me.'

'That's fantastic news, Jake! You're really having quite a day, aren't you?'

'If Angie hadn't spoilt things then maybe it would have been a hat trick,' commented Jake. He was beginning to realise that this new version of himself was a lot more daring than the previous one.

Jason roared with laughter. 'Well, in the words of Meatloaf, 'Two Out of Three Ain't Bad', right?'

'I guess so,' chuckled Jake. 'Anyway, I wonder how long it will take for this car to get here? It's coming from Arundel.'

'Don't ask me where that is. My geography isn't very good. You got time for a celebratory drink?' asked Jake, walking towards the fridge.

'I wouldn't mind a cup of tea,' admitted Jake,

assuming that his friend was about to offer another of his 'tinnies'. 'I'm sure there'll be some champagne flowing later though.' Jake was already imagining a big celebrity welcome awaiting him. 'Although come to think of it, neither Michael nor I ever drank alcohol, so we might be toasting with tea instead. Unless life in the fast lane has changed him.'

'You're such a light weight!' laughed Jason.

'Whatever happens - will you promise me something?' asked Jake. 'Can we always stay friends? I don't know what I'd have done without you these last few days and I feel like you've been a major part in this turn-around in my life.' He had tears in his eyes.

'Of course we can,' said Jason, winking. 'I'm not that easy to shake off. And I want an invitation to some of those celebrity parties. Imagine all the women I'll be able to meet.'

'Not to mention the men,' gasped Jake, giving his friend a mock punch on the arm. Jason had just opened a can of lager and Jake clouting him caused some of it to spill onto the floor.

'Careful!' Jason scolded.

'Oh sorry, dear, I don't know my own strength!' chuckled Jake, in a very camp voice. It was remarkable just how comfortable he was feeling with his sexuality now. It had virtually been an overnight transformation, although of course, he'd been aware of its existence for years. It had just felt too scary to do anything about it. 'Anyway, Jason, make me a cup of tea, please. I've got a glamorous new life waiting for me.'

Jason looked at him and rose to the challenge, shaking his head at the new brazenness of his friend.

'Of course, Princess. Your wish is my command!' He gave a little bow.

'If only,' laughed Jake.

'Anyway, you're not the only one with some news, although mine isn't good,' said Jason. 'I saw Madeleine earlier and she's made some progress, trying to track someone down at head office.'

Jake was intrigued. 'Oh, has she spoken with that strange woman? I know she was really keen to get hold of her yesterday.'

Jason shook his head. 'No response from her but Maddy has managed to speak with the wife of the guy she mentioned. Do you remember that she said that she sometimes spoke with him too, if she couldn't get hold of the weird woman?' Jake nodded. 'It seems he's left the country!' Jason concluded, shaking his head and pulling a face of disbelief.

'What do you mean, 'left the country'? Why would he have done that?' This wasn't sounding good at all and Jake was quite bemused.

'Apparently, he's admitted to having a gambling habit. His wife reckons she had no idea about it before. She knew he had a problem with drink and drugs and she'd been encouraging him to do something about it. She's told Madeleine that he's checked into the Betty Ford Center.' Jason pronounced the name of the institution carefully, like he'd never heard of the place before.

Jake took a sharp intake of breath. 'What? That's in America. That would be pricey!'

'That's what I thought,' agreed Jason. 'It doesn't solve the problem of where the financing for the cinema is going to come from though, and Maddy is more worried than ever now. The guy's wife has said that she can't help with that. She didn't even know that her husband was involved with a cinema. That might not be true, of course. You don't know what to believe in these situations. She could be making the whole thing up, just to protect him.'

Jake was standing there with his mouth open. 'Does his wife know any other way for Madeleine to contact the woman who heads up the cinema though?'

'She didn't even know about the cinema, as I said. It is all very odd. Maddy always took them both at face value. I've told her that she's just an employee and isn't responsible for any of this, so she could just walk away if she wanted to. But as you probably realise by now, my sister's not like that. I've got no idea where she thinks the staff's wages are going to come from. The suppliers will all need paying too - I'm not sure she's thought all of this through.'

'I agree - she needs to get out of there fast. Do you want me to speak with her?' Jake asked.

Jason smiled. 'That's a kind offer but if she won't listen to me …'

'So, what's going to happen?' Jake wasn't quite sure whether he'd be returning to his job at the cinema anyway, but he was still concerned for his two new friends.

'No idea,' sighed Jason, shaking his head. 'She said she's going to just play it by ear. I sometimes think she's a bit bonkers, especially in situations like this.'

'Does she make a habit of working for cinemas that end up being in dire straits then?' asked Jake, knowing full well that this wasn't what Jason had meant.

'You know what I'm saying. She's far too dedicated for her own good sometimes,' Jason commented. 'I'm nothing like her,' he added. Jake wondered if he was referring to just work or life in general.

'She sounds just the opposite of my darling wife,' chuckled Jake, realising that Sue was still quite prominent in his thoughts. 'Sue certainly wouldn't stick around in a situation like this.' Thank heavens he was out of that relationship now.

There was a knock on the door and they both jumped.

'That might be my car!' declared Jake, excitedly. 'I'm actually quite nervous.'

'Don't be afraid - he's your brother, after all. He's bound to be feeling just as nervous as you are. You'll have a fantastic time. Go on - your car is waiting, Cinderella! Just make sure you're home by midnight.' Jason was quite envious of what might lie ahead for his friend.

'I've got no idea when I might be back, to be honest, but I promise I'll keep in touch.' Jake was grinning from ear to ear.

Jason laughed. 'Yeah, right. I'll probably never hear from you ever again.'

'That's definitely not going to happen. Angie might not be around forever,' teased Jake.

'Get out of here!' chuckled Jason, giving his friend a punch on the arm as he followed him out of the kitchen.

Jake opened the front door to find someone standing there in chauffeur's garb.

'Are you Jake, by any chance?' the man asked.

'That's me!' confirmed Jake.

As he followed the driver out towards a very posh looking car, he turned and gave Jason a nervous wave.

The chauffeur opened one of the back doors of the vehicle and Jake climbed in. This really was the stuff of fairy tales.

'Goodbye, former life,' Jake sighed under his breath, as the car pulled away.

Chapter 22
Blood Brothers

Krystal was getting herself into a bit of a tizzy about the impending visitors. She had never met Jake previously but had heard so many stories about him from Michael during the time that she had been working for him.

'How long do you think Jake will be staying?' she asked.

'No idea,' replied Michael. 'I guess it depends on how well our reunion goes. Although judging by our brief telephone conversation earlier, I'm not anticipating much awkwardness on either side. I'd love it if Jake could stay for a night or two.'

Krystal thought it ironic that the rift in her own family could possibly be healing simultaneously with the one in Michael's. Pippa had promised to phone her mother later to let her know if Tim had agreed to his parents coming in to see him. Krystal had burst into tears when she'd heard about the accident and had been praying ever since that her son would allow her to visit him and that he would make a full recovery. Although she couldn't really think about anything else, for now she had to try to focus on Michael.

Being a keen baker, she suggested making Jake a cake, thinking that it might perhaps take her mind off things for a while. 'Shall I make one of my signature black forest gateaux?' she asked.

Michael knew how proud Krystal was of making her traditional German cake, based on a recipe that her mother had taught her as a child, back in Berlin. He had lost count of the number of times he'd eaten a slice of it over the years. However, he remembered very clearly that as a child, his brother's absolute favourite had been a pineapple upside-down cake. Their mother had made one for him without fail every year on his birthday. Krystal confessed that she had only ever made that particular cake once before, but didn't envisage this being a problem. She had all the necessary ingredients in stock, including a tin of pineapple slices.

Michael padded around the house nervously as he waited for his brother to arrive, looking out of the lounge window every so often, even though he knew that Ted couldn't possibly be arriving back just yet. He'd watched the car leave on the security camera earlier. He had been pleased to note that there was hardly anyone waiting outside now. Following his press release, the journalists had seemingly realised that there was no point in hanging around for any further statement.

Guessing that he probably had just enough time before Jake's arrival, Michael decided to put together a mix tape of favourite music from their youth. To bring things up to date, he included a couple of his own current favourites too. Michael and Jake had always had very similar musical taste and he hoped that might still be the case. He tried his hardest to remember some significant songs that they had enjoyed listening to when they were younger. He deliberately included a couple of his own hits too - hopefully this would bring a smile to his brother's face.

It wasn't long before he could smell the aroma of Krystal's baking and, when he'd finished making the tape, he went into the kitchen to see how she was getting on. She was just about to load the dishwasher and asked if he'd like to lick out the mixing bowl. He hadn't done this since he was a child and remembered how he and his siblings would take it in turns to do so whenever their mother made a cake. He licked the sticky mixture off the spoon and was surprised to find that it wasn't as appetising as he'd expected. If anything, it just tasted of the ingredients: raw egg, flour, sugar, butter and vanilla essence. Krystal laughed at the face he pulled.

'Not very nice?' she asked.

'I used to really enjoy doing this as a kid but my tastebuds have obviously changed over the years. No offence to your cake, Krys, but I think I'll give it a miss this time. I'm sure it'll taste much better once you've worked your magic on it and it's baked.'

Krystal smiled at him and shook her head, taking the bowl and spoon to rinse before putting into the dishwasher.

'It's going to be quite a day, isn't it?' Michael commented as he took a seat at the table. 'My brother is on his way and Alexandra is arriving later, too. Do you think I should have put her off until tomorrow?'

'She's obviously very keen to see you,' replied Krystal, not quite sure how she really felt about this new woman. 'Although from what you've told me about your brother, he's not going to have a problem with her being here.'

'Did I tell you that he's broken up with his wife?' asked Michael. 'I think it's quite recent.' Although he had never met Jake's wife, he didn't think she'd be someone he'd get on well with. 'From what he said, he's been going through a really tough time lately. It's going to be so good to catch up with him properly when he gets here.'

'So do you think he'll stay?' asked Krystal again. 'I mean, should I make up one of the guest bedrooms for him? Come to think of it, do I need to make one up for Alexandra too?' She gave Michael a cheeky grin. She didn't want to assume that his Swedish guest would be sharing his bed just yet.

'Well maybe make a bed up for each of them. It seems to be going well with Alexandra but we haven't actually slept together yet.' Krystal loved how open and honest he always was with her.

'You're such a gentleman, Michael.' Krystal was sure that lots of pop stars in his shoes wouldn't need much encouragement to do exactly the opposite.

'I don't want to assume anything. The last thing I want to do is scare her off.' Although Michael had been doing his best to sound excited about Alexandra, Krystal wasn't convinced. She looked at him, knowingly. Michael smiled to himself. Krystal could obviously tell that he was beginning to have doubts again.

'Well, you're always such a good judge of character,' she reasoned, trying to reassure him. 'I truly hope she's as wonderful as you say, because you deserve the very best.'

'It's funny how I met her, really. Ricky brought her backstage in Stockholm. She works as a make-up artist, although he'd never mentioned her to me before,' Michael explained. Krystal had heard all of this already from Ted. 'Did I tell you she came to Paris and did my make-up there?' Michael asked. Krystal nodded. 'She's very good at her job, not that I wear that much of the stuff on stage, as you know,' he continued. 'I also think it's a sign of how genuine she really is that she told me about Ricky introducing her to Alice.' Krystal wondered who he was trying to convince. She'd heard all about Alexandra's confession earlier too and was trying hard not to judge.

Michael seemed to sense this and continued to justify his reasons for letting Alexandra off the hook. 'Initially, she was trying to get information out of me about my childhood, for a book that Alice was allegedly working on,' he said. 'But she couldn't go through with it in the end. Isn't that nice?' He sat there staring out at the garden, taking in the true extent of his sister's loathing of him, and wondering yet again if he could really trust Alexandra.

Not wanting to rain on Michael's parade, Krystal still felt she had no choice but to voice her concern. 'Just promise me you'll proceed with caution,' she advised. 'Make sure you get to know this woman properly before getting too involved. I've obviously never met her but I'm a bit concerned if she's from Ricky's camp.'

Michael half wished that Krystal hadn't shared this thought.

'I might go for a walk around the grounds,' he said, pretending he hadn't heard her comment.

Krystal smiled. 'Ted will be pleased you're going out there because his team has been working so hard on the gardens whilst you've been away.'

'I'll make sure I take note of what's been done and mention it to him later,' agreed Michael, still trying hard to sound unfazed by Krystal's previous remark.

'Do you want something to take out there with you?' asked Krystal. 'A hot chocolate, perhaps?'

'That would be great!' Michael waited whilst his housekeeper made his drink, and proceeded to flick through a magazine to try to avoid making further conversation. He was secretly pleased to find a feature about himself within its pages and filled with pride as he read that they were now calling him one of the best-selling musicians of all time, quoting current estimated worldwide sales of a hundred million. The author of the magazine article was obviously a big fan, waxing lyrical about literally everything that Michael had ever released. *Who needs to pay for PR when a free article like this could generate so many sales*, he thought.

'Drink's ready!' said Krystal, putting it on the table in front of him.

Michael took it outside and sat on one of the benches that were dotted around the grounds. It felt strange that since he'd got home, so much had happened. He only hoped that there wouldn't be any uncomfortable feelings later. He should have probably given Jake some dedicated time on his own, rather than having his new lady friend arriving hot on his brother's heels. Hopefully, it would all work out fine. He guessed that Krystal did have a point about him taking it slowly with Alexandra.

He finished his drink and left the empty mug on the bench. He'd try to remember to collect it on his way back. He headed into a woodland area, past a row of pine trees, and saw that a hammock had been fixed between two apple trees in the middle of a clearing. It had turned out to be a nice, sunny day and Michael couldn't resist climbing into the hammock. It took him a few attempts but once he was in, he couldn't believe how comfortable it was. He had never been in one before but was sure he'd now be doing this quite often. With the gentle swaying, the lack of quality sleep he'd had the previous few nights and the warm sun, before long he'd fallen into a deep slumber.

Michael dreamt that he was in Central London. Everywhere he looked, people's hungry eyes were staring at him and he noticed that the bodies were getting closer and closer, all holding out their hands to try to reach him. He ran, finding himself in Trafalgar Square, next to the fountains. The mob was closing in now, and he ran towards St Martins Lane, passing the National Portrait Gallery, which had a big poster outside featuring his face. A group of fans ran out of the entrance, waving their arms and screaming, all trying their hardest to grab hold of him.

Michael sprinted towards a passing taxi, and the doors swung wide open, so he clambered inside. The driver turned round to look at him and Michael recognised Ricky's distorted face. He was looking at him greedily with pound signs circling in his eyes. His manager suddenly slammed on the brakes and the sides of the taxi fell away, with the fans outside now piling in. Michael screamed and suddenly woke up, with his heart racing.

He didn't know where he was at first but could sense that he was gently rocking from side to side. He felt quite giddy and disorientated. The sun was blinding but he could just make out a figure in silhouette standing next to him. He tried to focus and eventually made out the face of his brother, Jake, smiling down at him. At first, he thought he was still dreaming, but then realised that this was all quite real. Both of them started giggling with excitement.

Michael tried to sit up but failed miserably. He gripped the sides of the canvas to try to steady himself and after a few attempts at climbing out, he grabbed Jake's arm, laughing loudly as he begged for help. Jake held onto the hammock, which created more problems as Michael just fell to the ground, pulling Jake down with him. They couldn't get back up for laughing so much. Neither of them could remember when they had last been so hysterically happy and tears rolled down their faces. They struggled to get back up, still holding on to each other tightly, afraid that if they let go then they would end up being separated again. They stared each other out, both finding it impossible to unlock the other's gaze. They fell into a tight embrace.

'I can't believe you're here!' beamed Michael, finally breaking the silence. 'You haven't changed at all.'

'I have to say you've not changed either.' Jake had been half expecting Michael to look very different, as if he would have a special aura about him now that he was famous.

'Still the same old Michael,' laughed his brother. 'Welcome to Greengage Farm! I hope you'll feel as at home here as I do. Let's go back into the house. Have you been indoors yet?'

'I met your housekeeper - Krystal?' replied Jake, as they started walking, Michael with his arm around his brother's shoulders.

'I'd be lost without her,' confessed Michael. 'Although don't tell her I told you that!' he added, laughingly.

'This place is very impressive, Mike!' continued Jake.

'Ha! Nobody has called me that for years, but I love that you call me it, so don't stop.'

They walked back towards the house and went into the lounge through the open French doors. Krystal appeared through the door on the other side of the room and gave them a massive smile, asking if they'd like something to eat and drink.

'Is the cake ready?' asked Michael.

'Ooh cake!' gushed Jake. 'Now you're talking.'

Michael winked at Krystal as he asked her to bring them the champagne he'd put on ice earlier. Although he remembered that his brother had also been teetotal when they had last met, he hoped it would impress him nonetheless.

'Sit down,' Michael instructed his brother. 'I want you to tell me everything.'

'How long have you got?' sighed Jake. He explained how he'd split up with Sue after finding her in bed with their gardener. He then confessed that he'd been secretly struggling with his sexuality for some time and that recent events, including being free of his controlling wife, had led him to deal with it. 'I hope that's not going to change how you feel about me?' asked Jake.

'You're joking, right? Half the people I've met in the music industry are that way inclined. It doesn't make any difference to me at all. I love you for whatever or whoever you are, Jake. I bet it was hard being in the closet for so long though? You know, I did have my suspicions when we were younger. Hope you don't mind me saying that.'

'Not at all. In some ways I think it was a bit like being an undercover spy before I came out,' confessed Jake. 'Everyone assumed I was straight and I would listen to all their homophobic jokes and comments and wonder how they hadn't guessed about me.'

'That's a great description,' commented Michael. 'I get that completely. It's not good though.'

'I still can't believe that we didn't make any effort to get back in touch before now,' said Jake, sadly. 'My ex-wife would have given anything to have met you. Although she's not exactly your biggest fan, she'd have loved to have shown you off to her friends.'

'Well let's not worry about her now,' replied Michael. 'I think Alice was a key player in all of this. She told me some horrible things that you'd apparently said about me.'

'Like what?' asked Jake, concerned.

'That you'd said I was ugly and would never make it in the music business because of my terrible appearance,' laughed Michael. 'She told me you thought I was a terrible singer too.'

Jake looked shocked. 'Well that definitely isn't true! If anything, I always thought you were the good-looking one out of the two of us. And your voice is amazing! Actually, she did the same with me. She once told me that you thought that I was shallow. I bet that's not true either then?'

'What do you think?' asked Michael. 'But it's funny what you believe when you want to, isn't it? If I'm honest, I think maybe I was a bit blinded by the lights when I got my first recording contract. I should have known then that family was more important.'

'Well, I didn't make it easy for you, did I?' consoled Jake.

'That's all water under the bridge now, so let's look forward rather than backwards. Can you believe what they're saying about Alice fraudulently claiming benefits?'

'To be honest, I'm not at all surprised. Do you remember we used to think she stole from us as kids?'

'I'd forgotten that!' gasped Michael, as the memory suddenly flooded back.

'Well, let's hope we don't have to get involved,' said Jake. 'It's probably a good thing that we weren't in touch with her, because at least we can't be held responsible for any of it now. I hope it's not wrong of me to say that.'

'I agree with you,' nodded Michael. 'So, what's all this about you working in a cinema then?'

'I've only started there recently,' said Jake. 'But I have a horrible feeling it's going to be very short lived. I wouldn't be at all surprised if the cinema ended up closing down. The person financing the cinema has gone AWOL apparently, and the other person involved has taken himself off to Los Angeles to dry out.' He couldn't help but feel that this sounded very rock 'n' roll and wondered if it might earn him a few extra brownie points from his brother.

'I wonder if I know the guy?' commented Michael. 'It sounds like something someone in the music industry would do.'

'Who knows,' replied Jake. 'By the way, I want to say something, Michael. I'm really sorry about the way I acted when I asked you to lend me that money all those years ago. I realise now that you wouldn't have had much hard cash at that point in your career. I really didn't understand how royalties worked back then.'

'No need to mention it again, Jake.' Michael was determined to leave their disagreement in the past. 'I really can't believe all this about Alice though. Did you keep in touch with her for long after she fell out with me?' he asked, trying to change the subject.

'No, she cut us both off at the same time I think, when Mum and Dad got sick.' Jake was glad that Michael wasn't giving him a hard time about their fall-out. 'Looking back, I think it was all because she didn't want us to get our hands on any of their money. Didn't do her much good in the end though, did it?'

'That's very true,' agreed Michael. 'Actually, I'm going to tell you something but I'm not planning on sharing it with anyone else. When I was in Paris, on the way to the last concert venue, I think I saw Alice walking down the road with her friends. At the time I wondered what on earth she would be doing in Paris. But according to the police, that's where she was travelling back from. I regret not insisting that the driver stop to let me get out to speak with her now, but the traffic was really crazy and I seriously didn't think it could be her at the time.'

'If it was, I wonder what her reaction would have been if you'd approached her?' questioned Jake. 'I'm not sure you'd have got a great response, to be honest.'

'I've been thinking about that too. Sadly, I think you might be right,' agreed Michael. 'Unless she was

336

stalking me or something. I've also been wondering if she left a will. I guess you and I are her next of kin, unless there's a partner or a child we're not aware of. Not that I'm after her money, but it would be ironic if we ended up being her sole beneficiaries, wouldn't it? Especially after all the effort she put in, to try to stop us getting any of Mum and Dad's money.'

Jake hadn't even considered this. 'It would be so weird if we got to go back into our old family home. I assume that's where she was still living. I guess we just have to wait and see how it all pans out.'

'Yeah I'm sure it'll all come out in the wash,' commented Michael, just as Krystal entered the room, pushing a trolley.

'Michael tells me this is your favourite?' she asked, nodding towards the cake.

'It is,' beamed Jake. 'That's so sweet that you remembered.' He grinned at his brother.

'Not only do I remember that it was your favourite cake but there are a few songs that have always reminded me of when we were kids too. I've put some of them onto a tape.' Michael walked over to the hi-fi and pushed the play button on the cassette player. Boney M's 'Sunny' started playing.

'I love this song!' shouted Jake over the music, prompting Michael to turn the volume down.

'Yes, I know,' he winked. 'Hopefully you'll love all the others on there too.'

'Just to let you know, Ted has gone to the airport,' advised Krystal, as she positioned the hostess trolley in the middle of the room.

Jake looked at Michael, bemused. Krystal headed back to the kitchen, leaving them to help themselves to cake and drinks.

'I met this woman in Sweden,' explained

Michael, feeling a bit embarrassed. Although it felt like his relationship with his brother was already back on track, he did still feel a bit sheepish as he told Jake about Alexandra. He asked if he minded that she'd be joining them later.

'Of course not!' answered Jake, although he hesitated slightly. Michael realised his brother had been about to say something else, but had stopped himself.

'What were you about to say, Jake?' he asked.

'I was going to ask if you were expecting me to stay? I didn't want to assume anything.'

'You're welcome to stay as long as you like,' advised Michael. 'This is your home now too, if you'd like it to be. Where have you been living since you and Sue broke up?'

Jake laughed. 'Well, there's this guy at the cinema who's taken me under his wing. I have to say I was quite keen on him at first, but I found out earlier today that he's got a girlfriend.'

One of Michael's own hits, 'Out of My Head', started playing and Jake smiled. 'This is one of my favourite songs of yours! You won't believe how difficult it was for me to listen to your music with Sue around. I used to have to hide stuff away from her. I had a whole stash of videos up our chimney, believe it or not, including your latest tour video. I had to watch it when she was out.'

'Did she hate me that much?' asked Michael.

'I don't think she hated you,' explained Jake. 'In a way, maybe I was trying to protect you from her. She did keep telling me that I should try to get back in touch with you, but I always doubted her motives.'

'I hope I never meet her now,' laughed Michael.

'Your video was in very good company actually,' explained Jake, cheekily. 'I hid some naughty videos up the chimney too!'

'Don't tell me they're still up there?' gasped Michael.

'No, I took the guy from the cinema with me to rescue them when I knew that Sue would be at work,' explained Jake. 'We got all my clothes out too. The spare room at Jason's place is now crammed with all my stuff.'

'So why don't you just move in here?' suggested Michael. 'Not that you have to, of course. You might prefer to go back to your fancy man from the cinema.'

'He's very nice, but that relationship isn't going anywhere, is it? I'd love to stay here.' He was about to comment on the place being big enough for an army but bit his tongue. 'We've still got so much to catch up on.'

Michael handed his brother a glass of champagne and a plate with a slice of his favourite cake. 'I know neither of us drinks,' he chuckled. 'That is, unless you've started hitting the bottle since we lost touch?'

'Nope - nothing has changed there,' said Jake.

'Same with me. But I still felt we should toast our reunion with something stronger than fizzy pop, since this is such a big day for us.'

'That's a great idea!' agreed Jake, taking a sip and laughing. 'Do you think I could have a cup of tea now, though?'

Michael had hesitatingly tasted his champagne too and was thinking the very same thing. Especially since, in his opinion, tea went much better with cake.

'I agree. But hey, at least we sipped it.' They both laughed, returning their glasses to the trolley simultaneously. Krystal had guessed that Michael wouldn't be drinking the champagne and had put a pot of tea, some milk, mugs and spoons on the trolley too.

'She thinks of everything,' commented Michael. 'Do you still smoke, by the way?' he asked, proceeding to pour them both some tea.

'Very rarely these days, to be honest,' Jake said quite proudly. 'I used to get so stressed with Sue at times and I'd convinced myself that smoking would calm me down, but it never did. In fact, I'm making a vow to you now that I'm giving it up totally! Do you smoke?'

'No,' replied Michael. 'You can do this, Jake! I'll support you. Do you remember that Mum always said that she'd seen me smoking in the street with one of the older kids when we were younger?' His brother nodded. 'Well, she didn't. I've never even tried one. The press would have a field day with that one, wouldn't they? To be honest, this is about as outrageous as I get - tea and cake!'

'You might be a pop star, Michael, but it's good to see that you've not gone down the sex and drugs and rock 'n' roll route,' commented Jake.

'Well, certainly no drugs and not much of the other one either, to be honest,' he chuckled. 'There's been a lot of rock and roll though!' He looked at his brother with an exaggerated sad face.

'How can you say that when you have this woman flying in from Sweden?' queried Jake.

'It's not like that. She's lovely but …,' Michael hesitated before continuing. 'Well, we seem to be taking it very slowly. And that's fine with me, actually.'

'We need a code word for when something does happen,' teased Jake.

'And that, my brother, is another reason why I have missed you so much. There's nobody else in this whole wide world who I would accept to do that with.'

'Tesco!' suggested Jake. 'Let's use that word. Nobody will guess the significance of it.'

'Oh yeah - I'll just drop 'Tesco' into the conversation. Nobody will think it strange at all if I ask something like, 'Did you buy this cake from Tesco, Krystal?' Michael found the idea hysterical.

Jake was now really laughing too. 'I'll be listening out then. So, tell me some stories about being on the road. You must have met some amazing people. Did you ever meet the members of ABBA?'

'You're still a fan then?' asked Michael. 'Me too, funnily enough. But unfortunately, no, I've never met any of them. But I live in hope.' Michael proceeded to tell his brother the highlights of his music career so far and confessed that his main experience of it was of solitude and loneliness.

The time went so quickly as the two brothers chatted. The topics of conversation just seemed to flow, one after the other. They discovered that their current musical taste was very similar too and that they both loved George Michael. Fortunately, Michael had put 'Fastlove' on the mix tape.

Another song that got a good reaction was 'My Brother Jake' by Free. 'Do you remember how we always used to sing along to this one in Dad's car?' asked Michael.

Jake laughed. 'You used to say it was my theme tune.'

When the second side of the cassette ended, they decided to play the tape again. Michael was really pleased now that he'd made the effort to put it all together.

Having lost all track of time, Michael was surprised when he suddenly saw his car pulling up outside. He immediately ran out of the French doors to greet Alexandra, who leapt into his arms. Without speaking first, they fell into a passionate kiss. It felt to Michael like every nerve in his body was tingling.

'Oops, sorry about that,' blushed Alexandra, as

341

she pulled away.

'Please don't apologise,' said Michael, kissing her again. Eventually, Michael became aware of his brother in the doorway watching them, making him blush slightly. He took Alexandra by the hand and led her towards the lounge doors.

'Maybe I shouldn't say this,' Jake blurted. 'But the two of you do look good together.'

Alexandra held out her hand and Jake shook it. 'I think I like this guy already,' she said, as Michael introduced them.

Ted got out of the car. 'I'll take your luggage upstairs, Alexandra,' he told her.

'Krystal has made up a couple of spare bedrooms,' Michael clarified, not wanting his lady friend to get the impression that she was being pressurised into sharing a bed with him. She smiled at him coyly.

'At least you've got luggage,' commented Jake, trying to ease the awkwardness that seemed to have now descended on them. 'I only have the clothes I'm wearing!'

'Well, I'm sure we can sort that out, Jake. It's a good thing you're still a similar size to me,' said Michael. 'You can borrow some of my clothes for now. You're not having any of my lady's underwear though,' he laughed.

Alexandra looked shocked, so he felt the need to explain. 'I'm joking!' He noticed how easily he had fallen back into this harmless, playful banter with his brother.

'We could always pop down to Tesco tomorrow to buy some,' winked Jake. Alexandra looked puzzled.

'It's a private joke,' explained Michael. 'Just ignore him. I'm not sure we'll be going to Tesco just yet, but who knows.' He gave his brother an admonishing look.

'You may be speaking English but part of me thinks I'm not understanding a single word you're saying,' commented Alexandra. 'Must be a secret brother language thing.'

'Well, don't worry about it. Come and meet Krystal.' He took Alexandra by the hand and led her through to the kitchen, with Jake following close behind.

As was often the case, Krystal was busy preparing yet more food. She gave Alexandra a very big smile. 'So good to meet you,' she said, shaking her by the hand. 'What would you like to drink?'

'Did I see champagne in the other room?' Alexandra asked.

'You sure did and I'm guessing there's probably most of the bottle left, if Jake is as big a drinker as Michael is,' smiled Krystal.

'Thank you. Champagne is my favourite!' said Alexandra.

Michael's mind flashed back to the restaurant in Stockholm, when she had told him that she didn't drink alcohol. He hoped this hadn't been yet another lie. He tried his hardest to push this thought from his mind.

'A woman with good taste!' chuckled Krystal. 'Why don't the three of you go back into the lounge and I'll bring some more drinks through.'

Once they were settled, Michael told Jake what Alexandra had said about Alice trying to bring about his downfall.

'Have you told him about Ricky too?' she asked.

'Ricky? That's funny! I think that's the name of the man who has gone missing at the cinema,' said Jake.

'That's a bit of a coincidence,' responded Alexandra, looking at Michael. 'I don't actually know many Rickys, do you?'

'It's not an uncommon name,' Jake commented.

'Anyway, you're not going to believe this update,' declared Alexandra. 'I made another call to Ricky before I left Sweden to let him know that I'd told you everything, and guess what? The call was answered by his wife. She told me he's taken himself off to America to get treatment.'

'That's uncanny!' exclaimed Jake, not quite believing what he was hearing. 'That's what's happened with the guy from the cinema! It must be the same person, surely?'

Michael was concerned that Alexandra had tried to contact Ricky again, but was trying his best to put it out of his head. He suddenly had an idea though.

'Jake, do you have the name of the person who's managing the cinema and their phone number?' he asked.

'Of course!' He got up to fetch his phone. Alexandra looked at Michael, not quite sure what was going on. He brought her up to date with the story his brother had told him about the unfortunate situation at the cinema.

'Do you want me to speak with the person in charge there, so we can compare notes, to see if this really is the same man?' asked Alexandra. She was half hoping this might score her a few bonus points with Michael. 'I'd love to be able to help, if I can.'

'That might not be a bad idea,' agreed Michael, as Jake came back into the room, with his mobile phone in his hand.

'Jake, why don't you call your boss at the cinema and explain the situation and see if they're happy to speak with Alexandra to check that we're talking about the same Ricky?' Michael was mystified by the events that were unfolding before him. 'Use the house phone,' he said.

Jake couldn't get to the phone quickly enough. If he could help Madeleine in any way at all, then he was more than happy to do so, since she'd been so kind to him. This all seemed so surreal.

He dialled the number and waited for it to connect. As he did so, he told Michael and Alexandra all about Madeleine.

It was just a matter of seconds before his call was answered. Jake explained that he was with Michael and was relieved to hear that Jason had already brought Madeleine up to date with his revelation about his brother. Without giving Madeline the chance to say anything else, Jake jumped in with what Alexandra had told him and promptly passed the phone over to her.

The two brothers listened intently to the side of the conversation that they could hear, trying to fit the pieces together. Their minds were working overtime, doing their best to fathom out what was going on. As Michael sensed that the conversation was coming to a close, he mouthed for Alexandra to pass the phone to him. She nodded and explained to Madeleine that Michael wanted to speak with her too.

'Hi Madeleine!' said Michael, hoping that the woman wouldn't be too star struck. Fortunately, she sounded like she was taking it all in her stride.

'I wonder if Jake and I could come and visit you in the next couple of days?' he asked. 'Please don't tell anyone else we're coming though, as I don't want this to become a big media circus. Hopefully I can trust you with that?' Madeleine assured him that he could. 'I obviously need to know all the finer details but I'm wondering if perhaps I could help you out with the financing of the cinema in the interim?' he asked, beaming at his brother. 'Jake speaks very highly of you.'

345

Jake and Alexandra looked at each other in total shock.

'Oh Michael,' Madeleine stammered. 'That is the best thing I've heard in my life! I've not told anyone about the situation here apart from Jake and my brother Jason, so nobody else is aware of what's going on. There's no need at all for me to mention to another living soul that you're coming and we can arrange it for when I'm here on my own. Just let me know when works for you. Thank you again! I just can't believe it!' Michael could tell how happy his decision had made her. They finished the call and hung up.

'That's so kind of you to be doing this,' his brother gushed. 'I think you've made Madeleine's day!'

'I've always quite fancied being involved with a cinema,' said Michael. 'We can screen *ABBA - The Movie* on repeat!' The two brothers roared with laughter with Alexandra looking on. She loved how people could get so ecstatic about a pop group from her homeland.

'Do you remember that Mum took us to see that film three times in one week when it first came out?' asked Jake. 'And that you insisted on dancing along to all the songs in the aisle?'

'Embarrassing,' commented Michael, blushing slightly as he gave Alexandra a sideways glance.

She took another sip of champagne and thought how easily she could get used to this lifestyle.

Chapter 23
Family Reunion

Considering the fact that he'd initially given the impression that he wasn't at all interested in his parents coming in to see him, Tim seemed to be making a very big effort with his appearance and the state of the area surrounding his bed on the day that they were due to visit. Brian and Louis exchanged glances and while Tim was in the bathroom, they both agreed that this was a good sign. When he walked back onto the ward, Tim could tell they'd been talking.

'I suppose you find this hilarious?' he commented.

'I wouldn't say hilarious. I think it's quite sweet, actually,' replied Louis, prompting a scowl from Tim.

'I don't want them to think I've gone to rack and ruin since they threw me out,' explained Tim. 'Even if I have been in a car crash. But if my dad says anything that's remotely homophobic, he's out of here!'

'We know that and we're sure he knows it too,' said Brian. 'Just don't be too hard on him. Today isn't going to be easy for either of you.' Tim didn't reply but just carried on tidying around his bed.

Visiting time grew ever nearer. Both Brian and Louis could sense Tim's growing nervousness. He'd only played with the sandwich he'd been given for lunch, which was very unlike him.

They heard footsteps coming down the corridor and saw Pippa appear through the glass partition at the end of their side ward. She was pointing across at Tim and being followed by a couple in their late 50s who, judging by the striking family resemblance, were obviously his parents. As soon as he saw them, he started crying, sitting there on his hospital bed with his shoulders shaking. His mother rushed over, leaning across and taking her son in her arms as carefully as she could, afraid of hurting him. Brian and Louis both felt tears welling in their eyes too as Tim's father also reached Tim and put a comforting hand on his son's shoulder.

'It's OK, Son,' they heard him say. Pippa looked across at Tim's two friends and mouthed the word 'sorry' as she unfolded the screen that was standing next to her brother's bed and pulled it around her family, clumsily using a second screen on the other side of the bed to complete the enclosure.

Louis was already sat on Brian's bed. They had a whispered conversation about what they had just seen, only glancing up when the tea trolley was wheeled in. The man in charge of it, Will, poured a cup of tea for each of them and offered some small packets of biscuits from a wicker basket. Both boys took a pack of custard creams as Will nodded towards the closed screens.

'What's going on over there? Your friend taken a turn for the worse?' he asked.

'Just a family conference,' explained Louis. 'I'm sure they'd like tea or coffee if you're brave enough to ask. Or shall I ask them?' He really wanted to get a sneaky peak at the events unfolding around Tim's bed.

'Go on then! You sound a braver man than me!' chuckled Will, going back over to the tea trolley.

Louis hurried over to Tim's bed and shouted through the screen. 'Anyone in there like a cuppa?'

Pippa's head appeared and she smiled at Louis before proceeding to unfold the screens, revealing a perfect family portrait. Louis hurriedly retreated back to Brian's bed and then glanced back over.

Tim was sitting at the centre of the family unit, propped up in bed with a parent on either side of him, each with a hand on his shoulder. After a brief conversation with her newly-reunited family, Pippa walked over to the tea trolley and gave Will their order, waiting for the drinks and delivering them to her parents and brother. She then got one herself and came over to Brian and Louis, raising her eyebrows as she reached them.

'Well, that couldn't have gone any better,' she sighed with relief.

'It's still early days,' said Brian, hoping he wasn't putting a damper on things. 'But it looks very hunky dory at the moment, I have to say.'

'Once you've had your tea, why don't you come over and say hello to Mum and Dad?' suggested Pippa. 'They won't bite, no matter what Tim may have told you in the past.' She went back over to join her family.

After they'd finished their drinks, the boys slowly walked over to Tim's bed. 'Hi,' they exclaimed in unison.

'Mum and Dad, these are my best friends, Brian and Louis. I don't know where I'd be without them.' Tim was looking a lot more cheerful than earlier. 'They were both in the crash with me.'

'Nice to meet you,' nodded Ted, holding out his hand. The boys each shook it in turn and for some strange reason, Louis did a little curtsey. Brian glared at him. Both of them decided that Tim's dad didn't seem anything like the monster Tim had portrayed.

'We've asked Tim if he'd like to come and stay with us for a while,' said Krystal.

'You wouldn't mind, would you?' asked Tim.

'I'd still like to move in with you guys afterwards but I'm thinking I could stay with Mum and Dad for a couple of days first.'

Brian's heart warmed at how happy his friend looked. All the nervousness that Tim had shown earlier in the day had evaporated and he was now beaming from ear to ear.

'Sounds like a great plan to me,' Brian responded. 'Stay with your family as long as you like.' He noticed that his voice sounded deeper than usual and he wondered if he was subconsciously trying to beef up in front of Tim's dad.

Tim's face lit up. 'Thanks, Guys!'

'We'll go down to the TV room for a bit, to give you some space,' suggested Brian. He looked at Tim's parents. 'Please don't go without saying goodbye though.'

'We wouldn't dream of it,' responded Krystal. 'And thanks for being such great friends to our son!'

'It's not hard - he's a wonderful human being,' replied Brian, as he gently led Louis by the arm out of the ward.

Once the two boys had left, Krystal took the opportunity to address the elephant in the room. 'Tim, your dad has got something he'd like to say to you.'

Ted blushed and looked very shamefaced. He cleared his throat before speaking.

'I'm really sorry that I reacted the way I did when you told me and your mum … your news.' He looked quite awkward and knowing how bad his dad was at talking about his feelings and discussing anything personal, Tim realised what an enormous thing this was. All the anger he'd been feeling towards him seemed to just melt away and he burst into tears again. This was all he'd ever wanted - to have the acceptance of both his parents.

'Thank you, Dad,' he blurted out as he patted his father's hand. 'I really do appreciate you saying that and I promise I'm not going to be acting any differently from how I did before. It's just important to me that you know who I am and who I chose to love.' His dad nodded.

Tim looked at his mum who gave her son a satisfied smile. 'It's so good that our family is back together,' she declared. 'We really have missed you, Son.'

'I think my work here is done,' laughed Pippa.

Chapter 24
Secret Visit

For the first time in as long as he could remember, Jake had slept soundly all night. It was lovely and quiet in Michael's house and he had never experienced such luxurious, comfortable bedding before. Although he listened very carefully when he first woke up, he couldn't hear a sound, so assumed that Michael and Alexandra were still asleep. He smiled to himself, wondering if his brother's new girlfriend had spent the night in her own room or in Michael's. He had deliberately gone up to bed before them the previous night and had firmly closed his bedroom door for two reasons: to give his brother and Alexandra some privacy but also to give himself some time on his own to process everything.

Jake was enjoying his new-found peace of mind. He lay there evaluating the events of the previous few days. He really couldn't comprehend the massive transformation in his life. There had been moments in his recent past when he'd truly believed that his mundane, gloomy existence was the way things would always be. Yet strangely, he realised he had always had a faint glimmer of hope. He'd never completely given up on his dreams.

He contemplated getting up, since he'd been awake for a good half an hour or so already, but was just so comfortable. Finally getting out of bed, he headed into the ensuite bathroom to take a shower. It was just gone 8am but he still tried to be as quiet as he could, since he didn't want to wake his brother or Alexandra. Michael had sorted out some clothes for him the previous evening, which luckily fitted Jake perfectly. He'd also noticed that the bathroom was well stocked with toiletries, including a new toothbrush and toothpaste. Slowly turning the water on, it was immediately evident that he needn't have worried about making a lot of noise - the hi-tech shower was virtually silent.

As the water caressed his body, he couldn't remember when he had last felt this relaxed. His muscles seemed to be succumbing one by one to the pummelling from the jets of water. He was enjoying himself so much, in fact, that he found himself singing softly. It seemed quite appropriate that the tune that he was singing was one of Michael's hits, 'Fall to Pieces'. It had been on the tape that his brother had put together for them to listen to the day before and was such an earworm. He hadn't been able to get it out of his head since hearing it. They had played the tape three times in total, as Jake had kept insisting that Michael put it on again and again. There had been so many songs on that cassette that were linked to their childhood together and his brother had been so clever at selecting them. Jake had loved all the recent songs that had been on there too.

He dried himself with a plush bath towel and selected an aftershave from the bathroom shelf to liberally spray over his body. Everything felt so good and he concluded that he really hadn't been taking care of himself for a very long time. Things were going to change from now on though, and he was sure that his brother would support him with this new positive regime. He could probably get some tips from him too.

Jake carefully hung the damp towel over the rail and walked back into the bedroom to get dressed. He adored the designer clothes that Michael had given him to wear. Even the feel of them was expensive. He chose an outfit and checked himself out in the mirror. Wasn't it amazing what good clothing could do to change your appearance? He decided to head downstairs, even though he assumed nobody else would be up just yet. He didn't want to miss a single second of today and it would be quite thrilling to be waiting in the kitchen when his brother finally made an appearance.

As he made his way onto the hallway, Michael's bedroom door suddenly opened and out walked Alexandra. She looked at Jake in surprise and he responded with a big smile, hoping she would take it as a sign of his approval. He noticed that she was wearing a white, towelling dressing-gown, which was far too big for her. Jake assumed it was Michael's.

'I'm just going down to get a drink,' whispered Alexandra, 'Michael isn't awake yet.' Jake gave her a thumbs up and followed her downstairs.

They walked into the kitchen together and were both surprised to find Krystal getting things ready for breakfast. The house was definitely very well built as Jake hadn't been at all aware that someone was already busy working in the property. He noticed the remnants of the snacks they'd had the night before on the kitchen worktop, including the half-eaten plate of cheeses that Michael had fetched for Jake and Alexandra to taste. Krystal smiled at the two of them.

'Did the three of you have a nice evening?' she asked.

'It was lovely,' replied Alexandra. Jake smiled at Krystal and raised his eyebrows. He wondered what she really thought of the current situation.

'It was gone midnight by the time we got to bed,' he commented. He was tempted to tease Alexandra but felt that perhaps he didn't quite know her well enough just yet. He would catch up with his brother later, not that he really wanted to know any of the finer details.

Alexandra asked Krystal for a glass and helped herself to some mineral water from the fridge. *She's feeling very much at home,* thought Krystal, not sure if that was a good thing or not. She hadn't quite made her mind up about Alexandra yet.

'I'm going back to bed,' announced the young Swede, as she left the room. Krystal looked at Jake.

'Michael's not awake yet, apparently,' he explained, pulling a face, as if to say 'enough said'.

Krystal nodded and gave him a knowing look. 'Seems it was a waste of time me making up that extra room yesterday then. Actually, I'm really pleased for Michael. She seems quite nice, don't you think?' She hoped it wouldn't be too obvious that she was trying to gauge his opinion.

'Yes, she seems fine,' he replied, which he knew sounded very non-committal. He couldn't help but wonder if Alexandra had a cute, single brother back in Stockholm. *Easy, Tiger,* he thought to himself.

Krystal made Jake a cup of coffee, which he took outside. It was a very sunny morning and he decided to take a walk around the grounds, finding it hard to believe that his brother had done so well for himself that he could afford such an incredible property.

He took a seat on a bench in a clearing surrounded by fir trees and sipped his hot drink. His stomach rumbled and he wondered how long it would be before Michael and Alexandra would emerge for breakfast. As if on cue, he heard Michael's distinctive voice in the distance, calling his name. Jake felt a warm shudder run through his body. He hadn't truly felt part of a family for such a long time - especially not whilst he'd been married to Sue.

355

He jumped up and found himself running along the path leading back to the house. After the events of the previous evening, he knew that his brother was just as happy as he was about their reunion, and this filled his heart with joy. He couldn't imagine them ever parting company again.

The house came into view again and he saw Michael standing in front of the French doors, looking out for him. Jake waved and once he reached him, his brother ruffled his hair, asking where he had been.

'Just for a walk around your incredible grounds,' said Jake. 'It reminds me of a National Trust property! It must need so much work to keep it all in such good order.'

'You can thank Ted for that,' explained Michael. 'He takes care of everything, along with a team of helpers.'

They walked into the kitchen together, finding Ted sitting at the table. Jake couldn't help himself and started waxing lyrical about the gardens and how exquisite everything was, prompting Ted to nod his head, in acknowledgement of the compliment.

'You've worked wonders out in the gardens whilst I've been away,' commented Michael. 'I've got to hand it to you - you're a real asset, my friend. Thank you so much. You know I appreciate it, don't you?'

Ted didn't answer but looked quite chuffed with himself. Michael gave Krystal a smug look. He walked over to the fridge to refill his glass of water.

'I'll give you an extra veggie sausage for that,' Krystal whispered as he went past, which made him laugh.

'So, what's on the agenda today?' asked Jake, taking a seat opposite Ted at the table. 'Do we have to go to Tesco or have you already been, Michael?' He gave his brother a wink, hoping he would realise that he'd mentioned the secret word to acknowledge that his brother's relationship with Alexandra had now moved on to the next stage. Michael gave Jake a glare.

'Why would you need to go to Tesco?' asked Alexandra, confused.

'Oh, just ignore him! He's trying to be funny but is failing miserably,' chuckled Michael, giving his brother a dig in the ribs.

Krystal started to bring over plates of hot and cold breakfast items for them to help themselves to. Jake was astounded that there was such a feast on offer. This was a far cry from the breakfast he would normally have. He thought of the last breakfast he'd tried to have at home with Sue and the muesli which had ultimately ended up in the bin.

Michael looked around the table and smiled. He held up his glass of water to Krystal, who had just sat down.

Thanks for this amazing breakfast, Krys, and thanks to all of you for being here. Even you, Jake!' he said, which prompted a laugh from everyone.

'I could always leave again, if you'd prefer,' responded Jake, faking a look of hurt.

'Please don't do that!' insisted his brother, winking. 'It means the world to me to have you here.'

They all continued to chat away over breakfast, with just Ted remaining silent. He did smile from time to time however, to show that he was quietly enjoying the conversation.

Michael had originally proposed that they go to collect Jake's things from Jason's house at the same time as they visited the cinema later that day, but after giving it some thought, he'd suggested to his brother that it might be easier for them to send a courier instead. Jake was disappointed at first, since he was looking forward to showing off his celebrity brother to Jason, but he knew that this new plan made more sense. Once they'd finished breakfast, he phoned Jason to arrange a convenient time.

It was great to hear his friend's voice again. Jake couldn't resist jokingly asking if Jason had been tempted to examine the boxes of stuff he'd left in the spare room and whether he'd watched any of his secret stash of videos. Jason promptly assured him that none of them would be of any interest to him.

For Jason's benefit, Jake forced himself to ask how Angie was, even though he really didn't care.

They fixed a convenient time for him to visit and for his things to be collected and Jake said he would arrange everything with a courier company. He hung up and went back to the breakfast table to relay everything back to Michael.

'Jake, do you also want to call Madeleine and confirm it's still OK for us to go there today?' suggested Michael. 'And please make absolutely certain that she hasn't told anyone else about us coming.' He looked at Ted. 'And are you still around to drive us there and wait for us and then bring us back afterwards?' Although he knew that this was actually one of the tasks that Ted was employed to do, he still always liked to ask rather than command. Ted nodded his agreement. He was indeed a man of very few words.

Michael and Alexandra went back upstairs to get ready.

'They'll be a while,' laughed Jake, causing Krystal to chuckle. She really liked how cheeky Michael's brother was.

Later that afternoon, they set out on their journey to the

cinema. Michael was pleased to find that there wasn't a single person waiting outside the house when they left.

'I'm so relieved that the press seems to have given up on trying to get another quote out of me about Alice,' he commented.

'I bet!' sympathised Jake. 'Do you make a habit of reading the papers generally?'

'Not if I can help it,' Michael replied. 'Mainly because their stories often upset me.' His brother could see his point.

'Maybe now that Alice is dead, the stories will dry up,' suggested Jake. Michael had shared with him the previous evening that it had been evident from the content that a lot of the newspaper reports had been created by their sister. 'Although I've always thought that you came across very well in print, especially in interviews,' Jake continued. It was true, and he thought that his brother should know this.

'That's nice of you to say, but you're probably biased. I still appreciate it though,' Michael smiled.

Ted had the radio on softly and as they drove down the country lane, away from the house, the intro to ABBA's 'SOS.' started playing. It took the two brothers right back to their childhood and being in the back of the family car with Alice and Eve. They looked at each other and then sat there in silence, hoping that Ted wouldn't burst their bubble by changing stations or talking. The only sound in the car was Agnetha's melancholy lead vocal, interspersed with both girls singing the heartfelt choruses. They listened to the piano climax of the song and Jake sighed very loudly.

'Do you think their music will always remind us of Alice and Eve?' asked Jake.

'I think they'll always remind us of the happy times we had when we were kids,' replied Michael. 'And

I guess that includes our sisters. They're good memories though and we have to always focus on that. It was only in recent years that Alice turned on us, after all.'

'That's very true, actually,' said Jake. 'I can't help thinking how different things could have been, if she hadn't become so nasty.'

'Well, we can't change that now,' said Michael. He looked out of the car window and noticed that they were just joining the A27.

As they drove into the cinema car park, Michael commented on how much he liked the building's exterior and that he was pleased to see that there wasn't a crowd waiting outside. They got out of the car and walked in the direction of the cinema entrance, with Jake feeling like a child, about to show his parent around his school.

Madeleine was already waiting for them at the door. She greeted them and Jake could tell that she was really worried.

'It's OK, you don't have to curtsey,' he laughed, hoping that his attempt at humour might relax her a bit. He knew this was probably a big deal for her, meeting someone as famous as his brother. She locked the main door behind them once they were inside, explaining that none of the staff were due to start work for another couple of hours, which would hopefully give them enough time to chat without being disturbed. Jake was disappointed to hear that Jason wasn't likely to be making an appearance. She led them into her office. Jake said he would go and make drinks whilst Michael talked business with Madeleine.

'You might want to hear what I've got to say first,' said Madeleine, looking like she had the weight of the world on her shoulders. 'There's no other way to say this, but I think it's your sister who owns this cinema,' she stammered.

'What are you talking about?' asked Jake. 'It can't be!' He looked at his brother, hoping he might be making more sense of this than he was.

'What makes you think that?' asked Michael, trying to hide the anguish that was boiling up inside him.

'I've been working such crazy hours here that I hadn't even seen the news about Alice until last night. When I saw her face on the TV screen, I recognised her immediately. I only met her once and because of her surname, I obviously asked if she was related to you. I'm sorry to say she seemed quite taken aback. She said you would be the last person she would want to be related to.' The two brothers stared at each other, not quite believing what they were hearing. 'I realise now that she was just trying to cover things up.'

Michael was shaking his head, in total disbelief. 'So, how was she financing this then?' he eventually asked, dreading what the answer might be. There seemed to be no boundaries to his sister's fraudulent life.

'I've no idea. For the first few months that I worked here, money came in quite regularly from a company called Griffin Investments, which Alice told me was her business account,' explained Madeleine. 'But I've not received anything for about six weeks.' She was trying her hardest to be respectful towards Alice's two brothers and hated having to add to their grief. 'I'd been trying to call her for days but there was never any response. As Jake knows, I was getting quite frantic.'

'What will happen now then?' asked Jake. 'Does that mean the cinema has to be sold?'

'Not necessarily,' pondered Michael, who was still really struggling to get his head round it all. 'I believe it becomes part of Alice's estate, and should be able to carry on trading, unless there's something more complicated in the company's set up. I can get my legal team to check it all out, if you'd like me to?' he suggested.

'Oh, that would be amazing!' gushed Madeleine. 'I prepared some financial documents to show you before I realised that Alice was your sister,' she explained, nodding at her computer screen. 'I'm sure you're not at all interested in seeing them now though.'

'I would still like to see them,' Michael replied.

Michael suggested Jake go and make them all a drink as he dragged his seat round to Madeleine's side of the desk. He spent some time scrutinising the documents she'd prepared and realised just how little money was actually involved. He'd been expecting it to be a lot more, but didn't share this thought. He'd had a conversation with his accountant the previous evening and had ring fenced a much larger sum than what was now needed.

Looking up, he smiled. 'I think I can still help you out financially,' he said, 'at least in the interim. And I hope we can sort something out legally in due course too.' The look of relief on Madeleine's face was palpable. 'I'm sure the press would have a field day with this if they discovered that Alice had been financing a cinema,' commented Michael, 'so let's try to keep this between ourselves, if it's alright with you?'

'I can promise you I'm not going to be sharing it with anyone,' promised Madeleine.

'I trust you,' said Michael. 'Perhaps we can get my brother involved too' he added. 'He's got some legal training as well, which might be useful.'

Jake had just come back into the room with their drinks and overheard what Michael had just said. He loved how his brother was trying to big him up.

'Oh wow, that's very impressive!' gushed Madeleine, deciding not to mention that she remembered seeing this on Jake's CV.

'What do you think?' asked Michael. 'Do you think you'd be up for the challenge, Jake?' His brother gave a bashful nod of approval.

'Having you around would certainly ease things for me a bit too,' confessed Madeleine, still struggling to believe that this was all working out so well.

'I have got one question,' Jake interjected.

Oh no, thought Michael. *I hope he's not going to ask something that I'd prefer that we discuss privately.*

'I just wondered if Madeleine knew why it's called the Griffin Cinema?' asked Jake. Michael was relieved that this had been the main question on his brother's mind.

Madeleine pondered on this for a moment or two before replying. 'I do know that Alice chose the name herself but I'm not absolutely sure why. She did share on a couple of occasions that Midland Bank had always been very helpful to her and I know their logo used to be a griffin, so maybe it's something to do with that?'

'That would make sense, actually,' Michael agreed. 'Do you remember when we were kids that Alice loved myths and legends?' he asked his brother. Jake nodded. 'I remember she was obsessed with collecting leaflets and things from the bank, because she loved their griffin logo so much. She used to cut them all out and stick them on the wall. It used to drive our dad crazy.'

'I remember that too now,' chuckled Jake. 'We used to really rib her about it.' He looked at Madeleine. 'You have to agree it is a bit unusual.'

She smiled. 'Maybe not as strange as then going on to name a cinema after it.' The three of them were relieved to finally have something to laugh about.

'Well, that's everything settled then,' concluded Michael. 'I'll put you in touch with the guy who handles my finances and he can deal with all the finer details.'

Madeleine felt herself start to relax. They discussed Ricky again briefly, and Michael told Madeleine a few of his most outlandish experiences of him. Alice wasn't mentioned again.

After ten minutes or so, Michael looked at his watch. 'Do you need anything else from us before we leave, Madeleine?' he asked. 'Although I'd love a look round before we go, if that's alright with you?'

'Everything is perfect,' she replied. 'Thank you so much, once again, Michael.' She had really taken to him already and was impressed at how down to earth he was. 'Jake - do you want to help me show your brother around?' she asked, as she stood up and led them out of the office and back into the foyer. Jake reflected on how it was just a matter of days since Madeleine had shown him around the cinema for the first time too, although it felt like such a long time ago now, with everything that had happened since. Michael's tour of the building proved to be much briefer than the one that Jake had had.

As they said their goodbyes to Madeleine and went to walk back round to the car-park, Michael spotted some people standing by his vehicle.

'I thought it was all a bit too good to be true,' he sighed, taking a quick step backwards so that he could hide under the cinema's porch.

'Maybe they're just admiring the car?' suggested Jake. 'Shall I go over and ask Ted to pick you up over here?'

'Good thinking!' agreed his brother. 'Yes, let's try that at least.' Michael really appreciated having Jake around. It really did feel like he was looking out for him. He tried to peer around the side of the wall and watched his brother casually walk over to the car and get in. He noticed that he didn't speak to the waiting crowd. The car then slowly pulled over towards Michael, and he hoped for a brief moment that he might just be able to jump in. Unfortunately, the group of people followed the car over and got there before Ted did. As usual, they wanted autographs and photos, which Michael found himself going along with, as it felt far easier than making a big scene. He found it incredible that this group of fans had found out that he was here, when there had been no announcement of it anywhere. Interestingly, his *Secret Seven* fans, who usually found out about everything, hadn't made an appearance. Yet again, he was frustrated at not being able to move without being hounded. In general, the fans were very sweet and well behaved, but it was still suffocating not to be able to have a private life any more. Jake got out of the car and stood by his brother's side, to show his support.

Ted, ever the professional, got out of the car and waited by the door, prepared to open it as soon as he sensed that Michael was ready to leave. It was a good ten minutes before he was able to do so. Jake could see that his brother was getting quite visibly stressed.

When they eventually drove away, Michael shook his head. 'I've had enough of all this. I know they mean well and it's because of them that I have this amazing life, but I can't move now without being stalked. If I don't find a solution soon, I'm going to give it all up!'

Jake was flabbergasted. 'But you can't do that!' He sat there in silence, not knowing what else to say. 'How do other stars deal with it?' he eventually asked.

'I don't know. Maybe they're just stronger than me. Or more accepting.' Jake could tell that his brother was quite serious about the possibility of hanging up his microphone.

'We'll find a way, Mikey, we really will.' Jake

patted Michael on the leg. 'I hadn't realised that it was affecting you to this extent. But there has to be a solution.'

Michael wasn't convinced that there actually was, but was touched by his brother's optimism.

'Can you believe that Alice had the audacity to set up a cinema?' asked Jake, trying to take his brother's mind off his current predicament. 'Makes me wonder just how much money she must have had. And trust me to have found a job working there.'

'The more I learn about her, the more I think that she was capable of anything,' said Michael, shaking his head. 'It wouldn't surprise me if she didn't have a few more surprises up her sleeve for us yet.'

Chapter 25
The Letter

Alexandra had decided to go into Brighton to source a few things, whilst the boys went to the cinema. Michael had suggested they drop her off en route, but she was fiercely independent and quite liked the idea of taking the train. She set out before the boys and wasn't at all surprised to encounter two fans who were waiting for their idol outside the house. Smiling at them sweetly, she chuckled to herself, since they obviously hadn't recognised her from the many photos that had been published of her with Michael in Stockholm and Paris. She even cheekily told them that Michael wasn't at home, so there was no point them waiting for him. She was relieved when they didn't ask who she was or how she knew. They wouldn't have been at all impressed if they had known that she was Michael's girlfriend.

On the way to the station, Alexandra reflected on how well it was all going with Michael. She was really enjoying sharing his extravagant lifestyle. The best thing of all was that he had agreed to pay off all her outstanding debts and had even offered to give her a monthly allowance. She was now quite determined to find a way to help him escape the confines of his goldfish bowl existence.

Alexandra had the seeds of an idea for a disguise that she thought might work for Michael. There was a movie that she'd recently seen at the cinema and she had decided to use one of the characters in the film as her inspiration. She really wanted to create a new, anonymous look for him and had concluded that this was definitely worth a try.

In the film, which was called *To Wong Fu, Thanks for Everything! Julie Newmar*, Patrick Swayze played the part of a drag queen who'd won a competition to travel to Hollywood, to take part in a glamorous pageant. Alexandra had been astounded by Mr Swayze's very convincing transformation in the movie and how he had faultlessly carried it off. She could really imagine Michael getting away with a very similar look, since he had the same build and bone structure as Patrick Swayze. She truly hoped the disguise might work.

Having planned her route well, changing trains just once at Barnham, she hadn't anticipated the engineering works which inevitably doubled her journey time. She decided that she would definitely get a taxi back later. Michael would be paying, after all.

Alexandra was quite impressed with the shops in Brighton. She hadn't expected it to be such a thriving commercial centre and she fell in love with Kensington Gardens, a hidden gem tucked away at the back of The Lanes. She spent some time browsing round a bustling emporium there and couldn't believe the selection of vintage clothing they had on offer, at good prices too - not that it mattered with Michael's budget. It didn't take her long to find everything she needed, although she was slightly concerned that she might not be guessing Michael's size correctly. Now that she'd had the opportunity to examine his body close up, she felt that she had a fairly good idea though. With each item that she bought, her plan gathered momentum and in her mind's eye she began to see exactly how Michael might look. The only problem would be if he was too bashful to go along with her idea. She knew that for him to carry off a successful transformation, it did need to be quite radical and to disguise him as another man just wouldn't cut the mustard. He had tried going down the sunglasses and hat route many times before, after all, and it had never worked.

It was such a relief to take a taxi back to Michael's, instead of struggling with all the bags on the train. The house appeared to be empty when she got back, so after depositing her bags in the bedroom, she took a wander around upstairs. It was about time she acquainted herself better with this amazing property. She was really curious how things might pan out in the future, but decided that it was far too soon to consider that her presence here could become a permanent thing.

Alexandra walked into Michael's office and smiled when she saw the pile of what she assumed to be fan mail, waiting on the desk for him. On closer inspection, she noticed that there were two piles of post, and was surprised at how everything was very neatly stacked. She couldn't help but scan through some of the envelopes and was puzzled to discover that a large number of them were addressed to someone called Nicola Beth Hammel, enough of them in fact to cause her concern. Whoever this mystery woman was, she must play a very big role in Michael's life, judging by the amount of mail waiting for her. He had assured her that he'd not been in a relationship for some time, but she now began to wonder if that was true. Was he already involved with this Nicola person and just using Alexandra for what he considered to be a harmless fling? It would certainly explain some of the secret jokes between Michael and his brother too. Her mood darkened as she heard the two brothers coming in downstairs. She quickly tried to put all the post back into some kind of order and stood there, just staring at all the letters.

After a minute or so, Michael called out to her and she hurried from the office to the top of the stairs, taking a deep breath before making her descent. She really needed to speak with Michael about what she had just found but didn't want to do so in front of Jake, and certainly not within earshot of Krystal. She desperately tried to think of a way to get Michael on his own.

He kissed her on the lips when she reached the bottom of the stairs and took her hand, leading her into the kitchen. She noticed that both Jake and Krystal were already there and wondered how long the German housekeeper had been in the house and whether she'd been aware of her snooping about upstairs. Alexandra was now feeling extremely on edge and was tempted to feign a headache, but instead joined Michael and his brother at the kitchen table.

'All go well?' asked Krystal. Alexandra wasn't sure who the question was addressed to initially so remained silent. She hadn't shared her idea for disguising Michael with anyone yet, and wasn't even sure if she wanted to carry on with the plan now, based on what she'd just found in his office.

'Very well actually, apart from there being some fans waiting there when we left,' reported Michael. Krystal knew how much this would have bothered him and gave him a sorrowful look.

'How did they know you were going to be there?' asked Alexandra. Despite her inner turmoil, she was trying to act as normally as possible. 'Do you think the woman at the cinema tipped them off?'

'Your guess is as good as mine,' responded Michael. 'But I don't really think it was anything to do with her, to be honest. It's just the way it goes sometimes.' Jake was pleased to hear that Michael was sounding slightly less stressed about the fan encounter now, since it had really bothered him at the time.

'You wouldn't have any of this hassle with fans if you moved to Stockholm,' suggested Alexandra. Somehow, she could never resist singing the praises of her homeland.

'You just need to disguise yourself better,' commented Jake. 'I know you say you've tried in the past, but maybe you haven't tried hard enough.' Michael knew that his brother was only trying to help, but he obviously wasn't aware of the lengths he had gone to previously. 'Anyway, we had quite a shock when we got to the cinema,' continued Jake. Michael dug his brother in the ribs. He wasn't sure if he wanted to reveal this latest turn of events to anyone else just yet. Not until he'd had the chance to work it all out in his head first.

'Yes, I couldn't believe how many fans were waiting when we left,' Michael commented, looking sternly at his brother and hoping that he would pick up on his inferred message to keep quiet. Fortunately, it did the trick.

'Some more post arrived while you were out,' commented Krystal. 'There's a couple for you and one for Nicola.' Alexandra's ears pricked up. She couldn't believe that Michael's housekeeper was being so brazen about this other woman in front of her.

'Who's Nicola?' asked Jake, as Alexandra's heart skipped a beat.

'My secret wife!' laughed Michael, before noticing his girlfriend's face. 'Oh, darling, I'm joking. Nicola doesn't really exist.' He told her and his brother all about his alter-ego and how he had cleverly created an anagram of his own name to use for his charity activities. Alexandra felt the cloud lifting. She really shouldn't have doubted him so easily.

'Don't forget that neither Ted nor I are here

tomorrow lunchtime,' advised Krystal, changing the subject. 'We're going to pick Tim up from the hospital.' She'd had several conversations with their son on the phone since their visit to see him and had been busy getting everything ready for his arrival.

'That's come round fast!' exclaimed Michael. 'How exciting! Can't wait to meet him!' He'd heard so much about Tim from Krystal and had suggested that it might be nice for him to join them for meals in the main house, during his stay. 'How is he doing?' he asked.

'He sounds in really good spirits,' replied Krystal. 'His two friends are also being discharged from the hospital tomorrow. I might invite them to visit us at the weekend too. Would you mind?'

'I think that's a great idea!' responded Michael. 'I imagine it would be good for Tim's recovery if he had his friends here too.'

'Is he good looking?' asked Jake. Krystal looked quite taken aback.

Michael glared at his brother. 'You're a very different man from the one I used to know, Jake. Although I'm not complaining. It's quite refreshing, actually. I quite like this new you.'

'I'm only joking! You know me, all bark but no bite.' Jake looked a bit embarrassed and wondered if Krystal might now think of him as a potential predator where her son was concerned.

The house phone started ringing and Michael looked at Krystal, hoping she would answer it.

'Do you want me to get it?' asked Jake, taking them all by surprise.

'Yeah, why not?' said Michael. He loved how willing his brother was to help out.

They watched as Jake went over to the phone and picked up the receiver, using a voice that was a lot posher than his usual tone.

'Hambelton residence!' he announced. Although he didn't know this, it was standard procedure at Greengage Farm to answer the phone with a plain 'hello', to keep Michael's identity hidden. Michael's heart sank. But it was too late now.

After exchanging a few brief words with the caller, Jake beckoned his brother to the phone. 'It's Ricky!' he said, raising his eyebrows. He'd heard all about Michael's roguish manager and had taken an instant dislike to the man.

Krystal and Alexandra exchanged glances as Michael took hold of the receiver. He took a deep breath to try to calm himself before speaking.

'Hello! Long time, no hear!' he said, trying to sound as neutral as possible. He had been so angry with this man for such a long time, yet somehow, having Jake and Alexandra with him now, it didn't seem to matter quite so much.

Ricky sounded more buoyant than Michael ever remembered hearing him before. He apologised for going missing and asked Michael to forgive him for the way he'd been treating him recently. He had indeed checked into a substance abuse clinic in America and, as part of his therapy, had been told to contact all the people he had wronged in his life in order to put things right. Michael sat down on the stool next to the phone and gave the others a thumbs up, even though he was feeling a bit confused and wasn't quite sure where this call was heading.

His manager told Michael that he had already spoken with his wife and had confessed to numerous affairs. Unsurprisingly, she had taken this quite badly, and had told him that she wanted a divorce. Michael began to doubt the clinic's strategy, since it sounded a bit reckless for Ricky to be totally honest about everything so soon. He wondered if perhaps some things may have been best left unsaid.

What came next knocked Michael for six. Ricky told him that Alice had been on a mission to try to totally destroy him. Although he already knew about her book project, thanks to Alexandra, the way Ricky described it made it sound a lot worse than he had originally imagined. She had offered Ricky an unbelievable amount of money in exchange for his assistance. Ricky explained that he hadn't been in his right mind at the time and had agreed to co-operate with her, but was now convinced that this added pressure had pushed him over the edge. He had been in terrible debt when Alice had contacted him, due to a long-standing gambling habit, and had stupidly thought that working with her would be an easy way to restore his finances. Instead, it had just made things worse and he had hit breaking point. Michael sat there, listening to his manager in disbelief.

'You know that Alice has died?' asked Michael.

'I do. And I'm so sorry. But she really did have it in for you, Michael. She felt that you abandoned her after your parents died, although I know from what you've told me in the past that this isn't true.'

'She's the one who cut me out, and my brother too, actually,' explained Michael, determined to stress that the blame lay firmly at Alice's door. He chose not to mention that he was now reconciled with Jake and that he was actually with him in the same room.

'I guessed that was the case,' said Ricky. 'Funnily enough, I never actually met Alice, even though we were in this strange agreement together. Everything was done at a distance. She seemed a very odd woman, if I'm being totally honest.' *That's rich, coming from you*, thought Michael.

'She didn't used to be like that when we were kids.' Michael found himself saying, wondering why he was defending his sister. 'Although that all seems a lifetime ago now.'

'Well, I need to be selfish here and put myself first,' advised Ricky. Michael smiled to himself. Hadn't this always been Ricky's stance? 'Do you know she was financing a cinema?' he continued, obviously keen to dish the dirt. 'I get the impression she's left it in a terrible state, judging by the messages I've received.' Michael noticed that he didn't actually sound at all remorseful, especially since he was also involved with the cinema.

Michael wondered if he should put Ricky out of his misery and tell him that he now knew all about the cinema. He also chose not to mention that he and Alexandra were now an item. Ricky seemed to be on a mission to clean up his act but Michael still didn't trust him.

'There's something else I need to discuss with you,' confessed Ricky. 'I don't know if you realise, but my contract as your manager expires this month.' Michael was very much aware of this but remained silent. 'I think it might be best if we go our separate ways for now,' the guy continued. 'I'm certainly not strong enough to do the role justice at the moment.'

I don't think you ever were, thought Michael. Although he was still furious with Ricky, there was no point making matters worse. He would have loved to have given Ricky a piece of his mind but what would that actually achieve? In a way, he was relieved that his relationship with his manager would be officially over at long last, and that he could start looking for a suitable replacement now.

'As long as that's what you want,' said Michael.

'It is and I appreciate you taking it so well,'

concluded Ricky.

'Thanks for everything you've done for me in the past though, Ricky,' Michael uttered through gritted teeth. He smiled to himself. The only thing that he was thankful to Ricky for was introducing him to Alexandra.

'You're very welcome,' accepted Ricky, sounding very pleased with himself.

'Anyway, thanks for the call, Ricky. And promise me you'll take care of yourself,' said Michael. He guessed that there was still a part of him that did actually care about the guy.

'I will!' declared Ricky.

'Speak with you again soon,' said Michael, half-heartedly. He hung up and sat there in silence, trying to process the conversation they'd just had.

'So, what was that all about?' asked Jake.

'I'm not quite sure where to start,' commented Michael, as he went on to relay what Ricky had said. 'I guess that leaves me without a manager now,' he concluded. 'He wasn't very good but at least he was better than nothing.'

'Are you sure about that?' sniggered Krystal. Michael didn't respond.

'Couldn't I do it?' asked Jake, sounding very enthusiastic.

'It's a possibility,' replied Michael, not wanting to burst his brother's bubble. He knew that Jake wouldn't be aware of everything that was involved. The thought did cross his mind that he probably couldn't do a worse job than Ricky. 'I'm really shocked about Alice though,' Michael continued. 'I wonder if I'll ever get to the bottom of why she had it in for me? I bet she would have tried to get you involved at some point too, Jake, especially if she found out that you were working at the cinema.'

His brother's heart sank. He wasn't always the quickest on the uptake. 'I hadn't considered that.'

'What do you think about all of this?' Michael asked Alexandra. The words came out before he realised that it was obviously a delicate subject for her, since she had originally been part of Alice's scheme too.

'It's all a bit mysterious,' she responded. 'But sometimes things aren't that obvious, are they? There's a Swedish proverb that says, *in a good book, the best bits are between the lines*, and that seems quite appropriate right now.' Michael didn't quite see the significance of this but was finding Alexandra's Swedishness very cute.

Krystal went cold. She suddenly remembered that when she'd collected the post earlier, she'd kept an envelope to one side but had completely forgotten. She retrieved it and handed it to Michael. 'This looks important,' she commented. 'I should have given it to you as soon as you got back.'

Out of curiosity, Michael turned the envelope over and read the embossed seal: D. Patterson & Co. Solicitors. His heart sank; he really hoped this wasn't going to be another unwelcome surprise relating to Alice.

He sat back down at the table and tore the envelope open. He sensed everyone's eyes on him as he took out the letter and unfolded it. It reminded him of when he'd had to announce one of the winners at the Oscars ceremony a few months previously.

The letter advised him that Alice's inquest had been arranged for the following Tuesday. It also stated that the company was in possession of an original copy of her will, which she had had drawn up a couple of years previously. In it, she had left everything to her two brothers. As Michael read the letter out loud, he wondered what had changed in Alice's life for her to

---

377

leave half her estate to him one minute and then decide to try to break him the next. A lump came to his throat. Despite everything, she had still cared about him at one point.

The letter also stated that Alice had specifically stated that there should be no funeral service and that she wanted no-one to be in attendance when her body arrived at the crematorium either. Michael thought this quite sad, although he couldn't even imagine the media frenzy it would cause if he did attend. Maybe Alice had known this and had therefore planned it that way deliberately. The letter stated that a copy had also been sent to Jake's address.

He handed the letter to his brother, who read it through again and then looked at Michael, without saying a word. He was obviously struggling to make sense of this too.

'If that letter arrives at my home address, Sue is bound to open it and will have a field day,' he eventually said. 'Imagine if she sees that I have an inheritance coming,' Jake cringed, looking extremely concerned.

'Let's cross that bridge when we come to it,' suggested Michael. 'She won't know the sums of money involved. In fact, we don't even know that ourselves yet.'

'It's a shame we can't say goodbye to Alice though,' sighed Jake. 'Although maybe we can find a way for us to do something for her, just the two of us?'

'I'm sure we'll think of something,' said Michael, taking the letter back and handing it to his girlfriend to read.

'If this is meant to teach us anything, it's that we need to live our best lives,' concluded Jake. Michael remembered that his brother had a habit of coming out with profound statements like this.

'Never a truer word,' agreed Alexandra. 'And to

do that, I think we really need to find a way for you to live your best life, Michael. Are you going to let me work on this disguise, so you can go out into the big wide world without being recognised?'

'I can't even imagine that, but yes, I give you free rein to try anything,' Michael conceded.

'This is a lovely house and I can understand why you would want to spend so much time in it,' said Alexandra. 'But I really want you to be able to throw open the doors and live a full life outside these walls. As you know, I went to the shops while you were out this morning, because I had some ideas. Why don't we make a start this afternoon?'

Although Michael really couldn't imagine what Alexandra had in mind, he realised that she must have put a lot of thought into this. After the revelations at the cinema earlier, he really wasn't in the right frame of mind for trying new disguises. But he really didn't want to pour cold water on his girlfriend's ideas and felt he had no choice but to agree.

'Great idea!' he answered, taking her by the hand and kissing her. 'Let's go upstairs and make a start then.'

As they left the room, Jake looked at Krystal. 'I don't think there'll be much disguising going on up there this afternoon, do you?'

She chuckled. 'Want a slice of the Black Forest Gateau I made earlier?' she asked.

'You bet!' he replied. 'If Michael can have his cake and eat it, then so can I!'

Chapter 26
Patrick Swayze

Krystal had been very busy at home, preparing last minute things for her son's arrival. When she went back over to Michael's house, she was surprised to see someone she didn't recognise sitting at the table with Alexandra and Jake.

'This is my sister. I'm not sure if we mentioned that she'd be coming to visit?' explained Alexandra.

The woman looked vaguely familiar and Krystal was trying to work out whether there was any obvious family likeness with Alexandra when everyone around the table burst into hysterical laughter. Krystal looked at them all, bemused.

The visitor spoke first, 'It's me, Michael!'

Krystal blinked in disbelief. It certainly sounded like Michael but looked nothing like him at all.

Krystal stepped forward and examined the stranger more closely. She had red hair, piled quite high on her head, and was wearing an off the shoulder shawl, over a purple, high-necked dress. Even after closer inspection, Krystal still found it hard to believe that it really was Michael.

'It's good, isn't it?' commented Jake. 'I fell for it too. I can't believe what a transformation Alexandra has made. I might get her to do me next!'

'I can even do a new voice,' half-whispered Michael, in a high falsetto tone. 'Although I'm not sure how long I'll be able to keep it up for.' His voice broke and he coughed to clear his throat.

'We can work on that,' laughed Alexandra. 'I can always say you've just arrived from Sweden and don't speak much English, if we go out.'

'You'd never get away with that,' replied Michael, now using his normal voice again. 'I've never met a single Swede who doesn't speak perfect English.'

'Plus, Michael is very hard to shut up sometimes, so you wouldn't be able to keep him quiet for long,' added Jake. Michael shot his brother a glare and stuck out his tongue.

'Ooh, she's such a bitch!' scowled Jake.

Krystal was still trying to get her head round the fact that the fairly attractive woman sat at the table in front of her was Michael.

She shook her head. 'It's unbelievable, it really is. Well done, Alexandra! You've really fooled me and I imagine everyone else will be deceived too. I see Michael every day when he's at home, so you'd think I'd be able to see through the disguise, but I really can't.'

'That's the idea,' commented Alexandra. 'He … or should I say she … has promised to take me out for dinner tomorrow night to try out the new look in public.'

'Tim arrives tomorrow afternoon, doesn't he?' asked Michael, changing the subject and now having cold feet about going out in public.

'Yes, I spoke with him earlier. He's been having quite a nice time in the hospital with his two friends, believe it or not, despite still recovering from the accident. I know he's going to miss them both. Louis is going to stay at Brian's flat and I think Tim is a bit sad that he's not joining them.'

'We'll have to make sure it's fun for him while he's here,' suggested Michael.

'With you parading around the house looking like that, how could it not be fun?' chuckled Jake.

Krystal laughed. 'Oh, don't get me wrong, he is excited about coming and Brian and Louis are coming to see him at the weekend too.'

'That's great!' responded Michael. 'I'd like to meet them too.'

'It's going to be so strange having my baby boy living with me again,' beamed Krystal. 'Although, to be honest, I'm also a bit worried that Ted might accidentally say something out of place.'

'He doesn't have a problem with Tim now, though, does he?' asked Michael.

'No, not at all,' replied Krystal. 'But I guess this has been playing on my mind for so many years, that it's hard to suddenly accept that everything is now OK.' Michael got up and gave her a big hug.

'You might look very different, but you still smell the same,' chuckled Krystal.

Jake pulled another face. 'It's a good thing that the CK One cologne you're wearing is for both men and women. Imagine you looking all ladylike and smelling of Old Spice!' Everyone laughed.

Krystal looked down at Michael's feet and noticed that he was barefoot. 'Won't you need some ladies' shoes if you go out?' she asked.

'Alexandra has already thought of that. She's bought me a pair of very pretty flats and they fit perfectly. I'm glad she's not expecting me to wear stilettoes,' he replied. 'In fact, I can't believe that everything she's bought for me fits so well. She really is amazing. She didn't even measure me before she went out to buy all this stuff.' His girlfriend blushed, half-expecting Jake to make a smutty comment about her having already had enough experience of Michael's body to not need to measure him. Jake smiled at her mischievously but didn't say a word.

'Since we're going out for dinner tomorrow night, why don't you take the day off, Krys?' We can fend for ourselves for breakfast and lunch and Jake can come with us to the restaurant, if he wants to?'

'I've actually arranged to see Jason then,' declared Jake, proudly. 'I don't want to play the gooseberry with you two!' Jake turned his nose up as he looked at them in mock disgust.

'Suit yourself,' whispered Michael in a very camp voice, prompting them all to giggle again.

'Ooh, listen to her! She's getting all above herself already,' said Jake. 'She'll be mincing round the house like this all the time now, treating us all like we're her minions.' He studied his brother a bit further. 'Actually, Alexandra, I bet I know where you got your inspiration from.'

'Oh, here we go!,' laughed Michael. 'I dread to think what he's going to come out with now!'

'Patrick Swayze in *To Wong Fu?*' suggested Jake, looking very smug.

Alexandra nodded her head. 'You're totally right,' she admitted. 'I take it you've seen the film then?'

'I had to sneak off to the cinema without my lovely wife knowing,' reminisced Jake, sadly. 'Imagine what she would have made of me going to see a film about drag queens!'

'That's very sad, Jake,' consoled his brother. 'I'm sorry to say that I missed that film. I saw the other drag movie that was out at the same time though, *Priscilla, Queen of the Desert*.'

'I loved that one too!' gasped his brother. 'I bet you only saw it because of the ABBA connection though?' he added, laughing.

'I didn't even realise that there was an ABBA link before I saw it,' Michael replied. 'But it was an added bonus, I have to say. And what a great movie!'

Michael noticed that Krystal was staring into thin air, in total silence, seemingly lost in thought. 'Are you OK, Krys?' he asked.

'Yes, I'm just thinking that it would be really nice to have tomorrow off, if you're really sure?' she smiled. 'It will give me the opportunity to focus on Tim for the day. You'd better warn me when you're going to be dressing up like this again though. I'd probably prefer to introduce him to you when you look like a man,' she laughed.

'Oh, I don't know. Tim might quite like this new version of Michael,' consoled Jake. 'It's a big improvement on the old one.' His brother stuck his tongue out at him.

'Don't worry, Krys' Michael smiled. 'You can definitely take tomorrow off. And I hope Ted is taking my car to collect Tim. He should arrive here in style. We can get a local cab tomorrow night, when we go out for dinner.'

'How did I get to have such a wonderful, understanding boss?' asked Krystal.

Back in his room later that day, Jake decided to check his mobile phone. He was dismayed to find that there were several missed calls from Sue. She'd left him a couple of messages too. He listened to them cautiously and was instantly transported right back to the awful life he'd had with her. Against his better judgement, he hit the dial back button.

'It took you a while to call me back,' she spat. Her tone was accusatory to say the least and Jake's heart sank. He had been hoping that he'd never have to hear that voice again. The plan was that the solicitors would deal with everything, without him and his soon-to-be ex-wife having to have any direct contact ever again.

He tried to hold his nerve and to be as polite as he could, considering the circumstances.

'I got your messages. How are you?' he asked.

'I'll be better once I've got you properly out of my life,' she snapped. 'There's a letter that's come for you. I've opened it and your sister is leaving everything to you and that loser brother of yours.' Jake had been dreading the letter arriving but had known that it was inevitable. 'I know where you are,' Sue continued. 'I've seen pictures of you in the papers. You're staying with Mr Jumped Up Pop Star, aren't you?' She wasn't sounding best pleased about the situation, but Jake reminded himself that frankly, it had absolutely nothing to do with her now.

'I don't see why any of that matters to you,' he replied, defiantly.

'I suppose you think you're Mr High and Mighty now, don't you, hobnobbing with the stars?' Sue was sounding as bitter as ever. 'Well, I can only imagine just how much money that brother of yours has got and I hope you realise that I'll be going for half of that too. That'll wipe the smiles off your faces, won't it?'

For a brief moment, Jake wondered if Sue really would be able to get money from Michael. He decided he needed to end this conversation fast.

'I'm going,' he concluded, hanging up without giving her the opportunity to respond. He quickly turned the phone off and threw it onto the bed, before running downstairs.

Michael was still sitting at the kitchen table in his new disguise when Jake rushed in. He could tell by his brother's face that he was upset.

'What's wrong?' asked Michael, genuinely concerned.

Jake started crying. He sat down at the kitchen table with his head in his hands.

'Sue just called me!' he sobbed. Michael was shocked. He thought they'd agreed that his brother would leave everything to his legal team. 'She left me a message on my mobile phone, ordering me to call her back and I guess I got sucked in. But I'd forgotten how venomous she is. She says she's going to go for half of your money too!'

Michael laughed. 'There's no way she'll be able to do that, so don't worry. You're the injured party in all of this, anyway, after her bullying behaviour towards you and the fact that you caught her being unfaithful. Plus, she told you at the hospital that the house is in her father's name, so she's been misleading you all along too.' Jake looked at his brother, hoping that what he was saying was true. 'None of this is going to look good in court, is it?' Michael continued. 'If anything, you'll probably be able to claim something from her.'

'Do you really think so?' asked Jake.

'Listen,' Michael went on. 'I've been thinking about the solicitor's letter. I don't need any of Alice's money. You can have whatever she's left us. Although we need to make sure that Sue doesn't get her hands on any of it. We need to be quite clever here.' Jake was looking at him in disbelief. 'I'm guessing that our childhood home will be part of Alice's estate, along with whatever savings she may have had,' Michael continued. 'I'm not sure what will happen about the money she's fraudulently claimed from the state though. That might need paying back.'

Jake got up and threw his arms around his brother.

'You know you can stay living here forever, as far as I'm concerned, but you might like to have your own place sometime soon,' Michael suggested. 'You could probably even move back into our old family home, if you wanted to. You really don't have anything to worry about, Jake.'

His brother looked at him, still with tears in his eyes. 'Thank you so much,' he stammered. 'I really do love you, Brother.'

Chapter 27
Restaurant

As his father drove him through the impressive gates of Greengage Farm, Tim felt like he'd been transported into a parallel universe. One moment, he was saying a tearful farewell to his two friends at the hospital and the next he was being whisked off in a very flashy car to a massive, very imposing estate. He had already imagined just how awesome everything would be, but as he observed his current surroundings, reality was far exceeding his previous expectations. Brian and Louis had promised they'd come and visit him at the weekend and he couldn't wait for them to see this place. He wasn't intending to stay with his parents forever, but for now, he was more than happy with his lot.

Krystal rushed out to greet her son as the car arrived and hugged him gingerly. He did still look quite sorry for himself. But considering what the outcome of the crash could have been, his mother was very much counting her blessings. She had spent the last couple of days trying to make sure that everything would be just right for Tim's arrival.

As soon as he walked in, Tim felt at home in this new environment. He spent some time settling into his room and then had lunch with his parents in the kitchen. Krystal had been worrying about how things would go, especially with her husband and his less than tactful tongue, but she needn't have been concerned. There was no awkwardness at all

Once they'd finished their meal, Ted took Tim

for a quick tour of the house, and Krystal later found them snuggled up next to each other on the sofa in the lounge, watching a Tina Turner concert on TV. She remembered when the three of them had gone to see the rock legend at Wembley Arena, a few years earlier.

Ted and Tim both smiled at Krystal as she came in, before continuing to discuss Tina's amazing stage presence. It was so true that music broke down barriers, not that there seemed to be any between father and son now. Krystal squeezed in next to Tim on the sofa and found herself beginning to relax too, as she joined in with the easy family banter. After half an hour or so, she noticed that Tim had drifted off to sleep, which she took as a good sign.

The phone rang and Krystal jumped up to answer it, hoping that she might manage to get to it before it woke Tim. It was Pippa, calling to ask how her brother was settling in.

'Like a duck to water,' replied Krystal, sounding extremely relieved. 'He's in the lounge watching Tina Turner with your dad. Although he's just fallen asleep, which I'm pleased about.'

'That's brilliant news!' exclaimed Pippa. 'Do you think it will be OK if I come to visit sometime soon?'

'Of course, Darling! You know you're welcome here at any time!' The two women chatted for a while in German. Krystal absolutely loved being able to speak her mother tongue with both her children and wished that her own parents were still alive to witness it.

Once they'd finished their call, Krystal went back into the lounge and stood there for a moment, taking in the peaceful scene of her husband and son fast asleep next to each other on the sofa. It was so magical to be able to spend some quality family time with them and she was now looking forward to her daughter joining them too.

The following afternoon, Jake took a taxi into Lewes. Michael had offered for Ted to drive him there, but Jake had insisted that he was more than capable of taking a cab. Besides, Ted was needed by his family right now.

During the journey, Jake reflected on how much he was enjoying not having a car, although Michael had offered to buy him one, if he so desired.

Jake had agreed to meet Jason at the cinema and he couldn't wait to see both his handsome friend and Madeleine too. When he arrived, he was surprised to find just how busy it was with customers and lots of staff on duty. It was the busiest he had ever seen it and he made a mental note to tell his brother, who would undoubtedly be really pleased to know that he was investing his money wisely. He almost had to fight his way to the bar to see Jason, who seemed really happy to see him.

Things eventually calmed down once the majority of the punters started making their way towards the cinema's main screen to watch the latest Jim Carrey film, *Liar Liar*.

Jake was pleased to finally be the centre of attention and everyone was full of questions about his new life and especially about his brother. At first, he found himself bragging a bit, but then he saw the look of disapproval on Madeleine's face. He suddenly remembered how discreet she had been when she had met Michael, and realised that perhaps it would be best if he tried to take a leaf out of her book. He quickly turned the conversation around to discuss what everyone else had been up to, which resulted in Madeleine giving him a big beaming smile. He continued making small talk with everyone and it wasn't long before Jason finished his shift, and they were able to leave.

Jake had been really looking forward to spending some quality time with Jason and loved the way his friend drove like a maniac around the local streets.

Once they arrived at Jason's, Jake quickly checked on his belongings, deciding to get the task done straight away. He made sure that everything was in a fit state to be collected by the courier. Although he'd never technically unpacked, he had frantically rummaged in both cases during his brief stay there previously. By packing a bit better, he managed to fit all his videos into one of the cases. Once he was satisfied that everything was ship-shape for collection, he went back down to join his friend.

Jason had promised to cook them both dinner and Jake was relieved that Angie hadn't been invited to join them. He was also impressed that Jason was mindful enough to not even mention her name.

After eating, they spent the evening catching up on recent events. They lost all track of time and it was gone midnight by the time that Jake booked his cab back to Michael's.

Earlier that evening, Alexandra had got Michael ready for their night out on the town. It seemed to take her considerably less time than the previous day and within forty-five minutes, she had finished doing his make-up, hair and clothes. She guessed that this time, she'd known exactly what she needed to do. It was no longer a test, it was a *fait accompli*. She decided that Michael looked even more convincing tonight - maybe because he was getting into the role a bit more. He certainly seemed a lot more comfortable with his new disguise.

They had booked a cab to drive them into Arundel centre. Michael had been told that there was a really nice Italian bistro there, on the opposite side of the road to the castle, half way up the steep hill. Alexandra had reserved a table for two in a false name.

Over the years, Michael had heard so many good things about the restaurant, but had obviously never dared to venture there previously, knowing that he would be instantly recognised and bothered all evening by people wanting autographs and photos.

The taxi was collecting them from home, and just the thought of walking through the gates felt very scary to Michael. Under normal circumstances, he wouldn't ever consider doing this, since it would be nothing short of walking into a lion's cage.

When the car arrived to collect them, Alexandra took Michael's hand and he nervously triggered the gates to open. They stepped outside and started to make their way down the driveway, with Michael doing his best to try to walk like a woman. He almost forgot himself at one point and raised his arm to wave at three waiting fans, but Alexandra quickly noticed this and tugged on his hand, reminding him that he was in disguise. Michael chuckled to himself as they got into the car. The fans were totally oblivious as to how close they currently were to their idol.

The couple kept conversation to a minimum in the cab to try to avoid giving the game away to the driver, and when they did speak, they used hushed tones. Alexandra squeezed Michael's hand, reassuringly.

They'd asked to be dropped off round the corner from the restaurant and Michael continued to make a big effort to walk in a more feminine way. He felt he carried it off quite well, despite a couple of small stumbles. It didn't help that the restaurant was on such a steep hill.

They were given a table in the corner, which pleased Michael since it was away from the main area, where tables had been set up for larger groups. After browsing the menu, he let Alexandra order the food. He still couldn't believe that he was getting away with this. Everyone seemed completely oblivious to the fact that they had a global superstar amongst them. Time and time again, he forgot that he was wearing a disguise and flinched whenever anyone came near. He realised that if this continued to work, he would be eternally grateful to Alexandra for opening up a whole new world for him.

The evening was such a big success. Once they were safely back home, Michael completely forgot that he was still dressed as a woman and tried to kiss Alexandra. He was shocked when she backed off, insisting that they transform him back into his usual male persona before they considered getting amorous.

When Jake went downstairs the following morning, he was greeted by quite a crowd in the kitchen. Krystal and Ted had brought Tim over to meet everyone and they were all enjoying brunch around the kitchen table. Even Othello and Tobias were in attendance, sitting together under their preferred human's chair.

Jake stopped in his tracks. He hadn't even considered that Tim would be quite so good looking, even with the scars on his face. Jake joined the group and before long, as the newcomer, was the centre of their conversation. He quickly noticed that he and Tim had a lot in common. They'd studied the same subjects at A level and had both worked in cinemas. It was soon quite obvious that there was a rapport building between them and when Krystal and her family finally returned to their own property, Jake couldn't help but ask Michael what he thought of Tim.

His brother laughed. 'Down, Boy! You've only just met him.'

Jake was quite offended. 'All I'm saying is that

he seems like a really nice guy.'

'I think he is. Let's just give the poor man time to settle in before you pounce on him,' advised Michael. 'I'm sure we'll get to know him a lot better while he's here.'

Interestingly, Krystal was having a very similar conversation with Tim, who was equally smitten with Jake. She found it quite endearing that her son felt able to confide in her but was surprised at how enamoured he was with Michael's brother, after just one meeting.

She wasn't sure how she felt about a romance blossoming right before her eyes. She concluded that it would be nice if Tim could find some happiness in his life, especially after his recent traumatic experience. She just hadn't expected this to happen quite so close to home. Krystal couldn't help but wonder how Ted would feel about it. She decided that frankly, that was his problem, not hers.

Chapter 28
Unwelcome Guest

The next three months flew by. Michael and Alexandra's relationship had gone from strength to strength and it really did feel as if they had been together much longer than they actually had. Apart from a short UK promotional tour and a couple of very brief foreign trips, Michael had been enjoying his time at home.

Alice's inquest had concluded that she had died of brain damage, internal bleeding and broken ribs, as a result of the crash. The boys had been truly shocked by the extent of her injuries. Every day, they reminded themselves just how lucky they were to have survived such a horrific accident.

They were also glad not to be questioned any further by the authorities. They had been approached several times by journalists, keen to get the boys' inside story, but after a group discussion, they had declined the proposals, out of respect for both Alice and her brothers. They really had no interest in slandering their friend's name any further, even though the money offered had been very tempting.

Michael and Jake had been worried that perhaps they might be called in to identify Alice's body and were relieved when they were told that one of the doctors at the hospital had recognised her name from a previous meeting, and had subsequently been able to confirm that it was her. Having read all about their sister's antics in the press, it had become evident to the brothers just how often she must have visited local clinics and hospitals to substantiate her fraudulent benefit claims. No wonder one of the doctors had been able to identify her.

The date for Alice's funeral had been set, but as per her wishes, neither Michael, Jake or the other three boys were planning to attend. The two brothers had racked their brains to find a suitable way to celebrate Alice's life, which they planned to do on the same day as the funeral. When Brian had mentioned that he had a spare key to Alice's former home in Rottingdean, both Michael and Jake had thought the same thing: wouldn't it be fitting if perhaps they could spend some time in the garden of their childhood home to commemorate their sister's life and to reflect on much happier times. At first, Brian had been quite hesitant about letting them use the key, but he soon realised just how much this would mean to Michael and Jake.

Brian, Louis and Tim had subsequently asked the brothers if there would be any chance of them also coming along, since they also wanted to say goodbye to Alice in some way. Michael and Jake had readily agreed, keen to show their gratitude to Brian for making things easier by providing the key. Their only stipulation was that they be left alone in the garden for a while, so they could say their own, personal farewell to Alice. Brian was pleased with this arrangement too, since he wouldn't technically be handing the key over to anyone if he was also going to be in attendance. He signed the visit off with the solicitor handling Alice's estate, who agreed that as long as nothing was removed from the property and that the key was handed over to him for safe keeping afterwards, then there wouldn't be a problem.

Michael was extremely relieved that nobody had found out that he was going back to his childhood home. The street was deserted when Ted dropped them off. Rather than cause attention by parking the flashy car outside, he'd suggested waiting elsewhere until Michael called him to say that they were ready to be picked up.

They'd collected the other boys on the way and it felt very strange for all of them as they entered the house. Neither Michael nor Jake had been inside it for years. They wondered if they would notice any major alterations, but it turned out that Alice had changed absolutely nothing, although they suspected that this was down to convenience, rather than nostalgia. It all looked virtually the same as the last time they had been there. So much so that they even found their parents' clothes still hanging in the wardrobes. They also recognised the familiar furniture, wallpaper and even the bedding in all the bedrooms.

As the brothers went out into the garden, the others went into the dining room, preparing a cold buffet of sandwiches, crisps and cakes they'd bought that morning in the large Marks & Spencer branch in Brighton centre. The three of them had thankfully made a full physical recovery now and apart from a couple of small scars on their faces, which they were managing to cleverly hide with concealer, there was no obvious evidence that the accident had ever happened. They were still suffering from mental trauma though, especially Louis, and had started group therapy sessions, which Michael had insisted on paying for. It was definitely helping.

Michael and Jake noticed that the layout of the garden hadn't changed either, apart from the familiar bushes and trees looking quite a bit larger. In some ways, it really did feel like it was just yesterday that they had all been out there as a family. They took a seat on a bench at the bottom of the garden, where they couldn't be seen from the main house, and sat in silence for a while, each caught up in his own private thoughts.

'Rest in peace, Alice,' said Jake, eventually. 'I'm sorry things turned out the way they did. But we both wish you well, don't we, Michael?' He sounded quite matter of fact.

'We really do,' agreed his brother. 'And we have some wonderful memories of you,' he added. 'You'll always have a very special place in our hearts.'

Michael looked at his brother and smiled. 'Do you remember what Alice's favourite ABBA song was?' he asked.

'Of course I do,' chuckled his brother. ''Happy Hawaii'! I can still picture her face when we played it for the first time and she discovered that her name was mentioned in the lyrics.'

'Do you remember how we discovered the song?' asked Michael.

'Didn't we go through Mum and Dad's singles and find that some of ABBA's B-sides weren't on their albums?' asked Jake.

'Exactly that!' confirmed Michael. 'I think 'Happy Hawaii' was on the flip side of 'Knowing Me, Knowing You'.'

'I wonder if she ever got to Hawaii?' pondered Jake, jokingly.

'Well if she didn't, I guess she can go anywhere she wants now,' suggested Michael.

After a brief pause, Michael shared something that had been playing on his mind for a very long time. 'Do you think it's strange that Mum died so soon after Dad?' he asked.

Jake looked at him, slightly taken aback. 'I hadn't actually thought about that before.'

'Both of them were in their early fifties when they died. I've always thought that was quite odd. I just hope that, knowing what we do about Alice now, that she didn't do anything to precipitate Mum's death.'

'Surely she wouldn't have done that?' queried Jake.

'I hope not and I guess there's not much we can do about it now, anyway,' pondered Michael. 'Plus, there was an inquest after Mum died and I'm sure they would have discovered foul play, if there had been any. I think all this stuff we have learnt about Alice since she died just makes me question everything.'

'That's understandable. I think it's best we don't dwell on it though.' Jake replied. 'You could imagine all sorts, really. But it's not going to bring either of them back.'

They looked at each other and realised that being there didn't feel quite as emotional as they had expected. If anything, it just felt surreal. It was as if they had travelled back in time and were children again, sitting in the garden of their family home. They half expected their parents, Alice and even Eve to suddenly appear at any moment, and both of them would have given anything for that to actually happen.

The brothers had been beyond astounded when they'd learnt just how much Alice had inherited from their parents, since neither of them had been aware of any of their father's investments. The fact that she had been subsequently making fraudulent benefit claims for many years also, despite her enormous inherited wealth, chilled them to the core. How could their sister have been so conniving? Although neither of them had been involved in her illegal activities, they agreed that they both felt slightly guilty, in some kind of strange family association way.

Realising that their job here was done, they headed back into the house, where the three friends had already put all the food out, still in its original packaging, on the dining room table. Rather than make hot drinks in the house, they had bought some small bottles of water. Brian had been so paranoid about not touching anything that even making a pot of tea would have felt like he was breaking the rules.

It felt odd to be sitting around the dining table without Alice. Louis was brave enough to comment that she'd have really enjoyed this free lunch if she'd been there, which broke the sombre atmosphere and made them all laugh. It was obvious by the speed at which they all ate that none of them wanted to linger any longer than they had to, so within minutes, Brian was throwing the remnants of their lunch back into the Marks & Spencer carrier bag to take home with him. Michael called Ted to come and collect them.

As they closed the front door behind them, Jake found himself reflecting on something that Michael had said about him possibly moving back into this house. Although it was kind of his brother to suggest this, he had come to the conclusion that he would much rather sell it and buy a different property with the proceeds. He knew that he wouldn't feel at all comfortable living here again and shared this with Michael, who understood completely. The house contained far too many memories. Jake really needed to find somewhere of his own - a fresh start was the best thing, rather than trying to revisit the past.

Although Jake absolutely adored living with his brother, he'd decided it was only fair that he should now give him some space. He knew that he didn't want to leave the Brighton area, having only ever lived in Rottingdean and Hove. And since Michael had now put him in charge of the cinema in Lewes, commuting there from Brighton was very convenient too. Especially since

Michael had bought him a brand new Volkswagen Golf for his recent birthday.

Things at the Griffin Cinema had been going really well since Michael had taken over its finances. When he had first suggested that Jake become involved, his brother had initially planned on taking a back seat and letting Madeleine continue to look after everything. It wasn't long before Michael realised that she needed some on-site support though, and he managed to convince Jake that he should try to go in at least three days a week to help her. It would give him a purpose too, which Michael thought was what he really needed. Remarkably, the press hadn't picked up on the story of Alice having invested in the cinema.

After a couple of weeks of staying with his parents, Tim had finally moved in with Brian and Louis. However, he had very quickly started to feel like a gooseberry. His two friends had become romantically involved quite soon after leaving hospital, and even though they had been very discreet about it and made sure to include Tim in almost everything they did, he couldn't help but feel in the way. The fact that Tim had once dated Louis only added to the awkwardness. He had therefore moved back in with Krystal and Ted within days. Not only did he love living with his parents at Greengage Farm, but there was also the added advantage of being able to spend more time with Jake.

Michael's manager, Ricky, was now back in the UK. His treatment at the Betty Ford Center had gone exceptionally well and he was now feeling in fine form again. He had reunited with his wife, who had now somehow forgiven him for his affairs. He was still sticking with his decision to retire from show business.

Michael hadn't yet done anything about finding a new manager, although he knew it was something he needed to do fairly quickly, especially with a brand-new album about to be released. So far, he had been managing his day-to-day professional needs himself, with the help of Jake and Alexandra, although he knew that this wouldn't work at all once things started to crank up.

Ricky had asked for a meeting to be set up, so he could hand over some gold and platinum discs he'd been looking after, together with some fan mail he had for Michael. It was anyone's guess how long he had been in possession of these things and at first, Michael had been very hesitant to see him. He had eventually relented, and had suggested they meet at Greengage Farm. Ricky had happily agreed and had even asked if he could bring along his wife. Michael had never met Joan before, and was quite intrigued. Jake was very keen to meet Ricky too, after hearing so many crazy stories about him, so an afternoon tea had been planned.

Michael was still feeling very angry with Ricky but wanted to show him that the Michael Hambelton empire was still going strong, despite his lack of support over the last couple of years. He knew that Krystal would pull out all the stops to make everything just as impressive as if a top London hotel was hosting the event.

When Alexandra had heard that Ricky was coming to the house, she had refused point blank to be involved. She was embarrassed to face him now that she was in a proper relationship with Michael, and the last thing she wanted was for him to take the credit for introducing them. She decided to head into Brighton for the afternoon instead.

Although Michael's current opinion of Ricky was at an all-time low, he still felt very nervous as his soon to be ex-manager's arrival approached. He was pacing around the house like a caged tiger, despite requests from Krystal and Jake to sit down and relax.

When the doorbell finally sounded and Michael opened the door, he was shocked when he saw the lady standing next to Ricky. She looked nothing like the Joan he had pictured in his head all these years. Everything became clear once Ricky had inflicted his signature bear hugs on everyone. He still reeked of that awful cologne, as did everybody else now that he had crushed them with his embraces.

Ricky introduced the lady who was accompanying him as his 'business associate', Cleo de Mendes. Michael had always tried to make a point of not judging a book by its cover, but with her extremely low-cut top and a skirt that would probably best be described as a belt, he found himself thinking that there was only one type of business that Ricky was conducting with this extremely glamorous woman. She was from Brazil, and had met Ricky soon after he had left the American clinic, whilst she had been on a short visit to Los Angeles. Michael was very tempted to ask Ricky about his wife Joan, but decided that this would probably not be the best start to the afternoon's proceedings. It soon became quite apparent that Cleo wasn't exactly the sharpest tool in the box. She didn't seem able to keep her hands off Ricky for longer than a few seconds at a time either. Michael knew the man of old and was aware that he was very fond of splashing the cash where female company was concerned. She certainly wasn't with him for his sparkling personality or his good looks.

Ricky was in full bragging mode and at one point, he advised everyone present that he'd had the good fortune to win a substantial sum on the National Lottery, which had paid off all his debts and had left him with enough money to enable him to live a very comfortable life for the rest of his days. Michael had two thoughts about this: firstly, that Ricky's extravagant lifestyle would require a bottomless pit of money to sustain permanently, and secondly, what did this say about his commitment to give up gambling completely? No wonder Cleo was being so amorous - she may as well have had dollar signs in her eyes each time she gazed at her beau.

It was really sad to find that Ricky was still so shallow, since Michael had had such high hopes for him when he'd come out of the clinic. He guessed it was true about a leopard never changing its spots.

True to form, Ricky came out with several put downs during the afternoon. The first was when he first entered the house and, keeping his sunglasses on, commented on the property having such small rooms. He had only ever been there once before, and hadn't got further than the hallway on that occasion, after coming to hand over some documents for Michael to sign. He was still in the entrance hall today when he made his comment too, so it was anyone's guess what he was basing this observation on. In reality, the majority of the rooms at Greengage Farm were enormous, although Michael found himself questioning this after Ricky's throwaway comment. The man really did have such an annoying way of getting under your skin. Another ludicrous comment that he made was that you should never trust anyone with thin lips, as it was a well-known fact that this facial characteristic signified that the person couldn't be trusted. Needless to say, they'd all checked their lips in the mirror later that day.

As the afternoon dragged on, Michael concluded that, as usual, Ricky was enjoying having an audience. At one point, he shocked everyone by saying that it was such a shame that his former client had never taken his advice to have some facial work done.

'Your teeth are so crooked and discoloured, Michael,' he commented. 'You really should get them fixed. I've told you that many times before. There's so much that can be done to improve your appearance these days. They'd even be able to sort out your eye bags, I'm sure.' Michael was certain that he heard Krystal gasp at that last quip.

'Thanks, Ricky, I'll bear it in mind.' Michael didn't know how else to respond. He'd heard these kinds of comments from the man before, but still found them quite shocking. It wasn't as if Ricky was an oil painting himself. Rather than make a big thing of it, Michael chose to change the subject.

'So, what are your plans now?' he asked.

Ricky looked quite sheepish. 'I've not made any fixed plans yet. I'm just enjoying life at the moment.' Michael couldn't remember a time when Ricky hadn't enjoyed his life.

There was only one of Ricky's comments that Michael took particular exception to. When the food was ready, he had looked at the impressive buffet that Krystal had prepared for them, and uttered under his breath to Cleo that the standard wasn't very good. He had even implied, again in a stage whisper, that the only thing they'd be able to eat was the chips. Michael really hoped that Krystal hadn't heard this, and as soon as he got the opportunity, he whispered into Ricky's ear that if he really did feel that way about the food, then he would gladly show him the door. His manager, of course, denied having ever made such a comment and happily tucked in to everything on offer.

To say that everyone was relieved when Ricky and his lady friend left was an understatement. There was a communal sigh and Jake confessed that Ricky was far worse than he had ever imagined, with Krystal adding that he was probably the most horrible person she had ever encountered. They both agreed that Michael deserved a medal for having put up with him for so long.

Krystal also said it was a shame that Tim and Pippa hadn't been there to witness Ricky's outlandish behaviour, as they would have found it very entertaining. Tim was out with Brian and Louis, on a day trip to London. He had wanted Jake to join them too, but Jake didn't want to miss the opportunity to meet the infamous Ricky, so had declined the invitation. Michael had suggested inviting Pippa along to the afternoon tea, but Krystal had explained that she was currently in America, where her husband had business. He was very glad that Alexandra had ducked out of the meeting though, since he wasn't sure she'd have been able to hold her tongue, especially when Ricky had started hurling his insults.

Needless to say, Michael was very relieved to have got the meeting with Ricky out of the way, and it felt quite liberating to be able to officially cut ties with his obnoxious now ex-manager. But he still had the unenviable task of recruiting a replacement. He resolved to ask someone at the record company to appoint an agency to scout for possible candidates immediately.

Chapter 29
The Question

As summer approached, Michael encouraged Alexandra to give up her rented flat in Stockholm, since things seemed to be working out really well for the two of them, living together at his sumptuous home. She had been on several short trips to Stockholm since then, each time bringing back some of her belongings. Together with Michael, she was planning on joining a few of her cousins at the family summerhouse on an island in the Stockholm archipelago for midsummer, and had arranged to hand back the keys to her flat the day before. Michael had been hesitant about the trip at first, afraid as always of media and fan intrusion, but Alexandra had assured him that he wouldn't be bothered by anyone whilst there. He couldn't even imagine that such a place existed, but eventually gave in. Alexandra was also very keen to show Michael some more of Stockholm, so they had decided to spend three nights at the Grand Hotel at the beginning of their Swedish holiday.

It had taken Michael a matter of hours, after arriving in the Swedish capital, to realise why Alexandra loved her home city so much: the picturesque old town, the stunning architecture and the fact that you were never very far away from a beautiful waterside vista, all made this place heaven on earth. He'd been here on tour before, but had never really had the opportunity to explore the city properly. His usual experience of it was being holed up in a hotel room.

He very quickly learnt that far less people would

be hassling him here - just a few tourists perhaps, but certainly none of the city's residents. The Swedes seemed far too cool and respectful to bother with celebrities. They may cast a knowing look in your direction, but all interest seemed to end there. Alexandra had even persuaded Michael that there was no need for him to be in disguise whenever he went out, so chilled was the atmosphere of the Swedish capital.

It didn't take long for Michael to start imagining perhaps living there one day, although he decided not to share this with his girlfriend, in case she started to build her hopes up.

It felt weird to Michael that it hardly ever got dark at the height of summer in Stockholm. It started to get a bit dusky around midnight but then brightened up again within an hour or two. The weather was also very different from when he had last been there for his concerts, when there had been snow on the ground and it had been freezing cold outside.

For their first two nights' dinners in Stockholm, Alexandra had booked Berns, the restaurant where they had first got to know each other. On their last night, for convenience more than anything, they had decided to eat at the hotel. They had planned on meeting in the hotel bar, once Alexandra had handed back the keys of her flat to the landlord.

Michael was feeling very relaxed as he climbed onto a stool in the hotel bar. Since his arrival, not a single person had bothered him within the confines of the hotel. He glanced around the room and an idea suddenly came to him: he'd never really considered it before but why not propose to Alexandra tonight? There was no actual guarantee that she would accept but he was fairly certain that she wouldn't turn him down.

Michael ordered a 'Shirley Temple' mocktail.

He'd never tried this particular drink before but it came highly recommended by the barman. Even before Michael had taken his first sip, he had devoured the maraschino cherries adorning it. He was starving and made the decision to head into the restaurant for dinner, instead of waiting for Alexandra to arrive. He did wonder if perhaps he should try to be a bit more patient, especially since this could turn out to be a very important night for them, but concluded that he should try to act as if this was just another regular dinner. He took his drink and sauntered into the Veranda restaurant.

A very smartly dressed waiter showed him to a table and explained about the *smörgåsbord* that was on offer. Michael just needed to join the queue when he was ready and then select what he wanted from the sumptuous food on display.

It wasn't long before Michael gave in. He hoped his girlfriend would understand if he was already eating when she arrived. He was almost in ecstasy as he observed all the mouth-watering delicacies on offer, including healthy, refreshing salads, gravad lax, pickled herring and tempting cheeses to name but a few.

Snapping him out of his reverie, he heard a familiar voice behind him. 'The smoked salmon is delicious,' advised a slightly accented Swedish voice. 'I can really recommend it.' He turned round and chuckled. He hadn't spotted Alexandra coming in.

'Oh, can you now?' he asked. He kissed her on the lips. 'How did it go back at the flat?'

'Mission accomplished,' she declared. 'You'd better not throw me out now, or I'll be homeless!'

'Can you really imagine me doing that?' asked Michael, looking genuinely concerned that she might even consider this to be a possibility. If only she knew what he was planning to do later.

They put some food onto their plates and returned to their table. Alexandra recounted everything that had happened back at the flat and as she chatted away, Michael noticed just how much more relaxed she seemed, back in her home city, compared to in Britain. During the evening, he occasionally glanced around the restaurant and concluded that none of the other diners seemed at all bothered about having a famous pop star in their presence. He mentioned this to Alexandra who just beamed at him.

When they'd finished their meal, Michael suggested they get some fresh air, so led Alexandra outside into the cool Swedish summer's evening. The view was simply stunning with the Royal Palace opposite. Its golden reflection reminded Michael of an Impressionist painting, with bright colours like brushstrokes dancing in the water. He linked his arm through Alexandra's.

'I think you like Stockholm, don't you? she asked.

'That might be the understatement of the century,' he laughed.

They took a slow walk along the waterside, hand in hand. Michael loved how there was so much water in Stockholm and as he gazed at the view in front of him, he concluded that he was totally falling in love with this city. He was getting to know it really well now and could easily recognise some of the main landmarks.

'I feel like I'm in the middle of ABBA's 'Summer Night City' video,' he commented.

Alexandra loved how important ABBA's music was to Michael and how he knew their lyrics and videos off by heart.

'I wish they knew how significant they were to you,' she said.

'Well if we bump into them whilst we're walking along, you can tell them,' he laughed.

He decided that there was no time like the present for his proposal. He suddenly stopped, tugging gently at Alexandra's hand so that she would also come to a halt.

'What's wrong?' she asked.

'There's nothing wrong, my darling,' he smiled. 'I just want to ask you something.' With that he got down on one knee.

Alexandra gasped. 'What are you doing?' she asked, sounding somewhat flustered.

Michael took a ring off his own finger and offered it up to Alexandra. A couple of passers-by stopped, realising what was happening. One of them started taking photographs. For once in his life, Michael didn't care.

'Will you marry me?' he asked.

There were tears in Alexandra's eyes. 'Of course, I'll marry you, you wonderful man!' she spluttered emotionally. Michael had never seen her look so overcome.

He slid the ring onto her finger. 'Don't laugh! You can choose your own engagement ring, but I still needed one to be able to propose.'

Alexandra shook the oversized ring on her finger and giggled. 'That's a lovely idea. I'll choose the most expensive one in the shop!' She searched his face for a reaction but could only see pure joy in his eyes.

'If that makes you happy, then why not?' Michael got back up and held his future bride in his arms for the longest time as the nearby tourist continued snapping away.

Alexandra eventually broke the silence. 'I'm glad I brought you here now,' she whispered into his ear.

'Thank you so much for doing that,' he sighed,

easing back so he could look her in the eyes. 'I have to say that, like you, Stockholm has far exceeded all my wildest expectations. I don't think I ever want to leave!'

Alexandra smiled and snuggled up close to him. 'Who says you have to?' she asked, planting another kiss on his lips.

Chapter 30
Wedding Day

The British summer was being as unpredictable as ever. Over the last few weeks, there'd been a heatwave, followed by several days of heavy rain. There'd even been hailstones! Being his usual anxious self, Michael had been worrying about extreme weather ruining their wedding day - probably the most important day of his life - so was relieved when he watched the weather forecast on TV that morning and saw that a sunny day with average September temperatures was expected.

The news of Princess Diana's death in Paris at the end of August had briefly cast a shadow over everything. Although he had never met her, Michael had always been in awe of the princess and had been constantly touched whenever he'd seen reports of her charitable endeavours. He was sure that if they'd met, they would have become great friends, since they seemed to have the same mindset regarding humanitarian issues.

For Michael and his brother, Diana's death also opened up the still very fresh wound caused by their sister's death, just a few months previously. It was ironic that the princess had died in Paris, so soon after Alice and the boys' own fateful trip there.

Everyone at Greengage Farm had gathered around the television to watch the funeral service and they had all been in floods of tears, finding it incomprehensible that Princess Diana was now gone. Michael and Alexandra had been so heartbroken by the news that they had even considered postponing their

413

wedding at one point, but had eventually concluded that it was far too late for that.

'That reminds me of something that Princess Diana is meant to have said when she had second thoughts about her marriage to Prince Charles, the night before their wedding,' Michael explained to Alexandra, when they'd discussed postponing their nuptials as a mark of respect. 'Apparently her sister told her it was too late for that because the commemorative tea-towels had already been printed.'

Alexandra pulled a serious face. 'I wouldn't be at all surprised if there were commemorative tea-towels being sold to celebrate our wedding. Your fans will buy anything!'

'They're not quite that bad,' laughed Michael. 'Although I have seen some strange things for sale in the past that were definitely not authorised.'

The couple had decided to host the event at Herstmonceux Castle, in East Sussex. They had been very impressed with the venue when they had gone to visit it, and around 400 guests had been invited. The majority of Michael's fellow musician friends had confirmed their attendance and there was no doubt that the paparazzi would have a field day, snapping everyone as they arrived at the venue in their cars. A local security firm had been employed to assure everybody's safety. The couple had secured an exclusive deal with a celebrity magazine to cover the event and were planning on giving the proceeds to a local charity. The photographers had promised to be very discreet and Michael and Alexandra were going to pose for some official pictures once the wedding breakfast was over.

The wedding party had taken over the whole castle, which made Michael feel very relaxed, knowing that the chances of him being confronted by a stranger demanding a photo or autograph in the hotel complex were quite slim. So far, everything had been just perfect and the hotel staff couldn't have been any more accommodating.

The castle had been a feature of the Sussex countryside for centuries and had been restored at the beginning of the nineteen hundreds, after having fallen into disrepair. Its impressive turrets, moat and drawbridge gave it the semblance of being from a different era and the couple agreed that it was just how they imagined a fairy tale castle to be. The inside of the building had been refurbished to match the castle's history too and the Elizabethan gardens and parklands surrounding the castle were simply breathtaking.

The wedding ceremony was taking place in the hotel ballroom, with seats set out neatly in rows for the invited guests to watch the 'wedding of the year', as the press was calling it. A marquee had been erected in the grounds to host the wedding breakfast and subsequent party.

Jake had been over the moon when Michael had asked him to be his best man. Things had been going from strength to strength for him too recently, and his life was a far cry from his previous unhappy existence. Thanks to Michael generously donating his half of the proceeds of Alice's estate to Jake, he was now in the process of buying a lovely apartment in Kemptown, Brighton, with a beautiful sea view.

Although Alice couldn't be prosecuted for illegally claiming benefits now that she was dead, Michael had decided to give a large sum of money to a children's charity to try to exonerate his sister's memory. The press had initially gone absolutely crazy with the revelations about her fraudulent activities but, as was often the case with these sensational stories, they had eventually got bored with the story and moved on to something else. 'Today's news is tomorrow's fish and chip wrapper,' Alexandra had announced, showing off her perfect command of the English language.

In a strange twist of fate, Alice's family home had been snapped up, even before it had gone on the market, by Michael's ex-manager Ricky. Although everyone was expecting him to either pull out or declare that he no longer had the necessary funds, the sale seemed to be proceeding very smoothly and contracts had already been exchanged. Ricky had confirmed that he was well aware that if the outstanding monies weren't transferred in time, then he would be in very deep trouble. He had assured Michael and his solicitors that the funds would definitely be there. Completion on both Alice's home and Jake's new one were imminent and Tim was planning on moving in with Jake, once he got the keys.

Michael and Jake had arranged for a house clearance company to empty Alice's former home of all her personal effects. They had both thought it strange that no family photos had been found, but had put this down as just another of Alice's odd idiosyncrasies. Michael was relieved to hear that there was no trace of the alleged book which his sister had apparently been writing about him either. There were, however, a couple of pieces of jewellery which had been given to Michael for safe keeping. Ricky had asked if he could keep all the furniture, since his ex-wife Joan was being very difficult about him having anything from their marital home. *How the mighty fall*, Michael had thought to himself.

Michael and Jake hadn't even considered that they would also jointly inherit the Griffin cinema, with it being part of Alice's estate. Typically, although Ricky had been promised by Alice that he was also a stakeholder, nothing had been drawn up legally. Michael had been tempted to give Ricky a sum of money in compensation, but ultimately decided against it, thinking that it had been his now ex-manager's own stupid fault for not following it up.

Brian, Tim and Louis were so excited to be attending a celebrity wedding, and had clubbed together to hire a limousine to drive them to the event. On the way there, they discussed how grateful they were to their friend Nigel, who had taken great pleasure in dishing the dirt on Alice to the press. The three boys had spoken with Nigel very early on, and made it quite clear that none of them wanted to be involved in any shocking exposés. He had promised to contain things the best he could and seemed happy with the prospect of making a lot of money out of 'exclusive' interviews with the leading tabloids.

Although Michael was very excited about his wedding day, he was feeling extremely nervous too. It was a very different kind of anxiety to what he usually felt before going on stage though. The spotlight wasn't solely on him today for a start, and the pressure therefore didn't feel quite so great. All he really had to do was look good, smile nicely and repeat his vows correctly during the service, but that in itself felt quite daunting.

Unbeknown to Alexandra, he was planning on singing a special song for her later, during the evening reception. It was one of the couple's favourite songs, Savage Garden's 'Truly Madly Deeply', and had been released by the Australian duo earlier that year, around the time that Michael and Alexandra had first met. A string quartet had been hired to play both before the service and during the reception. They were going to back Michael when he performed his solo number too. He really hoped that emotion wouldn't get the better of him during his performance. Somehow he knew deep down that everything would go OK - even if he did get overwhelmed when the time came, he would just do his best to carry on and everyone would understand.

Alexandra had checked into a separate room on the other side of the castle earlier that day and Michael had found it strange waking up without his future bride by his side. Although she'd only been around since the spring, she truly did make his life complete. He could never have imagined that such happiness existed previously. It really felt as if he had finally found the yin to his yang. They were very different as people and yet they complemented each other perfectly. He couldn't imagine life without her.

Jake joined his brother in his suite and they started to get into their wedding suits, darting in and out of an adjoining room via a linking door, to fetch the various items of clothing they needed whilst listening to another of Michael's mix tapes on a portable cassette player that they had brought along. A recent hit, 'Wannabe', by Spice Girls, already a favourite of theirs, came on and the two brothers danced around the room like wild things.

Michael was wearing a silver chain, which had originally belonged to his father, and a gold ring, which had been his mum's. Both had been found when Alice's house had been emptied. He had promised the chain to Jake once today was over. He'd had to have the ring resized but it fitted him perfectly now. It made him feel that his parents were with him as he took this next big step in his life. He affectionately watched his brother as he pinned a white rose onto the lapel of his grey morning suit jacket.

'I'm a bit disappointed that you're not getting married in your Patrick Swayze drag garb,' grinned Jake. 'Actually, that reminds me. Have you been dressing up much like that, lately?'

'A few times,' chuckled Michael. 'Alexandra's idea was genius! I can't believe that nobody has recognised me in my disguise yet.'

'Well, I'm pleased for you,' replied his brother. 'I know how stifled you were feeling before she came up with that idea. Hey - maybe we should go out in drag together one day?' he joked. 'Did you ever see Erasure's video for ABBA's 'Take A Chance On Me'? I bet we could really rock that look!'

'Well, if that floats your boat, don't let me stop you,' scoffed Michael. 'But I'm planning on sticking with Patrick Swayze for now. Oh, by the way, I keep forgetting to ask you something too. Am I right in thinking that you've totally given up smoking now then?'

'Do you know, I've not even thought about it. How weird is that? If I can go without it for this long, then I'm definitely not planning on starting again.' Jake looked really pleased with himself.

'I'm proud of you. I really am.' Michael patted his brother on the arm.

'Thanks. I really appreciate it,' replied Jake. 'You can't even imagine how proud I am of you today.'

'Can you believe this is happening?' asked Michael. 'This time last year I'd not even met Alexandra and you weren't back in my life yet. This all means so much to me. I hope you know that.'

'Can you even imagine what this feels like for me, Michael?' asked Jake. 'I dreamed of us being reunited for so long, so the fact that we are back together again now and are closer than we ever were - it just makes me want to explode with happiness.'

'Oh, please don't do that. It would make a terrible mess on the carpet and we'd be charged a fortune for it to be cleaned,' laughed Michael.

Jake looked at him, and tears started to well in his eyes. 'You scrub up quite well really,' he beamed. 'And I much prefer your hair now that it's grown a bit longer.'

'Well, thank you, kind Sir,' blushed Michael. 'I'm proud of what you've achieved these last few months. I hate to kill the mood, but have you heard anything from Sue?'

'Not a word,' shrugged Jake. Their divorce seemed to be going through much more smoothly than he had anticipated and he couldn't wait to be finally free of her. 'Anyway, let's not think about her today.'

'I hope everyone has taken their seats by the time we go down,' said Michael.

'It's their problem if they haven't,' responded Jake. 'I've never seen you so jittery. Come on.' He led Michael back into the dressing room and they put the finishing touches to their attire.

They eventually made their way downstairs and found Ted and Krystal waiting for them, both looking very smart.

'Wow! Look at you two!' enthused Krystal. 'Alexandra is down already apparently, but has been hidden away until you're safely out of view.'

Michael looked at his brother. 'All set?' he asked. Jake nodded.

They made their way into the enormous ballroom and as they slowly walked down the central aisle between all the seated guests, a ripple of applause broke out. Michael looked at his brother and winked. Once Krystal and Ted had also emerged and had given the nod that Alexandra was ready too, the string quartet started playing an excerpt from Mozart's *The Marriage of Figaro*.

Michael kept his gaze to the front of the room but

the other guests gasped as they saw Alexandra appear and start to walk down the aisle towards her future husband. She looked stunning, in an ivory, off the shoulder satin dress, with a lace ribbon holding her hair up. She appeared to be floating, she was moving so gently. The couple had made the decision not to have any bridesmaids, since neither of them had any children in their respective families and if they'd asked one friend's daughter, then they would have had to ask them all.

After what felt like an eternity, Alexandra finally reached Michael's side and he turned to look at her. His heart skipped a beat. She truly was the most beautiful woman he had ever met. She took his hand and gave it a squeeze as the registrar approached and smiled at the two of them. The string quartet finished playing and for a few seconds, the room was silent.

The sound of a helicopter outside soon changed that.

The guests all started to crane their necks towards the windows, trying to see what was happening and Michael and Alexandra exchanged confused looks. They both hoped the paparazzi weren't trying to get aerial shots of the event.

The helicopter was hovering over a field, just beyond the parterre. It started to make its descent and everyone started whispering, wondering what was going on. The string quartet was very professional and started playing again as a couple of the security guards ran out to investigate. Michael and Alexandra stood frozen to the spot, not knowing quite what to do. The congregation had now started chatting quite loudly.

Everything became very clear within a minute or two and Michael couldn't believe his eyes. There was his ex-manager Ricky, marching as proud as Punch across the lawn, hand in hand with yet another new lady friend.

As the security guards escorted them into the room, Ricky gave a self-important wave at everyone assembled. He looked as dishevelled as ever, in a creased dark blue tartan suit. There was embarrassed laughter from everyone present as they noticed who it was. The couple were led over to their appointed seats and Ricky smiled at Michael and Alexandra as he sat down. He was completely unfazed by the fact that he had caused such a commotion by arriving late.

Michael looked at Alexandra. 'He'll never change,' he groaned, shaking his head. 'He probably thinks he's the most important person in the room.'

'You mean he isn't?' laughed Alexandra.

The quartet cleverly jumped to the finale of the Mozart piece. At long last, the ceremony could begin.

It all seemed to pass in a blur and before they knew it, the couple were walking back down the aisle, being showered in confetti. They were soon mobbed, as everyone came forward to congratulate them. Michael held tightly onto Alexandra's hand. He could feel tears streaming down his face - he truly didn't know if he had ever been quite this happy before.

His wife was crying too. She had vowed to herself that she would never share this with Michael, but over the last few days, she had been seriously considering returning to Sweden and calling the wedding off. To say that she'd had last minute nerves was an understatement. It was a relief to know that her money worries were now over, but she wasn't quite sure how she felt about being the wife of a global superstar. She truly hoped that she had done the right thing.

Jake eventually managed to get through the crowd and shook his brother's hand, before kissing Alexandra on the cheek. Ever the joker, he looked at his brother for a moment, with a glint in his eye. 'I have to

422

say that I'm surprised you didn't open the wedding with ABBA's 'I Do, I Do, I Do, I Do, I Do'. You really missed a trick there.'

'That would have been a bit too predictable, don't you think?' responded Alexandra, who had overheard. She still didn't get Jake's humour sometimes.

Tomas, Michael's new manager, who was also Swedish, came over to congratulate them too and was soon chatting with Alexandra in their native tongue. Michael was relieved that they seemed to have such a great rapport, especially after the awkwardness that she had felt with Ricky.

'I've just become aware of something,' Jake whispered to his brother. 'I've never noticed this before, just how much you look like Alice.'

'What do you mean?' asked Michael, quite taken aback. It was a nice thing to hear in a way, since of course they were siblings, but with everything that he now knew about his sister and the way she had conducted her life, he wasn't sure if he really wanted to be likened to her. 'I hope it's just an appearance thing,' he snapped. 'I'd like to think I'm not like her in my behaviour too?'

Jake shook his head, 'I don't think either of us could ever be quite as corrupt as she was. When you think of it, we were like chalk and cheese really. But I guess she'll always be part of our lives, whether we like it or not, and we do have some happy memories of her from when we were kids. I bet she's looking down on us now and wishing she was part of this.'

'That's very truc,' said Michael. 'In fact, let's make sure that the two of us raise a glass to her later.'

'Great idea!' agreed Jake, as his boyfriend Tim appeared at his side, grabbing his hand. He kissed both Michael and Alexandra, whispering 'congratulations' to each of them. Jake winked at his brother as he led Tim

423

back into the crowd.

Michael looked at everyone present and picked out those who meant the most to him. There were Krystal and Ted, his ever-faithful staff and reliable friends, standing next to their children: Pippa, who was with her husband Ranj, and Tim, who had just joined them with Jake. Tim's friends, Brian and Louis, were with them too. Even Michael's ex-manager, Ricky, who was busy introducing his latest blonde escort to everyone as 'his young lady,' was trying his hardest to put on a good show. Michael would hardly describe the guy as a close friend but he had been a big part of his working life for such a long time that it had felt only right to invite him today.

Michael watched his brother walk over to his friend Jason, who was holding hands with his new girlfriend, Andrea. Jason had apparently been very relieved when Angie had gone back to Australia, and had met this new lady, who hailed from Cologne in Germany, when she'd suspiciously come to the cinema on several occasions to watch the same film. It turned out that it wasn't the movie that she was interested in.

Madeleine and Pierre were there too. Michael had enjoyed working with them, albeit often remotely, since he had taken over the financing of the cinema and had found it hysterical how his brother would always flirt outlandishly with Pierre, knowing, thanks to Jason, that the man had a massive crush on him.

Standing to one side of them was Michael's childhood friend, Bowie, together with his wife and son. Michael had phoned his friend soon after returning from his last concert in Paris, but this was the first time that they were physically seeing each other again. Bowie insisted on being called Lee these days and it was hard to believe that he was currently employed as a share trader on the London Stock Exchange. He looked nothing like the rebellious teenager Michael had once known. With his shaved head and very smart suit, he was the epitome of conformity. His six-year-old son, who was standing next to him, was the spitting image of Bowie as a child though, complete with long hair and slightly goth clothing. There was obviously still hope for the continuation of Bowie's rebellious side.

In the distance, Michael spotted Alexandra's family, which consisted of an uncle and several cousins. They were here with a group of his new wife's Swedish friends, who Michael was looking forward to getting to know better. His new manager, Tomas, was standing with them. He had been the best candidate by far when interviews had been conducted and by a strange twist of fate, Alexandra had discovered that she had worked with him several times in the past and was able to put in a good word for him. Michael was already very impressed at how professionally Tomas had arranged the upcoming promotional tour for his new album.

'Are you happy, Mrs Hambelton?' Michael asked his bride.

'Are you?' she asked. 'How are you feeling?'

'Like the luckiest man in the world' he confessed. 'Welcome to our new life together!'

They kissed and Michael pulled her tightly to him, prompting an impromptu cheer from everyone.

Alexandra glanced across at Tomas, trying hard to catch his eye. He eventually looked over and smiled, giving her a thumbs up. She looked around at the assembled crowd and when she was certain that nobody else was looking, she gave him a wink and blew a kiss.

Today was the beginning of a whole new chapter.

Acknowledgements

Firstly, I'd like to thank you, the reader of this book, for buying it and for reading it. It means the world to me that you chose to read my first novel and I really hope you enjoyed it!

Writing this book has been a solitary task, as writing usually is, but it has also introduced me to a handful of already accomplished authors who have patiently answered my questions and encouraged me along the way. In particular, I would like to thank Marva Carty, Helga Jensen and Anthony McDonald. You have been totally inspirational and made me realise that dreams can come true.

I hope you enjoyed the ABBA references in this book. The members of the group have always played a significant role in my life and they definitely deserve a special mention. Agnetha Fältskog, Benny Andersson, Björn Ulvaeus and Anni-Frid Reuss - thank you not just for the music, but for always making my life brighter. A big thank you also to Rebecca Edwards at Universal Music for checking that I wasn't crossing any lines with my references to ABBA and their music.

I would like to express my sincere gratitude to Danny Cazzato, who not only designed the amazing cover of this book but also encouraged me tirelessly from the very beginning to get started on this project. Couldn't have done it without you, my friend.

Thanks to Jacqui Finch for putting me right with my hospital references and to Maggie Burton for making sure that I was on point grammatically.

I'm beyond grateful to Eileen Knowles for doing a virtual autopsy on my book and for spotting even the tiniest anomaly. I would have certainly ended up with egg on my face if it hadn't been for your eagle eye!

I'm indebted to the awe-inspiring Michael Price for painstakingly suffering both the original drafts and the multiple complete versions of the manuscript and for always giving your honest feedback. How you unflinchingly read the same story time and time again is nothing short of a marathon.

Thanks to my family and friends who remained engaged in this project throughout. You'll never know how much your genuine interest spurred me on and your constant enthusiasm has meant the world to me.

I enjoyed spending time with all the characters in this book, notably Alice, Jake and Michael. Thank you for amusing me along the way and for entertaining me with the twists and turns in your lives. Who knows what lies in store for you in the future? Oh yes, maybe I do …

I'm grateful to Classic FM and Heart 70s for your company during my many hours of writing.

Thanks to the staff at my local Original Copy Centre for humouring me each time I came in to print yet another draft copy.

Above all, thank you Lord God for giving me the inspiration to create and the energy to complete this novel.

Like Chalk and Cheese
List of Songs

Music has always played a very significant part in my life, especially the songs of ABBA, so I knew from the outset that I wanted to feature a lot of music in this book. Here are the tracks mentioned:

ABBA:
Chiquitita (Andersson/Ulvaeus)
Dancing Queen (Anderson/Andersson/Ulvaeus)
Eagle (Andersson/Ulvaeus)
Fernando (Andersson/Ulvaeus)
Happy Hawaii (Anderson/Andersson/Ulvaeus)
Hole In Your Soul (Andersson/Ulvaeus)
I Do, I Do, I Do, I Do, I Do
                  (Anderson/Andersson/Ulvaeus)
I Have A Dream (Andersson/Ulvaeus)
Knowing Me, Knowing You (Andersson/Ulvaeus)
Money, Money, Money (Andersson/Ulvaeus)
Our Last Summer (Andersson/Ulvaeus)
SOS (Anderson/Andersson/Ulvaeus)
Summer Night City (Andersson/Ulvaeus)
Super Trouper (Andersson/Ulvaeus)
Take A Chance On Me (Andersson/Ulvaeus)
The Winner Takes It All (Andersson/Ulvaeus)
Voulez-Vous (Andersson/Ulvaeus)
Waterloo (Anderson/Andersson/Ulvaeus)

Baccara:
Yes Sir, I Can Boogie (Dostal/Soja)

Boney M:
Sunny (Hebb)

Miquel Brown:
So Many Men, So Little Time (Levine/Trench)

Yvonne Elliman:
If I Can't Have You (Gibb/Gibb/Gibb)

Erasure:
Take A Chance On Me (Andersson/Ulvaeus)

Free:
My Brother Jake (Fraser/Rodgers)

Frida:
Även En Blomma (Glenmark)

Gina G:
Ooh Aah … Just A Little Bit (Rodway/Tauber)

Michael Hambelton (aka Colin Collier):
A Fool's Garden (Collier/Silk)
Fall to Pieces (Collier/Silk)
Kaleidoscope (Collier/Silk)
Out of My Head (Collier/Silk)

London Symphony Orchestra:
Adagio for Strings (Barber)
The Marriage of Figaro (Mozart)

Meatloaf:
Two Out of Three Ain't Bad (Steinman)

Mireille Matthieu:
Bravo Tu As Gagné (Andersson/Claudric/Ulvaeus)

George Michael:
Fastlove (McFaddin/Michael/Rushen/Washington)

Helen Reddy:
Angie Baby (O'Day)

Savage Garden:
Truly Madly Deeply (Hayes/Jones)

Spice Girls:
Wannabe (Rowe/Spice Girls/Stannard)

Robbie Williams:
Let Me Entertain You (Chambers/Williams)

Jackie Wilson:
I Get The Sweetest Feeling (Evelyn/McCoy)

Colin Collier has always been fascinated by words. He is trilingual, being fluent in both French and Swedish, as well as his mother tongue, English.

He was often writing stories and poems as a child and always dreamt of being an author. *Like Chalk and Cheese* is his first published novel.

Colin has been a successful singer-songwriter for the past decade and his music videos have had almost 100,000 views on YouTube.

Colin lives in West London, where he is usually found listening to music, reading books or meeting friends. He has been an ABBA fan since 1974.

Colin likes to keep in touch with his readers via:
www.facebook.com/Colin Collier - Author
www.instagram.com/colincollierauthor

www.colincollierauthor.com

Printed in Dunstable, United Kingdom